The Thirteenth GATE

A NOVEL
ESTER ZIRKIND

ISRAEL BOOKSHOP
Publications

Published by:
Israel Bookshop Publications
501 Prospect Street
Lakewood, NJ 08701
Tel: (732) 901-3009 / Fax: (732) 901-4012
www.israelbookshoppublications.com
info@israelbookshoppublications.com

Printed in Israel

Distributed in Israel by:
Tfutza Publications
P.O.B. 50036
Beitar Illit 90500
972-2-650-9400

Distributed in Europe by:
Lehmanns
Unit E Viking Industrial Park
Rolling Mill Road
Jarrow, Tyne & Wear NE32 3DP
44-191-430-0333

Distributed in Australia by:
Gold's Book and Gift Company
3-13 William Street
Balaclava 3183
613-9527-8775

Distributed in South Africa by:
Kollel Bookshop
Northfield Centre
17 Northfield Avenue
Glenhazel 2192
27-11-440-6679

Dedicated to all those whose connection is bruised. Know there is hope...!

ACKNOWLEDGMENTS

I t's odd. With this book, my second, there are less people to thank. Mostly, I really have to express my gratitude to Hakadosh Baruch Hu. He has given me the blessing of observation. And had He done just that, it would have been enough, but He also allowed me to perceive. And had He done just that, it would have been enough, but He also gave me the gift of feeling vulnerable. And had He done just that, it would have been enough, but He also provided me with thoughts and words, imagination, and the joy of expression. And had He done just that, it would have been enough, but He also gave me the time, the encouragement, a supportive environment, and the urge to bring it out into a neatly packaged manuscript. And had He done just that, it would have been enough, but He also sent me to Israel Bookshop Publications, who wanted this book out there in the world enough to take it on.

My gratitude is as endless as time.

Katonti mikol hachassadim!

To Humber School for Writers, who awarded me another mentorship with the awesome David Adams Richards. And of course, to Mr. Richards himself, who saw universals everywhere in my writing, who kept spurring me on to take more risks, and who—in the end—"got" my obsession with *Artzeinu Hakedoshah*.

To David Heubert, Lauren Nussbaum, Chana Perman, and Rivkah Meldung, who read through and critiqued different drafts of the manuscript along the way. To Dr. Loewenthal—the first reader of the completed manuscript—for his insightful support, encouragement, and guidance. Thank you as well to Miriam Webb, Andy Semiotuk, Fran Turner, Dew Williams, and Marg Krutow, all of my writers group, for their support and constructive comments when "workshopping" excerpts of this novel.

To my dear editor, Malkie Gendelman, who saves me from my own pitfalls, and does it with so much respect that I have never once been made to feel small for being too emotional/passionate/stubborn! My heartfelt thanks as well to Esther Malky Sonenblick, my incredible and devoted proofreader; Hindy Schwartz, the talented graphics designer who created the book's beautiful cover; and Liron Delmar, who skillfully managed the whole operation.

To my *kinderlach* and *eineklach, sheyichyu*, who fill my life with continuous wonderment and delight. I so deeply desire to instill within each of them an appreciation for, and a sensitivity toward, the walking wounded among us.

And lastly, to the other half of my soul, my cherished husband Shmuel Yosef, *sheyichyeh*, who consistently supports me along this unexpected writing journey—not to mention the fact that the whole genesis for this book grew from a *dvar Torah* he gave over at our Shabbos table! He is my anchor, without whom I would be hopelessly lost.

"The happiest people I know...
I don't know very well."

—Quote from a wise, old friend, Ruth Krevsky

"I wish I still knew,
What I used to know,
About what was what in the world.
The black from the white,
Which path led to light,
And which was ersatz and a fraud...

...When *did* everything get so muddled?"

—Opal Beaumont, circa 1883

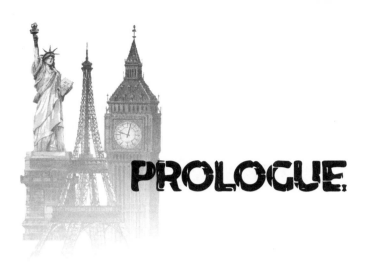

PROLOGUE

WEDNESDAY, MAY 27, 2015

The Sterns' van stood empty on the side of Highway 60, facing Jerusalem. From time to time, the beeping of an unseen phone could be heard from inside. It was not a fancy vehicle; in fact, there were rust stains growing over its back fender, and its windows were not even electric. But it had served the Stern family well for eleven years, taking them to and from their Ulpan classes, doctor and dentist appointments, and general errands. Now it had been about to return the *olim* to their tiny dwelling in Maale Adumim.

Eleven years earlier, with hope in their eyes and a dream in their souls, the Stern family had arrived on Israeli soil from Brazil. Mr. Stern spoke Portuguese as well as English, and he had just secured a new position in one of the small Sephardic communities sprouting up in Sderot, a relatively new city southeast of Jerusalem. The family was all set to move from Maale Adumim to Sderot on July twentieth.

Now, the Sterns' van's windows were rolled down and hot wind rushed through them. One of the tires was slit, and it sagged on the road. The windshield was smashed. How long had the van been standing there? No one could tell. The last time anyone had seen any of the Sterns was the night before, at around 8:30 p.m., when they had said goodbye to the families who were supposed to become their new neighbors, after a get-to-know-you bash.

A policeman, with gloved hands, delved between the back seat cushions of the van and finally retrieved the beeping phone. Every time another text came through on it, the smiling profile of Dorit Stern—the family's one and only daughter—lit up. The policeman turned the phone around in his hands, searching it for clues for the whereabouts of Dorit; her two older brothers, Shmuel and Amit; and their parents, David and Esther Stern. On the back of the phone, Dorit had pasted on a sticker, dog-eared with age, that read, "*Tizkeri: Lo L'daber Lashon Hara!* (Remember! Do not speak *lashon hara!*)"

Underneath the words was an emoji with zippered lips.

To: Henyaleipzig@sympatico.com
From: simah@gmail.com
Date: August 19, 2015
Time: 2:34 a.m.

Henya...please!

Stop ignoring me like this.

I like to think that the fact that we are born of the same parents means something to you. Surely shared history, shared blood, should triumph over perceived offenses. What I did, I did for Mummy. Not to spite you. Was it so wrong of me to want what's best for her? For us? Okay, so we disagree on what is best. Okay, so we have different opinions. Okay. I grant you that. But surely by now, even you can understand that some things were just plain wrong and needed to be set right.

For Heaven's sake!

If I would have known that through my actions, I had broken what I thought—naively, as it turns out—was an unbreakable bond, I might have done things differently. Now, hold on, don't get me wrong; I am not saying I would have abandoned my impulse altogether. This I will not say. But I may have done things differently. Oh, Henya, when will you forgive your fanciful sister?

You do realize that Tatte is *gone* now. *Ten years* in the grave. That his words to us, spoken so long ago, should not hold us hostage eternally. *The world is different today!*

If you only knew how many nights I am up, lying in my bed, unable to sleep. But Henya, one thing is clear on my conscience: I have no regrets. Not for one moment do I have regrets.

Only you, Henya. That's what I regret: the loss of you.

Please, don't keep up this silence anymore. It does both of us only harm, not good.

Henya, answer me this time!

Love,

Sima

PART ONE.

MONDAY, JUNE 29, 2015
LONG ISLAND, NEW YORK

It was an awful way to wake up on the first day of summer vacation. The phone just kept on ringing. It was the landline, a relic of the times—an appendage similar to the wisdom tooth: not much used but still somehow there. Sima Hertzberg, a woman prone to regularity, blinked unbelievingly at her watch.

10:04 a.m.!

What! How did *that* happen?

The ringing, a piercing abrasiveness, angered her. She reached for the phone with one hand, while fumbling about her forehead to straighten out her *tichel* with the other. There was an underlying urgency spiking her psyche that morning: a sharp little rubbing at her temples. She tried to account for it: the dream.

Only moments before she had been in a whole other place, experiencing one frustrating sequence after another, each one ending identically: without her making contact with her ever-elusive father, leaving her—as always—shattered. At one point he was standing surrounded by people she didn't recognize; at another, he walked out of the room just as she walked in. She was still trying to reach him when the phone's ringing punctured the illusion. It was too late. She would have to awaken and pick up the receiver, if just to stop its infuriating noise. And though the dream had hurt, she had wanted to stay with it a little longer.

"Mommy?" It was Tamar.

"G'morning, Tamar..." Sima coughed to clear the sleep that had caught in her throat. "How's it going? You okay?"

"Uh-huh. Did I wake you?"

"Yeah." She knew her daughter would think this strange. She, Sima, was known for the tick-tock precision with which she ran her life. It was why she had been voted head of PTA. It was what everyone admired and no one could replicate. It was what her children hated but secretly—according to her—relied on. "I must have overslept. Not to worry. Just tell me how you are."

"Good...I guess."

Sima sat up. "Just good? Just guessing? *Oy*, Tamar! That doesn't sound so reassuring." She regretted saying those words not as *soon* as she said them, but actually *while* saying them. It was as though her mind went in one direction and her lips in the total opposite. She decried herself, silently bemoaning her inability to pull herself together enough to say *useful* things to her teenage daughter; things she wished had been said to her; things she stored in her mind to say but forgot about at critical moments.

"No, Ma, it's good. Really. I'm happy that I came back."

"Okay, then..." Sima fell back against her pillow and into her dreamy state. "I'm relieved." Her mind rewound to the scene the Shabbos before, just after candle-lighting on Friday night, when she had wrenched out of her daughter the true reason she'd decided to go back to Camp Shoshana. The summer before hadn't been so smooth. There were girls there for whom Tamar hadn't cared, girls who had mistaken cruelty for a sport. Tamar had come back different. Sima hadn't been able to read quite how, but something was there, as though her daughter had sustained internal bruising that resulted in an almost unobservable, nebulous rift between the two of them. And while Sima had tried to reach out to Tamar, the girl had refused to open up to her. Sima had been sure that her oldest daughter would pass up going to camp the following year, but Tamar had surprised her by announcing that she wanted to go back as a lifeguard.

As Sima had heard that Friday night, it turned out that Tamar was experimenting, seeing if she could bypass insensitivity in others, and remain strong and unaffected. She said she had been doing that a lot in school recently, as it seemed the best way to function. She'd turned to her mother and said in a half-joking, half-serious tone, "You created a false world here, Mommy. You made us all so careful and caring, but that is not what the real world is like. It's harsh out there. I don't think you did enough to prepare us. We sisters have very few antibodies. I'm just working on fending for myself, that's all."

Taken aback at how much her daughter had grown, Sima had winced at the apparent indictment of her parenting. *Few antibodies, indeed!* She'd swallowed, silently applauding her daughter while shelving her own concerns.

"Ma..." came the voice at the other end of the line.

"Mmmm? What can I do for you, Tamar?"

"Did...did you read it yet?"

The streets surrounding the Hertzbergs' Long Island home were not identical to theirs, but not unlike it either. Each house stood on its own, with both a front and back lawn, and a driveway for two cars. Green was the predominant color of the parks-filled neighborhood. Sima had come under the spell of it when she'd realized that, minus the cars, it conjured up bucolic England, or Wharton's New York— reminiscences of stately homes from yesteryear.

Sima and Aryeh Hertzberg had arrived at this life in the late nineties, after Aryeh had established his computer support company that serviced most of the Jewish day schools in the two-mile radius of the Boro Park section of Brooklyn. His was a forty-five-minute, congestion-filled commute that he did not mind on most days, when he thought about the cleaner air and space that the move to Long Island provided for his family.

Five daughters had been born to Aryeh and Sima. And though

they both craved a boy, it was not to be. Sima's last pregnancy had ended with severe complications during a long and difficult labor that nearly cost the life of the little girl who ended the childbearing years of her mother. After enduring that near-death experience, Sima and Aryeh had made peace with the family that Hashem, in His great wisdom, had granted them, and they looked forward to having sons-in-law instead of actual sons.

Sima and Aryeh enjoyed the quiet of their lives, the fact that nothing much happened to them or their neighbors. Oh, there would be the occasional scandal, ruffling the carefully groomed feathers of this family or that, but nothing too indelicate to spice the nattering mouths of any local gossips.

After hanging up with Tamar, Sima got out of bed, slipping her feet into the Crocs near her night table. She glanced over at Aryeh's bed; she hadn't even heard him leave this morning. He was out so often these days, she felt she had to make an appointment just to speak with him.

Every morning, for the past four weeks, Aryeh was leaving early to shul, only to return there every evening, after his workday and supper were done. The shul had organized ongoing Tehillim and learning sessions in the merit of finding the Stern family—a father, mother, and three teenaged children who had disappeared on the way back from a party in Sderot, Israel—alive. Aryeh was very concerned, more so than Sima remembered him ever being before. She suspected that he was seeing himself in their faces, having spent the three best years of his single life learning in a yeshivah that was in the same area of Israel as where the Sterns' empty van had been discovered.

Sima threw on her pink fleece robe and opened the bedroom door. The house was silent, and the silence made her smile.

Ahh...summer vacation. The girls would still be luxuriating in their beds.

The Hertzbergs' home was lovely. Not grand, but certainly it was nicer than Aryeh or Sima felt they deserved. A wooden staircase, with a strip of maroon carpeting down the center, was tucked to the side of the main hallway that opened to the living room. Impressive bookcases graced the main wall of the room, holding court over large, inviting couches and throw cushions, and an elegant breakfront dominated the wall of the dining room, overlooking the polished table.

As Sima passed the mirror at the bottom of the stairs, she stopped for a moment to stare at her reflection. She did not look too bad for having just turned forty. Wrinkles were kept at bay by expensive organic creams purchased at the health food store. The skin around her blue-green eyes looked puffy most mornings, but she trusted that by the time she would be ready to go anywhere, the puffiness would have settled.

Where *had* she put her pocketbook?

It was surprisingly unlike her daughter to hand her such a carefully written letter; hard, silver envelope with a red "Mommy" penned in calligraphy. Sima had smiled deeply when Tamar handed it to her at the bus stop the day before. *Tamar must have seen this done by her friends*, she'd thought. "Read it tomorrow. Not now," Tamar had instructed her mother. Both curious and dismissive, Sima had popped the envelope into her pocketbook and out of her mind.

Recently Tamar had become quite testy with her mother. Sima put it down to normal teenage rebelliousness—individuation. *This too shall pass*, she would mutter, after unclenching her teeth and forcing her breathing to regulate itself, while the smoke from the exchange of fire still hovered between them; a slammed door wedged unnaturally tight in its frame.

Walking into the kitchen, Sima tried to remember what it was like to be sixteen and a half. How had her mother-daughter relationship fared during those rocky years of drifting passions and as-yet-unformed identity? There were moments of friction, for sure. And embarrassment. Sima could recall with wicked clarity the time when her mother—Greta Bulman—had once entered the school building, which also served as a community center, just as Sima and some classmates had been coming up the stairs from lunch. Greta had called out to her, unabashed in showing her delight in having this unexpected encounter with her eldest daughter, smack in the middle of her day. Sima could recall every hot detail: the way her heart had pumped with ferocity, how sweaty she'd suddenly felt, how she'd watched her friends take her mother in: Greta's short, curly wig; her lace-up shoes; her swollen leg; the stain, small and white, on the front of her navy-blue blouse. Sima could not match her mother's exuberant greeting and had continued up the stairs ashamed of herself, embarrassed of her mother, imploding with an awkwardness that would stalk her for the rest of the afternoon.

She wondered if everyone had to go through that rite of passage. She wondered how Tamar had handled it. Had she ever been embarrassed of her own mother? Perhaps it would be best to confront such feelings head-on. Perhaps Sima should ask Tamar about it when she came home from camp, if she could find the right moment…

In the kitchen now, Sima spied the strap of her pocketbook on the floor, jutting out of the open pantry door, and remembered dropping it there yesterday when she'd emptied the groceries. Not wanting to miss the fullness of this letter, Sima switched on the kettle and pulled a mug from the cupboard to prepare her morning coffee. She heard the footfalls of her girls as they trundled out of their beds above her. She thought about the day ahead of her, relishing the fact that not much was planned for it. Odel, fifteen, and Shana, thirteen, were scheduled to leave for camp on Tuesday, and she needed about an hour to take care of their last-minute shopping trips. Naomi, eleven, and Bracha, nine, were starting day camp on Wednesday, giving them today to fill how they pleased. From Wednesday on, Sima would be free, a notion that both excited and terrified her.

The kitchen had been renovated three years prior. Sima and Aryeh had argued over the countertops that now gleamed in deep, dark brown interspersed with a creamy peach. Sima wanted the less expensive stone, from a quarry in China, but Aryeh insisted on this Santa Cicilia, and it had cost them three times as much. He reasoned that since this would only be done once, it behooved them to do it right. *Behoove*! He'd actually used that word! And furthermore, Aryeh had pitched, the expensive countertops added value to the house. Sima was dubious about that last bit but made the compromise and let the matter drop. The payments for the renovations were to end this September, and she did enjoy the richness of the coloring of her kitchen. The pecan wood cabinetry, with its caramel hue, caused the dark granite to stand out sharply. Aryeh was usually the one to scrimp and she the one to splurge, so Sima felt it odd that their roles had reversed, and in such a feminine place, too.

Could it be the imbalance of females in their home that was speaking through him?

Rummaging around now in her pocketbook, Sima's fingers felt the coldness of the envelope, and she remembered why she had been so surprised by it the day before. This gesture, so unlike Tamar's modus operandi, was orderly and elegantly planned. A tiny tremor lit across her abdomen. She carefully opened the seal, sat down at the table, took a sip of coffee, and began to read:

Dear Mommy,

I really don't know how to begin writing this letter. I have been writing it in my mind a thousand times over this past year, but I never had the guts to put pen to paper. I still don't. But I see I cannot push it off too much longer. We have been fighting recently, and it never used to be like this. Remember? We never used to argue. I always listened to everything you and Abba said. Well, that's all changed now, and I think it is not fair anymore to hold back from you the reason for the change.

I know about your brother.

Please don't start with asking me questions. Just you should know that I know about him, and that I am so upset that you raised me—us—in ignorance.

For me, everything has changed because of this.

And before you get worried, no, I have not mentioned anything to the others, because that much respect I still have. Only Mommy, they deserve to know. Just like I do.

I hate to have to say this, but I feel betrayed by you. Why? Because I thought you stood for something, but I feel it was all a deception, a sham. You put such emphasis on family, family, family, but your own brother—my uncle—you give up for dead! But it's even worse, because you don't even acknowledge that he ever lived!

How can I trust you? How do I know you will not do the same to me? Or to Shana, or Odel, or any of us, if we are not able to meet your standards?

I don't yet have the words to explain how I'm feeling, which is why I've put off telling you all this for so long. I do know that this has been eating at me for some time now. In fact, I don't even remember what it felt like before, when everything was okay.

Mommy, I have been affected by this revelation on so many levels. During class time, I find my mind wandering; I can't concentrate like I used to. I am starting to have misgivings about things I never doubted before. I question everything these days, and I know it's been making my teachers nervous. It's been about a year now, and I still feel so unanchored.

I know, as I write these words, that you might feel anger toward me. I know that you will want to run to Abba and tell him. Please don't. In fact, can I ask you not to discuss this matter with him at all? It is not Abba who has let me down. It is you. I think that if things are to be repaired between us, you need to be honest with me and tell me the whole story, without relying on Abba to bail you out.

Mommy, I have just reread this letter, and even I am shocked at how I am speaking to you, but I am hurting, Mommy, and I want to know why you've done this! Don't you think you owe me at least that?

Can you at least think about it? You have time; I don't get back home until the end of the summer.

Love,

Tamar

Sima's white, trembling hands could not hold the paper. She laid it down gently on the table. Everything shifted for her as she stared at it. Her kitchen, her home, the sounds of her daughters fighting upstairs—everything lost its lustre, obliterated by the neat, handwritten missive lying beside her.

How long? she thought. *For how long has this been going on? How have I been so blind? So very, very blind?* She lifted her hand to shade her eyes, for the light in the room had suddenly become too strong, so swiftly had her inner world darkened.

So, she had not escaped this fate after all. She had tried. Hadn't they both tried? Had she been so wrong to shield her daughters from shame and horror, abuse and destruction? Was she as Tamar saw her, a betrayer? A liar? Suddenly the whole of her adult life, assembled with so much painstaking attention to detail, appeared before her eyes as a large, shiny, rainbow-colored soap bubble—enchanting, yes, but oh, so fragile and temporary.

Tamar was right in one thing: the *anger*. More like rage. It rolled over her, through her, settling in her gut. How *dare* Tamar call her out on something she could not possibly understand? How *dare* she judge her on decisions that had been made *for* her? *She knows nothing! Nothing! None of the wretchedness I carry!* Slowly, insidiously, Sima felt herself being pulled down into the hollow gulf from which she had tried to protect herself and her girls all these years. How was she to handle this, with no internal model? How could she succeed in making her child understand, when her own parents had failed so badly?

The front door opened. Sima looked up. She wasn't expecting anyone. The girls' footsteps were still creaking the old floorboards to life upstairs. She stood, unconsciously rewrapping the fleece robe around her as she took a few steps toward the dairy sink and peered out, past the back-splashed wall and into the hallway.

Aryeh closed the front door slowly. He turned to walk through the hallway toward the kitchen, his movements lethargic, his face ashen. Had Tamar written a different letter to her father, telling him not to let her mother know what she had just unloaded? Sima could not believe how quickly she had lost trust in the feeling that she knew her daughter at all. She walked around the dairy counter to greet her husband who should not have been home at this hour.

"I have bad news," he said, as soon as he saw her.

"I have worse," she responded.

"No. No, you don't."

His tone filled her with a dread so pure that, for the second time that morning, she felt herself go weak. "What? What is it?"

"They've been found."

2

MONDAY, JUNE 29, 2015
DEAUVILLE BEACH, NORMANDY, FRANCE

It's called a flashbulb memory.

Aaron knew right away what it was because he'd had it before: Fourteen years had passed since two planes flew into the Twin Towers in New York and everyone in the world lost their complacency. This felt similar. Sort of. Except that this time, his was not just another face amongst millions of listless, horrified faces staring at a screen. This time the listlessness he felt, he felt on his own. His body tingled and his peripheral vision interspersed with little lights. But when he looked around the bar for someone with whom to share his anguish, he understood that his aloneness was absolute. No one around him had stopped—even for a moment—to absorb what the newsmen were reporting. Only *his* movements slowed. Only *he* had been sucked into a tunnel, making everything else seem far away. Only *his* mind shut out any and all other stimuli, light and sound obliterated, focusing on the one thing that eclipsed everything else:

The Stern family had been found.

With sluggish indifference, Aaron wiped the last of the glasses and slid them, upside down, into their places. It was dark and cool in the bar area of Black Tie 33—one of many night clubs along one of the many cobblestoned streets of Deauville Beach, where Aaron had fled many years before in search of peace, anonymity, and complete severance from his childhood. He had been drawn to the beach town's quaint quietness, to the idea that no one would think to look for him there, while he could still be in close enough proximity to the shores of England to allow himself the satisfaction of a smug and contorted smirk every now and then. Now he walked over to the plasma TV suspended on the side wall and switched to the English-speaking channel; the newscasters had been speaking in too rapid a French for his tired mind to translate.

"The bodies of the missing Stern family, who disappeared just over four weeks ago, have been discovered in a small, remote cave along the southernmost tip of the Negev. The entrance of the cave was obscured by rockfall, that, after investigation, appears to be fairly recently formed, prompting the searchers to explore within.

"Following the discovery, Israeli Prime Minister Binyamin Netanyahu blamed Hamas for the murders, warning that the militant group will pay a heavy price for the deaths..."

He needed a drink. He shook his head. It would soon be the end of his shift. What he really needed was sleep—and to stop thinking about what was happening. *This will not end well; these things rarely do.* Yet every time the young, skull-capped immigrant brothers, with their auburn-haired, freckle-faced sister, flashed on the screen, his gut clenched.

He blamed Eitan and Uri for this new, inner turmoil.

Before they had waltzed into his life, he had been comfortably numb to all things Jewish. He shrugged now at the memory. Hadn't that suited him perfectly?

From the moment he'd first laid eyes on those two young men sitting on stools, speaking their Hebrew out loud, laughing, all without the least bit of the self-consciousness that was requisite propriety in establishments such as Black Tie 33, he'd wanted their friendship. And that was not a sentiment with which Aaron was familiar, having neatly dumped that particular urge during his turbulent mid-teens, when friendships were hard fought and easily betrayed. Aaron had not been *born* an observer; he had *become* one—of necessity. It was a survival tactic, a skill-turned-way-of-life for him, as his earliest memories of society were fickle and untrustworthy. *People*, he had concluded at the sagacious age of six or seven, *are dangerous and need to be kept at a distance*. Never *let them in your heart.*

This view was subsequently reaffirmed by his brief marriage when he was in his late twenties. After his divorce, it was easy to accept that his retreat from human companionship would be absolute. That is, until Eitan and Uri began to frequent the bar and show him what it meant to be safe in the company of others.

Was it kinship that first niggled away at the padlocks of his soul? A tribal affinity?

Had he not been successful at purging himself of the desire to have brotherly companionship?

Many gates needed to open before Aaron decided to try his hand at friendship. With so little practice, he seemed to need the honed skills of true Sabras to re-teach himself the norms and forms of alliance. Eitan and Uri, buddies enjoying a year off in France together after serving in the army, immediately set to work with Aaron, recognizing his hunger, coaxing him out of solitude and into the warmth of social embrace.

He had never wished for something so badly.

At thirty-seven, Aaron looked older than his true age. His thick, dark brown hair was prematurely graying at the sides, and receding slowly on top. He knew that by the time he would turn fifty, he would be bald—a gift from his father, Elchanan Bulman, along with a soprano singing voice, pale skin, and gray eyes—stormy gray, perpetually trapped in mid-winter gloom. Had Aaron let his beard grow, the likeness to his father would have been eerie, given that Aaron often thought of himself as his father's disgrace; his father, *gone wrong.* From his mother he had taken a hard jawbone and height. No, Aaron was not exactly handsome, but he had been described as striking by some. And, of course, there was his signature intensity; he seemed to be forever searching for redemption from the sin of disappointing his parents.

Eitan and Uri had woken in him a menacing sentimentality. In the eight months since they'd met, they had eaten together in most of Deauville Beach's restaurants, visited many of Deauville Beach's night clubs, and even gone on a six-day hike together, exploring old Roman roads and castles made by the Cathars, Montsegur, Peyrepertuse, and the Puilaurens; breathing in the restorative air there; and swimming in magnificent gorges. Best of all was when the threesome had visited the picturesque French town of Padern, in the Pyrenees, where they were able to clearly see into Spain.

It was a beautiful night when the three of them had downed the last of their food and knew that, come morning, they would be forced back to civilization. That night, around a small fire, staring at the star-filled sky, Uri described his childhood in northern Israel, up in the Galil. "Mountains bring me peace," he said. "That's where I go when I need to forget the day-to-day stresses." He stopped, and then threw out, "Did you know my mother didn't really want me?" He said it so matter-of-factly, like it was just another color in the palette of his life. "She was hoping to give me up for adoption, but my father wouldn't allow it." Uri played with the twigs by his feet. "I always wondered why she felt it necessary to tell me this. What a wonderful way to connect with your child, no?" He turned his face to both Eitan and Aaron, challenging them to humor him with a response.

Aaron was duly moved. Eitan, though, who had heard this before, simply pulled his cigarette from his mouth and blew a long plume of smoke into the air. "I can't relate," he drawled. "My childhood wasn't like that. It was all fun, freedom, and friends."

Uri looked hurt, and Aaron suddenly found his own childhood memories spilling from his lips.

"Y'know that moment, when you're a kid, and someone pushes you in the recess yard and knocks you over? Now there's that instant when you have not yet made contact with the ground. Your breathing stops. You know what will happen, yet you cannot escape. You know you will break skin and bleed—and there is *not a thing you can do about it...*" Aaron stopped talking. It was so rare for him to be sharing like this. He looked up at his audience and felt encouraged to continue by their silent absorption in his tale. "Well, I think of my whole childhood like that. That knowing, that surety, that I would 'bleed'—but having no way out..."

Silence followed for a few seconds.

"Care to explain?" *kibbitzed* Eitan.

Aaron shrugged and laughed. "No. I don't think so. Let's just leave it at that."

If only I could just evaporate, thought Aaron as he left the bar, squinting his eyes in the blinding sun. Disoriented by the range of emotions that fumed and fussed within him, he resented all this upheaval because a family he didn't even know had turned up dead in some cave, in a country he had been told was his by birthright, but to which he felt little, if any, connection.

Since May 27th, the news of the family's abduction had tugged at him daily. He did not pray; that was not his way. But those young, overly confident brothers and sister had wormed themselves into his heart, and he knew he would suffer for it. Perhaps they reminded him of himself. Perhaps it was their youth that struck a raw chord within him.

He badly needed sleep. It was too hot, too bright outside. Aaron decided to skip visiting Eitan and Uri and just head home. Maybe a shower, and then...blessed slumber. He turned right and walked uphill to his little studio rental, off one of the resort town's main arteries. Trudging up the back staircase to his bachelor digs, his mind wandered—of late it seemed to be doing that more and more—to his mother. If anyone would induce him to re-examine his life, it would be her. Her love was in her quiet presence. And however ineffective it was, at least it was consistent. If there was ever love in his life, she would be its holder.

He pictured her as he remembered her: a tall woman—not that she used what most women would be very happy to have been given. No, Greta Bulman stooped. At full height she was statuesque, but she'd often said how much she would have preferred to be petite. Aaron regarded his mother as devitalized—as though her life had been an endless series of errands and chores that she had to get through. Every day the same, its monotony draining her of vitality. Did she ever express happiness? Sing just because? Dance? He couldn't remember. And as quickly as it came, he quashed his easy condemnation, with its accompanying guilt.

Sleep, O sacred, intoxicating sleep! Bestow upon this lowly soul from your generous bounty! Lend this unholy being your fortitude, for the world has darkened and bears down all too strongly...

He let himself in and looked around. The blinds were down, but the sun still shone through the slats, picking up dust particles and making the place look lonelier than usual: his unmade bed, his quilt on the floor where he had kicked it the day before... This night-plus-half-day shift was wearying. He opened the refrigerator and pulled out a Jenlain-Ambree, thinking that a beer would help loosen his muscles, ease the ache in his neck, the tension in his shoulders.

He sat on his bed and slowly finished the beer. Shaking off his shoes, without bothering to remove his clothes, he lay back and allowed his mattress and pillow to release him of his body weight. With his eyes closed, the voices in his head—the newscasters, the footage blasting with sirens, close-ups of the weeping crowds, and, of course, the Palestinian kids' attack on the ambulance with rocks, as it drove the bodies away from the mountain—came into sharp focus.

There he was, in the recess yard, falling again...and he knew what was coming...that he would break skin and bleed...

...and there was not a thing he could do about it.

Of their own volition, his eyes opened and stared at the mold stain on the ceiling above his head. There it was: Rabbi Isaacs's face, smiling disingenuously, the droopy eyelids giving nothing away. When Aaron came upon this stain, during the first night he had slept in this apartment after signing the lease and moving in, he had made a spitball and hurled it, childishly, up at the mildewed face of the dean of his yeshivah back in London, the man who presided over the entire institution that included an elementary school, high school, and *beis midrash* program.

It hadn't reached.

Just as well.

Most days he tried to avoid looking in the direction of that stain, but today it was impossible. Those kids. Those dead kids and their parents would not remove themselves from his thoughts, making him look up at Rabbi Isaacs's moldy portrait with his infuriating smirk.

Either I should move, or just wipe that awful stain away.

Soon, he resolved, as his eyes closed sleepily. *I'll get to it soon.*

Just before slipping into slumber, Aaron tried to remember some better people. There *had* been better people in his childhood. Not everyone was bad, though somehow the rotten ones seemed to have more staying power than the others. There was Rabbi Gold, young Rabbi Yona Gold, with his small, neat beard and tailored suits, who had told Elchanan Bulman that his son was destined for greatness. Aaron remembered how both his father and Rabbi Gold had smiled down at him, nodding pleasantly.

"I mean it!" Rabbi Gold said excitedly. "I'm not just saying it. There is something special about your Aaron. His sensitivity...it comes from you, the 'Red Rebel.'"

Elchanan had laughed heartily at the mention of his old title. "I have not heard zis words in a long time." He coughed. With one hand on his broad chest and the other on his son's shoulder, he shook his head, as though telling himself off for dreaming. "Ahhhh," he hankered, "if mine Arele would grow to haff the man h'is naming after, I will be happy...haff the man... More zan zis—" he shook his head softly— "...I cannot hope."

Half the man...?

Oy, Tatte! Didn't you see?

I didn't stand a chance!

When the alarm on his phone started beeping, Aaron pulled it under his quilt to silence it. He peeked through the window slats. Night had fallen. He threw his quilt back onto the floor and glanced ruefully at his sleep-crumpled clothes, hunting around for cleaner ones. His shift would start soon, and he needed to speak with Eitan and Uri beforehand.

Hurriedly, he showered, dressed, and ran out the door. He had half an hour. Rushing to his friends' apartment building, he shot a quick look up at the balcony where the three of them had spent many a happy evening together, overlooking the sparkling English Channel.

Empty.

He ran inside, toward the elevator, tripping between other residents, slammed his whole palm on the up button, and waited for it to open. What his rush was he could hardly understand himself, but he needed to talk to his two friends, and hear what they had to say about the Stern family and what it all meant.

Alighting on the fifth floor, Aaron crossed the corridor and knocked on the familiar apartment door. He did not wait for anyone to let him in, opening the door himself. He stopped short only when he saw the suitcases that were standing, with military obedience, in the hallway of the cramped little French residence that Eitan and Uri had called home for nearly a year.

"What's going on?" Aaron called out.

Uri came out of the bedroom, hair wet, clothes comfortably casual, ready to travel. "We've got tickets to go home. Our plane leaves at five after twelve. Sorry this is such short notice, but our time here is done. For now, anyway." He threw Aaron a smile. "It's been fun. Remember us."

Eitan was on the phone in the bedroom. Glancing between the hinges of the door, Aaron could see an open laptop, keys, and a wallet on one of the beds, all ready to go into hand luggage. They must have been packing all day.

"How come you're leaving? Is it because of the Sterns?"

"Well, yes and no. Come. Come into the kitchen. We have some leftover chicken we need to get rid of, and you look like you could do with some food. Come. I'll heat it up for you."

Aaron followed Uri to the kitchen. It was just a small kitchenette really, that opened to an eating area with a large patio door leading out to the balcony where they loved to spend their time. He looked at the white table and six chairs—though mostly it would be just the three of them together, enjoying the view of the streets below and the sea further away—and felt, once again, a tightening in his stomach. Uri opened the refrigerator and took out a plastic container of chicken and rice.

"Why yes and no? Explain what you mean."

"What are *you* going to do?" Uri asked him. Maybe he had not heard Aaron.

"Do? What do you mean? Nothing."

"Right. I forgot. You are English."

"What is that supposed to mean?"

"Well, we are a country preparing for war." His use of the word "we" hurt Aaron. "More rockets were shot into southern Israel today, again. Do you even know what that means?"

Aaron shrugged his shoulders. "So this is why you are leaving. What do you do? In the army, I mean?"

Uri looked at him for a long time without saying anything. Then he turned back to the kitchenette.

Aaron went out to the balcony and stood by the wall, hands resting on the top of the railing. The dark sky was lit up with stars. The sea bobbed and flowed, moonlight bouncing off crests like fireflies. Below, on the street, some merrymakers were leaving an establishment, their carefree giggles contrasting with the mood percolating within the little apartment. It was strange, how the friends' relationship had so dramatically shifted in the space of one afternoon's announcement. Eitan and Uri were charging back to Israel as full participants in action, while Aaron was a mere spectator of a drama he felt he should have understood better.

Should have...should have...should have... A person could just die *under the weight of all the "should have's" of the world!*

Eitan opened the patio door wide. Like Uri, he was wearing jeans and an untucked shirt, open at the neck. Aaron whirled around to greet him. "So you're off," he said, his throat tight, making him sound woeful.

"We'll be back. We're not giving up our rent so easily. It's on a full year lease. You know, if you want, you can take it over while we are gone." Eitan was shorter than Aaron by a full half a foot. It was odd how some shorter men could command so much respect just by using their carefully perfected presence. When in Eitan's company, Aaron had the feeling of being summed up and placed by him. Eitan always seemed fully in control of any situation. Aaron, on the other hand, had never felt in control of anything, which perhaps was why he was so struck by Eitan in the first place.

"What are you expecting when you get there? Do you think there will for sure be war?"

Eitan smiled, and Aaron disliked him at that moment. "Of course there will be a war. It is inevitable."

"And that's why you two are heading back."

"War is never a good thing." Eitan sat at the head of the patio table and pulled out a cigarette. After lighting it, he added, "Especially not for Israel."

Uri came in holding a plate of food for Aaron. He laid it down on the table with a plastic knife and fork. "What are you two talking about?"

"In a war," Eitan did not even look at Uri, but continued to address Aaron, "as with any life situation, there are always multiple narratives. You will probably stay here. You will watch the news and you will see it from one side or another; whichever news station you will use will have their take. Know, Aaron, that on the ground, where the real battles are being fought, it will look completely different. Israel can never win."

"Aaron, sit and eat!" called Uri, before disappearing back inside.

"What do you mean, 'Israel can never win'?" Aaron sat down and put a piece of chicken into his mouth.

"The media war. On the ground, Israel will win. But the enemy knows better how to manipulate opinions. They know how to portray themselves. We lag way behind in that department. All our resources we pour into survival. Israel can never win on the world stage. It's a sad fact. Okay, eat up."

Aaron had not realized that he was not chewing. He turned away from Eitan and tried to eat, but the food felt rubbery in his mouth. Uri emerged once more with three bottles of beer. He handed them out. "Sorry to rush you, Aaron, but we have a plane to catch."

Aaron stood up. Eitan and Uri pounded him on the back, and they said their goodbyes. A few minutes later, he walked down the stairs and out into the street.

There was so much to process: an old, familiar feeling of abandonment, and another, very different, almost alien, emotion. Jealousy. And immediately upon recognizing the emotion for what it was, Aaron felt ashamed. How could he be jealous of two people headed for war, while he would be sitting pretty here in the north of France? He tried to wrest the feeling out of himself, if just to fling it across the street, but it was jammed fast somewhere between his thoracic wall and the organs therein.

He approached Black Tie full of dark thoughts. These two friends, who had reintroduced him to society, were leaving. The realization of how different they were from him hurt even to explore. Eitan and

Uri had an existence outside of themselves. They had reason to *be*. The contrast was bleak. A good day for Aaron would be if he had not gotten into any arguments with any patrons; if he had not fought with his boss; and if he had enough money in his pocket to get by.

He was thirty-seven, for goodness' sake! How had he gotten to this age with nothing to show for it?

Had he been asleep? Too busy getting through the days to remember about the years?

Aaron opened the side door and immediately felt repulsed by the throbbing vibrations of the music; the crushing, swaying bodies; and the smell of the whisky that he would soon be pouring. *Eitan and Uri*, he concluded, as his boss nodded to him from across the bar, *have purpose. Their time in Deauville Beach had always had unspoken boundaries and parameters.*

Now their country is calling them. And they can hear it.
While all I hear are the empty echoes of yesterday's footsteps.
I am running nowhere...
...but I drift everywhere.

The internal pendulum, rusty from inertia, slowly began to swing, its awakening, creaking and coughing, causing a massive dust storm within, beginning to sway with an urgency that could no longer be ignored.

Perhaps it was the grave of Elchanan Bulman sibilating, as the winds blew news to him in the Next World that resurgence of his son's spirit was imminent. And Elchanan, who had lost hope in the waiting that had gone on for far, far too long, could not continue in peaceful slumber anymore...

It was the fourth day of Chanukah, 1977, when Elchanan named his eight-day-old son Aaron Rephael Bulman, and wept over the squalling infant like he had never allowed himself to weep in his life. The small crowd who had gathered at the little shul in London could not have known the images and memories that bombarded his mind, generating his glut of tears. Greta, in the women's section, turned to her family and friends and nervously apologized for her husband's impropriety. Who could have fathomed that at that moment Elchanan was revisiting the moment he had last seen his father—the original Aaron Rephael Bulman?

It was 1948, and he was only six years old.

They had just sat down to eat, his mother, his father, and he, in their one-roomed home in a little hamlet outside of Rostov-on-Don, in southern Russia, when four of Stalin's pistol-touting, uniformed NKVD agents barged in and dragged the unsuspecting Aaron Rephael away. Just one of the 750,000 purged un-wanteds sent to an unknown destination, rumored to be Siberia—a place empty of life, a desert of snow and ice, where men perished in their sleep. His mother, expecting at the time, cried and begged, but was thrown down and did not ever seem to get "up" again after that. His father's parting words to his son were, *"Yetst bist du der ba'al habayis, Elchanan. You are the man of this house now. Take care of your mother. Learn Torah. Stay a Jew."*

That winter, two letters addressed to Elchanan's mother were all that came. Nothing more. They never knew what happened to him, how he died, where he was buried...nothing. And what was Aaron Rephael's crime? He was a *melamed*—a teacher who delicately and devotedly "indoctrinated" small children to rebel against Soviet G-dlessness:

Kamatz aleph...ah, kamatz beis...bah, kamatz gimmel...gah...

...This is how we read, kinderlach...

...This is how we pray...

...This is how we understand the world...

Kamatz daled...dah, kamatz hey...hah...

A few months later, Elchanan's mother gave birth to a stillborn girl whom she named Sarah before burying her in the local Jewish cemetery, right next to a thicket of birch trees, two meters in from the brook some used as a *mikveh*.

Ten years went by and in 1958, while the regime kept a tight noose around all Jewish activities, the now-teenaged Elchanan fought back. He organized underground schools for children to learn what his father had given his life to teach. Dancing in the face of danger, he built a few small matzah bakeries for the families willing to risk holding a Seder in a country that could send you to the dreaded gulags for twenty-five years for what they termed, *counter-revolutionary activities*. He set up clandestine synagogues in basements and hovels so that people would have where to pray. He even arranged a small sukkah crunched between buildings in every town within biking distance, and miraculously provided one set of *arba'ah minim*, so his fellow Jews would be able to fulfill the mitzvos on Sukkos properly. He earned the nickname, "the Red Rebel." People relied on him for their connection to *Yiddishkeit*, and because of that he refused to marry.

His mother grew old very quickly. For six years he cared for her, working small side jobs to pay for exorbitantly priced medications, massaging her rheumatic limbs, changing and laundering her bedclothes, until she died in 1967.

Alone now, at the young age of twenty-five, he grew despondent. Though he bravely continued his "rebel-like" mission, he applied for a visa to emigrate. At first he was refused, but after two years he was granted permission to leave the country. He packed a small suitcase of belongings—notably his father's compact set of Gemara and his mother's brass candlesticks—and set out. He arrived in England in 1969, without family, penniless, and with nothing more than rudimentary English, picked up from years of hearing from the American Jews who came to visit and supply inspiration to their fellow Jews left behind the Iron Curtain.

Friendless and fearful, Elchanan walked out of Heathrow airport with no address and nowhere to go. He hired a taxi and asked to be brought to any synagogue in London where he was sure he would find someone who could lend him the money to pay the driver. The driver was a Cockney gentile who thought he had picked up a fool, but good-naturedly brought him to the Jubilee Street Great Synagogue. There Elchanan indeed found the means to pay for the ride from the generosity of the old *rav*, Rabbi Yehuda Leib Levine, who not only paid his fare but brought him home to eat and sleep.

Elchanan never forgot the kindness of the rabbi and his wife, Chana Baila. He spent three years in their home, probably the calmest years of his life, working on his English and looking for suitable employment. Once these things were taken care of, Chana Baila set herself the task of finding a match worthy of the "Red Rebel," whom she had grown fond of and admired greatly for the stories he told at her Shabbos table; for his otherwise quiet manner; and mostly for the careful way in which he honored her ailing husband.

Greta Galowinsky, a nursery-school teacher at the newly established Jewish center in Chattersfield, a working-class district in southeast London, came highly recommended as a potential bride for this intense new immigrant who had served his Soviet Jewish countrymen so well. Greta was not pretty, but tall and impressive-looking. Still single at twenty-eight, she was considered a living calamity. Wagging tongues blamed her overbearing and highly critical mother, whom, so they said, had bequeathed to her daughter a crippling shyness. Who knew? Only in her nursery classroom did Greta Galowinsky shed her inhibitions and shine, as she took care of the youngest members of the growing religious populace of the area.

Greta met Elchanan in the living room of the Levines' home, and the two continued to see each other for four weeks, going out for walks or meeting in parks, before deciding that theirs was a good enough match, and setting a date for the wedding. They were in a hurry, as Rabbi Levine's health was declining, and he wanted to be present at the marriage of his protégé who had, quite literally, stepped in off the street three years earlier.

No longer alone, Elchanan cherished his new wife; she, conversely, held him at a distance, not quite believing that he was all he was cracked up to be. There was one thing, though, that Greta had been delighted to discover: Elchanan's singing voice. No one had thought to mention to her of its soft, stirring, moss-like quality; how Elchanan had been the *chazzan* at the Jubilee Street Great Synagogue now for three years; and how everyone had been mesmerized by his soothing, restorative timbre, a power made more so by its subtlety.

During the first Shabbos after their marriage, Elchanan was asked if he would honor the modest congregation in Chattersfield by leading them in prayer. Greta found her eyes watering with disbelief that it was *she* who had nabbed the owner of that most beautiful voice. The women of the shul surrounded her after the service was over and filled the air with accolades for his stirring rendition of the *chazaras hashatz*. He quickly became their shul's favorite *chazzan*, and with that title Greta found she could shed a few more of her social anxieties. Though she was never free of them completely, as time went on she learned to handle them better and better, and this was especially so after the birth of her first child.

It was a girl, and they named her Sima Rivka, after Elchanan's mother. And so Elchanan became a new father at the age of thirty-two, and Greta a mother at thirty. They both felt splendidly blessed that theirs should turn out a happy ending after all. All the love they both felt deprived of was now showered onto their firstborn. She was a fair-haired, chubby-faced, green-eyed treasure that they pushed around the neighborhood in a Silver Cross perambulator, looking and feeling as though their trust in G-d had paid off with dividends at last. They had never known happiness like this. The angels were smiling down on them, they were sure.

Slowly Elchanan and Greta learned to trust one another. They moved into a little house on Ashley Grove, a small street in Chattersfield. It had cost them a fortune, but Greta had been saving for years—ten pounds a week from her wages at the nursery—so they were able to pay a decent down payment and live off the salary Elchanan made as a bookbinder for the local Jewish printing house, Vashentroib and Sons, Ltd. Old Mr. Vashentroib spoke only Yiddish, with a strong Hungarian accent. He was mostly kind, but had a sharp tongue of which Elchanan was none too fond. Consequently, Elchanan was on the lookout to open his own printing house. Like his wife had done, he began putting away money every week to realize this dream, waiting for the right opportunity.

About two years later Greta found out that she was expecting again. Nothing about the pregnancy nor birth could have foretold that the child she and her husband were bringing into the world would overturn theirs. When Elchanan wept at his only son's *bris*, it surprised him more than anyone. He put it down to having come full circle, but in the later years he considered it portentous.

The baby was named after Elchanan's father. Greta had no complaints to her husband for hogging the names. After all, she hadn't lost any family members yet.

Though little Aaron Rephael was showered with the same affection as his older sister, his was not a happy infancy. Many a night Greta could be seen pacing through her home, cradling her fidgety, colicky baby, hour after maddening hour. By seven months, the baby seemed to have settled whatever it was that was bothering him, and got down to the business of growing, sleeping, eating, and observing. Greta was his ally in all things, as trouble began when he could not keep his hands off anything, so much more destructive in his explorations than his sister had been.

"It's a boy thing," Greta would say, trying her best to tame the tension, as a frustrated Elchanan patched together yet another *sefer* that Aaron had ripped. "Isn't this what boys do?"

"*Nein*, zis is not vhat I done vhen I vas a boy!" Elchanan would snap, forcefully shaking his head.

"Well, seriously, Elchanan, you can hardly compare..."

By the time Sima turned four and Aaron was eighteen months old, Elchanan was thirty-six, and deeply in debt. He had hatched a plan that would allow him to break away from the sting of Mr. Vashentroib's tongue, and provide greater wealth for his growing family. He'd borrowed a considerable sum from his local bank to purchase a fully functioning printing property about an hour east of Chattersfield. The problem was, he had no idea that the crumbling structure had been condemned the year before. Uncontainable black mold had been creeping from its drainage for years. His determination, coupled with naiveté, had blinded him. And of course, the sellers did not think it necessary to warn him. Though he appealed to the government, they would not allow him to pursue fixing the damage, as they claimed its toxicity levels exceeded their warrants and that the building was slated for demolition. Elchanan would have taken the two men he shook hands with to court, had he been able to track the address on the bogus contract he had signed in triplicate.

With his head almost touching his tail, he broke the news to his wife that for the next ten or so years not only would they have no extra income, as they had both dreamed, but each week a fat chunk of Elchanan's paycheck would have to go to pay off his irredeemable debt. Declaring bankruptcy was not an option, as neither of them cared for the tarnishing of their good reputations.

Humiliated, he returned to the Vashentroib family, who took him back but would not up his wages. Grateful to have been treated respectfully, he sulked quietly and constantly about where he was going to come up with the funds to keep the bank at bay and still cover the prohibitive costs of living. When he would come home at night, a tired Greta's list of Aaron's mischief-making did not cast the boy in a favorable light to his father, who was becoming more and more querulous and resentful.

It did not get better in kindergarten, where Aaron earned notoriety for punching and kicking. He even bit a boy. Once, after being placed in the corner for "time-out," he smashed one of the large windows overlooking the outdoor play area. He was sent home. He was five years old at the time and remembered nothing of what had happened that day, except that his classmates had formed a circle around him and chanted, "Aaron Bulman, stick him in the oven, turn it on, and you'll have bacon!"

By the time Aaron entered elementary school, he viewed his impulsivity as a monster living inside him. Fearing it and mistrusting himself, he found it hard to focus. The only thing he could be assured of was the unpredictability that filled his days.

Thus his childhood passed—with his father preoccupied with work and bills, and his mother softly dismissive, both not sensing any foreboding, letting all signs pass them by completely undetected.

It was a generational thing.

To: Henyaleipzig@sympatico.com
From: simah@gmail.com
Date: September 1, 2015
Time: 8:56 p.m.

Hey Henya, me again.

You know, I'm getting quite used to your silence. Something that should worry you a bit, no? I mean, all the texts I keep sending and the emails, and not a thing from you at all. Nada! Well, oddly, I don't mind it anymore. I'm pretty sure you're reading them, but it still makes me mad that you're being soooooo incredibly stubborn!

Meanwhile, I feel free to air my thoughts, and that is what I intend to do. Henya, do you remember that time when Rabbi Gold told Tatte that Aaron was destined for greatness? Do you remember how we all laughed at the time? I'm a bit ashamed of how I treated him. No, that's not exactly true; I'm actually much more than a bit: I'm *very* ashamed.

I think we—all of us—hurt him.

Oh, Henya, Aryeh just walked in and told me I'm crazy for keeping this up with you. But he has accused me of being crazy before, so, oh well. Anyway, he said to tell you that there is something called the Thirteenth Gate, and that if you don't know what that is, just Google it. Maybe then you'll change your mind about what I did, and about Aaron, and maybe, just maybe, we can put all this behind us. That's what Aryeh is sayng right now to me. I'm just typing relly fast to keep up with him, cuz he is in one of his rare passionate modes and is speaking reallly quickly and loudly.

Anyway, gotta go,

Sory for all the speling mistakes

Until the next time I write,

Au revoir, my dearest, most annoyingly wrong, sister,

Love,

Sima

5

"There will be war," Aryeh said from his study near the kitchen, his voice rich with unease and resignation.

Sima shook her head quietly to herself. *What, he thinks he's Churchill or something?* she thought. *All he needs is the cigar.*

It was early morning, and he was sitting at his desk, staring into his laptop. "Sima, you've gotta come see this...!"

Ever since the Sterns had gone missing, he would begin his day by finding out what had happened during the night. Today was the first day of Camp Menucha Hills, where the two youngest Hertzberg girls were signed up to attend, but Aryeh remained sequestered from all the busyness: the dressing, hair-brushing, scampering, packing, filling, sloshing, rollicking, and general hoopla. The very air wafted with Coppertone Water Babies sunscreen. It was a wholesome ruckus, but one that was utterly lost on Aryeh.

"What was that?" Sima called back distractedly, all attention focused on brushing the knots out of Bracha's dark brown, unruly hair.

"You have to come and look at this." Aryeh's eyes did not waver from the screen. "Israel is being goaded. It's sickening!"

"What's sickening?" Sima entered the study, pulling the tangled mush of hair off the bristles of the hairbrush and throwing it into the small garbage can near the door.

Aryeh pointed to his screen. "Nineteen rockets and six mortars launched against us overnight. And that's on top of yesterday's fiasco, at the funeral. I'm telling you..." Aryeh shook his head. "They *want* war. They *love* war." He looked at Sima, disgust burrowing lines in his forehead and around his lips, hardly seen beneath his sharp black beard. "Some people simply *thrive* on death and destruction."

Sima sat down on the chair across the desk, and Aryeh swiveled the screen toward her. "Look." He pointed to the headlines. She scrolled. Aryeh started to put on his jacket. Pulling the collar down, he said, "Better step up security over here."

She looked up. "Do you really think that's necessary?"

"Sima..." His taut shoulders went flaccid. "Of course it's necessary." He took a long, deep breath. "Don't you understand what is happening here? In any courtroom, including the courtroom of public opinion, 'truth' takes a back seat to 'what can be proven.' Hamas has been manipulating the hype for years. I can just see what's gonna happen now: Israel will retaliate, the world will scrutinize, and then before you know it, Israel will be charged. We've seen it all before. Look..." He went back and started working his laptop, clicking with quiet indignation. Finally, he found what he was looking for and opened it on full-screen mode. "Look, Sima."

She watched an ambulance driving around a mob of riled-up Palestinians. It screeched its brakes and hadn't even come to a full halt before it had its back doors opened. From the side came another mob carrying an injured man amid shouts and flying fists. They practically threw the stretcher into the vehicle.

"Now," Aryeh continued, "we will never know if that was staged or real, but just look at how they react when they see that the cameras are on them. They have been trained to do this: to make things look as dire as possible. We are just not going to compete with that. And that is one of the ways we *lose* and they *win*. *Every time...*" He started pulling at his black beard. "Hundreds of Palestinians have been arrested, homes demolished, and roads closed. Trust me: there are bound to be repercussions. Even in sleepy ol' Long Island. Hamas can always rely on the world's hatred. Happens every time."

"Aryeh...?"

"What?" He foraged around for his keys.

"If this is just about land, why don't we simply give it up? Land is a *thing*. And things are not *people*. Why not give them what they want and walk away with our lives intact?"

"Sima!" Incredulity spread across his face. "Don't you realize that this is *not* simply about land? And it never has been. This is about the Jews' right to *breathe*. Our right to exist on this earth! They hate us and just want us dead, no matter how much land we give them!"

Sima said nothing.

Keys found, he collected his papers and stood at the doorway looking at her. "Heard anything from Tamar?" he asked, as though a new file had just popped open inside his head.

"What?" She blinked, looking up. She scrambled for a moment, the sudden reshuffling of thoughts catching her unrehearsed.

"Tamar. Has she made any contact yet?"

"Not much. Why?" She pulled at her earlobe.

"Nothing important." He turned to leave. "Just wondering if you'd heard how she's doing up there. Last year was not a success, right? Just making sure there are no repeats."

"Ahhh..." Sima shook her head. "No. We had a quick phone call, but no real conversation."

Aryeh left.

Hmmm, Sima mused. *Tamar and her little "situation."* In the aftermath of the murders of the Stern parents and children, did anything else really matter? When she saw the pinched but trying-to-be-brave faces of their relatives, shouldn't she just feel gratitude that Tamar was, after all, alive? There ought to be a word for families who had been decimated by terrorism, like the word "orphan" or "widow" or "survivor."

Why wasn't there a word for such families?

Maybe there was.

Didn't the circumstance call for a *whole new* word?

She checked her watch. It would soon be time to go. She stayed a little longer, reading from the computer screen: The day before—the day of the funeral—Israel had more than twenty rockets fired at it from Gaza. On the day of the funeral, no less! Sima shook her head. She didn't want to read further, would have preferred to have stopped right then, but something she could not name made her continue: The IDF just shot an Ibrahim Al-Kazha dead during a raid. His family claimed he was carrying eggs; an IDF spokesman said he had thrown a grenade at the troops.

Who will the world choose to believe?

Once in the car, Sima quickly noticed the glaring contrast between her cheerlessness and the world outside. As she drove dispiritedly through the streets, she observed people going about their daily routines. They still shopped to Sixties hits that grocery stores played over the red, green, and yellow peppers. Camp buses still disgorged their charges to the outstretched hands of the teenagers hired to shuttle them from activity to activity. Women still gathered in clusters and admired one another's weight loss. *Wow, Mazy, you look amazing! Tell me, how did you do it?*

When Sima pulled up to the day camp to drop off Naomi and Bracha, she noticed Mimi Eisner, one of Tamar's friends, there. Her hair was in a messy bun, a whistle dangled from her neck, and she wore an I-Love-Camp-Menucha-Hills T-shirt. They exchanged a wave, and instantly Sima's head filled again with Tamar's letter.

Mimi Eisner kept looking at her. Did she know? Was the letter and its contents old news among Tamar's friends? Was it the classic case of the parents being the last to find out about something? She felt humiliation creeping up onto her face; her cheeks began to burn. "Hi, Mimi!" Sima called out, letting down the window and trying to keep her voice steady. "Having fun?"

"Hi, Mrs. Hertzberg. Did you hear anything from Tamar yet?"

Heard what *from Tamar?* Sima nodded. "She's having a blast up there. Shame you stayed in the city, but I understand. Moolah!" Sima rubbed her fingers to her thumb, and they both laughed.

As she drove off, she scolded herself. What did it matter if Mimi knew? Her knowing did not make anything any different. She—Sima— should be above that. But she knew, on a deeper level than she preferred to acknowledge, that it *did* matter to her; that she wouldn't be able to bear it if Mimi knew. And that just amplified the shame and the guilt.

"Mommy, for my next birthday can you buy me a horse?"

"Sure, zeeskeit." *Sima smiled and leaned over to kiss her oldest daughter's forehead. "But where would we put it?" They were sitting on the hammock on the veranda that overlooked the backyard, swinging so lightly, it was almost imperceptible. It was a rare, one-on-one moment wherein she was not rushing off with something to accomplish.*

"We could build a barn there." Tamar pointed to the furthest corner, where three pitch pine trees stood majestically conferencing with one another, their limbs intermingling, compulsively shaking hands on the deal.

"Our yard is not big enough, sweetie. A horse needs space to run and play. No?"

"I guess." Tamar lowered her eyes and snuggled closer.

Sima felt her daughter's disappointment in the increase of her body weight. "Tam?"

"Yeah?"

"Why do you want a horse?"

Tamar sat up and looked into her mother's eyes. "So when I ride it to school, I will be able to feel the wind in my hair."

"Mmmm, sounds lovely." Sima took her index finger and ran it slowly down from the center of Tamar's forehead to her nose, ending it at the very tip where she planted a kiss. "Maybe you can have that same feeling when you are biking to school."

"It won't be the same."

"No. You're right. It won't."

How old was Tamar then? Sima tried to remember. Seven, eight? *Was I missing the signals she kept sending me? Signs of her discomfort, of her claustrophobia, of her need for more space?*

Sima never thought the day would come when she would be out of touch with her daughter. That she, who had placed much responsibility at the feet of her own parents for the loss of Aaron, would now be stuck in the same quagmire. Was there something faulty in her DNA? Something woeful that traveled from her genetic code and into her offspring? Whenever she thought of Aaron—which was something she had struggled in the early years not to do—it was accompanied by a mild, but still potent, explosion. She had decided, long ago, to heed her father's advice and not mention his name to her daughters. As far as they knew, Mommy had only one sibling—Aunty Henya, who lived with her husband, Uncle Michoel, and their family in England, and visited occasionally.

Better that way, she had thought at the time.

Safer.

Now she was not so sure.

She paused at the end of the Camp Menucha Hills driveway, considering what to do for the next six hours of complete freedom. As the social worker at Magen David Elementary, the conservative Jewish day school that Aryeh and Sima did *not* send their daughters to, she worked five-hour shifts every other day. When she wasn't working, she was filling out reports. Consequently, summers, when she was off, were intensely anticipated. She glanced at herself in the rear-view mirror. *How indulgent would it be if I booked myself in for a massage later today?*

But once she was already on the road, Sima turned the wheel unexpectedly westward. Her car was making the decision for her. Destination: Aryeh's office building.

Brunch with Aryeh? Yes, that was a wonderful idea. Would she take the opportunity to tell him what was going on? Maybe. To figure this thing out together? Yes. *I cannot do this alone.* A sudden detonation of anger erupted inside her: Tamar had made her lie to her husband! That was wrong. And she was going to right it. Yes.

She sat back in her seat and enjoyed the few moments of clarity that always followed an executive decision. She was going to tell everything to Aryeh, and they would talk it through. Perhaps that was part of what was missing with her parents, she thought. Perhaps they had not talked things through enough. She remembered the feeling she had as a child, a choking, crushing feeling as she would gather all the unspoken words that littered her childhood home. Words she knew needed to be said: angry words, yes; explosive words, true; words with the power to destroy—but which would then lead to comforting words, receptive words, words with the power to heal.

Sima's mind wandered back to that Pesach, when Aaron appeared at the Seder table without his *tzitzis*—signifying the start of a more tangible estrangement. He had been uncomfortable for a long time, always asking issue-filled questions and striking out at his teachers when he wasn't satisfied with their responses. Elchanan had been called down to the school to meet with the principal. What they exchanged with one another would never be fully told, but that night, over supper, Elchanan had chastised his son with relentless heat, while Aaron looked down and did not move, and Greta stood by the sink, staring out at the mess and tangle they called a backyard.

Things had quieted down after that, but then came the Seder. When Aaron entered the dining room without his *tzitzis*, everyone in the family had done their very best to avoid eye contact. Greta fluttered around, setting everyone's places, trying so hard to compensate for an atmosphere gone awry, but Elchanan simply looked down—crumpled from the inside. Aaron, Sima remembered, just stared at a tiny protrusion on the wall opposite him.

Watching the spectacle with a growing alarm, Sima's porousness had soaked up all the wordlessness. She felt like lashing out at her brother. Instead, she followed the lead of her mother and said nothing that would draw attention to what Aaron was doing. In her gut, she knew it would not end there either. She knew that what she was witnessing was not about an absent pair of *tzitzis*, but about an ideology under attack: the old ways, and the struggle to preserve them, versus the appealing upchuck of that ancient yoke. She knew that what was happening was so much bigger than anything she could give words to. Fury grew with helplessness, and her heart hurt for her father, the "Red Rebel." Her father, the hero, who would now have the greatest battle of all, but who was so wholly and completely ill-equipped for it, having no weapon in his cache with which to duel. She saw defeat in him that night. Of all the adversities he had had to endure, she figured, Aaron had to be the hardest.

It was Henya, of course, who broke through all the restraint. "Aaron, you look weird. Where's your *tzitzis*—they disappeared?" Then she giggled. "That rhymes. Did you notice? I made up a poem. Aaron looks weird, his *tzitzis* disappeared. Aaron—"

"Enough, Henya!" Elchanan sputtered, his fist hitting the table, making all the fine Pesach china jump. "No more. Thank you."

A little more than two years later, Aaron was gone.

For good.

Sima popped a CD into the CD player to try to distract herself, but the music and the lack of traffic, unusual for this time of day, served to deepen her absorption. She steered the car into an unpopulated lane and turned on cruise control. How was it that she had turned out so differently from her brother?

When he was very young, Sima remembered, Aaron seemed to divide much of the world into two: in his childish lexicon, things were either "*goyish*" or "*Yiddish*": Men with ponytails were "*goyish*," whereas beards were "*Yiddish*"; long, messy, bleached-blonde, scratchy-dry hair on a woman was "*goyish*," whereas the simple pageboy cuts or curly ponytails were "*Yiddish*"; a shiny, slick, red sportscar was definitely "*goyish*"—"*That's a* goyishe *car, Mummy, right?*"—whereas a rusty station wagon or an old Volvo he called a "*Yiddishe* car." Even food—especially food: If they passed pig carcasses hanging in a butcher's window, Sima remembered Aaron pointing to it and saying, "*Goyish!*" And, of course, music. How many times did he block his ears in stores because the blasting, heavy metal music was too "*goyish*"?

Everything changed the summer of Matthew.

It was August, 1984, when they first discovered Matthew: the tall, skinny Nigerian boy from two terraced houses away on Ashley Grove. His family had lived on the street for three years before he befriended the Bulman kids. They hadn't even noticed him before. The day he came out through his hedge, Sima and Aaron both knew he'd been there for a while, like he'd been watching them. At first they were afraid, but Matthew disarmed them with his toothy grin. It was hard not to succumb to his charms. He had that otherworldly joy about him, a happy-go-lucky ease of being that drew the Bulman children to him.

Now Matthew was quiet. Really quiet. That was because he had a speaking disability. According to the parlance of the time, he was a mute. In the summers, his parents pretty much left him to his own devices. His was the last house on the block, so access to his backyard came from not only within his house—which the Bulman children were afraid to enter—but from the side, through the little alleyway that lined the west wall of his house. Sima and Aaron, who considered Matthew's home forbidden territory, had gotten as far as peering into the front hallway. The walls were painted a dark shade of colorless beige. The lights were rarely on. His mother wore florid orange and pink turbans on her head, with long crystals that swung from her ears as she went about her chores. Aside from her, there seemed to be no other color in the house. They rarely saw Matthew's dad. He was an important man, they surmised, because he always wore a suit, and if they were up early enough, they could spot him going into his car with his leather briefcase and driving off to work. He would return home at the same time every evening. From the house to the car, from the car to the house—always with his briefcase in hand.

At first, Matthew baffled both Sima and Aaron. He approached them on the pavement, just as they were drawing numbers for hopscotch on the concrete slabs. He held out his fist, but did not look ready to start a fight. His eyes searched out theirs; he was looking to make contact. The Bulman siblings stopped what they were doing and studied his outstretched hand in silence. Matthew grunted and opened his palm to reveal a small piece of fallen roof tile, bluish-gray with silvery lines shot through it. He grunted again and waved this treasure toward Sima, who felt more curiosity than fear.

"What do you want, Matthew?" Sima asked, unsure of how Matthew would explain himself.

"How do you know his name?" Aaron asked.

"I heard his mother calling him. He's not deaf, you know, just mute."

Matthew moved toward the beginning of the hopscotch board and stood with his feet apart, just beneath the slab that had the number "1" written in chalk. He smiled at the two children, showing irregular but very white teeth. They watched in silence as he gently threw the piece of fallen tile so that it landed on "1." Matthew then jumped, spread his feet and landed with his left foot on the slab that read "2," and his right on "3." He looked at the two Bulman children and beamed.

"He wants to play."

"Go on, Matthew. You can play with us."

They played all that day and every day that summer. When Sima brought out snacks, she brought out three. When Aaron brought out shovels, to dig for buried treasure in the Bulman backyard, he gave the best one to Matthew and settled on the rusty one for himself. When Matthew brought out drinks, the first time, he brought out three, but was forced to drink them all, as the Bulman children would not eat anything Matthew offered them—for fear of it not being kosher. Sima worried about offending him, but Matthew did not seem to mind. He did not seem to mind any of the tacit little differences between them, making it so that he was able to walk into the Bulman house, but the Bulman children would not have considered entering his. He did not seem to mind that Sima and Aaron spoke of him as though he were not there, even though he understood perfectly what they were saying. He did not seem to mind that every so often, Greta would hiss at her children that they should go up the block where the other Jewish kids played, and leave this unsuitable, ragtag of a playmate to his own devices.

"Why can't you just go up the street? Who is this kid, anyway? Trust my children to befriend the village idiot!"

Matthew would just shrug his thin shoulders and step away, waiting for the moment to pass.

And that summer, it always did. This was because there were many other things that worried Greta Bulman that summer: having a two-month-old infant at home with a croupy cough that flared and scared her every night, was just one; a husband who may or may not have been battling depression, after the electric company threatened to cut off their power if he did not submit the minimum fee, added to it. To top it off, Greta, who had inherited a rare genetic disorder called lymphedema from her mother, was suffering from the condition's fury caused by the confluence of pregnancy and summer heat. Her left leg was so swollen, she was unable to wear anything on that foot at all. Barely did she manage the household chores; leaving the house to go grocery shopping had become a faraway dream.

So Greta simply turned away from her two oldest children in defeat, with little Henya drooling down the back of her housecoat, and let fall what may.

Summer began to fade. The plane tree leaves, having grown so wide, drooped and slapped passersby. The rubbish bins emitted odors of an accumulated sap, maggoty in the late August mugginess. The slow-to-arrive dusks began creeping in earlier and earlier.

It was a Friday morning when everything changed. September was a week away. All of the block kids were kicked out onto the street to play, so their mothers could cook and prepare for Shabbos. Mostly the children stayed further down the block: the Lerners, the Litmans, the Shwebels, the Holtzes, and the Zimmermans. You could hear their hooting and whooping bouncing off the street's prewar brick walls.

Aaron and Sima had their end of the block to themselves. They knocked on Matthew's door, and Matthew came out, shirtless, wearing white shorts and brown flipflops. Sima and Aaron *never* went *any*where without proper clothing. Aaron didn't even *own* a pair of shorts. Black or blue pants, with a gray, blue, or white shirt during the school year and a colored T-shirt in the summer, comprised his weekday wardrobe. And never did he ever go without socks and proper leather shoes. But the Bulman children didn't care, much less notice, that Matthew dressed differently from them. Matthew was Matthew.

They found him captivating, though they never really found out his age. They'd asked him about it once, and he just smiled and tilted his head sideways, so they dropped it. Perhaps he himself did not know how old he was.

Matthew touched both children on the shoulder and motioned them to follow him around the side of the house. In truth, Matthew was the group leader. Despite his difficulties, he had charisma. Taller than both of them, and much, much skinnier, he possessed a magnetism, some magic ardor that rendered the two of them hopelessly enamored.

He brought them to the concrete part of his backyard. All the backyards on the block had a small concrete area first, and then grass. The cement was primitive and lumpy, like steel-cut oatmeal that had hardened. Many of the neighbors had chosen to paint over the bumpy platform, but nothing could eradicate the bulges and swellings of inadequately mixed mortar. Matthew pointed to his bike. It was turned upside down. The chain was off. Aaron immediately got onto the uneven ground and tried to manipulate the chain into place, but he couldn't do it. At almost seven years old, he may have known what to do, but his hands would not obey.

While the two boys tinkered, Sima looked around. It felt strange to see her house from this angle—the way others saw it. She glanced up at her bedroom window. Did she really live behind that glass? Those curtains? How fast does a change of aspect convert something so familiar into something so wholly foreign?

Matthew's garden was slightly smaller than the Bulmans', but better kept. The grassy middle was freshly cut and the concrete they stood on may have been cracked and lumpy, but it still was in better shape than the Bulmans'. Sima's parents put no effort to maintain the plot of land their house had come with. She meandered over to a wooden chair and sat down, waiting for the boys to give up fixing Matthew's bike.

Sima peered into the kitchen window. A pair of white eyes stared back at her, rhinestones glinting nearby. A tremor spirited through her. Her stomach curdled. Then she realized it was Matthew's mother, and that she was smiling at Sima—not in the least bit angry that the Jewish kids from two doors down had suddenly appeared in her garden.

All the same, Sima was unnerved.

"Okay, Aaron, when are you going to finish already?" she asked, feigning boredom to cover her fright. "The bike is not budging, Matthew. It's full of rust. You won't be able to fix it. You need to buy a new one."

Matthew nodded. His shoulders dropped and his head fell. He pointed to Aaron and grunted. "What?" asked Aaron. "What do you want?"

"Let him use yours," said Sima. "He wants to ride a bike, so let him use yours."

"Do you want to ride my bike, Matthew?"

The small grunts that followed were high-pitched, with a giggly undertone. Sima, Aaron, and Matthew filed out of the yard and down the street, all three disappearing down the Bulmans' cellar stairs, which could be accessed via the front garden. They emerged shortly after with two bikes. The red one Aaron had been given the previous fall for his sixth birthday, and the white one Sima had inherited from her cousin Sonia, the daughter of Greta's older sister, Aunty Breeya.

When Matthew got on Aaron's bike, it became obvious that it would not work for him. His limbs protruded, and he looked like an incognito superhero using an inadequate vehicle that would soon sprout wings and fly.

Sima offered him hers.

The children took turns riding up and down the block. Matthew was unmatchable in his speed and tricks. He showed them how to lift both hands off the handles and still keep the bike straight. He showed them how to do a wheelie, and then to jump—with both wheels off the pavement—and crash down without falling. Matthew had a lot of brains in him, even if he could not utter a word.

Suddenly Greta appeared at the doorway. She was holding little Henya, whose coughing the night before had sounded like tiny buildings being demolished. "Sima, please come here right now!" her mother yelled, in a tone that froze the gnats in orbit. Sima ran up the stoop. "Stay with Henya while I lie down for an hour, will you? I'm utterly exhausted."

Sima nodded, catching Henya in her arms as the baby almost fell out of her mother's. Sima went into the cool and quiet living room. Plopping down on the couch, she snuggled with her beloved little sister. She stared down at the soft perfection of her face, her beautifully plump red lips, the length of her blonde lashes, her dark brown rounded eyes that drooped a little in the outer corners, the invisible arc of her eyebrows, and of course, the smooth landscape of her pale skin, untouched by life's burdens, not a blemish in sight. Sima held her tightly to her chest. She began to softly sing, the two of them looking at one another.

Henya coughed. "Ahhh, Baby Henya," Sima cooed. "Hopefully you'll feel better very soon. And then later, when you're older, you'll run around with us outside." Henya just stared into Sima's eyes, blinked, and produced another small, weak cough, before falling into a gentle sleep.

Sima sank deeper into the old velvety softness of the couch and listened to the sounds of the house: the hum of the fridge, the ticking of the clock, the odd creak from here or there. She must have fallen asleep, but was woken up by strange noises that kept getting louder and louder. She realized, as the last vestiges of sleep left her, that they were coming from right outside her home. She sat up.

Still holding Henya, she walked quickly to the window. The suddenness of movement woke Henya, who whimpered in protest. Outside, it looked like a battle scene: The kids from down the block had formed a circle and were shouting. She could see Pesach Litman and Ari Holtz; Chanale and Zevi Shwebel—the redheaded twins; and Nutte Zimmerman. Lots of little ones were crammed between their older siblings' knees. A nasty ache formed in her belly.

She could not see Aaron or Matthew.

By now Henya had woken up fully and was crying, but Sima just tightened her grip on her and went outside, quickly barging through to the epicenter of the brawl. There she found Pinny Lerner pinned to the ground by—of all people—Aaron. His legs were holding down Pinny's shins, his right arm straddled straight across Pinny's neck, holding his face to the asphalt, as his left hand clutched enough of Pinny's hair to render him still. Pinny's yarmulke had flown a good few feet away.

She then noticed Matthew. He was sitting on the road, his bare chest scraped and bleeding, cuts on both of his knees and arms. He was crying, wiping his tears with his fingers, his mouth open, saliva dripping down his chin. Between sobs he pointed at Pinny and Aaron, grunting hoarsely. Of course no one paid him any regard; they were all concentrating on the two combatants who were silent and unnaturally still.

"What in the world is happening here?" cried Sima, her voice sounding horribly grown up, peculiar even to her own ears.

Zevi pointed to Matthew. "He stole your bike."

Matthew shook his head violently, emitting strained, high-pitched, desperate squeaks.

"No! He didn't!" screamed Aaron, tugging harshly at Pinny's hair. Pinny let out a pitiful moan.

"Aaron! Get off Pinny right now!" Sima ordered. "All of you, GO. Go away! Matthew is our *friend*. I *let* him ride my bike. Now, go away!"

Some of the children stepped back. They looked at Matthew, still crying, using his bare arms to wipe his face. Aaron released Pinny, who stood up and faced him. "We were *saving* your bike. We were *trying* to help you, but you are *so* messed up. No one can help you Bulmans."

Sima saw Aaron fill his mouth with saliva. "No, Aaron! Don't! Can't you see they were just standing up for you?"

The group high-tailed it.

Across the street, just behind his front gate, stood Reb Helfgot, watching. In the London of the eighties, it was still possible to live on the same street as an old couple whose childlessness was courtesy of the medical experiments they had endured in the Nazi concentration camps; in whose dark eyes haunted the ghosts of the families they'd lost, together with the certainty that, when death would finally claim them, two Jewish dynasties would come to an end. Reb Helfgot was a short, thin man who walked with a stoop. He had deeply sunken, hollow eyes and a long, wispy white beard, and could be found every early dawn shuffling along the street, clutching his *tallis* and *tefillin* bag tightly, the wind seeming to blow right through him. Mrs. Helfgot was a pale-faced, withered woman who wore a dark snood that stopped just above her tiny eyes. She could be seen from time to time taking out the garbage, or tending to her garden. Though the couple's eyes were lightless, they had always given the Bulman children a weak smile whenever they noticed them staring. On Fridays, it was the Helfgot home that gave forth the best smells.

Sima stared at Reb Helfgot now. *Had he been there all this time?*

She was still holding Henya, who had stopped crying and was watching her brother sitting in the street. Matthew too had not budged, but was wiping his nose on his bleeding arm. Sima had never heard Reb Helfgot speak before, could not relate to him on any level, but she needed him now. She beseeched him silently: *Do something.*

Reb Helfgot's empty eyes fell upon Matthew. He opened his garden gate and walked over to the trembling boy. He looped his arms under Matthew's shoulders, lifting him to his feet. From his pocket he pulled out a white handkerchief, which he used to tenderly wipe Matthew's face. Reb Helfgot lay his arm around Matthew's bare back, holding him under his armpit. The two walked together, slowly and a bit unsteadily, to Matthew's house, disappearing into the thicket of towering bushes that formed the garden fence.

Sima stepped toward the bike and tried to pick it up with one hand. She struggled. "Aaron, get up. I need you to help me. I can't do this by myself."

Aaron moaned.

"Come on! Get up and help me!"

Aaron sat on the dirty asphalt, reaching for a stone. "Pinny Lerner is going to suffer for this," he said. He threw the stone in the direction of the Lerner home, his eyes reflecting a new kind of anger.

Matthew did not join them again that summer, never opening the door when they came knocking.

Before fall officially began, Matthew's parents had put their house up for sale.

Only now, as an adult, did Sima wince at the memories. They didn't know the word *racism* back then. They couldn't possibly have understood all the layers that led to that bike episode. At the time, they'd all just brushed it off as an inconsequential spat.

Only once, after that, did the Bulman kids see Matthew again.

It was around six months later, when Aaron was seven, and Sima almost ten. The weather had turned cold. Sima was wrapped in a coat too big for her, but it was a beauty: blue fake suede, with white fake fur around the hood and cuffs. It was an indulgence made practical only because Greta had bought it two sizes too big, thus convincing herself that Sima could wear it for an extra-long time. And though her oversized coat made her the target of some jokes, Sima still loved it, not minding too much that it had become a bit of a trademark. Meanwhile, Greta was suffering another flare-up of lymphedema. Water had pooled so badly in her legs that she could not stand for more than a few minutes, deeming it necessary for Sima to pick up Aaron from school and walk home together with him.

What joy coursed through Sima as she strode into the boys' playground and picked out her younger brother from the crush of black yarmulkes edged in silver. Oh, the pride! She felt the stare of the *rebbi* on duty boring down on her as she took Aaron's hand in hers and marched him away, through the gates and into the street. She'd even saved a small snack from her lunch for him. What a great mother's helper she was! This was because, she was sure, she had shown her mother how responsible and mature she was. And now that her mother had placed her faith in her, she would not let her down. This was her sacred task: to bring Aaron home unharmed. For ten minutes she would be making all the decisions for the two of them. Of course Aaron had been forewarned to, "Listen to your sister!"

She had not considered any possibility of danger.

It was a Tuesday evening, just after four. The rain had been ceaseless all day, and a thin fog had settled over their little corner of London. When they reached the council flats, with its tiny, winding path that offered a shortcut to their street, a stone hit Aaron on his shoulder. It was too misty to see anyone, but Sima heard voices from behind one of the parked cars. She felt her limbs stiffen and her stomach contract. Her fingers tightened around Aaron's hand, and she pulled him closer to her. "Just keep walking," she whispered as she lowered her head, concentrating on placing one foot in front of the other.

"Hey!" A boy, not much older than herself, sprang out from between the cars and stood in front of them. "You Jewbugs?" The skin-and-bones boy had long brown bangs that covered one of his eyes. He wore a black bomber jacket, open in the cold, both hands burrowing in his pants pockets, elbows hanging loosely on either side. He was chewing what looked like a large wad of gum.

Sima faltered. To answer would be to invite more questions, but to ignore would be considered an act of war. Furthermore, she did not believe he was alone. In her mind, she envisioned many more stones in jittery hands behind the cars. "Yes," she finally said, pulling on Aaron's hand to indicate her intention to continue walking.

They passed the boy and crossed the road. Once across, she made the mistake of turning back to see if he was watching them. She tried to avoid it, but their eyes met. He made a quick, pullback gesture, as though he had another stone and was aiming it at them. Raw panic took hold of her, and she broke into a run, the likes of which she had never known. Aaron flew alongside her. Later, they would describe the hoots and whistles and frenzied laughter that followed them as they sprinted through the lamp-lit streets.

Just as the whole gang of stone-throwing youths was closing the gap, and the Bulman children were convinced that their legs would not carry them to safety, Matthew suddenly appeared. "Matthew!" they both cried. "Help us!"

The whites of Matthew's eyes shone as he surveyed the situation. Grabbing both their hands, he led them under a gateway they had never crossed before—never had the inclination to—into an old cemetery for war veterans. There, amongst the gravestones and crosses, the two trembling siblings tumbled through the dirt pathways before finding a massive monument on which was engraved the names of hundreds of fallen British soldiers whose remains had never made it back home. They crouched behind it and waited in terror. The cemetery was dark and thick with overgrowth. Sounds fell away, as though the foliage understood to stay respectful and silent. Yet Sima regretted having brought Aaron into this place, a place she would never have chosen for refuge.

Both children hadn't noticed Matthew leaving. He just disappeared. Then they heard him, his unmistakable grunts and barks, coming from the street. He must have crawled out and was facing-off their attackers. Sima wrung her hands, trying not to cry. Then she placed her hands over Aaron's ears, not wanting him to try playing the hero for Matthew. After all, she was the one supposedly in charge.

"Well, I'm blowed if I'm going in there..." they heard one hooligan say. "It's too dark."

"Com'on," said another. "Let dumbo alone."

They heard a clanging of the gates, and shuffling.

Then silence.

Then soft footsteps. Matthew was looking for them. They whispered his name. His head swiveled. He smiled his white, toothy grin and gestured with his hand that they could come out and join him. Aaron hugged him. Sima thanked him. He showed them a different path, obscured by excess weeds and abandoned shrubbery. They took it without question and were surprised when, after walking through it, they came to a double gate and found themselves on the southern side of the main thoroughfare leading to Ashley Grove, from which they could easily navigate their way home.

Running most of the way, they sprinted up the red-tiled path of their front yard and began pounding on the front door. Greta, hearing the frantic banging, rushed to open the door, swollen leg and all. Sima and Aaron flung themselves onto their mother. Greta decided not to barrage them with her questions until their breathing calmed, and for a full five minutes, all three stayed in the narrow hallway, rocking together softly from side to side. As the children's trembling slowly tapered off, she asked, "Are you going to tell me what happened? Was it a dog or *shkatzim* or both?"

"*Shkatzim!*" they howled in one voice.

"Did you do what I told you?" Greta looked into Sima's eyes, wondering if she had remembered her mother's instruction for this exact occurrence: *Look for the nearest door with a* mezuzah *and bang on it with all your might.*

Sima shook her head. "There wasn't time. They were *chasing* us." She started to cry.

"*Oy, sheifelach...*" Greta pulled them closer. They rocked a little more. "You must have been so frightened." The children did not look up. Greta did not know what to do: To track down her children's attackers would be impossible; to call the police would be a joke. There was truly nothing she could do to protect her children. "Did they hurt you?" she asked with her eyelids shut.

"They threw stones."

Greta pulled the children off her, holding them at arm's length, her eyes inspecting them wildly. "Did any stone actually hit either of you?" she asked. Finding no cuts or bruises, she led them into the kitchen. "Sit. I'll make us all some hot chocolate. Then we will have a conversation."

Greta brought the drinks and set them on the table, listened to them recite the *brachah*, and watched them take their first few gulps. "Now, can you tell me where you were and what exactly happened?"

"Matthew saved us!" cried Aaron.

"*Matthew?*"

"Yes, Matthew. Our friend."

"Yes, I know who *Matthew* is. How did he save you?"

They told her. She listened, shaking her head gently, her eyes lighting up as they described what Matthew had done for them. "Who would have believed? Who would have concocted such a story? Wow, really amazing..."

"Mummy..." Aaron was speaking into his cup. "Are all *goyim* bad?"

"Some. And some are not. Look at Matthew, for instance."

"What about *Yidden*? Are *Yidden* bad?"

"Some. But not like this. *Yidden* don't start fights with people."

"What makes a bad *goy* and what makes a bad Yid?"

"The things they do."

"What kinds of bad things do *Yidden* do?"

"Oh, I dunno. Things."

7

WEDNESDAY, JULY 1, 2015
LONG ISLAND, NEW YORK

Sima nearly stopped too late; she slammed the brakes just in time to avoid rear-ending a silver-blue Lexus with a license plate that read "Siberia." Sima read the word and laughed out loud. *A Lexus named Siberia!* Was that even *legal*? She had to overtake the car to see who was driving around in an oxymoron like that.

Pulling up parallel to the driver's window at the next traffic light, she shot a peek. A woman with chiseled cheekbones, enormous mirrored sunglasses, and rich blonde curls pouted her lips before turning away from Sima. Her interest piqued, Sima lowered her window and gave her horn a friendly pat. The woman turned back. "Why do you have 'Siberia' on your license plate?" Sima asked.

The woman smiled majestically, as though to a child, but she did not answer.

Sima persisted. "Isn't that where they put all the illegals and unwanteds?"

The woman laughed, revealing a set of impossibly perfect teeth. She shook her head slowly. "Siberia," she said, in a thick, smoky tone, "is beeeeaaauuuutiful!"

The light turned green and she sped away, leaving Sima slack-jawed.

■ ■ ■

1433 Ditmas Ave. Sima stared at the dilapidated building where East River Tech—the computer support company Aryeh Hertzberg had founded with his business partner, Shloimy Fass—was located. The company had six employees, including Aryeh and Shloimy, and was housed on the second floor of this small, three-story structure that had been built in the mid-fifties and never renovated once in all that time. The suite boasted an old and cranky refrigerator next to a counter with a sink. They referred to this area as the "kitchen." It had washrooms at the back where legions of bacteria, or so Sima claimed, had been given carte blanche to germinate in its cracks and grouts. Aside from those more obvious eyesores, the office was a jovial, if a little musty, workplace.

When Sima walked in, Aryeh looked up from his data-base—a three-paneled computer system that held the servers of twenty-one schools—and smiled. "Freedom looks good on you."

"Yup, don't it just." She flashed him one of her most brazen smiles. "And there is no one on this planet I'd rather take to brunch than you. And that is the truth, however cheesy."

Aryeh turned to Shloimy, the soft-spoken chassid who had been with him since ERT was just a piddly little idea in the back of Aryeh's mind. "You'd be okay if I went out on a date with my wife, right?"

Shloimy, whose golden *peyos* made him look too young to be the father of nine, considered the proposition with exaggerated solemnity. Sima blushed, though she needn't have worried. Since 1998, when Shloimy—then a newlywed with one small baby—had opened the fledgling company with Aryeh, the two had developed a brotherly bond. "Sure," he winked, "...so long as you remember to bring me dessert."

Aryeh got up and fished for his phone and jacket before leaving the premises. "My car or yours?" he asked, when they reached the bottom of the stairs.

"Yours." Sima was not smiling anymore. "I need to talk. I can't drive and talk about this at the same time."

"Oh." Aryeh looked at Sima as he opened the car door. "What is this about?"

"Start the engine."

They drove in silence for a few minutes. "Spoons," Sima finally said. "Let's go to that new place, Spoons. I like it there. We can sit in the back and have our privacy."

"Okay." Aryeh made an immediate left. "You know, you're making me nervous. Can you at least tell me the subject matter?"

Sima took a deep breath, held it, and exhaled slowly. "It's Tamar," she said, at the exhalation's tail.

Aryeh's eyebrows lifted. He stole a side glance at Sima, quickly returning his eyes to the road. "She's not in any kind of trouble, is she?"

"I wouldn't say trouble in the usual sense, but something has happened with her. We need to tread very carefully if we want her to come through it... Let's wait till we get to Spoons. I'll tell you everything I know there."

Sima looked at her husband's profile; his hard, thin nose; the way his dark mustache and beard vaguely met along the side of his mouth; his large black yarmulke peeking out from under his black hat, which was now tilting slightly forward, giving him intensity as his eyebrows knit close together. Her thoughts flashed at cyclonic speed as the moment of truth drew closer.

Was she right to betray Tamar's confidence? In light of how betrayed Tamar was already feeling, would this not just aggravate an already charged circumstance? Should she seal her lips around Tamar's new path, in the hope that it would turn out to be just a teenage phase that would ultimately dissipate? How could she be sure? Secrets were never a part of her and Aryeh's relationship. Her husband was practically transparent. He would not be able to keep so large a secret from her, so how could she from him? They had long ago agreed that secrets would be a disturbance to the peace they built and a corrosion of the trust they enjoyed.

Sima honored Aryeh's need for peace. There had been precious little of it in his family of origin—FOO, as he was wont to quip. One of twelve, Aryeh had seven rollicking and rowdy siblings above him and four below. This resulted in him having to put up with not two, but nine parents, seven of whom did not understand the disastrous long-term effects of corporal punishment.

On their wedding night, after all the dancing and endless photographing were over, the two of them had been taken to the tiny apartment that they had rented for two weeks. When Sima and Aryeh crossed the threshold, closed the door, and looked at each other, alone at last, Aryeh had lifted his hand, pointed his finger in the air, and said, "Sima, do you hear that?"

Sima's forehead had wrinkled with confusion. "What?"

"That?"

She'd stopped all movement. She was still in her bridal gown, so she waited for it to cease rustling. Still nothing. "No. What are you talking about?"

"It's a wonderful sound!" said Aryeh, beaming at her. "Listen!"

Thinking she might have married a lunatic, Sima shook her head slowly, hoping for something normal to come out of her *chassan's* mouth. "Please, tell me what it is you are hearing!"

"Silence," he said. "It's ours. Our silence. It makes me happy that together, we can create such peace."

Sima had smiled. Yes. It truly was a lovely sound.

Now Sima watched as Aryeh pulled into a parking spot in front of Spoons. The two of them left the car and entered the café together, making their way to the furthest table in the back corner. Sima sat down heavily, grabbed a menu, and began to peruse it. She felt uncomfortable in her *sheitel* that morning; the equivalent of a bad-hair day. The wig just refused to sit right. She maneuvered the top of it again, hoping to alleviate the pain from her widow's peak that must have been caught in the gripper.

Aryeh was staring at her. "When will you free me from the misery of speculation, Sima? Tamar seemed fine over Shabbos. She even gave me a hug before you took her to the bus on Sunday." He glanced at the menu. "Choose for me, Sim, will you?"

Sima ordered: a grilled vegetable Panini for Aryeh; California wrap for her. She rested her chin on her palms and waited for the waitress to leave them before looking up. "She wrote me a letter. Before she left to camp."

"So...?"

"Actually, she instructed me when to read it." Sima began rummaging in her pocketbook. "I thought it was going to be one of those cute I-love-you letters that kids sometimes write, so I stuffed it in here and meant to read it later, maybe in bed, but I got distracted and forgot about it, until she called the other day to ask if I'd read it." Sima paused. This was silly, this introduction. Why was she stalling? *Get to the point already.*

"*Nu*? What was in the letter?"

"Maybe you should read it for yourself. Hold on..." She continued to disarrange the contents of her handbag. "Hmmm, I thought I had left it here..." She stopped and faced him. "It's probably in the night table drawer. Anyway, according to her instructions, I'm not supposed to share it with you. So say nothing to her about it, please."

"Tell me what it was about."

"Okay..." Sima looked down at her hands, fingers spread on the table between them. "She wrote...she wanted me to know...that she knows about Aaron." Sima let out her breath.

"*What?!* How? When?"

Sima squeezed her eyes shut and shook her head; she wasn't finished. "There's more... She writes that she feels betrayed by me and...as a result...she finds herself full of questions and doubts. I think she means doubts in *Yiddishkeit*..."

Aryeh was silent.

"I think she blames me."

"For what?"

"For bringing her up on a lie?" The sides of her mouth trembled, and her eyes began to fill. She looked up at her husband to find his eyes closed in contemplation. His forehead was wrinkled, and he was pulling mindlessly on his beard.

"I don't know how deep she is with this, Aryeh," she whispered. "But do you realize the impact this could have, if it hasn't already? I mean, you don't really get it, because you don't know..." She tapered off.

"What? What don't I know?"

She pursed her lips. Why was he forcing her to articulate her deepest fears? "You don't know what it is like to live in a home where one of the children goes off the *derech*! You don't *know* that kind of pain; the helplessness you experience watching someone you love make all the wrong choices and fall, fall, and keep on falling. And how it weakens everyone else. It's not like I hadn't noticed her declining standards for some time. But now...now she confirmed it. In this letter."

Sima's hand formed a tight fist. "*Oy*, Aryeh..." Her eyes filled again. "I am so scared. For her. For us. I don't know if this information has done irreparable damage to my relationship with her. I mean...I didn't even know she *knew*. I didn't know anything. I would have told her. I would have. I would give anything to have that opportunity handed back to me. Had I known. But I didn't know. And now she is mad—so, so mad. And I can't blame her. I am the idiot here. I am the one who should hang my head in shame. What a fool I've been all these years." Sima gripped the sides of her head. "*Oy*, what a fool. I never should have risked this. Never. I should have done everything differently. Now what are we going to do?"

They sat together in dreadful silence.

Finally Aryeh spoke up. "I think this is a very unwise—even dangerous—place to go," he said. "The blame game. I mean, if anyone, *I* should be the one to blame."

"Why *you*?"

Aryeh shook his head slightly. "I don't know. Maybe I should have stopped the charade earlier. Maybe we should have asked *da'as Torah* what to do in this situation, instead of relying on our own decisions. We just let it go on for so long...both of us."

"Let's stop this," Sima asserted. "You're right. Blaming is not smart, not to mention irrelevant."

Aryeh turned his gaze from Sima to the windows overlooking the busy street outside. "Where have *I* been?" he said to himself, playing now with the napkin that was placed like a pyramid on the table. "How did *I* not see this coming?"

"She did mention you in the letter..."

"Oh?"

"Yeah. Something about her not wanting you to bail me out."

Aryeh looked confused.

"*Oy*, stop..." She exhaled. "We can fix this. No?"

"I'm not sure. Let's face it, Sima: if her life was great in every other way, would she still be running?"

"What do you mean?"

"Well...look. Tamar is a smart girl. She does not act from impulse, usually. She must have had some sort of something happen to her, some unpleasant incident, *something* connected to how she found out." He shrugged his shoulders. "I just don't know..."

Sima looked into her husband's stricken face, and winced. There is a special kind of pain that is experienced when someone close to you is in pain. It doesn't have a name—again, another un-named phenomenon. But just like that, their hopes for their daughter—their pride and joy, their eldest child—seemed now perilously threatened. In one moment, everything changed.

With one letter.

Sima decided to change direction. "I just saw Mimi Eisner. She's working at Menucha Hills this summer. Aryeh...?" Her forehead puckered. "I don't know who knows about this. My imagination is killing me. Every time I see one of Tamar's friends now, I start wondering to myself, *Does this girl know? Does that girl know?*"

"You shouldn't care about that," Aryeh said forcefully. "People knowing makes no difference right now. Our focus must be our own daughter, and her alone."

They both fell silent. There were so many unknowns. Where exactly was Tamar holding right now? How could they have both missed the signs that something was wrong? What could they do to change her course?

Precisely at that moment, two things happened simultaneously: the waitress brought them their food, and Yitzchak Rubner entered the café together with his glamorous wife Miriam—designer handbag, blue sunglasses, perfect makeup, and all.

Yitzchak's eyes swept over the mostly empty restaurant and landed on Aryeh and Sima sitting at the back. Immediately he headed over. Sima stiffened. In general, she found Miriam and her circle of friends to be too pushy; the gum-snapping, fancy type of women who dress up to buy eggs at the grocery. Sima became aware of a delicate swell of irritation, singed with vexatious intimidation.

Don't let her bother you, she tried telling herself.

"Aryeh Hertzberg! Good to see you!" Yitzchak Rubner hit him on the shoulder too hard, rubbing it now to soften the impact. Aryeh smiled. The two of them had been in yeshivah together, first in New York, then in Israel. They had gotten married at about the same time and were both fairly successful in their work. Yitzchak was the owner of two jewelry stores, one in Brooklyn and one in Long Island. He and Aryeh saw each other occasionally at *simchos*, but were not part of each other's lives on a daily, or even weekly, basis. "So Aryeh, what do you think, eh? We're headed for war?"

"I sincerely hope not," answered Aryeh.

Was it Sima's imagination or did her husband sound a tad hostile?

"Remember the Gulf War? When we were caught in the eye of the storm?"

"It wasn't the 'eye.' Kuwait was the 'eye.' We were just the 'brows.'"

Yes, thought Sima. *Definitely too hostile.* She willed him to soften up.

"If you want to know, I think of that war often, which is why I'm hoping that war can be avoided," Aryeh said.

"But how can it be avoided?" Yitzchak's head was swaying. "They just arrested four teens in Beit Shemesh for shooting Bibi bullets at passing Arab cars."

Aryeh's eyebrows shot up. "What? Sounds unlikely to me…"

"No. It's true. I just read about it. There is so much unrest in the region. I'm telling you, things are not looking good."

"Can't be!" Sima retorted, noticing the thickening of her English accent; that usually happened when she became agitated. "This is a media thing again. Shooting randomly at passing cars, even Bibi bullets, is not our way."

"Don't you read the news? It happened earlier today. A bunch of Israeli kids actually caused an accident because they were aiming their shots at the wheels, and one vehicle lost control. News outlets are dubbing it a 'revenge mischief.' Whatever. Point is, things are not looking good."

"Revenge for the Sterns because they were in their van?"

"I guess. Maybe. Hard to say what anyone would do when tormented. '*Under duress*,' it's called." As Yitzchak Rubner talked, saliva gathered in the corners of his mouth.

Sima wanted the conversation to end. She wanted to continue talking to Aryeh about Tamar. She certainly did not want the subject to permanently wander off to the Middle East. She also wanted to eat—she did not relish her food growing cold—but her English background would not allow her to eat while they had company at their table. "That's ridiculous. *Yidden* don't do that kind of thing, and you know it!" She picked up her fork and began to examine the side salad.

By now Miriam had reached their table, her heavy perfume making Sima feel slightly queasy. "Hi, Sima, how's it going? Everyone doing well? Good, because my head is pounding, and my every fiber is pining for caffeine. Can we sit, Yitz? We need to order." She pointed to a table near the window.

"Hi, Miriam, nice to see you. You look beautiful. As always." Sima reached out and gave her signature, soft English embrace. Miriam smiled and backed away.

Aryeh's phone rang. He glanced at it and mouthed to his wife, "It's Shloimy. Gotta take it."

Sima turned to Mr. Rubner and shook her head. "I cannot believe that Jewish kids did this. I will not believe it until it is proven."

"Well," Yitzchak took two steps back, "I don't know. It's hard to say what really happens in that region. We only get slanted stories. Always did, always will."

"But you still think it's true, don't you?"

"Oh, I don't think anymore if I can help it. I gave that up a long time ago!" A chuckling Yitzchak turned around to walk to where his wife was already sitting.

Yeah, I bet you did. Sima felt an internal curtain billow and fall as she gazed at the food in front of her.

8

Wednesday, July 1, 2015

Camp Shoshana, Seneca Lake, New York

Tamar:

I can't believe it's been a whole year.

You know what is really making me crazy? What one of my teachers said, just before the school year was over: "Remember, girls: nothing is ever lost." Now, to be perfectly honest, this teacher—Mrs. Batzinger is her name—is not too, too bad. But she has an uncomplicated life. So why should I listen to her? Still. That sentence really gets to me. I find myself thinking about it over and over again.

Nothing. Is. Ever. Lost.

Ever?

What does that even mean?

Dust? The gas we used for traveling three months ago? Last year's snow?

Do those things never get lost too?

What about people?

I know of someone who is very much lost.

Note to self: Don't be your mother's daughter, you coward. Four days have already passed, and you haven't had the guts to go back to the stables. Pathetic.

I need to revisit it. I promised myself. It is the sole reason I decided to *come back to camp. To revisit and revisit and revisit until I feel nothing. I. Will. Revisit...*

Soon.

Deep down, I think, I have always known that there was something wrong with us. With our family. Nothing I could actually pinpoint. Not like some other girls in my class, like Sari, who everyone knows is a bum, hanging around in a bad crowd; or Michal, whose father was busted for drugs. Total scandal! No. In my family, it's our precision. How Mommy does everything with slow and rigid movements, like she's always afraid someone might catch her out. Like she's always on guard. Like she's being monitored or something. Ever aware of the phantom tribunal, waiting to pounce on her for the smallest infraction.

She never, and I mean never, relaxes.

Sometimes I watch my friends and wonder what life would be like without a noose hanging over your head.

The other day, the length of my new skirt was the subject of another blow-up. Mommy lost it so bad she actually shouted, "You will end up in the gutter! And then what? You think I will come around and pull you out?" She covered her mouth so fast with her hand, you could almost see her tortured soul rise up and devour her. It would have broken my heart, if I hadn't been so angry.

And what would have cost me my little, dignified, square of sidewalk? What was it that would lead me to a life in the sewers? A few extra centimeters of fabric?

Really?

Give me a break!

Later that day, I stood outside their bedroom door and heard her crying to Abba: "What will everyone say?"

Is this what could have happened to my uncle all those years ago?

If only she'd told me. All this feigning perfection...this false life she handed down to us...my goodness! Mommy has a brother! Of whom nary a word was heard! If only I didn't hear about him from Raizy. That was the worst of it. Hearing about him from her. *What a risk Mommy took.*

Did she even think this through? Why did quashing the very existence of him seem like the better option?

In my best-case-scenario fantasy, she'd say, "Tamar, come into the living room. I want to tell you something," or she'd come into my bedroom one night, lie down next to me to let me know that I was safe, and then she would spill the beans. But no. She didn't do that. She chose to keep me and all my sisters in the dark. What was Mommy thinking? And, while we're on the topic, what was Abba thinking? He must have known. How could he have married Mommy? How could Bobbie and Zaidie have allowed their son to meet Mommy? Abba doesn't come from a blemished family; the Hertzbergs are squeaky clean. Maybe they didn't look into Mommy too much. Maybe their own gullibility held them back from uncovering anything, because they couldn't conceive of it.

My mother is "damaged goods."

I am "damaged goods."

Maybe, if I had been spared the humiliation, Mommy and I could still be close...

There they are. Not fifty feet from me. The horseless stables. Hmmm. Was it a good idea to come back? Not so sure now. I should text Mimi. She might help me stop trembling. Mommy doesn't know that Mimi knows. And that's a good thing. See, I'm keeping secrets of my own...

I'm at the stables again, I text. Let's see how long it will take for her to answer today. Oh good, she's typing:

-How r u feeling?

-Okay. Nervous. I'm outside. Shud I try to go in today?

-Only if u feel strong enough.

-Not sure.

-Do u need me to stay here with my phone?

-No. Thanks. I think I shud do this alone.

-K, let me know how it went. Good luck.

She sends me a heart emoji.

So sweet.

I walk up to the stable door and peek inside. The slats in the grooves slash stripes along the hay-strewn floor, just like they did last year when Raizy Kaplan and her acolytes cornered me. I want to go back in. I swallow. Did my resolve just leave? Didn't I tell Mimi I wanted to walk into those stables every day until I feel nothing? She laughed at me, but not in a mocking way. Maybe she just can't understand because she doesn't know what it is like to find out something about your family that changes everything. Should I text her again, just to see if she is still there?

-Hi. U still there?

Nothing.

'Kay. I'm on my own.

It's always the smell that hits you first: Stale horse smell, dried hay, scorn. Nausea washes over me like a wave. I must be sweating; the flies are buzzing around me like I'm a free-meal ticket. I want to bolt. Oh, I want so badly to bolt!

No, I won't.

Must be strong.

Must re-enter.

There. That's where I stood. It's surprising how fast Raizy Kaplan's nasal voice is reactivated. She was leaning against the back stacks, her knowledge supplying her with so much power. And I had nothing. No defenses. I am so, so mad, I could cry! Mommy...you did this to me. You set me up for this!

"Oh my gosh! I don't believe this! You don't know?!"

"Know what?" I asked, a mushroom cloud expanding in my gut.

"You don't know about your uncle?!"

"What...? I do know my uncles, thank you very much."

"No. Not your father's brothers. Your mother's brother."

I wanted to stop staring, but I couldn't. I wanted to close my mouth, but it just stayed open. All movement in me stopped. I tried breathing; how could I have forgotten such an elementary human function? The world suddenly became quiet, as though an airtight bubble enclosed us, not allowing any noise from outside to penetrate.

I felt like I would throw up.

"Oh my gosh! She really doesn't know!!"

"I don't know what you're talking about, Raizy, but you're crazy, okay?" My voice sounded too shrill, my naiveté leaking out all over the place.

Raizy looked over at her friends—Riva Slater, Carmela Goodman, and Shoshi Cohen—and my eyes also took them in, one by one. It was like a slow-motion film, how they all shared the same thin, crooked smile.

"So, your uncle, your mother's brother...he's a bit, you know..." Raizy laughed, drawing circles in the air. "He ran away—but not before setting his school on fire. Word has it that someone nearly died..."

"Aw, Raizy, why'd you tell her? Maybe her mom didn't want her to know. Can you blame her...?" Shoshi Cohen threw me a dry bone, hardly a flinch on that clear, porcelain face.

"Look...she's turning purple." Raizy would not endorse Shoshi's attempt at pseudo-compassion. "She's ashamed. Good for her. Her mother thinks she is the cat's meow 'cuz she's a therapist. My mother told me she has no business being a therapist when her own brother is as screwed-up as he is. And sorry to be the one to break this news to you," she continued, walking so close to me that I could smell the mint gum on her breath, "but if you think you're gonna marry anyone other than the pizza delivery boy, you should think again. Everyone knows about you and your family, Tamar Hertzberg..."

I shudder all over again. Is this what Mrs. Batzinger meant when she said nothing is ever lost? No memory, no moment, ever leaves us without a trace. Everything gets stored, somewhere. *They may mutate, deteriorate, sink, and decompose—but they don't ever, completely, disappear.*

Rabbi Yaakov Wechter saw him arrive from the corner of his eye. He saw him sit down, cross his legs and settle in, watching everything around him through discomforted eyes. He recognized the look, had seen it a thousand times: the look of hunger, of weariness and wariness, of one whose heart has taken a pounding one too many times. Rabbi Wechter turned his thoughts Heavenward and, as he had done countless times before, asked for guidance; another one of G-d's fallen had just entered his shul.

The day was petering out. It would soon be too late for Minchah. Aaron watched as the little rabbi glanced anxiously at the clock on the far end of the hall, hanging on the half-wall of the women's balcony, and shook his head. There were eight men. They were waiting for ten.

Then Rabbi Wechter approached him. "Can we rely on you for the *minyan*? Do you still remember enough?"

Aaron felt a burst of voltage dart through him; it started at the tip of his head and tingled its way down, prickling his whole body, shooting him into confusion. *Why did this short, white-bearded rabbi use the word "remember"? What if I am a complete stranger to the rituals and liturgies?*

What if I am not even Jewish?

How could this seemingly gentle man presume to know so much about me?

Aaron's confusion was perceived as a no. It suited his purpose. After all, it would be awkward to hear the Hebrew verses come from his mouth. Surely they would sound foreign and false. And further, to whom or what would he be praying? *No, let them think I am declining; let them think what they want to think. My silence is the best thing I have in my arsenal. It costs me nothing. It's durable. And best of all, it buys me time.*

Rabbi Wechter did not press. He rocked a little on his heels, looked up again at the clock, and asked those gathered, "Does anyone know anyone who is coming? Did Samuel Lacouf say he was coming? Can someone call him?"

It was almost dark when the afternoon prayers were over. The rabbi sat at a table with a large open book, humming and swaying. Three men sat down with him. He looked up at the others. Some trickled over. Soon the shul echoed with the sounds of their learning, filling the time between the slackening of the sun and the arrival of the stars. Aaron watched from where he sat. He did not move; he did not join.

After a while, he stopped watching and put his head down into his arms. He was exhausted. The anticipation of what he was about to do filled him with a familiar panic. These people, this moment... He wanted very much to get up and walk away.

He might have dozed a little, for the next thing he knew, the rabbi was standing very close to him, tapping him on the shoulder. "We are about to daven Ma'ariv. Would you like to join?"

Dazed and adrift, Aaron nodded. He stood up and walked over to where the rest of the men were gathered. Rabbi Wechter gave him a siddur and watched, appearing amused, at how Aaron leafed through the pages, reading the titles, and stopping when it read, *Tefillas Arvis*. A brief triumph was caught between the two of them, acknowledged by the tiniest hint of a smile exchanged. The newcomer had established himself; he was no *new*comer.

When the prayers were over, Rabbi Wechter took his time to put away the books and wish everyone a good evening. Aaron waited. Then the rabbi turned to him. "Come," he said. "There is much on your mind. Come walk home with me. My wife does not appreciate when I arrive late. She worries."

They left the building in silence, Rabbi Wechter locking the heavy glass doors, clanking the gates shut. Aaron walked a half-step behind the rabbi. Was it fear? Respect? Timidity? The rabbi beckoned him closer. "Walk with me. My hearing is not as good as it once was."

Disarmed by the rabbi's genuine kindliness, Aaron caught up to him. They walked a little in silence. "Now tell me..." The rabbi stared ahead. "What is it that is causing you so much grief? What is your name?"

Aaron found it difficult to talk. They continued down Paris's darkened streets noiselessly, both listening to the sound of their footsteps. "Sorry," said the rabbi, "I have forgotten to introduce myself. I am Yaakov. Yaakov Wechter." They continued walking quietly. The rabbi did not press.

Finally, Aaron cleared his throat. "My name is Aaron Rephael Bulman. How do you know I am grieved?"

"I don't. It was just a hunch. Bulman, you say? Was your father from the former Soviet Union?"

Aaron stopped walking. The old rabbi did not notice, but continued on a few paces, stopping three feet away. He turned. "As I thought. You look so much like him."

"You knew him?" Again, the voltage spiked. Aaron felt helplessly drawn. "He is dead, you know. He died ten years ago."

"Yes. I had heard. Come, let's keep walking." He gestured with his arm. "My wife. She worries." Rabbi Wechter continued to walk, a slow shuffle. Aaron followed.

"The Jewish world stands at a precipice, yes? It has stood at this difficult spot many times before. What do you think should happen?"

Aaron shrugged.

"You don't know, huh?" inquired Rabbi Wechter. "Yes, that is the wisest answer. Good. You have passed the first test." He smiled. "Now, you didn't answer my first question. What brings the 'Red Rebel's' son to my humble shul tonight?"

"Well, I...I didn't know that you knew my father..."

"Hmmm. We only met twice. But I never forget a face. I remember when he went to England. I remember because we had to find someone else to do all that he'd been doing for the *Yidden* left in his part of Russia." He stopped talking. Then he shook his head. "Ahhh, all that is from a long time ago. Tell me about your father. I am curious. How was life in England for him?"

"Good. I suppose. He had a job. He was a bookbinder first, and then a printer. He..." Now it was Aaron's turn to stop talking.

"Yes. He loved books. But you, you had a hard time? Being his son? Is that it?"

"Maybe. Possibly. I always thought he had a hard time being my father. I hadn't seen him for ten years before he died."

"You left home?"

"Yes." Aaron swallowed. "I ran away."

They came to a dark, four-story building with a courtyard in the center and windows—some lit, some black, some curtained with small beams of light peeping through. A heavy, wrought-iron gate stood between them and the open square of the building's center. Rabbi Wechter took out his enormous set of keys and fingered them until he found the right one. He slotted it into the lock until a small ping was heard. The gates opened.

They walked into the clearing. The rabbi turned left toward a staircase. Aaron stopped. He had not been invited to Rabbi Wechter's home. He did not want to assume anything.

"Please," said the rabbi, "don't be shy. I share history with your father. You are like family to me. Come upstairs."

"But your wife is not expecting me."

"That is never a concern. She is a true helpmate. She has weathered much with me. This will be nothing unusual for her."

Aaron was surprised by how much he suddenly wanted to meet Madame Wechter. What would she look like? How would she react to having an unexpected guest? How would meeting her make him feel? They walked up the four flights, painfully slowly, Rabbi Wechter stopping for a moment's rest between each floor.

"I hope I am not inconveniencing you in any way," said Aaron.

"Why should you think you are?"

"I just want to be sure that I am not in your way. You do not know me."

"You have made two incorrect statements. I *have* no way, except the way of the people I come into contact with. Your way, the path that has led you to me, *is* my way." Rabbi Wechter smiled to himself and then looked up at Aaron.

"And what is my second incorrect statement?"

"Aha, I was hoping that you would ask that." Rabbi Wechter's eyes had a glint. "The second incorrect statement is that I do not know you. I may not know you personally, but make no mistake: I know your kind."

My kind? Who are *my kind?* But Aaron said nothing. They approached the fourth floor, dimly lit by a small, pinkish fluorescent bulb mounted very high on the wall of the corridor. The door to the rabbi's apartment was slightly open.

Aaron was unprepared for what the smell would do to him. He stood very still in the hallway, breathing deeply through his nose an aroma that he had not savored since leaving home. They say that the olfactory glands lock in the greatest concentration of memories. Now, at the mercy of an onslaught of images, Aaron was unable to move, as hordes of reminiscences, unbidden, roared within him. He had all but forgotten the sensual delights of his mother's cooking, along with the smell of freshly printed words that would emanate from the Hebrew books his father would bring home... Yet with all the longing came the definite understanding that there was no going back, that that life was not available to him anymore.

For a long while Aaron just stood there, his eyes absorbing the simplicity of Rabbi Wechter's home while his nose continued processing the smells,

the smells,

the smells.

"Come in," the rabbi urged him. Aaron finally shook himself and entered the apartment.

To his right was the small dining area, lit up by a rustic, wooden, two-tier chandelier. The table was already set for two. Covering the entire back wall, behind the dining area, was an enormous and playfully chaotic bookcase. It seemed as though the books themselves resisted any order some hopeful person may have wanted to impose on them; as though they insisted on lying on their backs, stuffed between the tops of other books and the shelves above them. Some of them seemed to enjoy that their pages jutted out indifferently, sticking out their tongues to the world. Smaller books, stacked between larger volumes, relied on pressure to keep themselves from falling. The whole structure appeared edgy and unhinged, happy to keel over in its next breath. It made Aaron laugh inside, as he drew a contrast from his own childhood home; his family's bookcase had been as revered as an ark, the books standing to attention with military precision.

Aaron's eyes glided over the ubiquitous photographs all around the room, some framed, some held up with dog-eared tape. Most of the pictures were of young couples with children.

From the kitchen emerged a small and smiling, elderly lady in a light-blue dress, a mauve kerchief wrapped around her head. She carried an extra place setting and grinned generously at the tall, shy man her husband had brought home. "You'll stay and eat with us, yes?" she asked him. He noticed she wore a tiny bit of lipstick, some of which was smudged, and that her cheeks were smooth and warmed with rose-colored blush. Aaron smiled. *She must be very old*, he thought, *yet she still makes this effort*. Some things in life are so perfect, so absolutely perfect, it makes a person want to cry.

Aaron nodded and followed her into the dining area, sitting on the chair she indicated.

Rabbi Wechter was in the kitchen. Aaron could hear the faucet turning, the water filling the large washing cup, the spilling four times over the hands—one, two, one, two—the recitation of the first blessing, the towel being pulled from the hook. He felt a trembling in his stomach; his mouth seemed to fill up with sawdust, and his resolve buckled. How could he have allowed himself to come back? How could this rabbi endure him? He had not observed any of the practices and rituals since his youth!

He stood up. He wanted to leave before the rabbi would see him—without a head covering, without washing for bread, without *tzitzis*. It was too unbearable, this sudden feeling of being unclothed.

"*Nu, nu!*" Rabbi Wechter surfaced, beaming, making a questioning gesture with his hand, as though asking, "Where are you going?" It was too late. Aaron could not leave. "*Nuuu,*" he said again, pointing to the chair Aaron had vacated, letting him know with his eyes that it was fine that Aaron hadn't washed, fine that Aaron hadn't said any blessing, fine that Aaron couldn't bring himself to do any of those things.

Once he was sure that Aaron would stay, the rabbi looked around the table for something. Remembering that bread must be dipped into salt, Aaron glanced around too. He spied the little glass saltshaker behind a vase of wilting roses, reached over for it, and offered it to the rabbi. Rabbi Wechter's face lit up. *Aha!* his expression said. *So I was right!*

Aaron smiled. He had been unmasked...by salt!

Of all things!

The rabbi made a blessing with his eyes closed. He dipped his slice of bread into the little mound of salt he had made on the side of his plate, and took a bite. His chewing and swallowing were audible in the silence. Aaron did not know where to look.

"The Sterns, *oy*, the Sterns..." Rabbi Wechter spoke at last. "What a tragedy... What do you say? It is a sad state of affairs, Aaron Rephael, no?"

"Please, call me Aaron."

"Eat, Aaron. You are not eating. The food is good—it's warm and very good!" He winked at his wife. She pushed the steaming platter of meat and potatoes toward Aaron. He had not eaten cooked food since leaving Eitan and Uri's balcony. Grateful, he picked up the serving spoon and scooped a portion of the savory dish onto his plate.

Aaron took his first mouthful, and his eyes automatically closed. It was a simple dish—onions, carrots, potatoes, celery, stew beef, gravy—yet it made his mind fill with the image of his mother. For more than twenty years he had not eaten this type of food, and now one mouthful—and he was already pining for home. He could not open his eyes for a while; the pressure built up too strongly behind them. He was afraid. Too much had already been laid open. Would his eyes give him away? More than he had already given himself away?

When he finally opened his eyes, the Wechters were staring at him in compassionate silence. At once, all three felt a pall of awkwardness, and they began to talk in unison:

"The food is delicious. It reminds me of..."

"So what's the talk at shul tonight?"

"You'll be pleased to know that there was a *minyan* for—"

They stopped, looked at each other, and laughed. After that, the rest of the meal passed harmlessly.

Aaron learned that the Wechters had been born to second cousins living in the same small town in White Russia. They had always known one another, and their parents had made their match even before they were of marriageable age. How the two of them had made their way from the former Soviet Union to where they lived today in Paris, was an entire story of its own. The couple had four children: two sons living in Israel, one son here in Paris, and a daughter in Montreal. Neither of them asked Aaron about his own family.

After the meal ended, Madame Wechter disappeared into the kitchen, and Rabbi Wechter sat back in his chair. "*Nu*, Aaron... Tell me a little about yourself. What brings you here today?"

"I wish I knew," he said, more to himself than to his host. "I cannot explain why I am here, in the same way that I cannot explain why I entered your shul, nor how you knew my father."

"I didn't know him well," the gentle rabbi corrected him. "We corresponded for a while, back in the sixties. I was happy for him when I heard he got to England. I didn't know he'd gotten married or that he'd had children. I feel honored that you came to us. It is the last respect I can pay to your late father."

Aaron winced. It felt wrong to disturb the picture this sympathetic man had of his father. He fell silent again; he could not believe his own folly had brought him here. *I must make one sorry little picture*, he thought, *the son who refuses to adopt the lifestyle his own father would have died defending.* The old shame threatened to clamp his mouth shut. "The Stern family..." he finally stammered. "...I guess they've been on my mind."

"Ah, yes, you and every Jew, the world over. 'Never again' spiked anew. Schools, camps, Jewish businesses—everyone is on high alert. Anything could happen, and no one feels safe. All for a spot of land. When the world's map begrudges the wandering Jew his tiny sliver of sand."

"I guess I am a 'wandering Jew,' then." Aaron smirked. "Only I feel nothing for..." He stopped speaking.

"Go on."

"...for the land." He looked directly into the rabbi's eyes, waiting for the reprimand he was sure would follow. Only when the rabbi gave no inclination to speak did Aaron feel confident to continue. "I am ashamed to say it. Not a lot connects me—not to the land, not to the people, not to anything, really."

"Aaron, why are you here?"

Again the question, heard as an admonition. Aaron looked into the eyes of the rabbi, sure that this would end the meeting; that even this old, charitable teacher did not have unlimited reserves of patience; that he would, momentarily, abort mission. But in Rabbi Wechter's eyes Aaron found no shortness of temper, only endless storehouses of humanity.

"I'm here, I think, because I am seeking..."

"What is it you are seeking?"

"Maybe...I don't know...maybe, connection?"

"Then stop your search. You are already bound to us. What you mistake as disconnect is actually only connection bruised." A few moments passed in silence, until the rabbi spoke again. "Tell me about your past, Aaron. Tell me about what it was like to grow up as Elchanan Bulman's son."

Again, the familiar commotion stirred inside him. Aaron closed his eyes. His father, the image of him—angry, tormented, disappointed. There must have been tenderness, somewhere. Only he couldn't conjure it up. Perhaps it had gotten lost—a hug here, a chuckle there—in his profound resentment. It wasn't fair, he knew, but it was his truth.

"I remember a Seder night..." Aaron faltered.

"Go on."

"I must have been only around fifteen, but already I wanted to let go of it all. I had been quietly breaking Shabbos, in my room, writing or turning on and off the light. Once, I remember, I struck a couple of matches, just to see what would happen..." He laughed self-consciously, stroked his chin, and looked at Rabbi Wechter to see if it was all right to continue.

"Don't stop. I am eager to hear."

"Nothing ever did."

"What?"

"Happen. Nothing ever happened."

The rabbi seemed confused.

"From the matches. Nothing happened. I wasn't struck down because I kindled a flame on the holy day."

"Oh. Well. That's not how it works."

"Right." Aaron looked at him, and then continued. "I remember thinking it was time to make a statement, see what would happen if my parents knew. I finally plucked up the courage, and I came to the Seder without my *tzitzis*. I wanted to see if anyone would notice."

"And...did they?"

"Oh, yeah..." Aaron stopped again.

"Yes, go on. What happened at this Seder?"

"When I went to the dining room and I stood there in the doorway, I remember thinking how beautiful the table looked." Aaron's head swayed from side to side, as though he was trying to shoo the memory away. "Then my father saw me. At first he said nothing, just lowered his head. My mother made herself busy. I think my younger sister, Henya, laughed, but she was told off. Anyway, at one point, I had to go into the kitchen for something, and my father followed me. I turned around and he was there, right behind me, with his hand raised and his eyes full of rage. I hadn't been hit by him for a long time, ever since I was small.

"Then we both heard a yelp. My mother. He lowered his hand, but his dark gray eyes were still glaring down at me. He turned to my mother and said, 'Mebbe next he t'row bagel 'cross the table.' And then he stormed out of the kitchen."

"Where did he go?"

"Back into the dining room."

"He continued with the Seder?"

"Yes."

Aaron could not talk anymore. Something hard had lodged itself in his throat. He tried to free himself of it—swallowed, took deep breaths, shook his head from side to side. But the unbearable memory had deposited itself in his windpipe, constricting him.

Rabbi Wechter's stare did not waver, every trace of his being pointed toward his guest. "What happened next?"

Aaron coughed. "My mother stayed in the kitchen with me. She held me close and kept asking, 'Aaron, what are you doing? What are you doing?'" he whispered.

"Did you make it through the Seder?"

"Yes. But my father did not look again at me that night. He didn't even ask me to say the *Mah Nishtanah*, which is something all of us said out loud, one by one."

"Aaron." Rabbi Wechter's hands went flat on the table as he leaned back in his chair. "I want to tell you something about the Seder—about the matzah, or more specifically, the middle matzah. I'm sure you remember how we break the middle matzah, and then put it back between the two whole matzos? You remember that part of the Seder, when we break the middle matzah, yes?"

Aaron nodded.

"Well, we put the middle matzah, broken, back between the two whole matzos, right? And then we lift them all together. There is a question that is asked: why place the broken matzah between two whole ones? What does this symbolize? What does this teach us? You follow the question?"

Again Aaron nodded.

"Well, here is one explanation, Aaron. I believe you will appreciate it. Listen closely: Because when someone is broken, he requires two to hold him up, one on either side of him. You understand?"

Aaron stopped nodding.

"Your parents represent the two matzos who were trying to hold you, one on either side."

Aaron looked up, past the rabbi, past the crumbling bookcase with its messy collection, past the kitchen where the sounds of water could be heard and the clickety-clack of things being put away, past the narrow hallway at the end of which was a door that opened to a purple room. "Yes," he finally said, "that may be so, but what if..."

"What if what?"

"What if...they, too, are broken?"

"*Oy*, Aaron! We are all broken. One way or another. All of us."

I t was the rabbi who suggested to meet for a drink the next day.

"To speak things over, see if we can understand what is contributing to your discomfort."

Aaron had been hesitant. "Are you sure you can spare the time?"

"Of course! This is the fun part of my job. Let me tell you, next to disgruntled, complaining synagogue members, you are to me—how do you English say it?—like a breath of fresh air!"

It was a beautiful summer's day. A warm breeze blew softly, and the periwinkle sky was interspersed by cirrus clouds unfurling miles above, like lazy, sunbathing ghosts. The rabbi and his guest were sitting at one of the many outdoor cafés scattered along Campagne de Blocage, in Paris's left bank. It was a few blocks down the same narrow, artsy street that housed the synagogue where they had met the day before. Ancient masonry surrounded them, and the very air was scented with flowers and vanilla and cinnamon. Well-groomed couples strolled about, passively donating themselves to the famous European sense of orderliness and chic, appearing as though nothing could sully their confident worldview. It was impossible to be miserable in such a place, even if you were determined; in this place, relaxation was practically forced upon you.

Rabbi Wechter was clearly not a stupid man.

"Okay, Aaron," he announced, after making their orders. "Tell me your worst."

"Worst?"

"Yes. Your worst memory from your school days."

Aaron smiled inwardly. How guileless of Rabbi Wechter, to think that he, Aaron, would share the tipping point of his school career, the weight of which had remained suspended above him, subtly shadowing his every movement. The fire of his humiliation. *No, thought Aaron, I'll have to think of some other memory, something less scorching, less damaging.*

"I could tell you about the time my classmates decided I was too trashy for them, so they picked me up—we were around seven years old at the time, and I was always more height than heft—and threw me into one of the industrial-sized garbage bins that stood outside the school kitchens. I can never forget the stench, nor how I was allowed to go home to change—but had to be brought right back, in case I should, G-d forbid, miss any learning. For months after, none of the kids would go near me during recess because I 'carried the smell.' But we were kids, so no, I don't regard that memory as my worst."

"Go on, then. I want to hear your worst…"

Aaron took in a deep breath. "Once, in sixth grade, my teacher, Rabbi Zeligbaum…" Aaron stopped and blinked. He hadn't spoken this teacher's name in over twenty years. "Well…he entered the classroom holding a wooden stick. A two by two. I know by today's standards this sounds insane, but he had actually spent the evening before inscribing it with a motto…" He shook his head, the preposterousness of it hitting him again, fresh and formidable. His eyes lost their focus and seemed to settle deeper into their sockets. He stopped speaking.

"What had this teacher written on it?" The rabbi's face was lit with simple curiosity.

Aaron swallowed, knowing that he had nothing to be ashamed of, yet still feeling the shame of that moment as it reassembled itself in his cerebration. "I…I even remember how the words looked. He had used Hebrew double-letters. They were beautiful and precise, outlined in gold and filled in with black."

"Go on... What was written on it?"

"Well, forgive my not remembering it in the original Hebrew, but it went something like this: 'He who withholds the rod, hates his child.'"

"Hmmm..."

"He lifted up the stick for all of us to see, and then he announced, 'This is my rod. This will be broken over one of your backs today.'"

"Let me guess..."

"Go ahead."

"Yours?"

"Five times. Five times he slammed it over my back. Five times before it smashed in half, and then I was allowed to return to my seat. And do you know what the worst of it was?"

"No. Tell me."

"That not a single one of my classmates did anything about it. They watched. They sat in silence, without moving. Some, I believe, even snickered."

"And no one told the authorities?"

"Authorities? Please! What authorities? Rabbi Zeligbaum was the son of the administrator."

"*Oy-voy-voy!*" Rabbi Wechter pulled at the edges of his beard. "Tell me, did your parents do anything about it?"

"That's also complicated."

"How so?"

"We never told our parents anything."

Rabbi Wechter nodded. Same old, same old. Somehow the tacit message most kids of that time had ingested was to be grateful that they were not being persecuted, that their parents had had it worse, that their piddly little sorrows were nothing relative to what the previous generations had had to endure. So, shush...and eat everything on your plate.

"For how long did it hurt?"

"What hurt?"

"Your back?"

"Oh, that. I thought the memory. I remember I couldn't sit properly for a while, couldn't play in the recess yard." Aaron went quiet. He lifted his hands together into a ball and let his mouth rest on them. "I never showed the bruising to anyone. Didn't think to. It's funny, now that I think of it. Many people might have been concerned, only I didn't let anyone know."

"Why not?"

"I honestly didn't think anyone cared. Other than my mother. But I didn't ever want to bother her."

"And you regret that now?"

"Oh, I don't know." Aaron sat back in his chair. "I have many regrets but nothing specific, which would make things easier. No, my regrets come in generic packaging."

"Suppose I were to tell you that this Rabbi Zelig— What was his name again?"

"Zeligbaum."

"Yes, that this Rabbi Zeligbaum was suffering now as a result of what he did to you. Would that ease your pain?"

"You can't." Aaron's eyes turned cold. "He lives in Florida now. Apparently married to a lovely woman, bunch of kids, great position. Living the life." He suddenly became very tired. "Maybe this isn't such a good idea," he said, looking down at the table. "It dredges up some really unpleasant stuff."

"Okay. But suppose I were to tell you that the back injury was preordained for you that day, one way or another."

Aaron felt himself get angry; shoulders up, hands clenching at his sides. "You see, that's exactly the kind of piffle—excuse me—I *don't* want to hear. It takes away his responsibility. Rabbi Zeligbaum should be rotting in jail for what he did to me, and others, but you say I would have suffered this pain anyway. You see," he toned his voice down, leaned a little forward, "I know you are a good man, but I find this kind of talk aggravating, and—"

Rabbi Wechter's face went hard, blue eyes fixed sternly on Aaron's. "I am—in no way—exonerating Rabbi Zeligbaum!" he said, before letting his face soften again.

"Good to hear."

"What I am saying is this: G-d has many emissaries to do His bidding—a multitude. If a person has to experience some kind of defeat—a blow, a loss, an assault—Hashem can employ hundreds of thousands, millions even, for this errand."

"Hogwash. Excuse me."

"I hear you."

"Do you? Do you really?"

"Aaron, listen. Your back had to get hurt in some way. Playing soccer, falling from a window, tripping over your shoelaces. Rabbi Zeligbaum was simply the lowly minion chosen to execute the ghoulish deed."

"No. This is unacceptable. He is responsible."

"Of course he is."

"How so? You have removed responsibility from him."

Rabbi Wechter smiled. "No, no, no. That is where 'free choice' comes into the equation. It is up to every person whether they want to be G-d's envoy—a conduit of blessing or its counterpart. In *this* situation, your Rabbi Zeligbaum had the choice. He chose poorly. He is guilty. He will yet suffer, either in This World or the Next. But that is not our concern. Our concern, Aaron, is you, and what we can do for your healing."

"I'm afraid it's too late for that."

"Really, Aaron? Why are you here?"

The waitress came, and conversation stopped as she placed the drinks they had ordered on the table. Aaron grew quiet as he sipped his Coke, not entirely content with the direction this talk was taking.

"Now, Aaron. Tell me something *positive* from your childhood," Rabbi Wechter said, breaking the troubled silence. "Do you have any fond memories? Any friendships? Was there a time when someone was kind, in an extra special way, that sticks out in your mind?"

"Yes."

"Good. Tell me a bit about that. I am curious to hear."

Yisrael Thaler. He hadn't thought of him in so many years. Even now, just his name made Aaron crack a smile. Yisrael Thaler, who everyone thought was crazy, who nobody took seriously, who made a name for himself in the parks and streets of Chattersfield as a bum and a buffoon. Yisrael Thaler, whose parents had no control over him, who (according to a *most* reliable source) had dealings with the Mafia and was almost arrested. Yisrael Thaler, who now lived a quiet life in suburban Hendon. Aaron's only friend throughout those turbulent middle-to-high-school years; the only one who knew, with a small degree of certainty, that Aaron was still alive; the only one who had his contact information; the only one whom Aaron could trust would not give him away until he was ready, if ever, to come back. Yisrael Thaler: the kooky no-goodnik who was able (G-d knows *how* he did it!) to prove them all wrong, all the naysayers, all the tut-tutters, all the tiny people living their tiny lives predicting the worst for him.

"There was a boy, Yisrael Thaler..."

"Yes?"

Aaron grinned. "He was as messed-up as me, just about. We were classmates, chums." Aaron looked at his one-man audience, and then continued. "He was a little crazy...in some ways, worse than me. But he made good, in the end. He made good." Aaron paused and shook his head, as though to ask himself, *How?*

"Anyway, one time we were invited, my whole class—about sixteen boys all together—to a party in Rabbi Yona Gold's house. He was our teacher that year. He was actually one of the good ones. We were around bar mitzvah age, maybe some of us as young as twelve at the time. I was already a little shaky about my beliefs. And trust me, those boys were not exactly helpful with that..."

"Oh? How so?"

"Oh, man!" Aaron sat back in his seat, his chair rocking on its hind legs. "They were the most self-applauding phonies you could ever meet. They just loved to lord over those whom they deemed not righteous enough in their mitzvah observance. You see," he stared into the rabbi's eyes, "there was this great pecking order, a hierarchy, with obscure criteria. We were all subject to it, yet no one really knew how it came to exist. The measure could be anything: money, learning, how strict people were in keeping mitzvos. What made someone higher than others on this hierarchy? No one could say for certain. But of course, yours truly and Yisrael were relegated to the very last peg on it. You know what I mean?"

Rabbi Wechter had his head resting on the heels of his hands. "And that bothered you."

"Of course. At the time, anyway..."

"Why?"

"Isn't it obvious?"

"No. This kind of thing exists everywhere, in every culture. It is one of the many natural human pitfalls."

"You mean, you had such a thing too?"

The rabbi laughed. "Of course."

"And it didn't bother you?"

Rabbi Wechter paused. "I was not inclined back then, nor am I now, to pay heed to the approval or disapproval of others. I find it unhelpful and distracting. So, no. From a very young age, I disciplined myself to ignore much of the rumblings in the ranks, so to speak. It made not the tiniest bit of a difference to my journey."

Aaron laughed uneasily.

"But do go on with your story, all the same."

"Ahhh, where was I?"

"Rabbi Gold's house..."

"Yes. We were at Rabbi Gold's house. I remember that the table had been set with blue Magen David paper plates, matching cups, and napkins. Rabbi Gold had poured a little wine for each of us into those small, transparent, disposable cups, *keilishkes* we called them. But before we drank the first *l'chaim* of the evening, he had to leave the room to answer the phone. We were left alone for a short time."

Rabbi Wechter pulled a white handkerchief from his pocket, removed his glasses, and started cleaning them vigorously. "Go on," he said, looking up again.

"So there we were, on our own, with these small *keilishkes* of red, sweet wine, untouched by any of our lips, with our knees bobbing under the table in nervous excitement. Sitting to my right was Yankel Pomensky—a classmate and the son of a big *rav* in our community— and suddenly he announces, 'Rabbi Gold wants us to start without him.' Okay, big deal, you say. But Yankel was this big thirteen-year-old, husky pants and size-fourteen shoes. His father, Rabbi Shraga Pomensky, was terrifyingly large, too. I have nothing personal against Rabbi Pomensky, except that he had such a rotten kid..."

Rabbi Wechter's eyebrows climbed slightly.

Aaron ignored it. "Anyway, Yankel turns to me and says, 'Rabbi Gold wants us to make the *l'chaim* ourselves. I'll start.' He lifted his little cup and straightened his other arm high in front of his face, blocking my view. Everyone followed. They lifted their cups high and waited for Yankel to cue them in. So he says something like, 'On behalf of Rabbi Gold, who has entrusted me with the honors, we wish to commemorate this moment and make a *l'chaim*.' He tilted his head, shut his eyes, and swung his cup-bearing hand back. The rest of the group followed. I downed my little bit of alcohol and placed my empty *keilishke* on the table in front of me. Then I looked up and saw all the boys pointing and laughing at me, the only fool to have fallen for the trap.

"Mine was the only, lonely little *keilishke* that was empty. What entertainment! The boys held up my discomfort like a trophy. *Aaron Bulman downed his cup before Rabbi Gold. What a dope!*"

"Aaron," Rabbi Wechter grinned, "I distinctly remember asking you for something *positive*..."

"Wait. I'm not finished. So I'm sitting there, stewing, not knowing where to put myself, when I feel a nudge on my left arm. Yisrael, who had been quiet throughout, picked up *his* little *keilishke* and, in front of all those twits, gulped it down. When he was done, he set it down in front of himself and gave me a wink. The boys were hooting and carrying on, but Yisrael didn't care, and somehow, at that moment, neither did I. Does that satisfy?"

"Magnificently. Thank you."

Aaron looked at the wizened old face of Rabbi Wechter. "I don't know why you needed to know that. What does it tell you about me?"

"Quite a bit. Aaron, have you ever considered the possibility that you may be emotionally gifted?"

Aaron's features arranged themselves to express pure doubt. "What are you talking about?"

"I've been reading a lot lately about people who struggle to anchor themselves against the torrent of sentiments they are flooded with on a daily basis. Society tends to recognize the intellectual genius, but there is such a thing as emotionally gifted kids too."

Aaron did not react. His body remained still, legs crossed, elbows resting on the little table between them. He said nothing, but stared ahead, not meeting the rabbi's eyes.

Rabbi Wechter continued. "Most of us find strong emotions intolerably annoying, so we relegate them to extinction. But you, Aaron Bulman, I think you have been dealing with them all your life. This is your gift, but it is also your burden. And I believe it has left you with many, many scars."

Aaron, suddenly aware of how hot it had turned, pulled at the collar of his shirt. Perhaps he had topped his social quota for the day, week, year. Whatever. He needed space. He looked at his watch. Black Tie had not given him unlimited leave. He had to get back before his night shift started at ten.

"I have to go. Work. This has been...enlightening." Aaron got up. "I live in Deauville Beach, by the way. I tend a bar called Black Tie 33. The owner is Jewish, like myself, but...well...you know..." He checked his watch again, and then, despite himself, he asked, "How do you do it?"

"Do what?"

"Believe?"

"Practice."

"Practice?" Aaron blinked his eyes.

"Yes, practice." Rabbi Wechter looked up to see if Aaron wanted more. "Are you ready for a Hebrew grammar lesson?"

Aaron shrugged his shoulders and took a step back.

The rabbi rose from his chair. "The word for faith in Hebrew is *emunah*. Now, you must know already that Hebrew is an organic language. It grows of itself. *Emunah* comes from the root *uman*, which means *professional*. Which is really like saying, 'well practiced.'" He buttoned his jacket. "Did you never realize this before?"

"No. I always understood 'believing' to be something you're born into, or out of, or you choose to do, or not."

"Four mistakes in one breath. You are getting better." The rabbi smiled and aligned himself with Aaron as they both walked away from the café.

"So how did you learn your 'profession'? You had a mentor? You picked up tips? How did you become 'well practiced'?"

"Well, I have to admit, being born to a professional believer did give me a head start."

"I, too, was born to a professional believer."

"You can re—"

"No." Aaron stopped walking and swiveled around to face Rabbi Wechter, who was wearing a smile that looked, at that moment, too penetrating. "Don't get excited. Nothing is about to happen. Not now. Not ever." Aaron glanced again at his wristwatch and put out his hand. "Thank you for your time, Rabbi. But I must go now."

They shook hands, and Aaron walked swiftly away.

"Remember, Aaron, nothing is ever lost..." Rabbi Wechter called to his back. Aaron turned to face him once more, brows scrunched in confusion. He opened his mouth, then closed it, and turned and walked away again.

Rabbi Wechter watched as Aaron walked toward La Bastille,

crossing the street to catch the bus. "Hey! Aaron!" he called out. "Don't stay a stranger. Come visit again. Soon."

Aaron turned and waved as the bus drew closer and hid him from view. *If only*, he thought, *if only I could have met such a man years ago. Things may have turned out entirely different then. Oh, well...this is the burden of my lot.*

It was 12:05 p.m. His train was not scheduled to leave before 1:10. He had a whole hour to kill. He scanned the station to see what it offered, his attention automatically drawn to the book booth. He picked up a book, skimmed through its pages, and put it down again. Unable to concentrate, he looked at his watch again; could he risk a quick foray to Square Marcel Pagnol? Was it worth making the fifteen-minute detour, just so he could stroll in nature and clear his head? There *was* something distinctly disagreeable about how swiftly he had left the rabbi at the café. Something faulty in him.

A small, sad smirk settled over his face. He recognized the pattern. Proximity. He thought of his brief and terribly flawed marriage. Too soon into it, Aaron had begun to crave solitude, a craving that wiled its dark spell and stopped momentum. It wasn't on purpose. He simply couldn't navigate the constant presence of another person near him. Yet so many do it, and do it successfully, he knew.

Remember, nothing is ever lost...

What was that supposed to even mean? Nothing is ever gone from the world? Not even the mud on these train tracks? Wait a minute, did Rabbi Wechter mean to include the physical?

He and his ex-wife had surely cared deeply for each other when they'd decided to marry. Did those feelings disappear? If they had been there, and then fizzled out, then *some* things *do* get lost. Oh, this rabbi didn't know what he was saying. Of course things die and leave the world. Memories probably had the longest life span, but even those couldn't live forever. Surely they died with the person.

No?

The saddest part of all, Aaron realized, was that he didn't even miss his ex-wife. Not from the time they had separated. It was as though his signing the divorce papers was a simple acknowledgment of his having made one terrible mistake. And that very day he'd gone to a restaurant...alone. To celebrate.

There was definitely something messed-up about that.

He hoped she'd fared better.

He turned around and walked out of the station's main square, and then made a left. Yisrael Thaler. Aaron frowned at the thought of him. Had it been ten years now since that last phone call, when Yisrael had handed him the last opportunity to come back? He—Aaron—remembered the exasperation Yisrael had expressed after he realized it was a no-go.

In the beginning, Yisrael had been in touch almost weekly. Aaron enjoyed hearing community news, and Yisrael was happy to supply him with the colorful recounts. There had been the drunken tongue-lashing on Simchas Torah from cranky Nosson Kopshtimer, one of the big *machers* in the shul, who had been righteously indignant upon hearing that alcohol had been served, *to the ladies*; the crazy incident when some new and inexperienced driver had crashed her car into the wall of the boys' school, narrowly missing the youngest Schneider kid; and the medical scare when Kasriel Tropper, who was only in his forties, had had a heart attack.

But as the years passed, the calls had petered out.

So when Yisrael's call had come out of the blue that day, in the morning's wee hours, Aaron knew right away that someone must have died. And in the moments before Yisrael had spoken, he had closed his eyes and prayed, *Please let it not be my mother. Please, please, let it not be her.* Guilt had followed relief when Yisrael told him of his father's funeral. Then Yisrael had asked him, "Don't you think now would be a good time to come back...?" He had actually almost triumphed in breaking Aaron's resolve to stay away, but at the last second Aaron had simply been unable to get on the ferry.

Was that the last time anyone from his previous life had spoken to him? My goodness! How *was* everyone? Sima? Henya? He felt a tremor, followed by a fusillade. All the love he held for them, long banished to the furthest corner of his soul, where it could wring no damage, suddenly threatened to present itself. He teetered slightly, and then stopped walking altogether. The heaviest of dreads overcame him as the door to the vault of his memories—lying unreachable, beneath decades of dust and debris—now began thumping upon him from inside. Alarmed at this sudden disquietude, he stood very still, inviting odd looks from passersby. Had too many years gone by? Would he ever have the fortitude to go back and face the wreckage he'd left behind?

Aaron looked down at his feet and commanded them to continue walking. Turning right, he crossed over Rue de Rome and made his way to Square Marcel Pagnol. The musky-scented flowers, bobbing delicately in the breeze, were a sedative for the soothing of his spirit.

He had sat the requisite seven days of mourning, alone. Spent them drinking, thinking, sleeping. He'd called in sick, not wanting his boss to bother with any of the usual social etiquettes practiced all over the world for when someone loses a loved one. Aaron hated all aspects of forced kindness. He would rather do it alone. He only "sat" in deference to his father. *If I have chosen to live my life without all the stifling rituals of my youth, then that is one thing,* he had decided at the time. *But my father did not, and I need to respect that.* When he "got up" on the last day and went to work, it was as though nothing had happened. And nothing *had* happened, really. Had they not been lost to one another ever since the night of the fire?

Or rather, the morning after?

Throughout the park, visitors were offered beautiful strolling paths, speckled with benches and tables. Aaron sat on an empty bench and observed a Chinese family—mother, father, and three small children—sitting on another bench, eating hot dogs together. The mother handed each of her children a small carton of chocolate milk to drink. Aaron watched them with a fascination that surprised him, for how was it possible, after all these years, that he even acknowledged that they were eating meat and flushing it down with milk? It was something he himself had done and would do again without ever thinking. Why, now, was he suddenly noticing this?

The Chinese father stood up, picked up one of the children, and took him to the trash can to throw out his dirty napkin. At first the movement looked too swift to be loving, but then Aaron watched as the father kissed both cheeks of the child before returning him to the ground.

His own father had always been such a mystery. Did Elchanan love his only son? Aaron was never sure. Were there any small gestures of love? Was there ever a kiss? An intimate conversation? A quiet, private smile, just because? Yes, his father had zippered his coat for him when he was little, tied his shoelace, spooned his medicines, held his hand to cross the road, spoken to his *rebbeim*, showed him the place in the siddur at shul; but never had he tucked him into bed, scratched his back, tickled him, ruffled his hair, put him on his shoulders to dance with the Torah on Simchas Torah like all of his friends' fathers. Aaron had never gotten the feeling that his father was proud of him, only that he was his father's responsibility—as though to be born a Bulman was to be born liable.

Not wealthy or privileged—simply accountable.

Aaron glanced at his wristwatch. *I'd better head back now*, he thought, *or I'll miss my train*. He walked away from the footpath and turned to catch his last glimpse of the gardens at mid-day. Flashes of color in the sun's reflection squinted at him. He scrunched his eyes and made his way back up the Rue Rome toward the Gare St. Lazare train station.

WINTER, 1986
LONDON, ENGLAND

Elchanan was in a festive mood that Friday night, when he and Aaron, who was around nine at the time, returned from shul, closing their front door against the cold, blustery wetness. Elchanan was singing an old Russian army song that had been adopted by the Jewish community and used in one of their Shabbos prayers. It was an upbeat melody, charming in its vigorous pitch and rhythm, and putting everyone in a good mood. He had given Aaron a rare shoulder hug as he passed him on his way to the dining room, where the table had been set hours before with the family's good china, covered challahs, and lit candles. The girls slowly made their way to their seats, Sima putting down her books and Henya her toys with a stretch and a yawn. Greta came in from the kitchen, a platter of fish in her hand and a smile of contentment brightening her face.

After Kiddush and *Hamotzi*, and once the first course had been consumed and the bite of everyone's hunger had been soothed, Elchanan began a new rhetoric. It started simply enough: "You know, I'm tinking, de Jew and de voman, dey are verry similar..."

At first Aaron was not listening, his attention caught by the wind outside and the way the branches of the English oak tree on their front lawn were holding on so earnestly to their mother trunk. This was one of those evenings that gave him a good feeling of being safely cooped up in the house, while winter wrought its damage outside.

Elchanan was getting carried away. He lifted his silver wine cup. "To de Jew and de vomans!"

"Honestly, Elchanan, is this suitable Shabbos table talk? What are you talking about?" Greta was still smiling, but you could detect the slight lilt at the end of her sentence, depicting her confusion and a bit of irritation.

"*Nu*, Greta, is obvious! Everyvon agree that voman is superior to man. She is more viser, more...more... She know how to be human more better. *Eishes chayil*—vomans of courage." He held up his silver goblet. "To mine voman of courage, to mine vife, to you, Greta!" He drained the last of the Kiddush wine.

Greta pulled her head back and lifted her brows, the marks of surprise showing clearly on her features. The children were now all looking at her. She fluttered her eyelids at them. They chuckled.

"Vait." Elchanan placed the Kiddush cup back on the table in front of him. "I not finished..."

"Oh?" Greta's brows shot up again.

"De *kinderlach*. Deys growink so fahst. Ve needs to teach dem 'bout dis vorld, 'bout de dangers. No?"

Sima was staring at her father. Her eyes looked thrilled, but her lips betrayed an unease. "What dangers, Tatte?"

Aaron wished she had not asked. A hint of uncertainty began pinching at him.

"Listen, and you vill learn. Vhen de voman hold her dignity, she is precious, like jewels. Notink shine like she. Notink compare. But..." Elchanan threw a sharp look toward his daughters, a flash that Sima caught but that fell off Henya, who was paying more attention to a selection of miniature dolls she had lined up around her plate. "If vomans allow to fall to disgrace, she trash. No. She vorse dan trash. She got no vay out. She lose everytink: her sparkle, her future. Everytink!" He shook his head slowly and sighed, and Sima wondered if there was someone he had in mind. "It sad," he continued. "Very, very sad."

"Really, Elchanan..." Greta's smile had by now faded. "Is this Shabbos table talk?"

"Greta, Greta, ve needs to varn de girrrls. Dey needs to know. No?" He searched his wife's face for her permission to go on. Then his glance fell on the children, and that's when he saw it: Aaron sneering at his sisters, and Sima staring back. She was daring him to show weakness, daring him, through her stare, to break.

"Dat's enough, you two," Elchanan snapped. Aaron got a tap on the shoulder.

"Yes…that's enough now," repeated Greta, directing her words to no one, and to everyone. The children stopped. For a minute or two the family continued to chew, to pass around the salad bowls, to dip challah into horseradish mixed with mayonnaise. Only Elchanan had not—perhaps could not—let go.

"Aaron!" He used his most stentorian voice. Everyone stopped mid-munch and looked at him. "Don' tink dat juss 'cuz you a boy, dat you free. A Jew you born, and a Jew you be, all your life. Remember, ven de Jew behave like he should, he shine. He a blessing. But…Aaron, ven he allow hisself to turn rotten from inside, ven he greedy unt selfish, dere is no shmeck vorse dan his." Elchanan glowered at his son, harsh lines sprouting from his eyes and lips, disappearing under the thickness of his salt-and-pepper beard. "Guard yourselve, Aaron Rephael Bulman. Der shtink foon der rotten Jew can be shmeckt from all four corners foon der eard."

Sima threw a triumphant smirk at her brother, who did not care to notice as he and his father beheld one another in a trancelike state…

12

To: Henyaleipzig@sympatico.com
From: simah@gmail.com
Date: September 9, 2015
Time: 6:31 a.m.

HENYA!

Enough already!

Mummy speaks to me. She hasn't taken it the way you have. She's not mad anymore. Although...that too worries me. What if...? Uch! Doesn't bear thinking about.

Anyway, I think you ought to know—not that you've shown much interest, but still, I think you need to know—that the letter turned out to be quite important after all. It revealed something that none of us would have guessed, and Tatte became so much more human to me than he ever seemed before. I think that says a lot. Of course, since I don't have it, I can't send it to you, but I do look forward to the time when you will have read it, and then I think we should have a talk. Just the two of us.

You said Mummy was wasting her energy over that letter, but I disagree. Meanwhile...still waiting...!

Love always,

Sima

13

Monday, July 6, 2015
Long Island, New York

Peel, shuck, eye, and scrub; chop, grate, dice, and sizzle. *Oh, my eyes are stinging.* Peel, slash, taper, cut, gore out the bad stuff, don't leave it in, makes the food rotten, dig it out, clean it, slosh the water over it...potatoes, carrots, celery, and onions, what about the yams? Do it, do it again, do it again and again, a hundred times, a thousand, a million. Clean away the dirt, hallow out brown spots, black spots, purple spots. Check for bugs, mold, old and unusable... get rid of the tainted, the wormy and the worthless...

Rid thyself. Eliminate all that is tainted; eradicate all that is impure, infested, and disgusting. Yes, dig deeper, ever deeper, way beneath what eyes can see.

Rid thyself.

Rid thyself.

I am trying, whispered Sima to herself. *Confound it, I am* trying*!*

Oh, Tamar...

She had spoken only once to Tamar since reading the letter. "Let's not deal with this over the phone," she had suggested.

Mercifully, Tamar had agreed.

"Sima, come! You've gotta hear this..." Aryeh's voice, from his study near the kitchen, relieved her of her ear-wormy incantation.

It was early evening. The girls had returned from their sun-splashed escapades, settling in the unfinished basement to play computer games until supper, their squeals reaching the main floor every now and then. Sima left her cooking, wiped her hands on the wet dishtowel hanging on the oven door, and walked toward the study. She stood at the doorway, noticing her husband's bent back as he scrolled and scrolled, squinting at the open laptop. He didn't look up, just swiveled it toward her and clicked *start*:

An interview on SkyNews. A stocky, bald, skull-capped member of the Knesset answering questions that were being asked by an unseen, female British voice: "Can you comment on today's violence? What do you think will be Israel's response?"

"The provocations are mounting daily…" the man said, his intense, challenging brown eyes not leaving the camera for a moment. "How long does the international community expect Israel to remain silent while rockets are raining down upon us?" He held up a map. She started another question, but he stopped her with his raised hand. "Just a moment, please," he said. "I want, if I may, to show your viewers how many seconds an Israeli has to run to safety each time the siren is sounded."

"Okay," the disembodied voice replied. "Go ahead."

In his hand, the man held a laser pen, pointing it at the map. "Anywhere from 180 to eight. Seconds, that is. As you see, the areas closer to Gaza, superimposed with a red tint, here," he pointed his laser, "the people in that range have the least amount of time. Eight seconds is all they are given to find a bunker or safe house." He put down the map. "Now let me ask you, would the people of Britain expect the British government to exercise restraint if rockets were to rain down on, say, Birmingham?"

"But there are those who will say that you should not be living there, that you are occupiers, and for that reason the rockets come…"

"Please, we ask the people of the world to stand aside right now. We don't need permission to defend ourselves, thank you very much. We are not looking to the international community for advice, since they cannot understand the predicament we live with day to day."

"Well, perhaps if you were to—" she tried.

But he was having none of it. "The Jewish people are not going anywhere. Neither are the Palestinians. If the international community wants peace, they are welcome to try to arrange it. But let me make one thing clear: thank G-d we are no longer easy victims. This is our land. We have the oldest document in the world to prove it, the Torah. And G-d will help us continue to remain true to our land, come what may!"

Aryeh looked up. "What do you think? I think he did good. I like him. Hope people are listening."

"Who was that?"

"Sam Ben-Sasson. Decent guy."

Sima grew quiet. Her hand rested on the top of Aryeh's desk. She waited a few minutes, thinking. She was afraid to speak. It wasn't Aryeh she was afraid of; it was her thoughts.

"Aryeh?"

He was scrolling down the news channel. "Yeah?"

"Do the Palestinians have the right to be there?"

Aryeh looked up. "What do you mean?"

"I mean, weren't they there first?"

"No. We were there way before them."

"Yes. I know. But then we were kicked out. And they came in."

"So?"

"So...was it right of us to come barging in and claim that it's ours?"

"Are you kidding me?"

Sima did not respond, but the look on her face told him all he needed to know.

"Sima, Eretz Yisrael is our *home*. It has always been our home. Being kicked out—temporarily, I might add—does not make it any less our home." He shook his head slowly at her, incredulous. "That's it, Sima—I am booking tickets. It is time for you to travel to Eretz Yisrael. Okay, maybe not this summer," he said, watching her eyes grow wide, "but soon. You need to experience the land. Your *neshamah* needs it.

You will see, Sima...you will see for yourself how you will react when finally allowed to experience what being home feels like."

She sat without moving. For too long she had resisted—without knowing why—Aryeh's gentle urging that they travel together to visit the Holy Land. Perhaps the time had come. Perhaps she had misread her own inertia. They had skirted with this issue before, always arriving at the same place: Aryeh claiming that since she had never stepped foot in their ancient homeland, she could not possibly understand its effect upon the Jew; and Sima resisting any attempt by him to get her to join him for a visit—always begging for postponement, another year, another time, next season...maybe. If she would have the courage to look, she might have understood the anguish she was avoiding. Aryeh's time there had left him with a permanent ache to return. She was not about to welcome that misery inside her. No. America would do.

At least for now.

"Please, Aryeh, hear me out. I mean, before the Holocaust..." She paused, then ventured further. "I mean...they were there...living there...no?"

"So? What about *us*, Sima? We were living in Hungary, in Poland, in Germany, in France. Oh, we had homes—but they were taken from us. The only home that cannot be taken from us is the one given to us by Hashem Himself. We belong *no*where, *but* there. That is all."

"But Aryeh...if we do to others what was done to us, then we are no better than them! No?"

"Sima." Aryeh looked suddenly tired. "We *had* no place else to go. Where should we have gone, if not home?"

"So it was a question of right versus right?"

"No! It was a question of death versus death."

"Come on, Aryeh..."

"Look, Sima," Aryeh tried to explain, "after the war, when that motley bunch of bleeding survivors went back to their pre-war homes, homes they had paid for or built with their own hands, others were living in them. And we had no voice, no way of telling them to leave, of claiming our property back. It had all been stolen from us. In Poland, Ukraine, Holland, Hungary—you name it—we lost our buildings, our land, and could never reclaim them. Why? Because we are Jews. We are not Polish, Ukrainian, Dutch, or Hungarian. We are Jews, and the only place that is ours is Eretz Yisrael. So we took a lesson out of *their* book and reclaimed what is *ours*."

"But that is exactly what I am saying. We learned a *bad* lesson! We adopted a *bad* idea from the *goyim*. How can this be right?"

"*Sima, we were slated to die!*" Aryeh all but yelled. Sima covered her face with her hands. "*And we chose to die there, in Eretz Yisrael! And not on the foreign soil that refused to recognize our humanity.*" Aryeh stood up, wiped the sweat from his forehead, and looked out the window behind him.

"But Aryeh…" Sima still could not quash her thoughts, her terrible, hideous thoughts. "That still doesn't answer the question: If *they* were there, what right did *we* have to take it from *them*? To make *them* refugees?"

"Stop it, Sima!" Aryeh placed both hands over his ears. "Sometimes you are too much. I can't take your liberalism, especially when you are so ignorant of the facts."

"I am *not* ignorant of the facts. I know my history, thank you very much. I am still entitled to question the morality of my peop—"

"Oh, yeah? Well, did you know that at the time, there were more *Jewish* refugees from *Arab* lands than *Palestinians* from *Israel*?"

"Huh?"

"Yup. It's odd, isn't it? How everyone tends to forget that little nugget of history. No one ever mentions them. Hundreds of thousands of them. Turned out of their homes, their businesses snatched, their bank accounts seized, arriving by the boatload from Tunisia, Morocco, Iraq, Lebanon…you name it. Fleeing for their lives with two thousand years of history behind them and just the clothes they were wearing."

"So how come—"

"It was a whole reshuffling of people. Tons of Jews were made into refugees during those turbulent years. Yet you never hear about them. You know why?"

"Go on..."

"Because they didn't *stay* refugees. In fact, over half of today's Israeli population descends from these people. But you wouldn't know it." Aryeh pulled at his tie and turned to face her. "And that's what really gets me."

She waited, stunned at her own ignorance.

"What really gets me is how this situation of limbo has been allowed to continue for so long. It's ridiculous already!" His frustration contorted his face. "The international community, spewing invectives from their moral heights, ever quick to condemn Israel. They should have found a solution by now! For crying out loud, there are tons of landscapes more than capable of absorbing these Palestinian people and giving them the lives they deserve. But no! And you know why, don't you?"

Sima remained still.

"Because it serves their purpose to perpetuate these conditions." He ran his fingers through his neat, dark beard.

"But it still doesn't answer my question. Is it a matter of wrong versus wrong? Or right versus right? However you want to word it?"

"At the time, Sima, morals weren't the point. *Survival* was."

"But we are supposed to be *better* than that!"

Aryeh smiled. "Sima, Sima, why is it so difficult for you to understand? There is a huge difference between them and us: They seek our destruction, while we do not seek theirs; they crave a heroic death, while we crave to live in peace." He stood up and looked at her. "I could go on and on."

She shook her head. Slowly her hands came together, and she rubbed her left thumb along the knuckles of her right fingers. "And now?"

"And now we pay the price, *have been* paying the price, all this time."

Aryeh saw her first. She was staring stiffly at him from the hallway, her thick brown bangs falling into her wide-open blue eyes, her thin face pale. His startled expression made Sima swirl around. In a flash she felt a zing of electricity spark from her heart and diffuse itself throughout her body, ending with the telltale prickling of her fingers. She stood up, not flinching when the chair fell behind her. "Bracha, what's wrong?" she cried, opening her arms wide to her youngest daughter.

Bracha rushed to her mother, falling into her embrace. Entwined, the two stood together, Sima rubbing as much warmth and reassurance into the child's back, while throwing a long and condemning look at her husband. From under her enfoldment they both heard Bracha mumble, "Mommy, is there gonna be a war?"

Sima rubbed her daughter's back harder. After a few seconds, she pulled her out from inside her encirclement and leveled her face so that they could both see one another's eyes. She kissed both sides of her daughter's cheeks—noting the coldness of her skin—and hand-brushed her bangs out of the way before speaking. "Bracha, sweetie, nothing's gonna happen here. This is all happening far away from here."

"But what about in Eretz Yisrael? What about our cousins there?" Her lips quivered slightly. "Aunty Judy and Uncle Bryce... Fetter Shmuel and Tante Rivky and all their children... What about...?" She didn't finish.

Sima grew quiet. What about all of Aryeh's siblings who had chosen to live in the Promised Land? What about them, truly? She eyed Aryeh as he shut down his laptop, the impact of his indiscretion sinking into his facial muscles as he sat back guiltily in his leather chair, a fortieth birthday gift from his wife. No one spoke for a while.

"Bracha," offered Aryeh, "none of us knows what will happen. We have to believe that everything will turn out for the best. We have to trust that Hashem knows what He is doing, and that He will keep our family members safe. We can help them, by davening with more *kavanah*, by being nicer to our friends, and by having *bitachon* and not being afraid."

"But I *am* afraid, Abba."

Sima straightened her chair, sat back down, and pulled the girl toward her, tightly grasping her shoulders. "Bracha, do you remember when we went to England two years ago? We were on the plane, and the pilot turned on the seat belt sign in the middle of the flight, because we had turbulence. Do you remember that, Bracha?"

The girl nodded, but kept her eyes on the floor.

"Well, do you remember how afraid you were, and what we did together that made you feel better?"

Another nod.

"Do you want to do that again? Will it make you feel better?"

Bracha looked up, her blue eyes getting bluer as the whites turned pink. "Yes," she whispered.

Sima took her daughter's hands, hooking one into Aryeh's elbow and placing the other on her own cheek, not letting go. Together the three recited a *perek* of Tehillim, asking Hashem to help all those families in Eretz Yisrael whose safety seemed in danger. They did not drop hands when they were done, but continued to hold them together in silence, until Bracha broke away, seemingly satisfied that those she loved would be protected.

"We'd better be more careful in the future. The girls don't need to feel this so closely," Sima said, sitting back down after closing the door behind Bracha.

"Where did you learn that trick? That hand-holding trick?"

Sima smiled. "It's from a long time ago."

"Now I'm really curious," Aryeh said, grinning. "Tell me! Don't leave any details out!"

"Okay." She returned his playfulness and crossed her legs, enjoying the moment, before beginning. "I had to have been around nine, Aaron was about six, and Henya was just a baby. We went to a Chanukah concert as a family—a rarity for us." She tipped her head and squinted her eyes. "I remember it was held in the Hornsey Town Hall, about a half-hour's drive from where we lived. I think our shul must have been part sponsors; otherwise my father would never have gone. My mother would have taken me, maybe Aaron—but the fact that we *all* went makes me think our shul had something to do with it.

"Anyway, the whole of Chattersfield was there; at least that's what it seemed to me. And also people from other communities, including some more modern types. It was exciting to be there. Of the concert itself I don't remember much, but as the music was winding down, the conductor of the band turned to the audience and announced in a strong Israeli accent, 'Ladies and gentlemen, I invite you to join me in *Hatikvah*, Israel's National Anthem, which we will follow with a moment of silence in recognition of all the fallen Israeli soldiers. Please, everyone will rise.'

"Well, pandemonium broke out. People got up from all around us, grabbed their children, and walked out. Some sat silently. A bunch of people did get up to sing along. My father, of course, was one of the ones who stood up to leave. He gestured to my mother, but she would not budge. I remember pulling her skirt, trying to get her to move down the aisle because Tatte had such a strange look on his face, but she wouldn't. Truth is, he looked ready to burst, but Mummy was stalwart and would not yield!

"Until that moment I had never witnessed my parents really argue. It scared me. I remember thinking that the world would collapse if my mother refused to follow my father's orders. I was near tears by the time the song finished, but relieved to see that my father, though stewing, did not leave either, but stayed close to us.

"The whole way home, they fought—my mother, who was sitting in the back, next to the baby, and my father, who was driving, though nearly getting us killed, he was so livid. The gist of the argument was about things I couldn't understand at the time..."

"*Dey monsters, Greta, monsters! Resha'im gemurim. Allowed haff of Hungarian Jewry to die in de gas! Vhen dey could haff done sometink! Saved dem! Eichmann vas ready to talk, ready to deal. But no! 'Ve don't vant beards in de New Israel. No shtetl Yidden in modern state!' Ve should haff valked out, Greta! Vhy you make us stay?"*

"They were wrong, Elchanan, but that's not the point."

"Not the point? Bloisen kop? *No hint of G-tt in de whole song? Don't you know, Greta, dere cannot be future vhen G-tt is not invited!"*

"I agree, although nebach, *they don't know that yet."*

"Dey vill never to know, because...because...dey don't vanning to know. Dey puppets, unt dey haff chosen Vashington as deir gott. And good luck to dem! Oy! I cannot beleef you made us to stay. I cannot beleef you do not care."

"I do care, Elchanan."

"About vhat, Greta, about vhat you care?" He was shouting now, *really worked up.*

But she shouted right back at him. "About dead soldiers, Elchanan— that's what I care about! Sons lying dead in the battlefields in Eretz Yisrael. Sons who will never come back to their mothers! I agree that they founded the modern state on the terrible ground of secularism, but those who gave their lives for it still deserve our respect and recognition!"

Sima took a deep breath. "I remember crying quietly in the car, too shaken to move or make a noise. Only later, in my teens, could I process what they were fighting about, and could I understand both sides. And only then could I fully appreciate how hard it must have been for my mother to make such a decision, to stay and pay respect; and how torturous it must have been for my father, to have his wife see things a bit differently from him."

"So what's with the hand-holding thing? When does that happen?"

"Oh, yes. I forgot why I was telling all this to you. Yes, so later that night, when Aaron and I were in our beds, well, of course we could not sleep. I crept over to his room and sat on his bed. We were talking about what had happened, and Mummy must have heard us, 'cuz she came in and joined us, sitting on Aaron's bed and all. I think he was even more traumatized than me, 'cuz he started crying—really hard—and I remember him saying something like, 'Why did you say that sons are lying dead in the field, Mummy? Is that what's going to happen to me?'

"When my mother heard that, she went out and came back with my father. He was still smoldering from their earlier argument, but he sat down where she told him to sit, at one side of Aaron's bed, while she sat at the other, and all of us held hands and together said some Tehillim, and when we were done, we just sat quietly until Aaron broke the chain and lay down to fall asleep." Sima's eyes were full as she got to the end. "I remember thinking that my mother had to be the best mother in the world for what she had done that night."

Aryeh nodded slowly. "Wow," he said. "See, your father couldn't be all that bad if he listened to your mother and came to comfort you and Aaron, even though he was still so upset at her."

"Yup. Anyway, that was my first introduction to the complexity of being a Jew. It's hard, you know—we have enemies from without, *and* enemies from within."

Sima returned, troubled, to her kitchen. Was this at the core of Tamar's rebellion? Was this splintering of the Jewish nation what she saw and could not abide by? The splintering of her own family?

In a way...who could blame her?

TUESDAY, JULY 7, 2015
LONG ISLAND, NEW YORK

"Siiiiiiiiiiima!" Henya's primitive method of communicating her angst catapulted through the airways and landed on the hair cells of Sima's cochlear like volcanic lava.

She pulled the phone away from her ear and stared at it disgustedly. *Oh, goodness*, she thought, as the shrill of her sister's hysterics continued ricocheting in the labyrinth of her inner ear. *What now?* She shook her head and tried for a reasonable tone. "Hello to you too, Henya. What is it? What happened?"

"You *have* to come! Mummy *fell*—again! We just had the doctor here. He wants to take her in, says she keeps losing her balance, wants her in for tests. But she's refusing. Naturally. She *needs* you, Sima. She keeps asking for you..."

Her abdomen tightened up, rigid as glass. "Okay, okay, stop *scream*ing, Henya. Just tell me, *calmly*, how bad is it?"

"It's bad," said Henya, bringing the clamor down to a more audible, but still poignant, ululation. "She is in a *lot* of pain. Fell down on her side in the living room, early this morning, while getting up to answer the phone, of all reasons. Missed the old coffee table by an inch. I always felt we should get rid of that thing. Such a nuisance..."

"Was she taken to a hospital?"

"No. I just told you: she point-blank refused. We wanted to bring her in, but you know Mummy..." They were both quiet, but not for long, as Henya had little tolerance for conversational lulls.

"They sent us a nurse and did some bloodwork," she blabbered. "We're waiting for the results, but..." Sima heard her blow her nose and wondered if Henya was crying. "Oh, Sima, the doctor said it might be her heart medication that's affecting her. She gets all dizzy. He said this was bound to happen sooner or later. He doesn't think she's broken anything, but he is sure there is internal bruising. I've been with her all morning; haven't been home today at all. I'm not complaining, but...I mean...could you come in? Aren't you off work now for the summer, anyway?"

"I'll see what I can do," Sima promised. "I was planning to come visit Mummy sometime soon anyway. It may as well be now." She bit her lip, wondering if a change of scenery would help prepare her for when Tamar came home...

"Good. Great." There was a pause. And then, "Maybe I should warn you..."

"About?"

"Just that...I mean...you need to be careful here, Sima. London has changed."

"In what way?"

"It's not safe. Well, it's never been completely safe, but things have gotten worse. It seems we are free game these days. Last week some girls were walking home from school—right here in Chattersfield— and they got ambushed. One of the girls had her schoolbag emptied all over the street. I mean, that's just a small thing, but it makes us all nervous. Then yesterday Yanky Hellerstein—you know, Sara and Laibel's oldest? The one with the cleft lip, remember? Anyway, he was on a double-decker bus, the top deck, and some *goyim* started taunting him. So he got up to go down the stairs, and then they pushed him. He went flying, hit his head, got a real knock."

"Blood?"

"Yep. The bus driver saw the whole thing, through that mirror thingy they have, and wouldn't carry on driving. It was a whole palaver. Police came and everything."

"And what exactly did the police do? Any arrests?"

"No. Of course not. The troublemakers had scarpered by the time the police arrived."

"*Oy.* It's always like that. I will never forget that time, a few months before you were born, when Mummy and I were at home and…oh, never mind. I have to go and do carpool. Okay, Henya, I'll see what I can do," Sima repeated, and replaced the receiver quickly. It jiggled a little before settling into place. She put both hands on her temples and tightly massaged the area. *One more thing,* she thought, *just one more, and my head will spontaneously combust.* She thundered the names of her two youngest girls and ordered them into the car.

It was late. The traffic, like her life, coagulated and refused to budge. She used the time, as she always did, to think. England. The streets at twilight and the terrible dangers that seemed to stalk their every step, on their way home from school. She slipped a CD into the stereo system, changed lanes, and slowly drove straight into her childhood living room in London…

When the knocking came again, it was harsher—short, angry strikes. The glass within the wooden-framed front door rattled in protest. One or two more blows, and it would surely shatter. In the living room, Greta Bulman stood very still and kept her eyes on her children, her face pale with fright, lips empty of color.

The man coughed, his catarrh buildup making it sound more like explosions, with rumblings between each spasmodic eruption. Sima, eight at the time, peered out of the living room and down the hall to see what she could make out of their intruder, through the front door. A large, dark bulk shadowed the entranceway. He was so close!

The guy had one grimy hand plastered against the frosted pane. Blackened fingertips. She watched the fuzzy image of his other arm lift and tug at the mezuzah *affixed to the doorpost. But it proved too hard for him to negotiate, to extract the nails from the brick. She crept back.*

"He's still there," she whispered to her mother. "I think he is trying to steal our mezuzah."

Greta's blue eyes grew larger. "Sima," she rasped, "don't go out of this room again."

"Why would he want our mezuzah?" she asked her mother, still keeping her voice low. "It's not worth anything to him!"

"Don't worry," whispered Greta. "If we stay very still, he won't know we are here. The mezuzah will protect us. You'll see."

Her words did nothing to alleviate the dread collecting in Sima's heart. "But he only knows we're Jewish because of the mezuzah, so how can it protect us? It gave us away!"

"Oy, so many questions, Sima! Just keep quiet!" Greta put her finger on her lips, warning her daughter to stop talking.

But Sima couldn't stop. "Maybe we should take down our mezuzah. It's like a yellow star. It lets people know we're Jewish." She had heard about the Holocaust from some of her friends, who had proclaimed during one recess that having great-grandparents means you are not Jewish. Distraught, she'd gone to her teacher, who explained to her that her mother's grandparents had been born in England, and that was why they hadn't gotten killed in Nazi Germany; but that of course she was very much Jewish.

"No, mammela." Greta pulled Sima to her and gripped her shoulders lightly, lowering herself to her daughter's eye level. "This yellow star we wear with pride! You will see how it will protect us. You will see."

The knocking started again, this time flat-palmed, accompanied by shouting—mangled sounds that struggled to form themselves into words, expletives dangling at odd ends.

Greta covered her ears with her hands. Her eyelids fluttered. Sima watched her mother's lips chattering a prayer like a recording stuck on the turntable: "Hashem, get him away from us. Protect us. We are Your children. Make him go away. Protect us. We are Your children... Hashem, listen to me, we are Your children, get him away from us..."

Aaron walked over and pulled at his mother's skirt. She turned to *him, slowly shaking her head from side to side so he should understand. "Don't make a sound, Aaron. He mustn't know we're here."*

Another bang. They winced in silence, bracing themselves for the inevitable explosion of glass, Sima and Aaron forming a stiff barricade around their mother.

Miraculously, the door held.

They heard the intruder kick the wooden frame, turn, mutter to himself, and finally shuffle away—but not before hurling a mouthful of phlegm at the window. They heard him make his clumsy way down the three-step stoop and then, mercifully, they heard the clanging of the gate at the end of their front yard.

Too frightened to move, they stayed perfectly still for one, maybe two minutes. Then Sima, holding her breath, walked over to the living room window and softly opened the lace curtains to see what she could of their would-be attacker. Forever she would claim that she opened the curtains just a smidgen...but it was enough to invite the devil. With a juvenile lack of guile, she presumed that beyond the gate, the intruder no longer posed a threat. She heard her mother call her name through tight lips, but pretended she hadn't. She was mesmerized by the man, as he sat on the garden wall, his long, unwashed hair falling over a greasy, dark-gray trench coat. She could not take her eyes off his rounded, filthy back.

Greta Bulman came behind her daughter and pulled her sleeve. "Come away from the window!" she hissed. "Come away right now!" But Sima was unable to stir and waited a moment too long.

The man spun around, his eyes instantly meeting hers. Sima smiled at him uncertainly, but her smile must have slapped him. Jumping off the wall, he picked up a stone. Sima ducked just in time as the small rock smashed through the window and into the lace curtain above her head.

She screamed.

Greta became hysterical. "I told you to come away! You showed him we are home! What did you do that for?! How many times must I say something before you listen to me?!"

The man's ghoulish laughter streamed into the room. Greta, dropping all caution now, faced him directly from the empty space where the window had been. "I am calling the police!" she cried, her voice unrecognizably high.

The man had the wildest eyes Sima had ever seen: wide-open, with the whites shining out from within the bloodshot edges. They were framed with red, rough, and concertinaed skin. The same skin surrounded his laughing, malicious mouth, the corners of which were collecting spittle. Ultimately it was his mouth that stupefied her, rendering her completely at his mercy. The words that disgorged themselves from his broken, blackened teeth. Terrible, horrible words. Words she had not yet heard before: "Jewbugs! Go back to Palestine! Filthy Jewish pigs! Get out of 'ere! Go back to Palestine!"

Sima smiled now at the memory. *No problem, Mister! Sure thing!* Then her forehead scrunched. She turned the corner to enter the parking lot of the camp building, thinking, *But if that tiny strip of land is the acknowledged home of the Jew—even to a British drunkard—then why is our ownership of it so contested by the world?!*

Her mind, of its own accord, suddenly brought up another scene, a news clip from a few years prior that someone had shown her.

Her face—very pink lips, very pink-rouged cheeks, and the wrinkles around her very blue eyes—lifts up toward the camera. She is a sweet old lady, smiling in the mid-day sun, enjoying a conversation on the White House lawn. The month is June, the year 2010. She is giving advice on her subject of expertise: journalism. There is laughter all around her. She is relaxed. Genial and chirpy. Helen Thomas doesn't know it yet, but she is about to make the greatest blunder of her nearly-sixty-year career. A blunder so catastrophic that it will cause her to resign soon after, infamous and disgraced.

A man's voice is heard, reverent. He is excited to have crossed paths with the one-time dean of the White House press corps. "Today we're covering the Jewish Heritage...eh...eh...month. Any comments on Israel? We're asking everybody today. Any comments...?"

And without a moment's pause, still smiling, still carefree, she replies, "Tell them to get out of Palestine...!"

Chuckle, chuckle.

Sima parked the car, walked the girls through the big double doors to the building's main entrance where the campers were gathered, and waved to them, staying for a few minutes to watch each find her group.

Then she walked back to the scorching lot, turned her car around, and made her way back home.

15

That morning, like every morning since the Abney Hill cemetery incident, Aaron placed the compass he'd stolen from his sister's cheap geometry set into the pocket of his trousers and covered it with his sweater. It made him feel safer, offering thin protection for himself and his sister, should the need ever arise again.

No one but he knew it was there.

Later, during Chumash class:

How does he know that "mashkof" *means* "lintel"? thought Aaron, as Laibel Hellerstein read the passage with a flawlessness few could duplicate. *And what is a lintel anyway? It's as though a little bird is whispering all the answers into his ear; a bird that will not, no matter how much I want it to, perch on* my *shoulder and sing all the answers to* me.

Aaron stared at the back of Laibel Hellerstein's head. *He just knows everything. So no one ever starts up with him.* Aaron looked down again at the text on his desk, focusing on the page, the black ink, the white spaces between the words. He willed the verses to reveal their secrets to him, burning the letters with his eyes, brandishing them with his zeal—but they remained silent to him, cold and distant, as though turning their backs to him.

Suddenly a silver coin appeared in front of him.

He looked up. The *rebbi's* eyes were all crinkled up as he stood smiling down at Aaron, his unkempt beard trailing down past his collar, silver filigree bobbing as he nodded. "That's the way, Arele," he said, using the moniker of affection and tapping him on his shoulder. "Look inside, find the right place, and stay with us. Keep doing it. Finger on the place. This will make you smart." That was Rabbi Strauss, a crusader for the excoriation of lingering Dickensian ghosts within those classroom walls, instead seeing every student as equal to the other. Phantom castes would wilt into nothingness under his warm protection.

"Yes, Rebbi." Aaron looked down again at the unyielding print, his fingers already clasped around the money. He found the place, and for much of the rest of class held it; though the meanings of the verses still hid themselves from him, a mush of words that, perhaps, only needed separating to be understood.

That recess, in the dank yard surrounded by the school's three buildings, two pairs of hands grabbed Aaron's shoulders, and before he could regain control, he was whisked to the back alleyway. He sniffed the air; a malodorous smell drifted up from the green stain on the concrete corner near the main building. A pipe, running down the wall, ended just before the ground, above a metal drain that was caked with mud and fragments of leaves. The smallness of the space and the stench from the drain felt inhospitable even without Pinny Lerner and his posse staring at him.

Aaron blanched. Though they attended the same Jewish day school, and were even lucky enough to be in the same class, he and Pinny had never bonded. In the two years that had passed since the summer of Matthew, Pinny had grown taller and stronger than the rest of the kids on Ashley Grove. Aaron avoided him most days, walking home alone or with Sima. But there was no dodging him now, especially as he had reinforcements—Shalom Gordon and Chezky Leibowitz—acolytes sworn to loyalty, standing on either side.

Aaron, aware that his heart was pumping double-time, felt inside his trouser pocket. The compass's needle jutted into the palm of his hand.

"...*What kinds of bad things do* Yidden *do?*"

"*Oh, I dunno. Things...*"

Though Shalom and Chezky moved behind him, blocking any escape attempt, Aaron puffed out his chest and yawned loudly to disguise the fear that spread through him, and turned to leave.

"Where do you think you're going, Aaron Bulman?"

"What's it your concern?"

"It will be your concern if you don't stay and hear what I have to say."

"So, what do you want to say?"

"What's the rush? Can't we have a neighborly conversation?"

"Pinny, just say what you wanna say. I don't want to be here all recess."

"Give us your coin," Pinny demanded, throwing a knowing look to his appendages standing behind Aaron.

"No!"

"I knew you would say that, so I have a deal to make with you, Aaron Bulman..."

"Look, move aside and let me go please." Aaron turned to leave. "You're not getting my coin, and that's final."

"Not so fast. See, we've been watching your sister..."

Aaron stiffened. Never before had he considered his attachment to Sima, but suddenly he was unprepared for this level of vulnerability. Still, he tried to cover his nervousness with a nonchalant grin. "So...?"

"Got herself up all fancy in that blue coat, with the fake fur collar, don't she?"

"So? What about it?"

"How would you like it torn to shreds? Maybe, even, with her inside..."

"You wouldn't dare..."

"Oh, yeah? Try us." Pinny stood up to his full height, accentuating their height disparity.

Aaron's eyes turned cold. The fingers of his right hand fondled the double rod of the hidden compass. He said nothing. "So...Aaron Bulman, wanna strike a deal? We do nothing to no one, on condition that you pay. You understand. For protecting her."

In a flash, before anyone could hold the moment down, Aaron darted for Pinny. Grabbing him by his neck, their faces touching, he thrust the pointer of the compass through Pinny's open coat, into his shirt, sinking it deep in his chest. There was the sound of an earthy grunt, and Pinny's eyes grew enormous, the whites around the irises visible on all sides while his mouth formed a silent 'O.' Flaccid debilitation followed, and Aaron let him go, dropping him over the crate he had been sitting on, while he—Aaron—stepped back, fingers in mouth, and watched. Even at that moment, he could not relive the steps it took between Pinny's last words to him and the thrust of the compass—a tiny shard of eternity lost to him.

Within slow seconds, Shalom and Chezky appeared in his periphery, as though a great distance away. One of them—he did not know who—enunciated what all three were thinking: *"Did Aaron Bulman just kill Pinny Lerner?"*

Finally, Pinny coughed. The compass point was still inside him, hanging wretchedly toward the left side of his chest. Aaron reached up and pulled it out. A dark red circle grew on Pinny's shirt, Aaron's terror growing with it.

Shalom was the first to move. He ran out of the little cranny, shrieking all the way to the *rebbi* on duty in the front of the yard, a black and timeless silhouette. "Aaron Bulman just killed Pinny Lerner. Aaron Bulman just stabbed Pinny Lerner in his heart. I saw it, Rebbi. I saw it with my own eyes." Every soccer kick, every cricket ball throw, every conversation, halted. All eyes were on the *rebbi*, as he rushed after Shalom to the back of the yard, where Pinny was still lying over the crate, blood oozing between his fingers as it covered his wound. Aaron was now standing above him, holding the compass— its pointer very, very red. The *rebbi* bent over and pulled Pinny up.

Aaron silently begged Pinny to stop coughing, his panic reaching a crescendo when Pinny's lips turned blue.

Pinny Lerner did not die that day, nor any day after that.

The only damage done that day was the kind no eye could see: a punctured lung for one boy; a punctured self-image for the other. Hospitalization for one; suspension for the other. Heroism for one; ostracism for the other.

Greta never got out of Aaron what made him do it. She tried, over the next few weeks, to have him go over to Pinny Lerner's home and apologize properly, but he wouldn't. From that day on she maintained a strained relationship with her neighbor from down the road. Even when Pinny's little sister, Shoshi, was killed in a car accident three and a half years later, at the tender age of ten, the Lerners made sure that Greta felt unwanted when she came over to be *menachem avel*.

Elchanan never spoke with his son about the incident. Instead, a subtle distance settled between them, like a thin crack in a stone wall.

16

WEDNESDAY, JULY 8, 2015
LONDON, ENGLAND

"Well, thank goodness you're here!" Henya wrapped Sima in her arms and planted a large and loud kiss on her cheek. For a full thirty seconds they held one another and ignored the world, inviting English disparagement as the two of them obstructed the flow of arrivals down the slope of Terminal One at Heathrow airport.

Sima loved her little sister, who stood three inches taller than her and had no qualms whatsoever about expressing exactly what she was feeling, at any given time. The youngest of the three Bulman children, Henya had come after a gap and so never had to stake out her place; she'd always known how much she was wanted and loved. It was Henya who had gone to pieces after their father Elchanan had died. Henya—who had never even *considered* moving away from London; who had married Michoel Leipzig, the son of a wealthy English businessman, and was now a busy mother of four children, ages two to twelve; who hated traveling (especially to New York, with all of its noise and speed), and who loved her parents without reserve—was the one who had fallen apart at the funeral in a way Sima couldn't. To Henya, their father was exempt from criticism. After all, he'd had a hard life. If he was moody, so be it; he'd earned the right. If he was distant, harsh, demanding...well, okay. Look, he'd grown up eating potato peels in a *shtetl*, with no running water, no father, and a sick mother to worry about. What did you expect?

"How is Mummy?" Sima extracted herself from her sister's firm embrace and stepped back to take her in. Henya belonged to that group of women who instinctively knew how to put themselves together. As if born wielding a mascara wand, they flutter expertly made-up eyelashes, serve five-course meals to twenty guests on fine china, and never, but never, leave the house without having made sure each of their children had made their own bed that morning. Granted, such women can be tiresome, but Sima had been shunting any irritation she may have secretly harbored for her one and only sister for so long, that she was simply unaware of its existence.

To be sure, Henya had put on a little weight, but otherwise she held tenaciously to her beauty. Her silky brown *sheitel* was fashionably styled, and dangling crystal earrings played peek-a-boo in its hairs. Today she wore a lightweight, wraparound white cardigan over a coral blouse, and a white and coral skirt. Her face was expertly made up in peachy lips, brown eyeliner, and the sort of blush that had a shimmer to it. Henya was the unofficial beauty of the family. Even her walk was graceful. Next to her, Sima always felt impossibly dowdy, but she would push that sentiment out of her mind. It simply did not matter enough.

"Oh, she's still not doing great, but the doctors say to give it another week or so, and hopefully she'll be back on her pins again. I'm just so glad you're here!" She squeezed Sima again. "You should make a point of coming in every summer, now that Mummy is getting older. Not just once in a while, but every summer. It makes sense. I mean, aside from me and Aunty Breeya, she's really on her own."

The two walked through the revolving door toward the parking lot—or car park, as they called it here. Sima stopped for a moment as a waft of fresh British air encircled her; she closed her eyes and breathed it in. *Nothing quite like a summer breeze in England*, she thought. *Purified by its travels across the Channel from France... It's no wonder the British hail it curative!*

Henya continued talking. "So how was the flight?" Not noticing that Sima had stopped, she went on, "Did you get a kosher meal, or did you book too late for that? You must be—" She finally noticed that Sima wasn't with her. "What's the matter? Why are you stopping?"

"British air!" gushed Sima, incandescent with joy. "You don't know the value of it till you live out your summers in humidity, always rushing indoors for climate control. Gosh, Henya, what a marvelous country this is, to breathe such magnificent air!"

Henya smiled. She'd missed her quirky older sister. Who else could extol so plebeian a commodity, and not look cheesy? Sima had always been the more bookish of the two. Both girls had done well in school, but while Henya had packed away the last of her schoolbooks on the day she graduated, without so much as an intimation that she would ever leaf through anything printed again, aside from magazines, Sima went to bed every night with a book in her hand and three on her night table. She loved both reading and learning. Every so often Sima would call Henya to share an epiphany or something nice that she'd read, but while Henya enjoyed listening to the orbit of her sister's associations, she could never be bothered enough to make her own discoveries.

"Come on." Henya tugged Sima's sleeve and walked on. "We need to get back. I left Shloimele with my mother-in-law, and I told her I wouldn't be too long."

Sima walked alongside Henya for a few quiet minutes while Henya searched for her car. Each time she came to England, it always hit Sima at the airport how everything in that country was so much more compact than on the other side of the Atlantic. Space was at a premium, with every parking spot fashioned to combine utilitarianism and aestheticism. That seemed to be the theme of the whole country. And it worked too, to a degree. After about a hundred-point turn, they pulled out and swiveled the car around the spiral roadway down to the ground floor. Sima felt sure that her corner of Henya's black Honda would scrape against the concrete barrier, but it never did. Sima yelped a few times, while Henya only laughed.

"So, how long are you planning on staying?" Henya asked her.

Sima smiled. "That's the good news: Aryeh booked me an open ticket. The girls are all in overnight or day camp, so life is rather lackadaisical back home. I'm feeling a bit giddy at the moment, y'know: free! Let's make plans for some good times while I'm here."

"For sure! I want to take you shopping. I've found some warehouses that sell last year's fashions for really good prices. Oh, and before I forget, Aunty Breeya wants to invite you and all of us to a Sunday supper. Like old times..."

Sima's smile deepened. Aunty Breeya held a special place in Sima's heart. Like a time-worn but faithful icon on the desktop of her computer, Aunty Breeya had just been clicked, and the multilayered file spilled open inside her. Aunty Breeya had been her savior. The two shared a unique affinity, she having rescued Sima from the depths of naiveté on more than one occasion. Greta's elder by five years, Breeya was the more outgoing, slightly mysterious, but disarmingly open matron that the dilettante Sima was chartered off to when she entered adolescence; to whisper of things too blush-worthy for Greta to manage without permanently lopping off the young maiden's innocence and inserting her own annoying paranoias.

Sima sat back in the car and allowed her mind to float back to the time when she had been sent to Aunty Breeya's house, after asking her mother one of "those" questions again. It was just that Greta could never handle the types of questions that plague young girls, and Sima was always left feeling like she had wounded her mother just by being curious. Greta would turn to wood, her cheeks donning the proverbial pin-cushion red in their centers, the color leaking and spreading all over her face and down her neck, just because Sima had asked, "Mummy, what do couples speak about on a date?" Or, "How did you know that Tatte was the right one?" Sima had long forgiven her mother's awkwardness, especially since it was Greta who had suggested that she "call in the cavalry" and get Aunty Breeya involved. Aunty Breeya had an ease about her; she shied away from nothing.

Those two sisters were so different, and it was incredible to watch how they dipped and dove around each other, perfectly compensating for whatever one of them lacked. Sima loved her aunt but revered her too, never quite free of a subtle pressure to seek her approval whenever they were together. She chastised herself for it, involuntarily readying herself for the encounter.

"Good old Aunty Breeya! How is she?"

"You mean since her stroke? *Baruch Hashem*, she's doing amazing..." Sima's cheeks reddened. How could she have forgotten about her aunt's stroke? Henya didn't notice. "We've become quite close. Well, she was always family-oriented, but recently she and Mummy began spending every Wednesday afternoon together. Sometimes I join them. They are such dears."

"Speaking of which, give me the low-down. What should I expect when I see Mummy?"

For the next ten minutes, Henya regaled her with details. "Well, first of all, don't be alarmed by her appearance, because she probably will look older to you than the last time you saw her. But she is doing okay, I am told. She has a hard time hearing, but didn't she always? Only now it's worse. She stays in bed all day, but with some encouragement she will do her exercises. She doesn't like to go it alone, though. The day nurse is very vigilant, but the night nurse couldn't care less... Anyway, she believes, as we all do, that this is just temporary and that she will get back to herself once all the bruising heals. At least that's what they're telling us.

"Her house is pretty much under control. I have my cleaning help go over there two to three times a week. Also, I've had her eyes checked within the past few months, and Dr. Gimple—you remember him? Always in need of a shave? Yes, that's the one, down at Middlestreet Market—so he recommended a stronger prescription, but he said we could take our time with that. Oh, I forgot: because she isn't eating all too well, we've had to add Ensure to her diet, but she resists the stuff..."

"And her spirit?"

"What do you mean? Her soul? How on earth should I know?"

Sima looked amused. "No, silly. I mean her spirits, her emotional well-being. How's that doing?"

"Oh. Well. It's hard to say. She was never the life of the party. She is a bit of a puzzle, isn't she?" They were at a traffic light, and Henya looked hard at her sister. "Don't get me wrong, I love her and all, but she and I never speak of anything important—like feelings. I mean," the light turned green, and Henya continued driving, "I'm sure she has them, but with us it's only been…you know: duties, appointments, daily routines. She doesn't open up to me. Never has. I put it down to my being the baby of the family, so she never learned to trust that I can be there for her in that way. It makes me sad when I think about it, actually…" Henya pulled a face as she swerved to avoid a bright red car that moved too close.

"I wish we could be more honest with each other, but there is always that barrier between us. I had thought that we would become closer, you know, when Tatte died. It was me she had called first that morning, to tell me that she'd found him dead. I'm telling you, Sima, she never sounded so broken. I know, I know, you've heard all this before. But really, I mean, I just thought, what with you back in New York after the *shivah*, and with Aaron…well…you know…it would be just me and her together, and so maybe our relationship would…you know…work its way into more depth. But it never happened for us, and I don't want to push for it anymore. I love her. I do. But we are just not very close."

"Does she ever mention Aaron? You know what I mean?"

"Of course I know what you mean. No. She never brings him up. But I know it's gutting her. It has to be. Even though she would like to think she is doing a great job hiding her feelings. What is it with us British, that we think feelings are for wimps?! Anyway, I want to tell you something…"

"What?"

"Don't you think it's weird how things happen in around ten-year intervals?"

"What are you talking about?"

"Look, in 1995, Aaron leaves. Ten years later, in 2005, Tatte dies. Now it's 2015. I know you can't compare, but Mummy has a bad fall! I don't know. Stuff! It gives me the heebie-jeebies."

Sima stared out the window. The diminutive vistas of an English town rushed past her, row after row of gridlocked, two-floored terraces, bantam doorways and windows, asphalt pavements, a lonesome tree, a red pillar post-box, a corner fish-and-chips shop, a newsagent, a Ladbrokes betting shop, a small bank, smaller dress boutiques, and, of course, the ubiquitous and always busy pubs—double doors wide open, potted plant off to the side. What surprised her was how quaint she found it all—now, at this age.

How come I didn't appreciate this landscape when I lived here? How come I had always thought these streets ugly? Only now do I see them differently—the way they are built at a slant, the laundry hanging in the backyards, the curtains billowing into the little bedrooms, the empty chairs on narrow decks, waiting for the evening when someone will sit on them and enjoy a smoke... How come I ignored all of this enchantment growing up? And now, all I see is symmetry and elegance.

Have I turned into a doddering sentimentalist?

I wonder what it would be like to actually live the lives of one of these people. Wouldn't that be a magical experience? To be someone else, if only for a short period of time?

"Sima?"

"Yes. Sorry. I'm a little tired from the trip. Yes, you were saying how odd it is that something seems to happen to us every ten years. I agree. It is odd."

Don't say a word.

Don't say a single word about Tamar.

Sima's first thought—after dropping her suitcases in the tiny hallway and running up the narrow, green-carpeted staircase, flinging open the door to her mother's bedroom, and throwing herself into her mother's outstretched arms—was: *G-tt in Himmel! She's become so gaunt!* Although for those few moments, she reveled in being a daughter again, the awkward positioning of her elbows and knees put an end to the ebullient embrace. Cognizant of Greta's pain, Sima straightened herself and took stock of her mother, the room, and all the little changes that had happened in her two-year absence. By the time Henya entered, Sima had made decisions about what she would be doing to the curtains, the closet door that was slightly off-kilter, the linen on her mother's bed, and the smell—slightly sweet, like overripe cantaloupe—that drifted up from the bed, enveloping all three of them in a vapor of faint neglect.

Henya, jolted into observing her mother through Sima's unaccustomed eyes, kissed Greta's cheek and held her frail shoulders. "Mummy," she said, "has Deepa not changed your linen today? Maybe Sima and I can lift you onto the couch for a few minutes while we change it?"

"Oh, surely it can wait! I'd like to spend a few minutes with Sima first!" Greta held out her hand, and Sima grabbed it. "How have you been, my love? Tell me about your girls! How's Tamar?"

Huh?

Why did she single Tamar out?

"Great! *Baruch Hashem* everyone's doing well. No big news to report."

"Ahhh, that's good. You know how terrible I feel about all that I miss out on, not being there while they are growing up. You bringing them occasionally is not the same. It's not the same at all." Immediately, Greta's eyes began to fill.

Sima searched around for a box of Kleenex. "No. It's not the same." She handed her mother two tissues. "*Baruch Hashem* the girls are blossoming. Tamar is a lifeguard at the same camp she always goes to, Camp Shoshana. Just can't get enough of the outdoors, that one. I didn't think she would want to go back after her previous year. I told you about that, right? She had some friend-trouble. But you never know with kids. They have greater resilience than we adults, don't they? Odel and Shana are living it up in teen camp, and Naomi and Bracha are at Menucha Hills. Can't complain."

"And Aryeh?"

"He's wonderful, as always, *baruch Hashem*. He is taking some time off work so I could make this trip. It really works out well, because summer is his slow season anyway. Mummy, tell me how *you* are. Fill me in. Gosh," she gushed, "it's so wonderful to be here, to see you!"

Greta pointed to her hip. "Ooooh, so much has been happening..." She winked and tipped her face toward Henya. "Your sister here has been a real lifesaver. I cannot tell you how awkward this has been, this falling. I had to pull myself to the phone. And then subject myself to indignity after indignity, what with all the doctors and nurses' prodding and whatnot. I'm telling you, Sima, I never thought this kind of thing would happen to me."

"It's called old age, Mummy. Ain't none of us immune, you know."

"I know, I know. But you are never quite ready for it."

"So," Sima sat on the side of the bed and took her mother's hand again, "what's the alternative? Huh?"

"But it is so humbling..."

"I know..."

"Mummy," Henya interrupted, "I have to go and get Shloimele from my mother-in-law. Can I bring him here so we can all be together? While Sima's jetlag hasn't yet hit her?" She was standing by the open door, one foot out.

"Good idea. But bring him some things to do. I don't want him destroying the house."

Sima called to her before she disappeared, "Any chance you have a spare laptop, Hen? I would love to set myself up with Wifi while I'm here."

"Sure." Henya smiled. "I'll get Michoel to come by tonight and wire you up with his old one. Nothing wrong with it. He just wanted to upgrade." A moment later, she was gone.

Greta turned to Sima. "Henya's been marvelous, she really has been. It's such a wonderful thing, you know, to have a daughter living close by. Come, Sima, come close. I want to tell you something." Greta beckoned for her to lean in. "She wants me to go to the Keller Care Center for the Aged," she whispered, as though Henya was still in the house, though both of them had heard the front door close only moments before.

"I can't. I simply can't." In her mother's eyes, Sima saw the anguish Greta must have lived with. "You can understand that, no? All my life is here. Tatte, Aaro…" Greta stopped mid-syllable and held her breath. Sima held hers. For a while the shrouded silence overwhelmed them, a canopy that only existed in Henya's absence—impenetrable to anyone outside of the two of them. Every time Sima made the trip back, or any time Greta came to visit them in their Long Island home, there was always a moment of shared silence within which the name "Aaron" need not have been said.

"Still nothing from him?" Sima finally broke through, looking into her mother's watery eyes.

"Nothing." Greta's eyes seemed to sink into their sockets a tiny bit, unperceivable to the uninitiated. "But he's alive. I know it."

There was a shuffling at the door. A thin, albeit muscular, woman entered the room, wearing blue scrubs. She had caramel-colored skin; long, shiny black hair; round brown eyes; and a heart-shaped mouth. Walking over to the bed, she patted Greta on the shoulder. "Time for a washup, Mrs. Bulman. Then we change linens, yes?"

Reclaiming her vitality, Greta opened her eyes fully and, smiling, introduced the two. "This is Sima Rivka, my eldest daughter," she said, with more pride than Sima could justify. "All the way from America. And this," she turned to Sima and gestured to the day nurse, "is Deepa. She's from Zimbabwe originally. Can you believe it? Zimbabwe!" It was incredible, this seamless transitioning her mother had perfected over the years. Sima did not think she had mastered this skill, still feeling herself stuck in the bog of the earlier moment, still staring at the newly-shut window of Greta's disconsolateness, unable to unfasten herself from it.

"Sima, darling, step out a minute, will you? While Deepa gets me respectable…"

Incredible.

She brought her suitcases to her old room. It always unnerved her to walk into her old bedroom and find it so completely unchanged. It was the room she had shared with Henya. To be sure, the beds were stripped of their linens, which she found easily, in the same place as always—the large storage closet in the hallway. She made her bed using her childhood bedclothes: pale blue and pink unicorns flying through clouds of dusty purple. She touched the surfaces of her room and stared through the window, relishing the old view: the backyard of her youth, and Matthew's backyard a bit further away. Of course there was no sign of Matthew or his parents anymore. Now a busy young family was living in that house, judging from the laundry clothesline outside and the swing-set and broken toy cars strewn about on the haphazard grass.

She hung up her clothes in her former closet, which still smelled faintly of wood and glue. She sat at her old desk, smiling to herself, touching the curled photographs she had hung on the walls around her little space: a picture of her two best friends from high school—Sara Wolf and Chani Swissa—both now married and living in the States, like herself; the family around the dining room table, messy with *mishloach manos*. She and her siblings had dressed up as pirates that year. In the photo, she had her finger in her mouth, her eyepatch tight on her forehead; Aaron was holding out his hand for something; Henya was smiling at the camera; and Tatte had his head down, trying to make order from all the chaos. There was one photograph of her and Greta at her graduation. Sima recalled the jitters of that day; having won the English award, she had to give a speech. Oh, the nausea she had battled over that! Graduation had come five weeks after the fire that had branded all the Bulmans as pariahs. But scores were scores and hers had been the highest, so—she had to give a speech.

And before she could shut it down, a memory of the morning after the commencement ceremony suddenly sprang to her mind. She had been walking with Sara and Chani out of the school building, through its double doors, when Mrs. Pomensky—a teacher and one of the big *rebbetzins* of their community—happened to appear just then, on her way into the building. When she noticed the girls, her face grew sunny with joy. "My graduating girls!" she'd exclaimed. "My beautiful young ladies! My Sara and my Chani..." She'd grabbed the two girls and given them a powerful embrace. Sima remembered slinking off to the side, forever left wondering if Mrs. P. simply hadn't seen her, or if she had been deliberately turning her into a persona non grata. She'd never shared the experience with anyone, and was irritated now at how that scene still came with its accompanying shame and ignominy.

Surely there had been growth since then...

She spied the plastic Fisher-Price typewriter that her mother had bought for her, after her fifth-grade English teacher had told Greta at PTA that Sima was a girl with "deep thoughts." Now it sat looking forlorn in the corner, dust covering it like a mantle.

Sima remembered Greta whispering into her ear, *"One day, you may want to write down those 'deep thoughts' of yours. I thought I should give you a head start."*

"Do you ever write down your *thoughts, Mummy?" Sima had asked her.*

"Me? Whatever for?" Greta had laughed.

Sima picked up the typewriter off the floor, set it down on her old desk, and punched down on the letter K. The metal rod slammed against the ribbon. It still worked! She opened one of the ill-fitting drawers beneath the little desktop, found some paper, and fed the typewriter, punching some random letters. A faint print appeared on the whiteness.

She sat back and suddenly remembered why she had come. With a sigh and a wry smile, she got up and knocked on her mother's bedroom door.

"You know what kills me?" Greta had on a fresh robe and was sitting up now in crisp, clean sheets. "I saw it happening, right in front of my eyes, and could do nothing about it." Deepa had left them alone after placing a tray on the night table with tea and biscuits.

Sima had heard all this before, but she let her mother talk. This was her grief. And because she—Sima—had been there throughout it all, nothing was hidden between them.

"I saw how miserable he was, and Tatte, too, for that matter— but what could I have *done* for them? Oh, Sima, if only I had had the resources, the open-mindedness to seek the help they both needed. You know, worse than seeing your loved ones hurt, is the knowledge of your own helplessness. By the end, when he left, it was inevitable. The very air in this house had become poisoned."

Sima nodded and looked out of the window, where a single tree, blessed with excessive foliage, almost scraped against the windowpane. She hadn't remembered that tree so large. It had grown, forming a protective shade for her bedridden mother from the bulk of the July sun. It was now almost noon, and if not for that tree, the room would have been sun-drenched. "I remember," Sima finally said, "and it's true. What could you have done? Nothing." Then she made one small pitch for redirection. "When was the last time you sat in the garden?"

"Sima, don't!" The whites of Greta's eyes were showing.

"Don't what?"

"Don't treat me like a child! I *want* to talk about it. I *have* to talk about it. And you are the only person with whom I *can* talk about it." She paused. "I will come with you to the garden. We don't have to talk about it now, on your first day here, but Sima..."

"Yes?"

She paused before speaking. "There is something I want to tell you."

Sima tilted her head, very slightly. "Oh...?"

They both heard the noises of Henya's re-entrance, followed by Shloimele's whooping sounds as he recognized where he had been brought.

"Not now..." Greta whispered, and arranged her face so no hint of inner conflict showed. *Aha,* thought Sima, *so that's how you've been doing it—easy as pie, and isn't life great? You, by your brilliant acting, and I, by running away to America, each of us trying to protect ourselves and our loved ones, hardly daring to examine what lies beneath the surface...*

Sima got up and opened the bedroom door wide. She walked to the top of the stairs and called down to her youngest nephew. He looked up at her, lifting both hands above his head, showing off his toy. She ran down the stairs and picked him up, hugging and kissing him and throwing him into the air. Henya laughed.

"I want to take Mummy into the garden," Sima said, catching her breath while still holding Shloimele. "When was the last time she was outdoors?"

"Oh." Henya bit her lower lip. "I haven't taken her out at all since she fell. That is bad of me. I just didn't think she would be able to navigate the stairs. But you are right. She should go out for fresh air. Let's see if we can persuade her."

They went up single-file along the narrow staircase. Sima, not willing to let go of her nephew just yet, entered their mother's bedroom again. Greta beamed at them, noting how calm and happy Shloimele seemed in his aunt's arms. "He looks tired. Do you think he's going to fall asleep?"

"I hope so," said Sima. "Then I get to hold him longer." She looked at Henya, who was checking her makeup in the huge mirror that sat on the triple dresser along the wall opposite their mother's bed. "I really miss this age..." She tightened her arms around Shloimele.

"Sima," Henya turned to them, "what are you waiting for? Get Tamar married off, and poof!" She snapped her fingers. "You'll be a *bubby!*" Sima felt herself sway at the mere mention of Tamar's name. Shloimele was becoming heavier in her arms, as he snuggled deeper into her neck and shoulder.

"Mummy," Henya continued, "Sima mentioned that you might want to go out into the garden. What do you think? Can you manage the stairs?"

"I think I'd like that. Deepa could help me with the stairs. You two just stand by if I need you."

It took the combined efforts of Deepa and Henya to maneuver Greta down the stairs. Her howls and facial contortions made Sima doubt that their good intentions were sufficient to warrant such recklessness. When, triumphant, they finally arrived, Greta collapsed into one of the garden chairs. Sima waited; the verdict hung on her mother's first words, as she held her face up to the sun. "Lovely!" she exclaimed, allowing a smile to warm her face. Sima breathed again.

They sat on the patio. It was paved in smooth, white concrete, which reflected the heat from the sun, instantly making them feel like they could be in Italy or southern France instead of in the backyard of their modest little London terrace. In the last fifteen or so years, the mess of the Bulmans' backyard had undergone a makeover. Now flowerbeds lined the three walls, recently planted with pink and purple impatiens and petunias, and the center lawn had lush green grass, a frill that held no space in Sima's childhood memory bank.

No one spoke for a while. The soothing sun massaged its potions into their muscles, caressing them into semi-slumber. Shloimele fell into a deep sleep; Sima breathed in the Johnson's baby products emanating from his hair and neck. Greta, in worship pose, had her eyes closed toward the sun. Only Henya, who wasn't created with the capacity to "live in the moment," pulled out her phone. Her face instantly darkened. "*Oy gevalt!*" she blurted before, hand over mouth, she stopped herself quickly and threw a guilty glance to Sima.

"What is it?" Sima mouthed, making sure Greta was still basking in the rare but glorious rays of the English sun.

"There's this new neighborhood chat, just so we can monitor the safety of the community," she whispered to Sima. "Here..." She dropped her phone into Sima's hand.

Sima read from the screen:

–Yosef Englander, nine years old, was jumped on this morning by five teens on Fountain Road as he was walking to school. Witnesses say the teens chanted slogans against Israel while repeatedly kicking him in the stomach and head. As of now, he is in Homerton hospital, and is said to be in critical but stable condition. Please say Tehillim for Yosef Kalev ben Yocheved Sara. We will update as soon as we know more.–

Sima stared at Henya, shaking her head, repulsed by this new low, while thinking of her girls in America and how they had *no* idea... Henya scrolled down the myriad of anxious posts, muttering a *perek* of Tehillim under her breath.

"Do you know," Greta spoke up, without opening her eyes, "that I have only good memories of this garden? Tatte was the one who originally put in the flowerbeds. He contracted the concrete patio. Nowadays I just pay someone to come and maintain it. Breeya arranged it." She opened her eyes and addressed her girls. "That reminds me, will you two be going to Aunty Breeya for supper on Sunday?"

"I would love to go; it would be like old times. But..." Sima hesitated. "Now that I'm here, I want to stay with you as much as I can."

"Don't be silly!" Greta shuffled herself deeper into the cushioning, holding on to the armrests and closing her eyes again as she turned her face back to the sun. "Of course you should go. It would make me happy to know that you two went over there."

"Sima just wants to enjoy being a daughter while she is here. Right, Sima?"

Sima smiled deeply, and felt a flush rise to her cheeks. "Oh, give it up, Hen," she said, playfully slapping her sister's forearm. "Although maybe there is some truth to that." She looked at her mother. "I guess I just envisioned sitting here with you, as long and as much as possible. At home, I'm always someone's wife or mother, never daughter."

Greta lifted her head, eyes wide. She took in her oldest child, whom she had relied on for too long to think of as having needs. "Wow. So I still provide you with something. Even at this age. Even by actually doing nothing."

"Yes. Of course you do! You are the only person in the world whom I can..." Sima stopped talking.

"Go on...I would love to hear..."

Small prickles perforated the backs of Sima's eyes. Her throat tightened. She swallowed. "Mummy," she said softly, "I cannot believe you don't realize how important you are to me. Perhaps the fault lies with me. I don't tell you enough how much I value you, and everything you stand for."

Henya giggled. Sima turned to her and scowled.

"So I am not a burden?" Greta did not appear to notice Henya's gaffe.

"Burden? *G-tt in Himmel*, no!"

Greta touched Sima's sleeve. "Thank you for that," she said, in earnest, and then added, "Still, I would like you to go to Aunty Breeya on Sunday. It's four days away. Who knows, maybe I'll even join you then."

That Friday night Sima and Greta sat together in Greta's room. A makeshift table was set up near the bed, adorned in white lace. Sima had pushed the small couch closer to her mother's bed. When they were all little, that now-frayed couch had served as the children's sick bed. Sitting on it unleashed many a sweet memory for her. As they ate, they spoke of old family memories and new discoveries that would help steer them through life. The candles on the dresser were reflected by the mirror and shone double bright. Sima had prepared simple Shabbos food—gefilte fish, chicken soup with noodles, potato kugel, and schnitzel—but Henya turned up half an hour before Shabbos with a slew of gourmet delights in Tupperware containers:

mock liver, fried eggplant in a cashew sauce, sushi, and a salad that included arugula leaves, roasted pears, and candied nuts. She had laughed at Sima's childish glee as she unwrapped the delicacies and demanded, "Henya, when did you learn how to *cook* like this?"

After they had eaten and Greta proclaimed that she could not find space for one more morsel, she looked over at Sima. "I've been meaning to tell you something for a long time," she said, with a weak semi-smile. "I was always waiting for the right moment, but it never seemed to come. But I think, perhaps, now would probably be best." She motioned to Sima and lowered her voice. "Come closer to me."

Sima just leaned in, smiling to herself; there was no one else in the house. Who could be listening? "Go on..."

"I have a letter. Did you know about it...?"

"No. What letter?"

"I've had it for ages."

"From who?"

"From Tatte."

"Tatte?!" Sima sat up. "You're kidding! When? When did he write a letter?" Sima tried not to say, "*How?*" but it was difficult to picture her non-erudite father penning a letter. He hardly ever wrote, preferring to have his wife take care of the correspondence for both of them. "Who is it addressed to? Why have I never heard of this letter before?"

"It wasn't something he wanted to share with anyone."

"This is freaky, Mummy. You do understand how freaky this is, right?" Sima's animated response was not well received. Greta looked at her blankly; this was not an aspect of her daughter she enjoyed. Her face must have darkened, forcing Sima to adjust the effusiveness of her tone. "I mean, all this time... It's like a letter from the dead. So... when can I see it?"

Greta shook her head. "You can't. It's not for you."

Sima's eyes grew wide as her thoughts slowed down. "Aaron?"

Greta nodded her head, watching and weighing Sima's reaction. "I am not giving it to you, Sima," she said firmly. "I haven't even read it myself. So don't even try to wrangle..."

"Then why are you telling me about it?"

"I just thought you should know. That is all. In case anything should happen to me..."

Sima remained very still while electricity flowed through her. She waited for the tips of her fingers to stop tingling. When she spoke, it was in a whisper. "Mummy. You shouldn't think like that..."

"Of course I should. It wouldn't be responsible of me not to. I have to consider..." Greta closed her eyes just as two lone tears escaped their corners. Sima watched them make their clumsy way down her mother's cheeks, while the two of them became ruminative to the point of abstraction.

Sima was the first to break the silence. "Do you at least know what the letter is about? Is it a will or something?"

"No." Greta's eyes were still closed. "I mean, I know what was on Tatte's mind during the time he wrote it. I know what he wanted me to know, but I don't know the letter's contents. I've been holding on to it. Waiting..."

"I see." They both surrendered again to silence. Sima sank back into the couch. Realizing how dry her mouth had become, she lifted her glass of water and took a few sips. *Little wonder Mummy still holds out hope for Aaron; she has a letter to deliver. Who knew? I wonder if Henya has heard of this letter. If only I could get my hands on it! To hear what was going through his mind so many years after catastrophe struck!* "Mummy," she had to ask, "how close to the end did Tatte write this letter?"

"Close. A person knows when he is near the end. At least he knew. That I can vouch for. Was it a month before, or six weeks...what's the difference? He knew. And when he handed the letter over to me, in a way, so did I."

"*Oy,* Mummy..." Sima stood up and grasped her mother's thin, trembling shoulders. Twenty years of tension pulsed from Greta's veins and seared into her own. In that embrace, Sima was given a taste of what Greta had had to endure. They held one another for one, two, maybe even three minutes, during which Sima prayed never to have to come any closer to this kind of pain.

What was it that Tamar had once mentioned to her, something her teacher had said about nothing ever getting lost? How is that true? Now she questioned herself: When should she have told Tamar about her uncle? Why had she never found the right opportunity? Was she right to have held her silence? Was it too late now?

Tamar...dearest Tamar...please...let's talk...

17

For days there had been a lot of *shushking*. For days Greta Bulman had either been on the phone or crying, or crying on the phone. Henya walked through the house, frightened. No one would tell her what was going on. After all, at nine, she was just a child. What could she understand? She had walked into the room she shared with Sima and found her older sister red-eyed and heaving on her bed. And when Henya questioned her, even *she*—Sima—was silent. Life on Ashley Grove became oppressive, as though every day required each member of the family to push a boulder up an incline, just to get out of bed.

Bubby and Zeidy Galowinsky moved in, abruptly taking over all kitchen operations previously executed by her mother. As for her father, his presence became ghost-like. He was there, then not. She didn't see him at suppers. He barricaded himself in the master bedroom, and the meal trays Bubby left for him outside the door were usually untouched.

People came. They would stand around, not expecting to stay long. They would be offered tea and biscuits, but most shook their heads and begged off. Then the people stopped coming. When the rabbi of the shul came, he stayed longer, and they closed the living room door so Henya heard only mumbling.

In school, the girls kept their distance. Only her best friend, Kayla Messinger, stood by her. It was enough. She didn't feel like talking, and Kayla didn't demand anything but companionship, which Henya was still pretty good at providing. Recesses came and went, with few exchanges of snacks and words. Her Hebrew teacher took her to the side, one day soon after, and offered herself as a listening ear—if she was in need of one. Henya did not know how to respond to this sudden, dark, and ominous attention. Her English teacher, on the other hand, carried on as before, which Henya preferred. Maybe she didn't know what had happened. Maybe she hadn't been told. Henya hoped that was the case. This, together with the fire incident that had occurred shortly beforehand, was providing her first taste at being branded, a stigmatization of unpalatable offensiveness.

Henya would forever remember this as the darkest period of her life: when her brother Aaron vanished. Her brother, whom she did not understand and had little to do with, had left a small note on his unmade bed. She never asked to read the note. It was as though she'd already told herself that to survive, she would have to disassociate. She didn't need her father to warn her about that; her instinct had done a fabulous job all on its own. As time went on, anger replaced what had once been some affection. She grew angry with Aaron for taking what little laughter there had been in their childhood home. She grew to hate him for what he had done to her parents. She felt robbed by him, as though he had taken her childhood with him. She grew determined to rid herself of any and all vestige of her unreadable and distant older brother.

So when the sun rose exactly one month after his disappearance, and she heard her father's voice summoning her and Sima into the living room, the dread that seized her lifted as soon as he announced his game plan: eradication of all memory of Aaron. Relief. Soaring, searing, penetrating relief. She gave her father no argument, and was furious at Sima when she did.

"Tatte, what do you mean? To remove him from my mind and heart? I can't!"

"Sima'le, Sima'le, you must. He only bringing to you more *tzaros*."

"But Tatte..." Sima began again, stopping when her chin and lips shook too severely to articulate. Henya watched, horrified, as Sima attempted to upset what seemed like the best of all possible arrangements. *Stop protesting*, she begged her older sister. *Tatte is right*. "He is my brother, and I will always love him. Even now," said Sima, with her head bent and her tears freely falling.

"I know. I know. But I varning you: Don't try to find him. Try to forget. Soon, you vill see it is for de best."

And Henya did just that. She managed to create an uncluttered, even elegant life for herself. When asked about Aaron, she didn't flinch. "He's gone away to yeshivah, overseas." She would say it so naturally, no one questioned her. And then there came a time when everyone stopped asking. Tatte was right; life really was better when all thoughts and feelings regarding Aaron were removed.

18

Three texts.

The third came during his Saturday night shift at Black Tie:

   -When are you coming back to Paris?

Aaron could not make up his mind if he was grateful or annoyed. Did he want to make a friend of Rabbi Wechter? Perhaps it was a mistake to have given him his number. He could always switch numbers. But he didn't. Not yet. There was something the rabbi had, something he could give him, something that made him—Aaron—not want to break off their tenuous connection. Not just yet, anyway.

Eitan and Uri were gone, with no one miraculously appearing to replenish the void of their absence. Gauche in the mores and lores of long-distance relationships, Aaron slid quickly into familiar withdrawal. Since their abrupt leave-taking, Uri had sent him five texts, of which he had responded to only one. Eitan had just texted a picture of himself in uniform, standing by a UH-60 Blackhawk, his army cap sideways, a cigarette dangling from his mouth. Aaron sent him back a thumbs-up. On the other hand, in the couple of weeks since Aaron had drifted into his shul, Rabbi Wechter had texted him two simple salutations that had not required anything from him in return, until yesterday evening.

Aaron looked at the text again. He turned his phone around in his hand, then drew out his thumbs:

-Would tomorrow be all right?

-Certainly. What time should I expect you?

-5?

-Shall I tell my dear wife that you will join us for supper?

-Yes, please, replied Aaron, before his demons could stop him.

Upon awakening on Sunday afternoon, he turned on his phone and clicked the Headlines icon, as he had been doing every day since the Stern family had gone missing. He jumped from one news site to another, primarily to find out what *had happened* during the day and then to see *how it was being presented* to the world. The discrepancy, often staggering, had the effect of pseudo-asphyxiation, reverberations of Eitan's media warning spinning around inside his head. Not that he felt his understanding of the situation was complete—and who could make such a claim?—but it did absorb him. The day's yield; the calls for peace; the broken ceasefires; the terrible toll placed upon the citizens of Gaza; the torment of the Israeli population forced into battle; the paltry and awkward attempts of American politicians who were clearly inept at sailing these virulent seas.

A token from Washington.

Nothing more.

Aaron thought about the group of Jordanians he had gotten to know. Regulars at Black Tie. They were good people. Never gave anyone cause for concern. But since this whole mess had started, they hadn't been showing up. Aaron hoped it had nothing to do with anything, but he noted it.

Nevertheless.

When he got off the train, Aaron checked the time and decided to skip the bus and walk. It was only 4:10 p.m. Strolling along the elegant streets, he slowly became aware of an acrid tension in the air; the sky, white and heavy with unshed rain, a wearable humidity that inched its way under his clothes; an eerie absence of people, strange for a summer Sunday afternoon in one of Europe's most beautiful capitals; the stores—usually open at this time—closed; an isolated car here or there. Every few minutes came blasts of noise—mechanical voices, followed by roaring and popping—and then silence.

As he neared Place de la Bastille, where he had planned to turn right and walk along the picturesque Campagne de Blocage, he groaned. No one had warned him of a pro-Palestinian rally. Perhaps it was so spur-of-the-moment that no one—not even Rabbi Wechter—had known about it. The crowd of veiled women and jittery men seemed to deepen and expand the closer he got to the square that freedom lovers everywhere call home. Dominant over the sea of people were the red and green colors of the Palestinian flags. There were many keffiyehs bobbing in the crowds, the white glaring behind the chain-linked black patterning. Even more disconcerting to Aaron were the fake Fajr-5 rockets, painted symbolically with blood dripping from them.

The demonstration was well underway. Some members of the crowd were calling out through megaphones from the circular platform at the bottom of the Colonne de Juillet. Some lithe participants had made it to the top of the monument and could be seen draping their flags high in the air.

Aaron questioned his rationale for coming today, but how was he to know that today, two days before Bastille Day, would be used to urge the "boycott of the racist State of Israel"? He steered an early right and power-walked down a street he did not know but trusted would bring him to a path leading to Campagne de Blocage and Rabbi Wechter's little shul there.

It was quiet as Aaron arrived. From the street, the place looked deserted. Not one person was standing by the white fence that protected the synagogue's inner courtyard. He walked through the wooden doorway. This time, looking up, he saw that above the double glass doors was a white, concrete, trellis wall made up of interconnected Stars of David, in the center of which lay a black stone engraved with the Ten Commandments. Besides being attractive, it made him feel safe, at home. *Thou shalt not kill*, he thought as he opened one of the glass doors and walked straight through the foyer and into the main sanctuary.

Although he had been here once before, he hadn't noticed the room's simple yet impressive structure: The ceiling was made up of five or six indentations, each one ending with a different stained-glass compilation, lending a calming grace to the room. The ark, at front center, was of classic, grained wood, with a navy velvet curtain drawn over it. Embroidered on it in gold were the words *Shivisi Hashem l'negdi samid*. Aaron smiled. Not only could he still remember how to read the words, but he also knew their meaning: "I place Hashem before me always." *I guess not everything was lost on me, after all*, he mused. Two white pillars were posted on either side, standing guard to defend the scrolls within. The women's gallery, he observed, jutted out from above, taking up over half the airspace, but did not detract from the room's aerial dimensions.

He felt good about being in this place. It was not even faintly reminiscent of the shul of his youth. *Where are all the books?* he asked himself. His old shul back in London had bookshelves lining most of its walls. Here, more emphasis was placed on aesthetics.

Very French.

Someone coughed and fidgeted in a squeaky chair. Aaron walked to the front. The rabbi was bent over a large volume of the Talmud, concentrating intently on its open page, his fingers gently hovering just above the print. Deeply engrossed, he hadn't heard Aaron enter. Aaron took a chair and waited for him to finish. He may have sat there eternally had the clock not chimed, making the rabbi sit up, check his watch, and whisk his torso around, white eyebrows shooting up as he took Aaron in.

"Aaron! How long have you been here?"

"Only a few minutes. I didn't want to disturb you."

"That would not have been a problem. I needed disturbing. I'm having a hard time understanding this particular Gemara, and a break would probably be quite helpful right now. Have you eaten yet?"

Aaron smiled. "No. But it's okay. I'm not hungry. I had a large coffee before catching the train."

"So, Aaron," Rabbi Wechter said, motioning to a seat next to his table. Aaron moved to that seat. "Have you been doing any more of that soul-searching you seem so fond of? Any breakthroughs?"

Aaron looked amused. "I am not fond of soul-searching. It's more like, it is fond of me."

The rabbi closed the great text he had been studying. It shut with a tiny, but not insignificant, wallop. He looked up and gestured for Aaron to go on.

"I just...often think...that some people..." Aaron began, faltered a bit, but carried on in a quiet voice, "should never teach."

"I quite agree."

Aaron looked up, a flush on his cheeks. "I have often...well... thought that the world would be a better place if some of my old teachers had opened up a shoe store...or something." The rabbi laughed. Aaron just smiled.

"Why stop there?" Rabbi Wechter spurred him. "Why not have them sell stocks and shares and get rich playing the market? Or hire themselves out as party magicians? Or invent a back-scratching device and sell it on eBay? Point is," he stopped, but only for a moment, "you are in pain." Their eyes locked. "Aaron, why not just tell me what happened? Why did you run away?" the rabbi asked in a low, conspiratorial whisper.

"I..." Aaron began, but once again faltered.

"This must be really hard for you," Rabbi Wechter said gently.

Aaron nodded.

"But you know, until you let it out, it will only bring you misery."

Aaron looked tired. He nodded again. "I know," he said. "Here is the thing. I ran away because...I set fire to my principal's office."

There was a pause.

"You did?"

Aaron nodded. His eyes blinked twice.

"Not an accident?"

He shook his head. "No."

"Anyone hurt?"

No response.

"Someone died?"

Aaron shook his head. The rabbi blew out a long breath. On Aaron's face, Rabbi Wechter could see the frightened boy hidden for so long behind the façade of nonchalance. The shame he had schooled himself to conceal came pouring out from his eyes.

"Who got hurt?"

"Arkady. The janitor," Aaron whispered.

"Of the yeshivah?"

Aaron nodded. "I had no idea he was in the building." He spoke while looking down, his voice controlled and very low. "Apparently he slept upstairs, directly above the office. When they found him, he'd already lost consciousness. Spent a week in the hospital. Worst week of my life. His lungs were permanently damaged. Well, he was a chain smoker. Now do you understand?"

"Is that all?"

"What do you mean, 'Is that all?'? I could have *killed* him!" His face was drained of color now. "I should have gone to jail, or at least a juvenile detention center. Do you know why I never went to jail?"

"No. Tell me."

Aaron looked directly at the rabbi. "Because the community I left refused to report on me. The man I targeted, the principal of my yeshivah, put out a gag order stopping anyone from contacting the authorities and identifying me. But they all knew..." He looked away and repeated softly, "They all knew it was me. I was kicked out of yeshivah. My life there was over. I was only seventeen. And not a single person asked me why I did it..."

"Aaron, why *did* you do it?"

Aaron's shoulders slumped. "Because I hated him. Rabbi Isaacs. I still hate him, twenty years later."

From behind them, the entrance of the sanctuary opened and closed. Footsteps. "Rabbi Wechter...?"

The rabbi stood up, looked to the great double doors behind them. "*Oui?*"

A man in tweed pants and a light blue shirt stood at the corner of the center platform. He began speaking in rapid French to the rabbi, his expression anxious.

"Ahhh." Rabbi Wechter waved dismissively, returning a few sentences of his own in French.

The man shrugged and gave a short nod to the rabbi before leaving the room. Rabbi Wechter turned to address Aaron. "One camp does not know what the other camp is doing. They want to cancel the meeting this evening—a solidarity meeting, mind you, for Israel. They are scared of the rally up at the Bastille. You know, the usual. I say we continue. We must not allow ourselves to be intimidated. The meeting should go on. Anyway, you were saying...?"

"What?"

"Aaron, you're not a madman. Why did you do it? What is the backstory?"

Aaron's lips thinned as he pulled them in, crushing them with his teeth. The repugnance and hostility he felt toward the memories that were surfacing distressed him. He blew out a long breath, an attempt to calm himself. *Now or never*, he thought. *Where to begin?* "I think...I think it started two years earlier..." He paused.

"Go on..."

"He walked into our classroom..."

"Who did?"

"Our principal."

"Who was your principal?"

"I told you already: Rabbi Isaacs. He was my principal for as long as I can remember, both in elementary and high school. The yeshivah I went to was big, with a few different departments. Rabbi Isaacs was the dean, really. I guess that's what you would call it. He had other principals for each department, but he was the head of the whole thing. Anyway, when I was in ninth or tenth grade, he came into our classroom one day and told us to stay behind after English classes, as he had something important to discuss with us. Turns out that he had selected some of the boys in our class to attend a very important, posh event in the city, as representatives of our school."

It was late. Arkady, the Polish caretaker, was already making his classroom rounds, mopping the floors. No one knew much about Arkady, where he lived, if he had family. He was just there—part of the landscape. His red-rimmed eyes and unshaven face went mostly unnoticed.

Aaron and his classmates sat watching the swirling of the mop on the floor in the bleak light of an early fall evening. They were restless, annoyed at themselves for caring so much about the upcoming dinner. Told not to leave until dismissed, they lolled over one another's desks, feigning contempt for their predicament, making a show of indifference.

When the door opened, they all rose soundlessly.

Aaron was the first to try sitting, but Yisrael Thaler elbowed him sharply. Rabbi Isaacs was eyeing the boys in that way that made them feel guilty and confused. A short man with an unusually straight back, Rabbi Isaacs had been hailed as the shining star of Chattersfield in his youth. People said of him that he learned the whole day straight, plus half the night; that eighteen hours would swim past without him taking so much as a snack break; that the sefarim *he learned from could cover the London Bridge. But in the half-light of the early evening, the esteemed dean looked like an icicle, and it made no difference to the boys what anyone said of his scholarliness.*

Rabbi Isaacs had not yet nodded that they should be seated. The boys stood and bit the insides of their mouths to stop themselves from giggling, staring straight ahead. Aaron grew more and more wary of Rabbi Isaacs as he watched him walk slowly to the teacher's desk at the front of the room. He sat down, coughed, and finally, finally motioned with his head for the class to be seated.

Rabbi Isaacs cleared his throat. "As I mentioned to you earlier, boys, there is to be a large event in two weeks' time—a dinner in honor of the Jewish contribution to British culture. Our school has been chosen to be representatives of the education department, and after much deliberation, this is the class that has been selected to attend the dinner. But only the boys who are zocheh *will be allowed to attend. Many* askanim *will be at this event, so it is of utmost importance that we make a good impression. To this end, I will be picking only those boys who are deemed worthy, who are* zocheh. *Those picked should go to the office for a note that will need to be signed by your parents."*

A shift occurred in the room, as the boys sat up straight in their black hats and jackets, their necks straining to add another centimeter to their posture. In that tiny moment, they placed their entire self-worth on being one of the chosen few, a ploy Rabbi Isaacs had counted on.

He took his time. He toyed with his beard, slipping it between his fingers, surveying the classroom, making eye contact randomly. Aaron stifled a snicker and shot a glance at Yisrael, who was not looking at him but following the dean's eyes. Huh? He would never be chosen anyway. Aaron put his head down, but picked it up again quickly when Rabbi Isaacs cleared his throat for the third time.

"Levi Weiner, you are zocheh," *he said to the boy in the far-left corner. "Tzemach Kushner, you too are* zocheh." *As each boy's name was called, a swell of deliverance enveloped him; his shoulders dipped, neck elongating, followed by an exhalation of exaggerated proportion.*

"Shalom Steinberg," Rabbi Isaacs continued, "not zocheh." *A cry flew from Shalom Steinberg's mouth as his face fell into his folded arms, and his shoulders slumped. Rabbi Isaacs continued, impervious, "Shmuel Kantor,* zocheh." *Shmuel did not stir, did not move a muscle, not even to smile. Rabbi Isaacs continued down the rows.*

"Yisrael Thaler..." He stopped and looked for a long second at Yisrael, who cast his eyes upon the floor, not daring to look up. "Not zocheh." *Yisrael could have wept, but he managed to contract his despair to a small and dignified nod of his head.*

"Aaron Bulman..." Again Rabbi Isaacs chose to stop and think.

Aaron closed his eyes, feeling all the attention behind him boring holes into his back. Get on with it, *he silently pleaded.* "Not *zocheh."*

"So, you weren't *zocheh?*" Rabbi Wechter repeated.

"Do you understand what that does to a kid of fifteen? Rabbi Isaacs takes the place of G-d Himself. And the kid thinks, *If Rabbi Isaacs doesn't consider me worthy, neither does G-d...*"

"That's a very strong, and very twisted, statement."

They sat in silence for a minute or two. "Is that it? Is that all it took to turn you into a criminal?" Rabbi Wechter asked.

Aaron smirked. "No. There's more."

"Okay. Before you go on, I want to share with you a different story: Once, the old Lubavitcher Rebbe—have you ever heard of him? Not the one everyone knows, but the previous one—Rabbi Yosef Yitzchak Schneerson." Aaron nodded.

"I am not a Lubavitcher myself," Rabbi Wechter winked, "but some of their work is to be admired. In any event, this Rebbe had a secretary. Chatcha Faigin was his name. What a name, eh? Anyway, one day the Rebbe tells this secretary to select the 'best of the best' students from his yeshivah to come to his office for a special audience. Now this Chatcha Faigin was in a pickle. How would he go about the selection? What would it be based on? Academic achievement? Refinement of character? Community work? He was in a bind. So, here is what he decided to do: He told the entire yeshivah that the Rebbe wants to invite them all for a special audience, and they are all to prepare themselves, in their own ways, to receive this honor.

"At the appointed time, the Lubavitcher Rebbe approaches his office, and is shocked at the size of the crowd. He can hardly enter. He turns to his beloved secretary and asks the following question, taken from the morning prayers: '*Kulam ahuvim? Are they all beloved?*'

"To which Chatcha Faigin replies from the same verse in the same prayer, '*Kulam berurim. They are all flawless.*'

"The Rebbe is not satisfied. He continues to ask, '*Kulam kedoshim? Are they all holy?*'

"Chatcha answers, '*Kulam osim b'eimah u'v'yirah retzon konam. They all perform the will of their Maker with fear and awe.*'

"At that the Rebbe smiled, entered the squashed room, and gave over his precious words to everyone there.

"Why am I telling you this story, Aaron? *Yesh v'yesh*, there are these and there are those. There is good and bad in everyone, and there are good people and bad people everywhere. You happen to have been handed a bad batch. Chatcha Faigin was my kind of guy. Thank G-d, those who had a hand in my education were mostly good people... though I don't mean to make small of your pain at all."

"It's not that." Aaron's face was empty of all expression. "It's just that for every story I tell you, I fear you will have another story to counteract it. You realize that this will get both of us nowhere."

"You are right. I am no psychotherapist." Rabbi Wechter let out a long sigh. He stretched his arms behind his back before settling into silence for a little while. "Aaron," he finally said, "how can I help you? Please...tell me how."

"I don't know. I wish I knew."

"What happened afterward? How did your father react to your 'not being *zocheh*'?"

"Well, you can imagine the scene at home once my father found out. He heard about it in shul later that day."

"Hmmm. Yes. So, what happened next?"

"That was just the beginning. After that, I put no energy into learning at all. I'd been having doubts about Judaism in general even beforehand, but after this story, those doubts began multiplying exponentially, and my behavior reflected that. But the fire... That came about from something else." Aaron stopped talking. He looked up. "Are you sure you want to do this with me? Now, today? When there is so much going on in the streets?"

Rabbi Wechter smiled softly. "It's hard, isn't it? Talking about these things."

Aaron sat back in his chair. "If I am to be honest—and at this point, why wouldn't I be?—I think that was the day that the 'fight' in me—you know, the natural 'fight' that is within everyone—started to erode."

"What do you mean by that?"

"I mean, I started to stop caring. About who I was. About my place in society. About...anything really. I recognize that this was extreme, and I know you will say that any extreme is not good. But that was how it was. For me, anyway."

"Do you feel now that you do have a place in society?"

"No." Another shrug. "And society seems to be carrying on just fine without me."

Rabbi Wechter chuckled. "*Oy vei iz mir!*" he sputtered. "On a day like today, with half the world blowing each other's brains out, he says society is doing just fine! Aaron, how did it happen? What turned you into a man of violence?"

Once again Aaron looked down, noticing the way the table leg was boring yet another hole in the carpet. Over and over the scene had been replayed in his mind; by now his internal rewind button had been worn through to nothing.

He cleared his throat. "So...there had been a series of break-ins in our school. I give you my word that they had nothing to do with me, but you can believe what you want. Fact remains: they had nothing to do with me.

"One morning, when I arrived, everyone was staring at me, talking and sneering. I was embarrassed..." Aaron found it difficult to make eye contact with the rabbi.

"...I remember having no idea why the sudden attention, the alienation, the shift in everyone's attitude toward me. Nevertheless, I went upstairs to my classroom, and on the way I passed by Rabbi Isaacs's office. There it was—a note, apparently written to me. It read:

"*Dear Aaron B.,*
Please leave it as you found it!
Signed,
Rabbi Isaacs."

Rabbi Wechter inhaled sharply. He had thought that nothing could shock him anymore. But now, looking at his young friend, accused and deemed guilty without trial, without defense, he thought, *No wonder he harbors such hatred. No wonder he feels so unmoored. How do I help him? What words do I say?* He chose not to say anything.

"I spent that entire day stewing. I could not concentrate, could not eat, could not even defend myself, because I knew my anger would blow up inside me so badly that nothing I could say would sound coherent. That night, when I stole into the building, I hadn't planned what I was going to do. I wanted revenge, but I did not know how to achieve it.

"The office was easily accessible, laughably so. I danced around a bit, you know, in-your-face style, when the glint of the gold-topped lighter which Rabbi Isaacs always used during his lectures caught my eye. I tried it. It sparked easily. I fell under its spell. Setting fire to his chair seemed the natural next thing I needed to do, the only thing that would give me the satisfaction I thought I needed at the time. It was an organic impulse, growing out of itself. And let me tell you, while it burned, I saw him burning too—in effigy.

"Who knew the carpeting was so flammable? I was lucky to escape with my life. I was the one who called the fire department, from the office phone, before sneaking out the same way I had come in, and running back home.

"But the stench of smoke followed me. Of course.

"My mother knew. They all did. My father came home from shul the next morning and beat me. It was Yisrael Thaler who told me about old Arkady in the hospital. No one knew he slept in the attic. There was nothing for me to do but leave. It was hard to live with what had happened. The things I caused to happen and the things I didn't. It was Yisrael, too, who told me about the gag order. My gosh! It might have been hard for me to live with scorn, but it was absolutely impossible when that scorn was glazed with pity."

The rabbi nodded in silence.

"By the way, I still have the note."

"You do?"

"Yeah. I tore it down and stuffed it into my pocket. It's in my apartment right now, in Deauville Beach. I keep it with me. You know...to remind me why I can never go back."

"Come, Aaron." Rabbi Wechter suddenly got up. "Walk with me a little," he said, stretching his torso.

The heat from outside seemed to thicken around them.

"Walk with you?" Aaron got up too. "Where to? I don't know that the streets are safe right now." He worried that he had spoken too freely during this meeting, revealed too much from his past. Would he be punished for having spoken so carelessly, for having shared memories too scorched with shame to be aired?

"Nonsense. We've seen all this before. I need to purchase some refreshments for the event that will be soon. Nothing fancy, just some drinks, chips, pretzels and the like. You could give me a hand." They reached the main doors, passing a small staircase on the side, which Aaron assumed led to the women's gallery. Rabbi Wechter opened the door, and Aaron followed. The rabbi locked the door and turned left.

"As I was saying, Aaron, I am no psychotherapist. But I *do* want to help you."

"Yes, but…"

"But what?"

"It gets annoying sometimes. When you defend them. Or G-d. They hurt me…whatever."

"Hmmm."

They continued walking, stopping at a little corner shop where they bought what Rabbi Wechter needed. As they left the establishment, a group of demonstrators, who had splintered from the main rally, stared at them. One of them yelled, "*Itbah al-Yahudi*," and thrust his fist in their direction. Aaron instinctively stood in front of the rabbi and was about to yell back, when he felt a nudge on his side and heard the rabbi mutter, "Let it go, Aaron. Just let it go."

At six the shul was half full. Aaron chose a seat in the third row from the back, so he could watch the proceedings without being noticed. He was in no shape to participate.

The crowd settled noisily. After a small eternity, the rabbi rose to address everyone.

"We've come together for a meeting of solidarity," he said in French. "Solidarity for our beloved brethren, living in our beloved land. Once again, a war is foisted upon us. Once again, we are faced with the eruption of the oldest hatred known to mankind: anti-Semitism. We, the Jews of France, need to come together. Children are afraid to leave their homes. Supermarkets have become a place of grave hostility. If one appears physically Jewish outside, he is in danger. Many of our youth are determined to put on a brave face, walking out wearing their yarmulkes, though it encourages the beast. As we know, in cases of *pikuach nefesh*, when one's very life is in danger, we are obligated to suspend most laws of the Torah in order to save ourselves. But what constitutes danger? Is what we have here in Paris danger? These are the questions that will be hashed out tonight. But first, let us say some *kapitlach* of Tehillim."

Rabbi Wechter led the attendees through some chapters of Tehillim. Aaron found the words comforting, which was not what he had expected. For so long Hebrew had annoyed him. Its letters chastised him, holding themselves above him, regarding him with mockery and contempt. An *aleph* could have had horns instead of crowns; a *beis*, a lashing tongue instead of a dot. But today the letters and words seemed calm, almost welcoming. When the rabbi softly sang the time-worn verses, Aaron felt something close to nostalgia well up in his chest.

He looked around the room, surveying the crowd. The men around him were mostly well-dressed, wearing suits, although some were more casual, in jeans and open-necked shirts, the glint of a chain here and there. There was a pervading sense of prosperity in the room, of groomed, courteous people. No young children were present, obviously, but some of the community's youth hung back in the last rows. They were fidgety, unable to quiet themselves, garnering harsh stares every now and then from those up front.

When it came, it was so sudden that the entire body of people became instantly still. There was a loud thwack, followed by a shattering of glass. No one knew which window had been smashed. Murmuring began, before another wallop took the window behind the trellis that overlooked the courtyard, and then another window, and another one, and before anyone knew what was happening, the women up on the balcony were shrieking and running for cover, and the men had gotten up and were dashing toward the double doors.

Immediately the police, whose presence had been requested at the meeting, stepped in. "Stay where you are!" they ordered in French.

Through the noise, Aaron could make out the sounds of the mob outside—lots of guttural shouting. "*Mort aux Juifs! Sortez de la Palestine! Allahu akbar!* Death to the Jews! Get out of Palestine!" When the police left the courtyard, he got a glimpse of the street for a second, through the open door, but artificial smoke clouds, white and red, obscured his vision. As the police shut the door behind them, Aaron found that he was trembling.

Stuck in the belly of a riot, the Jewish youths lunged for the doors, but the adults yelled, "*Gardez-les enfermés! Gardez les portes fermées!* Keep them locked! Keep the doors locked!" Many pulled out their cell phones and called loved ones, issuing what they hoped were not dying orders and last words. Aaron, by instinct, ran up the stairs leading to the women's gallery. Once there he joined the crouched people who had taken up spots by the half wall of the enormous broken window, trying to get an aerial view of what was happening on the ground.

It was hard to process what his eyes were telling him. Hundreds of young Arab men, keffiyehs wrapped around their heads, were swarming the area, chanting and hurling stones at the synagogue. Directly below him, on the street in front of the shul, he could make out a group of young, angry Jewish men who were determined to protect their house of worship from the marauders—but were terribly outnumbered and haphazard in their planning. They launched a stampede, howling and marching, only to run for cover behind the police and their plastic shields when the pro-Palestinians counterattacked them.

Aaron felt his stomach lurch at their inefficiency. A dangerous combination of shame and anger quickly swelled within him.

His mind ricocheting, his instincts on full throttle, Aaron sped back toward the stairs, raced down them, past the silent, morose, unmoving crowd inside the main sanctuary, where Rabbi Wechter was directing his congregants to face whatever was coming with pride. Before anyone could stop him, Aaron took the glass double doors in both hands, flung them open, and shut them behind himself.

He strode through the little courtyard and banged on the white wooden, fence-like door that stood there. The young Jewish men in the rabble opened it, shuttled him through, and locked the door again. They looked up to face him, the only person who had dared leave what little protection the building gave. He nodded to them, and they turned from him, waiting for the next attack.

The street itself, Aaron noticed, was a mess. When had all this bedlam happened? Chairs and tables from nearby cafés had been thrown down, their contents spilling onto the pavement; there was broken glass and puddles of drinks; an abandoned handbag; a muddied and trampled jacket. Windows of stores and buildings were smashed; car roofs were dented. And everywhere, there was smoke. Besides smoke bombs, a number of tires had been set aflame, their rubber doused with oil, and the black smoke they emitted felt dangerous to inhale.

The posse of Jewish youths was temporarily protected by the plastic shield barrier held up by the French police. For a moment, everything was eerily quiet, so quiet that Aaron could take note of how his heart was pounding and how sweat was running down the backs of his knees, over his calves, and into the rim of his socks. There seemed to be nothing to do but wait on this days-before-Bastille Day, 2015, where once again in Paris a cowering crowd anticipated a storming—this one of a different kind.

From beyond the smoke came guttural war cries. They came in waves—reaching and dropping, reaching and dropping. Soon small objects penetrated the clouds of mist: rocks, glass bottles, the limb of a chair. The Jewish youngsters stirred and began emitting their own high-pitched battle cries. They jostled with the police and infiltrated the plastic shields, armed with their own stones, their own glass bottles, limbs from their own chairs.

Aaron stood, transfixed, watching his people become what they were not trained to be: ruffians, thugs, toughies. It filled him, this sight, this upending of roles. Some of the younger, newer generation of French Jews, who would not cower as their parents had, and their grandparents before them. "*Never again!*" they cried in French, as they marched toward the hate-filled horde, armed with a table, a garbage can lid, the chain from the flush lever of a toilet. Their battle cry was louder than their numbers, and as the smoke cleared, the pro-Palestinians could plainly see their measly foe. In that defining moment, they realigned themselves and rushed forward, falling upon the Jewish combatants with ardor. Vociferous and shrill, the shouting arrived first; then metal tables, unmoored garbage cans, crudely-made firebombs...all whistled through the stratosphere before landing with a small blaze on cars, storefronts, and people.

And inside Aaron, a fury unleashed: the persecution of his forbearers; his father's broken childhood; his grandfather's shameful arrest and execution. As their potent contents poured into his soul, a war yowl ejected out of him, incoherent and apocalyptic. He threw himself into the line of fire. Dodging a firebomb, he picked up a piece of broken pavement and slung it toward the oncoming assailants. Then, running toward the danger, he chucked whatever he picked up off the street, rock after rock, glass bottle after glass bottle, anything he could get his hands on.

Lying on its side on the patio of a corner café was one lonely metal chair. Aaron grabbed it and lifted it high above his shoulders, yelling as though bringing down the walls of Yericho. From behind him, two pairs of dark arms seized the legs of the chair, and before Aaron could catch a glance at the men who had hemmed him in, he felt a searing pain in his forehead, just above his left eye. He tried to stay standing, but darkness—red and heavy—pulled him down to the ground. He felt his ribs being kicked, twice on one side, once on the other. Someone's foot smashed his head.

Blackness.

Aaron Bulman, you are not zocheh...

Silence.

ima cut off the bottom of the Romaine heart. She was about to throw it into the garbage when her eye caught its flowerlike structure, and she lifted it for further inspection, its perfectly placed petals startling her. *Hashem is so detail-oriented*, she thought. *If man were to recognize the hand of Hashem in nature, we would spend all of our days in perpetual rapture. But it does not happen like that, does it? We expect. We presume. We discard. We pander to the worst of ourselves. We are like dreamers—ambling and meandering, hardly realizing that throughout all of our lives, G-d has been communicating with us. Take this lettuce—*she held it to the light. *Its leaves are spaced just so, each one at an exact distance from the other; like a rose, a pale green, stunted, but beautiful rose. How can G-d stand to be ignored and forgotten for so long, by so many?!*

"There you are, Sima!" Henya called out, interrupting her sister's lofty contemplations. She glided into the room, wig pulled back into a high half-pony.

However did she do that? Sima wondered. She put down the lettuce and took in Henya's appearance: frosty pink lips and green, shimmery eye shadow; green and gold, casual maxi-dress, gold shoes, and around her neck, a chunky green necklace that only the poised could get away with.

"I've been looking for you," Henya said. "I see Aunty Breeya put you to work already, eh?" Holding Shloimele's hand, Henya rooted about in her handbag for something. "I'm so happy Mummy decided to come," she said to the inside of her bag. "This is a big thing for her. First time out in a very long while." Her hands found a wad of tissues, and she looked up. "Why are you so down in the dumps, Sim? Anything wrong?"

"What makes you say that? I was just noticing the bottom of this lettuce. Look." She lifted it up. "It could be a flower."

Henya half-smiled, and Sima decided against catching the momentary condescension.

Sima returned to the salad. *You know, it would be a great relief to share my burden with someone,* she thought, staring into the half-filled bowl. She had already diced the red and orange peppers into cubes, along with unpeeled English cucumbers and tomatoes. After the lettuce, she just needed to thinly slice the pink onion, and it would be done.

"Henya...I actually *do* have something on my mind..." Her incertitude was exposed by her hesitant, faltering voice.

"Oh? Does this have anything to do with Tamar?"

Sima's jaw dropped. *How transparent am I?* "What makes you say that?!"

"Nothing. Just a hunch. You've mentioned her twice, and both times your tone was tense. I'm...sorry. I shouldn't have said anything."

Sima shook her head. "You know me too well..." she muttered.

Henya placed a bangled arm on Sima's shoulder. "Then you must talk to me about it. You know I won't let on to anyone." They shared a small smile. "Okay," she said, squeezing Sima's forearm. "We'll talk later." And she went back out to the garden.

Sima returned to the lettuce, feeling relieved. She would speak with Henya that night. Wasn't that what sisters were for?

Her disquietude over Tamar now in check, she found that she could suddenly enjoy the moment. After all, she was at Aunty

Breeya's, and the place had not lost any of its happy-home vibes in all the years she had not been here, chock-full as it was with good memories for her and Henya. For Aaron too, she was sure. How many Sunday afternoons had they spent frolicking in their aunt's garden! The two mothers/sisters would be sitting on deck chairs, chattering on about this or that—solving the world's problems, they called it— while the three Bulman children would be splashing about with their cousins in their wading pool. There was a small pond at the end of the garden, filled with goldfish that had suffered severely from time to time when the adults hadn't been watching, and two great climbing trees to which Uncle Zvi, may he rest in peace, had affixed slats of wood, to create makeshift ladders. After that, even the youngest kids had been able to climb the trees, at least to the lowest limbs.

When Greta and Elchanan had taken their one and only trip to Israel, in the mid-eighties, it was to Aunty Breeya's house that the three children had been packed off. Aunty Breeya was notorious for her fly-by-night meals: eggs and chips, French toast, or "bangers 'n mash." Often she could be found opening a can of peas or boiling frozen florets of broccoli for the vitamins she felt guilty not providing for her kids. She would laugh everything off; she had a great laugh. Infectious. Not at all like her sister Greta, whose appetite for anguish seemed at its peak during those years. She'd definitely improved since then. Aunty Breeya had once warned Sima, "Everyone morphs into a better or worse version of themselves. People don't change their basic nature—but they can improve or deteriorate. Happy people become happier, miserable people become...well...y'know."

Over the years, the two sisters grew to resemble one another. Both of them were tall, and though once slender, they both started inching their way toward well-padded. All through her growing years, Sima never remembered her mother bothering with her appearance. Only in the last decade and a bit, by Sima's calculations, her mother had begun making more of an effort in putting herself together, her wardrobe becoming more colorful, her short, curly wig regularly combed.

Aunty Breeya, though, had always gone the extra half-mile to make herself attractive. She wore shoulder-length custom wigs with delicate wisps around her forehead. Her clothes were always better made, and her shoes would sport a gold buckle or a leather bow or, when it was fashionable, rhinestones. There were a great many ways in which Sima enjoyed her aunt more than her mother, enduring a bitter-tasting lump of guilt because of it.

For instance, in the days before her wedding, when Sima had been questioning herself and panicking if she was doing the right thing by marrying Aryeh, it was at her aunt's door that she'd knocked. Sima smiled inwardly at the memory.

It was already dark. Greta had driven Sima to her sister's home in Golders Green, because a kallah *in the last seven days of her singlehood should not be out driving herself. She was greatly worried. Was her daughter about to break off the engagement because she, Greta, had been unable to provide her with enough "kitchen-table" wisdom? Biting her lips, she had waited in the car, listening to classical music from the radio in a futile attempt to calm her nerves, while her daughter and her sister sat together on the pink sofa and spoke about marriage.*

"How do I know if he is the right one? If we can have a good marriage together, truly care for each other the way a husband and wife are supposed to? I mean, he's scheduled to arrive tomorrow..." The skittish bride's hands covered her mouth. Her eyes peered out over them, wide and terrified. "You must think that I'm crazy, asking this now!"

Her aunt chuckled. "You want to know what is unknowable. Isn't that it, Simale?"

"Well..." Sima floundered. "How is a girl, who knows nothing about the world, supposed to know how to make such a big decision? I have no experience in these matters. I am...I am...I don't know...anything!"

Aunty Breeya looked into her eyes. "You know, Sima, it strikes me that what you do *know will be enough, and what you* don't *know may not be worth knowing."*

"What do you mean?"

"Oh, you young girls...I think I understand. You feel that you are missing something, that you are coming to marriage unprepared. You wonder, deep down, if maybe the goyim are better prepared for marriage, since they date for years and years before making any commitment. So surely they are more certain and confident that they are marrying the right one. Yes?"

Sima's face reflected the truth of her aunt's words. Yes, this was what she had been thinking, but had not been able to articulate, even to herself. She did not stop her aunt, but just stared into her green eyes and felt the sting at the back of her own.

"You are wrong, my dear niece," Aunty Breeya said, taking Sima's right hand in both of hers. "The Torah's way of dating and marriage is the best possible way there is. You will see this for yourself, though it may take some time for you to realize it."

"But is there any way I can know now, for sure, that Aryeh is for me?"

"Tell me, why did you choose Aryeh, from all the others you dated? Why him?"

Sima wanted to cry. "I don't know. I thought I knew, but now I don't think I do!"

"That's okay. I will help you know. Now...didn't you say that he was the only boy, from all the others, with whom you felt comfortable to be yourself?" Sima nodded. "He made you laugh?" Sima nodded. "He was the only boy, you said, that you respected and that you could see yourself growing old with. Yes?"

"Absolutely. But, Aunty Breeya...is that enough? To be married to him, and love and respect him, for my entire life?"

"Sima, what you've told me is all that you need to be reassured. You have all the ingredients necessary to have a wonderful marriage with Aryeh. Take it day by day. A real relationship, real closeness, does not happen overnight. It does not come in a flash of pink rose petals or a sunset over a glistening horizon!" She chuckled.

Still uncomfortable, Sima stayed silent.

Her aunt continued, "True closeness comes in little increments of time spent well, together. It is born out of the little things we do for one *another: the supper we make because it's his favorite, or the way he sets the shoes on the shoe rack, neatly, because that's what makes her happy. Or his putting the kids to bed with a story, or the two of you going for a walk together, or shopping at the local twenty-four-hour grocery in the middle of the night. Everyday moments of life-building, together: vacuuming, opening the bills, holding on to one another's secrets, respecting privacy, not mentioning things that hurt the other. Or talking about them, but safely. All these things are learned, over weeks, months, years..."*

Sima stared as her aunt delivered each point, her thespian tendencies on full display: chest heaving, arms spread, face reddened. Then suddenly Aunty Breeya stopped. An absent look seeped slowly down her face, her eyes watered, her cheeks became flaccid. Sima was afraid to breathe. And then her aunt smiled, breaking the silence.

"I want to tell you something else," she said, swiveling her body to meet Sima's gaze. "When I was first married to your Uncle Zvi, may he rest in peace, I was ashamed of his grammar mistakes. Here I was, an educated woman, working in the center of metropolitan London, and I had gone and married a foreigner who couldn't even speak the language correctly. Every time we went out in public and he would address people, I used to cringe.

"But something strange happened over time. The two of us became so close, such a team, that eventually I began finding his rudimental errors to be actually endearing! They gave me a warm feeling. Yes, it's true." She was grinning now, her teeth gleaming in the lamp-light. "Your Uncle Zvi, who couldn't even string a decent sentence of English together, was my best friend. We had the most wonderful marriage. You'll see. You'll feel the same way with Aryeh. Just give it time."

And she was right, Sima realized, as she drizzled the olive oil onto the salad. So very, very right. Wasn't every marriage a risk? Would it have helped her to have known Aryeh better before marrying him? Even those who date for years before tying the knot cannot guarantee success. She pictured Aryeh taking care of things back home. How grateful she felt for his reliability, his soothing presence there. Not every woman could pick up and travel abroad with such peace of mind.

Sima stood still for a moment, envisioning her Long Island dining room: Aryeh at the head of the Shabbos table, making Kiddush over the wine. She smiled as his tuneless-ness reverberated in her mind's ear. Aryeh Hertzberg might have been the other half of her soul, but to music, his tone was a death knell. In her vision he was smiling at her, and the vision became so powerful that Sima felt his warmth and encouragement surround her, until she felt herself relax, releasing the tensions she had not realized were there...

"You done with that salad, Sima dear?" Aunty Breeya's summons caused her to jolt. A tingly sensation washed over Sima. She looked up, nodded, and brought the salad bowl out to the patio, setting it in the center of the table, between the platters of lox, cream cheese, and bagels. Then she sat down on the deck chair nearest her mother, checking to see if Greta was enjoying herself.

"Our Sima is looking wonderful, isn't she?" said Aunty Breeya. It was a proclamation more than a question. Sima turned, and instantly she was once again a blushing, unsure bride, under Aunty Breeya's magnanimity.

"Need anything, Sima? I brought lemonade—would you like some?"

"No. I'm good. Thanks."

"*I'm good,*" repeated Aunty Breeya to the group. "Such a curious American expression: *I'm good!* Only in America can misuse of language sound...so...elegant."

"How is that misuse of language?" piped up Greta. "The adjective 'good' is being used to describe the pronoun 'I.'"

"Oh, yes," Aunty Breeya acquiesced. "Still, it is not an expression we English would have concocted."

A ping sounded from Henya's phone. She glanced at it, and then read the text more carefully. "*Oy vey,*" she murmured. "There's been another attack. This time in France."

21

Later, after Henya drove Greta and Sima back home to Ashley Grove, and both sisters had gotten their mother safely tucked back into her bed, Sima invited Henya into their shared childhood room. Henya sprawled herself out on the only made bed and scratched underneath her *sheitel*. "So? Let's hear. What's going on with Tamar?" she asked.

Sima sat down at the desk in the corner, fingering her old typewriter. "To be fair, I'm not exactly sure I should be doing this..." She paused and began to chew her right index fingernail.

Henya looked at her sideways. "You're making me nervous. Spill or be still, but stop dithering."

"Well, to begin with, she has somehow found out about Aaron." Sima stopped talking and waited to see what Henya's reaction would be, making it the deciding factor for whether or not she should disclose anything else.

Henya did not disappoint; she sat straight up. "What?! How?!"

"I wish I knew. I don't even know *what* she knows. All she told me was that she knows I have a brother, and that she is furious..."

"With what?"

"With me."

"Why?"

Sima looked hard at her. "What do you mean, why? Because I led her to believe that you are my only sibling. That I kept Aaron's very existence from her. She sees it as some kind of betrayal."

Henya made a face. "Oh, please. She's reading into it too much. So what that you have a brother! You don't need to tell her everything. It's your prerogative."

"You don't get it, do you?"

"Get what?"

"It's made her doubt…"

"Doubt what?"

"Everything. Her *Yiddishkeit*. Her faith. Everything. Who knows if she even wants to be *frum* anymore! *Oy*…" Sima leaned her head forward into her hands and continued to speak through them. "Henya, I'm really hurt by this! It's thrown me completely." She took her hands away from her face and looked across the room at her sister. "I can't believe I missed all the signs. And I tried so hard not to repeat the mistakes of our parents. You have no idea how hard I tried…" She looked angry for a moment, and then shrugged. "And it's all come to this! I know it's crazy thinking, but sometimes I feel it's as though I'm tainted, as though there is no clemency for me."

"A bit dramatic." Henya's eyebrows were raised. "No clemency? You make me laugh. Don't you think that Tamar is being a little… you know…overwrought about this? You've been such a good mother. Besides, I *do* know how hard you've tried."

Sima rubbed her eyes vigorously. "Go on," she said. "Tell me how you know. How have I not repeated the same dumb things that were done to us?"

"It's unavoidable. We all do. We're programmed to…"

Sima struck the Q lever. It flew up and hit the ribbon, forming a hazy image of itself on the paper she had put there on her first day here. She remembered reading an article about "internal models" in one of the papers she needed to study for her master's in social work. "You mean internal models?" she asked.

"Huh?"

"I read somewhere about 'internal models.' That they can only be planted inside a person during childhood. After that, most of us search for external models, to compensate for perceived gaps." Henya gave her sister a bemused look, but Sima went on. "Basically, it said that whatever you leave childhood with are your 'internal models'; they will form the basis of your behavior all throughout your life. You can adapt and adopt other models later on, but those models will always remain external, and by definition, will never be as strong."

"Sima!" Henya shook her head, exasperated. "I don't know what you're going on about. All I wanted to say is that *any* teenager— *anyone*, really—can have doubts in *Yiddishkeit, chas v'shalom*. It doesn't matter how hard parents try."

"But why? Why do you think this has happened to Tamar? Why did she have to find out about Aaron?"

"Why do you think figuring that out is going to make any difference?"

"I thought I knew her..." Sima looked at her shoes. "I know it's foolish, but I guess, unconsciously, I expected her to be a certain way—as though I had rights to her because she came from me. As though we, me and Aryeh, should be the ones to dictate the forces of her life. Foolish, foolish, foolish! Oh, Henya, I had such hopes for her. Such high hopes. Now she has opened herself up to goodness-knows-what. And what am I supposed to do? Just sit by and let her make bad decision after bad decision?"

"It doesn't have to be like that."

"What do you mean?"

"She's a smart girl. She'll come to her senses sooner or later."

"What, like Aaron?"

They stared at one another, each sensing the potent mordancy that hit them, like an arctic wind, and that stiffened their bodies and froze their words.

"You'll work it out." Henya stood up and walked toward the door. "You and Aryeh," she said, grabbing the doorknob. "The two of you have such a close bond. I'm sure you'll work it out."

Sima gave her sister a small smile, and Henya left the room. Sima heard her go into Greta's room, wish her a good night, close the door gently, and then walk down the stairs. Still feeling the frigidity, Sima did not move for a while. She questioned whether she had done right. Could Henya really fathom the depth of her fear for her eldest child? Had it been worth it to have broken Tamar's trust?

◼ ◼ ◼

"Have you checked the news?" Aryeh sounded tired. "Feels like madness is the order of the day…"

"No." Sima yawned. "I've been busy. Besides, Henya is really into it and keeps us all informed. For better or for worse. Though she tends to lean harder on the *worse*. Tell me about the girls. How are they doing?"

"Oh, they're doing fine, *baruch Hashem*."

"How was Shabbos?"

"Shabbos was boring. Both girls went off to friends, and I was left on my own the whole afternoon. I took a nap until my *chavrusa* came at around four. How about you?"

"My Shabbos was actually lovely. Quiet. I stayed home with Mummy. I thought of going to my old shul, but I didn't want to leave her. Any word from Tamar?"

"Yes, she called. She sounded okay. Made no reference to her letter. I stayed neutral, as you told me to. If you hadn't said anything to me about this whole thing, I would never imagine anything was amiss. We raised an actress. Who knew?"

"Did she…did she ask about me?"

"Yes."

"What did you tell her?"

"I can't remember. Nothing heavy."

"Well, did you tell her I'm in London?"

"Can't remember…" In the background, Sima could make out the high-pitched voices of their two youngest daughters, both vying for the phone. "You wanna speak with the girls? They're right here driving me crazy."

"Hi, Mommy!"

Sima tried to make out who it was by voice, but in the next second she heard a muffled, "Go away! I got it! I got it first!"

Sima chuckled inwardly. "Hello, *mammela*," she said, trying to restore order over the phone line. "Tell your sister you will each have a turn..."

◼ ◼ ◼

It was late, around midnight, by the time Sima sat in front of Michoel Leipzig's old laptop. She did not feel tired. Bothered, yes, but not sleepy. She checked her emails. Nothing pressing. She clicked on a news site to see what was happening in Eretz Yisrael.

Oh, the horror! The insanity! She clicked on headline after headline. Aryeh was right. It was a world gone mad. The tiny Jewish state, apparently, had no right to defend itself against Hamas rockets. Look at what was going on! The Palestinians were firing their rockets from areas where, even in targeted retaliation, the most civilian damage could be wrought. And the world was up-in-arms! What a ploy! It took devilish genius to craft so heinous a mechanism of war. Sima clicked on footage of women and children ordered to stand on the rooftop of the very building the IDF had warned would be struck, because multiple rockets had been fired from that exact location.

So Israel is forced to corrupt itself.

Her hands shook as she redialed her home number. The machine went on. Oh, right, Aryeh had taken the girls out for a pizza supper. Hanging up, she suddenly remembered an old Golda Meir quote. She opened a new tab on her screen and typed it into the search box. Here it was: *"We can forgive the Arabs for killing our children. We cannot forgive them for forcing us to kill their children. We will only have peace with the Arabs when they love their children more than they hate us."*

So...this strategy was an old one.

What was this? Sima's eye caught a flash of moving color in a little box at the bottom-right corner of the screen. Ahh, yes, the attack in

France: "Violent Anti-Jewish Riots Rock Paris Synagogue." Alarmed, she clicked on the story, and then the link that would provide her with the latest footage.

She watched as members of the Jewish Defense League gathered outside a white wooden fence, defending a synagogue with baseball bats and glass bottles. It was hard to see much, as drifts of colored smoke kept falling over the screen. Still, she could not stop herself from watching. A door within the white fence—was it to a courtyard?—opened. There, full-frontal, for just two or three seconds, stood...Aaron.

Stupefied with shock, her entire body went stiff. Blinking away the twinkling stars that started appearing in the corners of her eyes, Sima slammed the pause button. Was her mind playing tricks? She was afraid, aware of her primal desire for a neat, uncomplicated existence. Was she conjuring up salvation where there was none to be had?

She clicked replay. There he was again, emerging from the white, wooden door in the fence. She was certain it was him. It was her father without the beard. She caught her breath and slammed the pause button again, reset the clip to the beginning, and watched her brother appear over and over again through the gate, after which he mingled with the crowd of young defenders. She could not stop herself from clicking the reset button, not wanting to go any further than when her long-mourned-for brother suddenly appeared, in a white shirt and gray slacks, in a little clip that someone got paid a small fortune to forward to the news site, on this, the twelfth day of the month of July, 2015.

Something seems to happen to us, every ten years... It gives me the heebie-jeebies...

So he was in France. How ironic. He wasn't even far.

All these years of not knowing that he was just "next door"...

Sima's mind raced. *I could have done something ages ago! No, I couldn't have. I would never have been able to find him. He didn't want to be found. Who am I kidding? Besides, Tatte was pretty clear with his intentions, so what chance did I have? But now... Should I tell Mummy?*

Henya? Whom should I tell first?! No. I've got to think. I've got to think. Too much time has gone by. If I act carefully, maybe I could make things right again. Could I?

Oh, Aaron, Aaron, Aaron! Have you any idea how happy I am to see you?! Mummy always knew you were alive. She never gave up hope. Not like myself. I have to admit to you, Aaron, my dear brother, I did not think I would ever see you again. Oh, I let the footage go on. Oh, well, I may as well watch what it contains. The camera is moving and jerking. It's difficult to watch; it's making me dizzy. The cameraman is running... there are many feet, many faces... I do not know who is Jewish and who are the ones who hate us. I wish the camera would stop jerking about.

Oh, no! It's Aaron again, but he is in the street. Get out of the street! What are you doing, Aaron?! Can't you even see the danger you're in? They are coming at you from behind. Aaron, Aaron! Get out of the street! What's that noise? Is it you or them? I can't think. I can't watch...

Noooooooooooooo!

Sima stood up.

"I'm going to Paris!" she whispered out loud.

PART TWO

22

"So...hello," the man said, bowing his head slightly as he reached out his hand. When Elchanan shook it, it felt warm. Too warm. He—the man—was wearing an old white shirt, under a pilled, maroon knitted vest, and non-descript dark, crumpled pants. He sat down on a weathered leather rocker and crossed his legs, indicating Elchanan to take his place on the armchair across from him.

Musty, unventilated air suffused the room. A coffee table between them was piled high with artifacts from voyages Elchanan could only guess about: stone elephant heads with sparkling silver eyes; a group of pipes made of cornhusks, wood, and metal; a platoon of dusty pink sea urchins; and more. An heirloom-style, oversized bookcase, groaning from the weighty tomes squeezed into its shelves, stood behind where the man was sitting. In the corner, on a small accent table, a lamp was propped up beside a wall, casting a shadowy light on the lint both in the air and on the ground. It was daytime, though you wouldn't know it. Three tall, thin windows shed little of the sun's rays, as though it had skipped over the house, not thinking anyone cared enough to invite it in. Dust covered everything. It didn't bother Elchanan; after all, it wasn't *his* dust.

Hanging on the walls were flat, chiseled sculptures of African women carrying baskets on their heads. Was he permitted to stare at these female sculptures? Elchanan lowered his eyes.

"Let's start with your full name, shall we?" the man said to him.

Elchanan did not respond.

"Hello?" The man, who appeared to be about Elchanan's age, grinned sagaciously, his eyes looking over his glasses. He had sunken cheeks, sparse gray stubble, and pale-blue watery eyes that glinted in the scanty light of the gloomy room. "Shall we begin? Let's fill out this form together, all right? Let's begin with your full name..."

"My name is Elchanan Bulman." Elchanan's voice sounded raspy. He couldn't remember ever feeling this much discomfort. His heart pounded so strongly, he felt ashamed of the noise it was making. He closed his eyes and tried to force its submission. *Stop banging, mine hartz*, he commanded, *or I get angry.*

"Your number, please...?" the man continued, while scribbling.

"Seven, zero, three..." Elchanan stopped talking. The man looked up. Elchanan's eyelids were shut. Tears—real and alive—were flowing down and disappearing into his full beard. His hands were flat on the wide, dark armchair, on either side of his thighs, and he was rocking—forward and back, forward and back, like he was praying. Forward and back, forward and back...

The man put the clipboard down on the floor next to his rocker. "I see..." he said. "Let's skip the forms now, shall we?"

This was not Elchanan's idea.

Meshugge idea.

Never is gonna to work. Why she make me do this? Why, Greta, why? Just 'cuz your sister Breeya think is good idea... This I cannot do. I am a man. This is for woman. I must to stop crying. Wait, Mister. Let me stop crying. Don't say nothing now, please. I am shamed. I need to stop crying first. Mebbe I leave.

Elchanan got up. "Sorry. I wasting your time," he said, and turned toward the door.

The man stood up. "Please...you are not wasting my time at all. Elchanan, this is what I do—"

Elchanan turned swiftly back to him. "Vat, vatch old mens cry?"

The man smiled. "No. Sit down. I will tell you what I do." They both sat back down, the man shifting into his preferred position, Elchanan mechanically clutching the armrests. "I admit. I have an odd job. All I do, all day, is ask questions…"

Elchanan's brows lifted, his cheeks still wet. "This odd. True. But you making alots of money from these qvestions, so is good. No?"

"Good, but not easy. I don't ask the easy questions. I ask specific questions. Questions that no one else will ask. And your job, Elchanan, is to answer them." The man eyed his subject carefully.

Elchanan stared at him. "What if I not knowing de answer? I getting lower grade?" He snickered and shook his head slowly.

"Why are you shaking your head?" asked the man. "What are you trying to tell me?"

"Mine vife, Greta, she is…this her idea. They thinking…she and her sister, Breeya, they thinking I need help. They thinking I depressed. I says to her, *'So what I depressed! I have good reason. No? Nothing making it better. So I die depressed. So what? You think they not gonna let me into Heaven just because I depressed?'*"

"So you know that you are depressed. That's good. Have you ever spoken about it to anyone aside from your wife?"

"No. Vhy should I? No one needs know mine business. Peoples always talking about other peoples. Making me sick. I don' talk about others, and I don' likes it vhen peoples talkin' about me…or mine family."

The man leaned forward, considered his next move. "Okay, I think we are ready for the first question."

Elchanan nodded timidly and took a deep breath. "All right…"

"When was the last time you felt happiness? Do you remember?"

He thought for a bit, scratched his chin beneath his beard. "Four years 'go ve making vedding for our oldest girl. Now she is mother. She has two small girls. Pretty girls. Oldest is blonde, like mine own daughter, when she young. I am grandfather. This making me happy. Vhat else you vanna know?"

"Sounds wonderful. Sounds like you have every reason to be happy, Elchanan. So, can I ask, why were you crying before?"

Elchanan stopped moving. *Vhy I should tell this man? Vhy I should trust him? This meshugge. Nothing's gonna help anyvays.* He looked up. The man was waiting. Elchanan felt the silence, like it was sucking the oxygen out of the room, like it was strangling both of them. Yet still, he remained silent.

The man spoke again. "Your wife has made a few appointments in the past, hasn't she?"

Elchanan nodded.

"Yet you have never shown up. Why is that?"

Elchanan did not move.

"So why, today, have you come?" The man stopped talking and stared into Elchanan's face. The silence built up around them again, like a pressure vault. "Take your time, Elchanan," he said eventually. "Take your time. I'm in no rush."

Elchanan knew he would fold eventually. He let his shoulders down, held the gaze of his interrogator, breathed out, and said in the tiniest whisper, "I don't know vhere is mine son..."

The man blinked twice. "Aha," he said. "Well, that's gotta hurt."

MONDAY, JULY 13, 2015
LONDON, ENGLAND

"No way!" Aryeh sounded, at first, mildly amused.

"Excuse me, what was that?"

"Sima, sorry, but there is *no way* I am going to give you my blessing. France is a cesspool of anti-Semitism. You must be crazy to want to go there just because of some blurry image you think is Aaron." Then he suddenly became authoritarian. "No, Sima. And that is my final answer."

Sima grinned; she hadn't expected anything less. "Gotta love how you sound when you speak like that, all dictator-like. But it's not going to work. I must go. That is all."

"Sima..." Aryeh couldn't find the words. "You know you get like this. So hyper-focused, you miss all warnings..."

"Warnings? Of what?"

"If you think it's bad in England, Sima, France is way worse. *Way...!*"

"Aryeh, *noth*ing is going to happen to me!"

"How can you be sure? What if...?" He would never forgive himself. "Sima, please think. Be reasonable. You cannot be certain it was Aaron you saw."

"Yes. I. Can! Aryeh, please! *You* think! I mean, twenty years of not knowing... *Twenty* years! And now I have a lead. I have some light. I am going, Aryeh. I cannot NOT go. I just wish you would understand!" She wanted to hang up. She wanted to scream till she popped a vein. She wanted to pinch herself till she bled.

"Why can't you just call him? Why do you have to *go* there?"

"*G-tt in Himmel*, Aryeh! Don't you *get* it? He may run away again! Besides, I have nothing—no phone number, no contacts, no anything of his! Come on, Aryeh! I have to go. I need to just show up. Then he will be forced to speak to me..." A rush of intensity made her stop talking.

"Okay. Okay. I hear you. Can we discuss this tomorrow?"

"Not really." She sighed. "I'm hoping to catch the early ferry from Dover to Calais, so I am not sure we will be able to talk." She heard him take a deep breath. "Aryeh...please try to understand where I'm coming from."

"I guess you've made up your mind."

"I have. But...I can't go without your blessing."

"Okay...but please, Sima, be careful. Stay alert."

"I will. Thank you," she said, and hung up the phone, making it jiggle as it settled in its cradle.

Please, Hashem, let me not be too late!

Things went comparatively worse with Henya a little later:

"Are you *mad*?" Henya bellowed. They were standing in the little front yard on Ashley Grove. "You must be *crazy* to risk your life for an image!"

"Shhhh..." Sima pointed in the direction of their mother's open bedroom window. "And don't be so melodramatic!" she whispered, immediately regretting taking Henya into her confidence. But she had figured she needed her sister to cover for her absence. "I'm risking *noth*ing. France is not Iraq, for Heaven's sake..."

"It is now!" Henya hissed.

"*Rubbish!* Look, I just have to go..."

"And what about Tatte? What about his wishes?"

"*Oy*, Henya, please don't make this harder than it is already. I can't think about that right now. Would you give me a ride to Victoria station?"

"No. I'm not helping you out, Sima. You wanna do this, do this yourself."

"I *can't* believe you. I *can't* believe you would cut me off like this!"

"Listen to me, you came here for Mummy—not to go gallivanting after a dream. Besides, Aaron is trouble. You know he—"

Sima stepped back, her disgust reaching a ferocity level even she feared. "So you really are not going to help?"

Henya shook her head. "No. I will not be complicit in this."

Sima sucked in her breath and held it for a few seconds, adjusting her expectations. "Okay, then. I will just have to do this entirely alone," she said, and she stepped back inside the house, stopping for just a moment to listen to Henya slam the front-yard gate closed. Sima turned toward the stairs and stopped for a moment, her mind already concocting the tale she would have to spin, as she went up to her mother's room.

That night, sleep was slippery.

So many, many thoughts badgered about, heckling and baiting, that Sima pondered if madness would claim its hold on her long before the rising of the sun. *Courage*, she remembered reading in her favorite young adult book, *To Kill a Mockingbird, is not a man with a gun in his hand. It is the knowledge that you are licked before you begin, but you begin anyway.* Her ferry was leaving at ten the next morning. She had been to France once before, for a two-day high school graduation trip, the summer of the same year that Aaron had left. The incongruity of them, perhaps, being in the same country at the same time, without even knowing, did not make her smile. It just felt more wrenching.

Lying in bed, she considered her predicament. She did not know the French language, currency, or transportation. How would she get around?

Alone.

She listened to her mother's rhythmic breathing from the room next door. They had spent a large part of Monday together, Sima actively storing up on time, in advance of her desertion. She was careful to sound casual when she informed Greta that she would be leaving for a few days. "I'm going up to the countryside, Mummy, to a spa retreat I've been eyeing. They are having a promotion, and it seems too good of an opportunity to waste. Would you be okay if I take off for three days, at most? Henya will take me over…" She noted the slight shift in her mother's facial muscles that only showed disappointment, not alarm.

"Go," Greta granted. "It'll be good for you. I can manage. You know, I'm getting better every day, *baruch Hashem*."

"Mummy…" Sima's back was to her mother while she went through the day's mail, but she could see her in the reflection of the large triple mirror atop the dresser. "About that letter…"

"What about it, dear?"

Sima watched how Greta's eyes made swift contact with the bottom drawer of the dresser before settling on her daughter's back. She felt something turn inside her. She hated what she was doing: lying to her mother. "Haven't you ever had the urge to read it, Mummy?"

"Of course I have. Many times I was tempted. But then something would always stop me. I think it is the fact that this is the last thing I could do for your father. To carry out his last wish and deliver the letter, unopened. No, Sima. It is meant for Aaron, and Aaron alone."

Well, thought Sima, as she lay awake, waiting for sunrise, *it may be for Aaron, and Aaron alone, but how is he ever going to get it, if no one takes any risks?*

At 3:25 a.m. Sima had had enough. She got up, tiptoed out of her room, and stood by her mother's bedroom door, listening. Stealthily, she turned the doorknob and slowly opened the door just a crack. She stood very still, making sure that her mother's breathing continued as musically as before. Her heart clobbering, she inched her way into the room and made her way to the drawer at the bottom of her mother's dresser, where she could have placed a bet that her mother stored that letter.

All at once, inner voices blasted through her, voices that only she could hear:

You are taking the destinies of your father and brother into your hands.

But how else could there be closure?

Your mother will be furious when she finds out.

She will never find out.

Yes, she will. She will look for the letter and find it missing.

I will bring it back when I return.

What if Aaron insists he wants to keep it?

I'll cross that bridge when the time comes.

What if it is not the letter of your dreams? What if Tatte wrote scathingly in it, about his anger toward his one and only son? What if it seals Aaron up for good? Maybe read it before you go traipsing off on an iffy quest, thinking that you are some heroine in some thriller novel...

No. Don't read it. If Mummy didn't see fit to read it, then neither should you.

With trembling hands, Sima crouched low on the floor and opened the bottom drawer. In the light provided by the streetlamp, obscured by the overgrown tree whose branches cast stormy shadows on the wall behind her, she rummaged through the neatly folded nightgowns that her mother preserved with uncanny attention to detail. She stopped breathing when her fingers hit something hard. A small box, like those made in Cuba for cigars. She smothered the clicking sound of the metallic opener with her thumb and forefinger. Inside the box was a largish, white, unopened letter. On it was inscribed, in fading black ink: *To Mine Son, Aaron Rephael Bulman.*

Sima brought the letter to her chest. Guilt hit her hard. To what had she reduced herself? To a prying little thief, who would sell out her parents because of some highfalutin fantasy that she could set everything right again. Maybe Henya had a point, after all. Maybe she should leave well enough alone...

Sima closed the box and clicked the latch into place, replacing it between the folds of the nightgowns. She slowly closed the drawer and quietly slipped out of the room.

There was no one on the street when she left the house early Tuesday morning. The silence was so complete, she could hear her pocketbook rhythmically banging her hip. She feared that the sound of her small suitcase's wheels grinding the pavement behind her might wake the sleeping neighbors. The letter—a small but potent firearm—was nestled in that suitcase's front pocket.

Her mind churned. *Aryeh thinks of France as a foreign, war-torn country. Rubbish! France is no more war-torn than New York. Riots or no riots, France is a modern, free commonwealth.*

Why had Aryeh been so against her doing this? True, she had never done anything remotely like this before, but there comes a time in everyone's life when circumstances dictate a radical change...

I will be fine, she almost said out loud.

Chattersfield's Main Street was eerily deserted, roads and stores looking like an empty set in a movie studio. Two or three black-garbed, bearded men shuffled in the distance, on their way to an early Shacharis *minyan*. A young woman in a nurse's uniform jaywalked in the background. Sima waited at the crossroads for the little green man to appear on the traffic light before realizing it was not necessary; there were no cars out this early.

And then there is Henya! Sima thought as she reached the bus stop. *How could she still be so hung up on Tatte's warning? Would he not have wanted some kind of reconciliation? Surely that was what he had written about in his letter.* She tugged at her little suitcase. *Should I have told her about it? Would it have changed her mind?*

When her bus came, she got on and smiled gratefully at the driver, to whom she felt indebted just for being another person. Once they got to the Seven Oaks tube station, things picked up. There were lots of coffee-drinking, business-suited travelers—briefcases leaning against their shins—standing on the black platform, breathing in the dusty, gasoline-laced air. In typical English fashion, no one spoke a word. Still, their presence calmed her.

By the time Sima reached Victoria station, it was 7:30 a.m., and the sun was shining through the glass slats in the roof, casting its glow upon the white floor speckled with gold. She felt a bit more encouraged. "Dover, please," she told the man at the ticket counter. "Open return." *Dover*, she thought, *gateway to Europe*. She felt of sizzle of excitement, the tiniest tremor of adventure.

Spirit of Britain was the name of the ferry. The vast deck upon which she stood was crowded. She looked back at the famous eight-mile stretch of white cliffs. England, a land she considered home, was shrinking from view. France, a country she did not know, a culture she never had any reason to understand, rose menacingly along the horizon. Her knees jellied.

She looked around for somewhere to sit. The gleeful vacationers she had accidentally joined, with their laughter and their selfies, grated on her nerves. Wasn't there any quiet corner where she could rest? Wandering through the doors into some kind of lounge, where bluesy background music played, she found a small alcove with a coffee table and two winged chairs. Grateful for the more reticent atmosphere here, she settled into the chair nearest a small circular window, through which England could still be seen, and soon succumbed to the vibrations of the engine and the gentle rocking of the enormous ship.

She could not know for how long she slept, but she was woken by a small group of teenage girls in the midst of a brawl right beside her. Their screeches robbed her of what little peace she'd salvaged. She turned away from them and thought of Tamar. Where was she holding emotionally, and in her *frumkeit*, right now? Why had she, Sima, never considered speaking to her oldest daughter about her uncle? How long did she think she could keep up the pretense? Why *hadn't* she, the one whose own brother had gone off, read the signs that something was wrong? They say, *A shoemaker's child goes barefoot...*

Sima turned again to observe the shrieking teenaged girls. She took in their ripped clothing, their piercings, their tattoos...their *un*happiness.

...Mommy, I have been affected by this revelation on so many levels... I am starting to have misgivings about things I never doubted before. I question everything these days... It's been about a year now, and I still feel so unanchored...

Was Tamar going off the *derech*? Did she know enough to act responsibly, to stop herself before she spiraled too far down? Did she have limits? At a lecture Sima had attended recently, in her capacity as a school social worker, she'd heard it repeated many times: when the religious go "off the *derech*," they often lose all sense of boundaries. Once the upchuck of constraints has occurred, they rebel in the worst possible ways. Anything that feels remotely confining is scoffed and dumped, and many do things which they spend the rest of their lives regretting.

Oh, Tamar, tell me that none of this will happen to you. Tell me that you're okay.

Tamar...

Sima suddenly felt sick. What was she doing on this ferry? Crossing the channel to chase an image? She should be home, working on a plan to reclaim her daughter, not meandering around France following some wild hallucination! *Aryeh is right. I should be focusing on Tamar, not on Aaron. Aaron is the past that cannot be changed. Tamar is our future.*

A terrible dread rose up inside her, settling just beneath her throat. She had chosen poorly. She should turn back. The moment her foot touched Calais, she had to arrange for her return.

She should call Henya.

And admit she was wrong.

It was noontime in sunny Calais. Tired and hungry, Sima stood on the promenade, unable to decide what to do. In front of her, a large blue sign directed passengers to the town center and Calais Ville train station. It would be a fifteen-minute walk to pick up the train to Paris. All around her, happy people milled about, buying souvenirs, pulverizing the French language, savoring the local cuisine. Sima relished none of what France had to offer. One call. One call to Aryeh, and she would know what to do. She pulled her phone out of her pocketbook, turned it on, and stared at it.

No.

She turned it off again, slipped it back into her pocketbook, and walked down the path toward the train station. She had come this far. She could not leave without trying. The next few days would inform her of what to do next.

The next few days were all she had.

24

AARON:

*I*t's dark. Really dark. How come it is so terrifyingly dark? And what are those sounds? Is it daytime? I hear...daytime sounds. Sounds of light. Oh, dear, I feel a panic coming on. I need to control it. Or just give in to it. Where am I, for Heaven's sake? What's happened? Can someone tell me what's going on?!

Aha.

I hear footsteps. Soft footsteps. Someone in sneakers. And there is clanking. Is that beeping? Am I in a hospital? Am I awake? Gosh, I can't open my eyes. Why can't I open my eyes? This is hideous! Hello! Hello! Can anybody see that I am awake? Ohhh...I'm in so much pain. Perhaps I should try to speak. Yes. Someone may hear, and explain what is going on...

"H-hello?"

"*Excusez-moi. Tu es réveillé?*"

Who is that? Is that a nurse? I should nod. I can't nod.

"Y-yes."

"Do not move, Mr. Bulman. You have been badly hurt. You will recover, but for now it is best if you do not move. As for your eyes, you were lucky. Above your left eye, you have a large laceration, much bruising, and swelling, but your right eye is fine. We have bandaged them both for now, while the stitches heal. You will see again—don't worry. But you must be patient."

Cough. "How long have I been here?"

"Since yesterday evening. You've been sleeping, mostly. The blow to your head caused a concussion. But your MRIs are good. You also have two injuries to the chest, presumably from being kicked. That was some fight you had, Mr. Bulman."

Aaron could hear the smile, then soft footsteps again.

No! Don't leave. Stay with me.

Oh, well…maybe I should just go back to sleep. There is nothing else to do.

Beeeeep. Beeeeep. Beeeeep.

Am I awake again? Is anyone here? What are those sounds? Am I dying? Beeeeeep. *This is frightening. Am I still in the hospital? Am I still in Paris? Where is that nurse?*

"Hello! Anyone there?"

I hear movement. Shoes. Leather shoes. Someone is coming, walking at an even clip. Good. Get me out of here…!

"Aaron? Are you awake?"

Yes! Rabbi Wechter! I want to nod. Oh, dear, scratch that—I shouldn't move my head. I'll pick up my hand instead. Up, yes, a little wave.

"Rabbi Wechter? Is that you?"

Yes. My hand is being held. By someone's warm hand.

"Aaron, Aaron, you are our newest hero."

Ahem, what?!

"Really. Everyone is talking about it! About you."

What is he talking about? Why on earth am I a hero? I want to let go of his hand. He won't let me.

"It is true, Aaron. Everyone is talking about this stranger who went after the enemy, who fought for the freedom to be a Jew. I only found out it was you when they came to tell me that someone was badly hurt and no one knew who that someone was. I went with you in the ambulance. You were not alone. But don't worry, no one knows your name."

Oh, my goodness! Was it in the papers? Are people looking into me? What a disaster. No, no, no! My head! It is throbbing! Throbbing! Nurse! I need pain medication. Where is the nurse?

Cough. "Rabbi...my head... I need medication. Medicine."

"Yes. Yes. Certainly. Wait here—I'll go find the nurse."

I wish I could nod.

She had morphed into the proverbial "wandering Jew." Not the plant, the actual Jew. She shrugged as a faint reflection of her face appeared in the dust-encrusted window of the bus, catching her unawares. She did not like the whiteness of her complexion, the way her eyes announced that they were searching. She had never been good at hiding. *Transparent* was what they called her. As though being transparent was a great sin, in whose wake echoed unkind laughter.

She closed her eyes and opened them again, just as they rounded into a square so beautiful, she drew in her breath. At the center of this square stood a column. She stretched her neck and strained her eyes to follow the column up to its tippy top, where a golden angel looked as though it were about to take off. The bus driver called to her, "Campagne de Blocage."

She had no address. All she had was the name of the street. She was suddenly seized by the realization that she was repeating a journey her father had taken when stepping onto British soil for the first time: Without the language—check. Without lodging—check. Without a clue as to how to find the basic necessities of life—check, check, check. How frightened her father must have been, without a soul in the world!

She thanked the driver and got off, enormously grateful to spy the sign that did indeed read *Campagne de Blocage*. She thought again of Aryeh, and how worried he probably was about her right now. Oh, how secure he made her feel—just in the knowledge that he was there, that he existed, and that he would be there when she got back.

She was starving, not having eaten a thing all day. Noticing a small grocery store, she went inside. There she found chips and apple juice with a kosher stamp on their packages. Once outside, she tore the bag open and wolfed down her paltry meal. Now, where to go from here?

She stopped the first man who passed by. "Excuse me, where is the synagogue? Could you direct me to the synagogue on Campagne de Blocage? The one..." The words died on her lips. She found herself afraid to mention the riots. Who was this man? An ally or an enemy? Aryeh's face took over her, his warning words...

The man pointed. "Keep walking straight. You will find it." He spoke so gruffly before walking off, it made her insides shrivel.

She walked down Campagne de Blocage, noticing everything: broken pavement; stores with wooden planks where glass should have been; garbage bins still on their sides; shards of beer bottles and bits of burnt tires; limbs from demolished patio furniture—the top of a chair; a napkin holder; an exquisitely carved, rounded surface of a bistro table, minus its legs. A beautiful, high-heeled woman's shoe had settled in a gutter. *Put me to rest*, the strewn-about items seemed to say. A stinging, caustic smog hung in the air. Sima blinked away the grit from her eyes, and wrapped her arms around herself. Had it suddenly turned cold?

Then she saw it, and her mood lifted: the white fence. A little sunken from the rest of the street—appearing bashful between two taller buildings. She recognized the trellis above it at once. Her steps quickened as she made her way toward the yellow police line that was strung from one end of the synagogue entrance to the other. Was it forbidden to enter? After all this effort?

She approached the two policemen standing at the entrance. "Excuse me, do you speak English?"

"Certainly. What can we do for you?"

"Is the synagogue closed?"

"Yes. There was...a little trouble here this week."

"Yes. I am aware. I was just wondering if I could speak to somebody inside. I am looking for someone..." Sima felt her eyes fill. She power-batted her lids to rid herself of any inconvenient tears.

"Madame, there is no one in the building."

"Why? Did the inside get destroyed?" she asked, peering beyond the policemen, above the fence, up at the concrete lattice, which she could now clearly see was made up of little concrete Stars of David. "Is it dangerous to enter?"

The policemen smiled. "No. The building did not get destroyed inside. But we have strict orders not to allow anyone in. Well, except for the rabbi or the other staff members here."

"Oh," said Sima. A silence followed while she calculated her next move. "So, have they stopped all services?"

"What do you mean, Madame?"

"I mean, are they not continuing to pray here? The Jews? The community? Where do they pray now?"

The policemen shrugged their shoulders. "We do not know," they said, and turned away from her.

Sima stood around for a little while longer. She ran her fingers along the white painted slats of the gate she had seen Aaron walk through. They felt smooth and cold. She looked to her right and left to view the sights he had absorbed. Was this *his* shul for the past twenty years? Was this where he had made his life? Would this community be *his* people?

All she needed to do now was wait; surely the rabbi or some other staff member would come by. She looked for somewhere to sit. There was nothing. Two soldiers came out from a nearby café, armed with machine guns. They joined the two policemen. She leaned against the white concrete side-post, her eyes drifting about. She scanned the pavement for any signs of blood. Then she shifted her position and pulled her luggage closer to her, wishing her mind into nothingness, so she could get some respite from her constant over-thinking.

"Excuse me, Madame?" It was one of the soldiers.

"Yes?"

"What are you doing here?"

"Waiting."

"Oh." Silence. "For what?"

"For someone."

"Who?"

"Why? Is it a problem?"

A car pulled up, before the soldier had time to respond. A man with a neatly-trimmed, white beard opened the passenger door, said a few words to the driver, shut the door behind him, and turned to walk through the fence-gate, passing—but not noticing—Sima and the soldier.

This is it. This is my chance. "Excuse me," she called out, her voice tapering off to a high-pitched bay.

The man swung around. His eyes fell upon her, and he immediately gestured for her to follow him, as though he had been expecting her. He nodded at the police and soldiers and ushered her through. A path led to glass doors. She noted the Ten Commandments affixed to the trellis that the two of them walked under. Then the man pulled out a set of keys and unlocked one of the doors.

Once in the building, the man turned to her. "I am Rabbi Wechter, the rabbi of this synagogue. Now what can I do for you? Who are you?"

"I am looking for someone."

"Oh?"

"He got hurt in the riots on Sunday."

"Does your 'someone' have a name?"

"Yes. His name is Aaron. Aaron Bulman." She looked into the man's eyes. "Do you, perhaps, know him?"

The man took a few moments to examine her before asking, "And what are you to him?"

"I am…" She could not get the words out; her throat constricted so tightly, she had to fight it to open. "I am his sister…" she whispered, finally permitting the tears to slide down her cheeks.

25

A ryeh looked at his watch. It was 4:35 p.m. "Thank you very much," he said. "Yes...certainly...I will drive up tonight. No. No worries. I will be there...I'm guessing, around nine thirty, maybe closer to ten."

"Thanks so much for your understanding, Mr. Hertzberg. I am sure it is nothing, but we cannot take any chances, if you know what I mean..." The woman on the phone sounded distracted.

"May I ask where Tamar is right now?"

"We've put her in the infirmary," she said quickly. "Our physician spoke with me after examining her. He thinks she may be fighting two things at once. Neither is anything serious, on its own, but the two things together...it's a little harsh. A few days at home, with some rest and relaxation, and the doctor believes she should be fine."

Aryeh felt himself get irritated, but could not fathom why. "Thank you for taking such good care of her," he said, as he watched his two youngest daughters wander through the front door and make a beeline for the fridge. "I, er..." He scratched the back of his ear. "I will have to arrange for a babysitter. My wife is in Europe." *Why did I need to mention that?* "But I'll try to get there as fast as possible. Thank you again."

By the time Aryeh got to Camp Shoshana, it was already dark. He parked in a grassy field, next to the camp vans, and made his way to the building marked with a makeshift wooden sign that had the words "Main Office" scratched onto it. He knocked on the door and turned the handle.

Three young girls looked up. Each one wore a whistle around her neck and a baseball cap that had the camp insignia on it.

"Hi," said one of the girls, who was sitting near a phone and computer. "Can we help you?"

"I'm Aryeh Hertzberg. I've come to pick up Tamar."

"Oh, Tamar's father? Nice to meet you," she said. She stood up and walked toward the back of the room. "Come," she said, in a friendly tone, as she opened a door Aryeh hadn't noticed was there. "Your Tamar had been really under-the-weather over Shabbos, and then this rash broke out. It was my idea to call you. Sometimes people just need a break. Some rest and relaxation. You know what I mean?"

If one other person uses that expression, I think I'm going to explode! Aryeh thought. "Yes. I know exactly what you mean. Has she been working very hard?"

They were walking along a string of footpaths outside the office cabin. Small flying insects vied for landing spots on both of their faces as they passed pools of light from overhead lamps. A couple of the pesky gnats landed on Aryeh's lips. He slapped his mouth and stopped himself from spitting. He had never been to the campgrounds at night before. Although he and Sima trekked up here every year for visiting day, they had never stayed past dusk. The air smelled sweet, but it was so thick that it hung around them like floating goop.

"To be honest, I wouldn't have thought so." The girl's voice came to him after a small pause.

"Sorry, what was that?"

"You asked if Tamar has been working hard."

"Oh, yeah..."

"Maybe she has been, but she isn't the only lifeguard, so I wouldn't have thought her workload was especially hard or anything. Though, come to think of it, she *is* always at the pool..." She stopped walking and looked at him, biting her lower lip. "It's like she doesn't believe in shifts. I didn't realize. Maybe I should have been more vigilant."

"Oh, I'm sure that she did it by choice." He heard cheering in the distance. The shriek of a whistle. Announcements on a megaphone. Crickets. The dirt road was uneven, and he felt cloddish in his city shoes.

The path abruptly turned, and three wooden structures suddenly appeared in front of them. As they passed the first, the girl pointed and said, "Assembly-hall, slash, center-for-the-performing-arts." Aryeh looked it over. It was of imposing height, with a triangular roof made of long wooden beams.

They passed the second structure. "VIP Bunkhouse," the girl said, pointing. Smaller than the first one, this bungalow-of-sorts had double doors that swung noiselessly with the slightest breeze.

"VIP's?" Aryeh asked.

"Yup! The two oldest bunks. They get special privileges, y'know..."

Finally, they came to the third structure. "Infirmary," she announced. "I'm Rivka Grossbard, by the way. One of the head counselors. Anyway, I'm glad I could help." She opened the door for him, before giving a nod and retreating back up the many convoluted paths.

Aryeh stepped into what would pass for a small, square lobby. To the right and left stretched narrow corridors. Behind him, on his extreme right, was a tiny kitchenette, lit up by an exposed, dangling bulb in the center of the ceiling. It was the only light available in the place.

He felt awkward. This was, after all, an all-girls camp. Not for the first time, he bemoaned Sima's absence. If she were not in England— or France, actually—it would have been *her* coming to get Tamar, and he would not be left feeling quite so gauche.

"Excuse me..." he called out. "Anyone here?"

He heard shuffling and turned to face a matronly woman who was wearing a bluish-gray kerchief around her head. Her plumpish face looked up at him, thin lips set in a seemingly perpetual smile. When she entered the square in which Aryeh stood, the space quickly diminished by more than half. He took two steps back and bumped against the wall behind him.

The woman strode past Aryeh and into the minuscule kitchenette. "I'll be with you in one moment. I just need to wash my hands," she called. He heard the faucet turn on, and a strong stream of water splash against a metal sink. "You must be Mr. Hertzberg, Tamar's father. Yes?" The woman smiled as she dried her hands, standing under the lintel.

"Yes. She is here, right? Somewhere." He peered down the corridors. "I'm taking her home for a few days. Were you the one who called me?"

"I am. I'm Gabby Menashe. I've been nurse at the camp for ooooooh, too many years!" She flapped her hand and chuckled. "Come this way; I'll bring you to her. Don't be alarmed at how she looks. The doctor was here today, and he said the rash should go away on its own."

Of all the non-reassuring sentences, "don't be alarmed" has to be the worst, Aryeh thought.

They walked down the narrow passageway to the left. It occurred to him that although Tamar had spent at least five summers here, he had never really showed much interest in her camp. He thought now of the letter he was not supposed to have read:

...Mommy, I have been affected by this revelation on so many levels... I am starting to have misgivings about things I never doubted before. I question everything these days... It's been about a year now, and I still feel so unanchored...

It was like dirt that builds up slowly in the crevices of a house, not making any waves, and thus never being treated to a good scrubbing. Only the occasional guest, who comes after a long absence, will witness the house's slow decline. That was what may have happened to his oldest daughter. The fissure—hardly a crack—grew so lazily, creeping over the days, weeks, and months, that he simply hadn't noticed it. And now he was beating himself up about the fault that had been placed at his feet.

They came to a door. The nurse knocked lightly. "Hey, Tamar, can we come in? You've got a visitor..." Again, Aryeh found himself annoyed; was it the condescending lilt in her voice? His teeth subtly clamped together in quiet exasperation.

He walked in.

Tamar sat up. She was a pretty girl: blue eyes, long blonde lashes, and usually a healthy complexion. She opened her eyes wide now, taking in the apparition that was her father.

"Abba...?" Her throaty undertone expressed a mix of surprise and weakness. "I can't believe you came!" She blinked rapidly for a few seconds.

He considered her greeting. A dancing demon closed in on him, nuzzling at his ear. "And why wouldn't I come?" he asked, keeping the demon out of range. "You're sick. I care. I'm here."

Her hesitant smile hurt him. "I just expected Mommy. That's all." Tamar stretched her neck to see if anyone else was coming up behind him.

"Ahhh. No. Didn't I tell you? Something came up, and she had to go to England." She frowned. He caught it. "So..." He watched her every nuance now, feeling bereft. All the trust he thought they had, *poof,* seemed to be gone. "...I've come instead. Hope I'm a good substitute."

Her stare seemed to light up his incompetence as a father. Then he remembered: her beef was not with him, but with Sima. *Still, it is because of both of us that she feels let down. And I can't even say anything about her letter or any of this topic... Oh boy! This is gonna be a long night.*

"England?" she interrupted his thoughts. "Mommy never mentioned to me anything about going to England."

"She didn't want to worry you, I suppose. It's Bubby. She fell. Hairline fracture on her hip." Slowly, his eyes digested her rash. It was as though someone had slapped both her cheeks and pulled violently on her neck. An allergic reaction? An insect bite? *I'll have to find a dermatologist tomorrow, get her in for an appointment...*

"What's a hairline fracture?"

"A break so thin, it can't be seen."

"Ahhh," she said, squinting at him, as if trying to decipher whether or not this was another lie.

There it was—her admonition of him. He tried to ignore it. After all, he wasn't supposed to be aware of anything unusual going on. "Nothing to do for it. It just needs to heal on its own." He tried to smile, but it came out floppy. "Meanwhile, Tamar, you need to come home for a few days. Look at you..."

"I know." She rubbed her eyes. "Are you shocked to see me like this? I have strep, too, you know—did Mrs. Menashe tell you that? My stomach has also been really crazy these days. I haven't been able to keep much down. I'm a mess; I won't argue about that..." She turned from him and looked down at the two hills of her knees, under a thin blanket. "Okay, so I guess I'll pack up some of my stuff and come home with you for a little bit."

The roads were ethereal. A thin mist had settled in parts. Aryeh slipped a music CD into the stereo, and they both allowed its rhythm to lull them into comfortable silence. Between them, a surplus of pink elephants crowded the car, cramping its quarters, making only small concessions of space for its occupants to think. Neither knew how to relax in the exclusive presence of the other. It *had* been too long since they had spent some "alone time" together, Aryeh realized. His mind sought a conversation starter. He wanted to talk to her—to have her talk to him.

"Tamar?"

"Yeah?"

"Tell me about camp, about you, about...oh, I don't know...about anything you like, really." He hoped he sounded casual.

"About myself? I'm good. Why?"

"And camp? How's it going?"

"It's also good. Why are you asking?"

"You don't think you're getting tired of it? Ready to do something else with your summers?"

"Maybe next year. I'll have graduated by next year. I might be thinking about other things by then. Why? Do you have anything in mind?"

"Maybe a family trip to Eretz Yisrael next summer? How does that sound to you?"

Tamar turned to her father. "That would be amazing!" she said. Then she frowned. "How *are* things over there? Every day in camp they make announcements about what's going on there. We have Tehillim assemblies all the time for the *matzav* in Eretz Yisrael. It's so scary."

"*B'ezras Hashem*, everything will turn out okay. You'll see. Our People have been through this before."

"Abba, is it true that there are riots all over the world because of what's happening in Eretz Yisrael? Some of the girls were saying something like that..."

"Yup."

"In England?"

"Hmmm, I see where you're headed with this. Yeah, so Mommy said England has had some pretty bad attacks. Apparently on buses. But she isn't afraid. Well...you know Mommy."

"Sure." Tamar smiled knowingly. "I'm not afraid either." She sat back, arms crossed over her shoulders, nails digging in.

"That's good," he said, watching her in his peripheral vision.

They drove in silence. The music changed. It was a slow piece now—a weeping violin, a strident cello, a harp that sounded like the softest of bells. Aryeh hummed along, but Tamar scrunched her face, so he stopped. "Tamar?"

"Yeah?"

"Are you happy?"

Tamar turned again to him. "Why do you keep asking me these questions?"

"No reason. I was just wondering, that's all. Look, Mommy's being away gives me a lot of time to think. I haven't had a decent conversation with you in a long time. You're my daughter, and I just want to know how you're doing. That's all."

"You've read my letter." It was a statement.

He turned to see her face. She did not look angry. Not even upset. Even so, he felt himself break out in a sweat. He did not respond.

"Well?" she asked. "Have you?"

"What letter?"

"Abba..." Her face softened. "I know what you are trying to do—to protect Mommy. But, the truth is, I expected nothing less."

He breathed out. "Okay. I admit it. I did read that letter. Look, your mother is, understandably, very cut up about it. As am I. But before we go any further, could you do me the favor of just answering this one question: are you happy?"

"Why?"

"Is this how it's going to be from now on?"

"What do you mean?"

"You giving vague answers, not really allowing yourself to have a normal conversation with me..."

"Well, what do you want me to say?"

"The truth. Please. And don't over-think it. I just want you to say the first thing that comes to your mind. Are you happy? Do you ever think about it?"

"About being happy?"

Aryeh nodded, keeping his eyes on the dark country road ahead. The CD stopped playing its soulful sounds, veering into electric instrumentals. He switched it off. The silence told them both that they *had* to proceed, whether they liked it or not.

"Well...I actually *do* think about happiness—the pursuit of it— quite a bit. Am I happy? I'm not sure. Is a person ever sure?"

"Good point."

"The thing is: I *was* happy."

"Oh?"

"Yes. Things changed. But I do remember *being* happy. And I remember when and why it all changed."

They drove a little longer in sullen stillness. His stomach knotted.

She reached out to switch the CD back on, but he put out his hand to stop her. "No. No music. Tell me. What happened?"

She did not look at him. "Mommy has a brother she never talks about." Aryeh's mouth opened, automatically. "No," Tamar said. "Please, hear me out first. I was told about him, last year, in this same camp, by a group of nasty girls who enjoyed my ignorance and loved to torment me. Well, as you can imagine, the news shook my world.

"I asked around a bit. Mommy's brother's name is Aaron—Aaron Rephael Bulman—and he did some terrible things. I'm not sure what. But here's the thing, Abba: *She* cut him off. Just like that. She acts like her brother never existed! Does anyone deserve that?! I can't believe my own mother, whom I love, would do something like that. I can't come to terms with it. To think—" she looked at him now, her hand hitting her forehead— "...I have an uncle who is probably alive somewhere, but for all practical purposes, pretty much dead. Don't you think that would make me question Mommy?! And you, too, for that matter?! I mean, you must know about him too, right?"

26

SPRING, 2000
LONDON, ENGLAND

By the time Elchanan left the man's office, the heavens had opened. As the deluge poured down, he fumbled for his keys and got his back pummeled by hail—an onslaught of tiny, pricky pellets. Protected only by a white shirt over his *tzitzis* and undershirt, he was soaked through; his gray hair and beard clung to his scalp and face. He stopped short, closing his eyes, and concentrated on the tiny, sharp pings running along his shoulders. A strange hypnosis entered him and settled for a few, elongated seconds. Momentarily awakening, he glanced back at the tall, thin windows. The man had been watching him, his mug of coffee still in his hand. Although he himself wasn't aware of it, Elchanan's mouth was open, and his eyes had turned cold with guilt.

Whatever words he had spoken inside that room, Elchanan realized, were never the whole truth...

It was raining heavily that morning too, back in 1995. Then too, there had been a raging hailstorm. Elchanan had walked home in it from his daily minyan, *from speaking with Hashem, from trying—oh, how hard he tried—to communicate with the Divine. But there was a cyclone roiling in his gut that day. Precipitation had begun with the whispering he'd had to swallow, and the forced quietude he caused wherever he passed. Groups of nattering men behind him, in front of*

224 | **THE THIRTEENTH GATE**

him, and on every side cast their eyes briefly at him before swiveling their faces away. Something had happened, something regarding his son, and—naturally—he would be the last to know.

Something about a fire...whole office destroyed...Arkady in the hospital...smoke inhalation...nearly died. The Bulman kid. It was him? Yes... He's always been a little odd... Yes, yes. I can promise, it was him... People saw him...he did it... Arson... No way...! He could do time for that... Look, shhh, there is his father... Poor thing... Immigrant mentality...never really found his place...

It was Rabbi Gold who had come through for Elchanan. Young Rabbi Yona Gold who informed him of the hubbub surrounding his son, of the event the night before, of the damage done to the school building and to Arkady, the janitor, who lived in a small room in the attic directly above Rabbi Isaacs's office, and who had been taken by ambulance to the hospital. Yona Gold also told Elchanan about Rabbi Isaacs's gag order.

"I am only telling you all this because if I was the father, I would want to know, Mr. Bulman. But please don't be angry with your son. He is young. He does not realize the magnitude of what he did..."

At first Elchanan felt numb. But then a quiet rage began to rumble, as he mouthed the words of the morning prayers, wrapped in tallis and tefillin and silence. A roar rose from his abdomen, a roar that only he could hear, so loud, so merciless. He went through the motions of davening that morning as if on auto-pilot, sweat building beneath the black leather straps bound around his left forearm and fingers, rubbing against his skin, reacting to the inner turmoil only he was aware of. His breath turned rotten as his insides churned.

It was a flogging of a different kind.

Now, seeing the man standing by the window, Elchanan wanted to tell him about it, to reveal to him what he had done that day. Every detail of it. To be both witness and judge. Using metaphoric tweezers, he wanted—needed—to lift up the flap, carefully, and see, for the first time, *really notice*, the look on his son's face while he beat him that morning; to hear, for the first time, the hoarse screams of Greta behind him, breathless from running up the stairs with her swollen leg.

To Elchanan's relief, the man slowly nodded at him. Elchanan tilted his neck in question: *Can I come back?* The man beckoned with his free hand. Elchanan pointed to the building. The man nodded again. Elchanan walked back inside.

"Something came up?" the man asked, gesturing to Elchanan to sit back down in the seat he had just vacated.

Elchanan remained standing. He did not reply.

"Would you like to extend today's session? I could manage another few minutes."

"I...beat him." Elchanan's knees turned soft, his humiliation as strong as the violence in his anger had been then.

The man regarded him for a moment. "Okay," he nodded, slowly. "Many fathers do. How bad?"

"Doss it matter?"

Silence.

"Do you remember why you beat him?" asked the man. Elchanan was wet, cold, and uncomfortable. He shivered, but did not move. "Sit," the man half whispered. "Tell me what happened."

Elchanan burst inside the house, red-faced and furious. "Vhere is he? Vhere is Aaron? Still sleeping? I bet he is!" Flecks of his saliva shot in every direction, some settling on his beard. The front door remained open; rain and hail pelted the carpet. He saw his wife put down the kitchen phone hurriedly, her eyes wide with the confirmation she had dreaded since she'd first sniffed the air in her home that morning.

"Vhere is he? De criminal, de hooligan, de vorst of de vorst! I cannot even beleef dat I am his tatte! *Dat from me he come! Vhere is dat shtik drek?"*

Taking the stairs two at a time, he didn't even hear Greta shrieking his name. "Elchanan, no! Elchanan, stop! Don't!" His rage was too developed by then.

She trailed up behind him just as he bashed the bedroom door and found his son still in his bed, blinking as he sat up, unready and unwilling to play a role in whatever was supposed to happen.

Thwack! The first blow hit him right across his face. A flat-handed slap. Thwack! The second one matched the first in ferocity. Great big welts in the shape of Elchanan's fingers began to appear on both sides of Aaron's face. And if the blows weren't bad enough, the words that followed sealed the death of any reconciliation.

"I vish you had been never born!" Thwack, the third strike. "Oy, Tatte, Tatte!" He lifted his eyes to the ceiling. "Und I give him your name!" Thwack, the fourth. "You are not mine son. You are piece of drek! Get out! Get out foon mine house!"

"Stop it!" Greta screamed so hard, her voice cracked. "Stop hitting him!" Her fists struck the wall, the door, anything to divert her husband's attention.

Elchanan finally stopped. He straightened himself and looked down at his son. A trickle of blood slowly crept out of Aaron's right nostril. They both watched how Aaron lifted the back of his hand to wipe it off.

"Zere vill come ze day of reckoning, Aaron, and zen vat you vill say to the Ribono Shel Olam? Tell me. Vat? I vant to hear! Ehh...?"

"What happened after that?"

"I never seen mine son again."

"Did you ever try to find out why he did what he did?"

Elchanan did not respond at first. He just stared at the pictures on the wall behind where the man was sitting, and shifted in his seat. Now, he understood, was the moment to be honest. He opened his mouth and closed it again. He looked down at his hands, disgusted by what they had done, made him do; they seemed to him like foreign objects. He tried again. "At de time...I didn't tink it vas important..."

"You didn't?"

Elchanan shook his head.

"And now?"

"And now...I tink...maybe I make mistake..." Elchanan's eyes filled. How many lies we tell ourselves. Why do we do it? To live. Simply to live. He inhaled deeply and looked into the eyes of the man. There was something else he needed to say, something he had puzzled over all these years, something that frightened him so much, he had never discussed it with anyone.

"Mebbe, Mister, mebbe you tell me someting. I remember, when I hit him, it vas vith all of mine strength. I hit hard. I could have done damage. Mebbe I *did* do damage. I don't know. But here is someting: He never defend himself. He never put up his hand to save himself from my hands. Vhat kinda person do that? I never understand. I never figure out. Vhy he don't vant to save himself?

"Mebbe you tell me, eh, Mister?"

27

I t wasn't as though Sima hadn't considered this moment before; twenty years is a long time to mull. But of the myriad of visions she'd entertained over the course of the years—a wedding, a jail, a funeral—she had never pictured her reunion with Aaron to be in a hospital room. Though now it seemed the most likely of places.

Rabbi Wechter cautioned her to wait outside. She wondered why. What state was he in that she couldn't just barge in? Was he that delicate? Or was this rabbi just being overprotective? Would her sudden presence be too much for him? She felt the familiar jellying in the muscles right above her knees and, spying a chair across the hallway, she lowered herself into it.

Memories play havoc.

She'd spent years trying to tidy them up—ironing them, folding them, and putting them away—only to have them just swirl about all haphazard again.

His bar mitzvah Shabbos would have been unmemorable if not for her observing his translucent discomfort, his sheer nervousness, and the words that went unspoken between them that morning. They were both in the kitchen of their home on Ashley Grove. He was sitting quietly, looking sharp in his new, double-breasted suit and shoes that shone too much, when she had walked in. She was fifteen and a half, and life was complicated enough; she hardly even noticed him sitting there at the foot of the table. He was so quiet, he just seemed to suck in all noise around him.

It was a cold day in December, and she could still remember standing at the kitchen sink, looking out into the backyard, at the end of which, on the other side of the grim brick wall, were two very tall conker trees. She remembered how the very top of those massive branches rippled crazily in the breeze.

Then Aaron got up. She watched him fill a cup of hot water from the urn and make himself a tea. He cut off a huge piece of chocolate cake, put it onto a paper plate, and brought it back to the far end of the table where he would eat it—in solitude. The living room door must have opened, because she remembered lively chatter suddenly pouring out of there: Bubby and Zeidy were having tea and cake there, and Aunty Breeya and Uncle Zvi, and Mummy and Tatte.

"All this fuss over your thirteenth birthday," she'd said to him.

He'd just shrugged and spooned a morsel of cake, made the brachah, *and brought it to his lips. So many years later, and she still remembered how red he had turned when, at the last second, the piece had dropped onto his lap. She still remembered how he'd scowled at her, picked it up by hand, and stuffed it into his mouth, his head turned away.*

Then Tatte had walked in. "Aaron, you come now?"

Aaron had stopped chewing. "Soon," he'd replied, swallowing what was in his mouth.

"Today...your big day!" Elchanan had looked happy. "Come, soon as you can."

She remembered watching those large gray eyes as they stared at Tatte's back, never wavering even when Tatte had left the room. When he saw her staring, he'd scowled weakly, and gone back to eating his cake and tea.

Later that morning in shul, as she'd stood in the women's gallery, holding the lace partition curtain tightly against her face so she could peer through its many holes, she'd watched her brother being called to the Torah. Aunty Breeya and Bubby, together with a couple of Greta's friends, had gathered in a circle around their mother when Aaron had taken his place at the bimah. *Uncle Zvi, Aunty Breeya's husband, had placed both his hands upon Aaron's head and mouthed,* "Yevarechecha Hashem v'yishmarecha..." *From the corner of her eye, she'd seen her mother wipe her eyes with a white tissue.*

She remembered trying to find Aaron again a few minutes later, but he'd been surrounded by so many men, it wasn't possible. At one point, though, he had looked up, and she thought their eyes locked. She remembered wondering: Does he feel as lonely as he looks?

Rabbi Wechter suddenly materialized, looking unsettled. She stood up.

"He is sleeping. Do you want to stay here until he wakes up? Perhaps you should wait until morning, when both you and he are refreshed? Tell me, how long has it been since you have last seen your brother?"

"Twenty years..."

"Another night won't make or break it."

They were standing in the corridor. Brown wooden doors broke the monotony of the cream-colored walls at around ten-foot intervals, with nursing stations at both ends. The nurses were swift and economical in their rebuke: "Please move aside; find someplace else to talk."

"We cannot stay here. Perhaps...perhaps I can offer you food and a place to stay for the night? My wife does not insist on prior booking." The rabbi's small blue eyes glinted concern above his neatly-trimmed white beard.

Sima looked down the corridor again. She shook her head. "No. I need to see him now," she said, and turned toward his room.

Rabbi Wechter followed. "Don't be alarmed at his appearance." He spoke in an undertone. "The bandages over his eyes are only there for protection. He did not lose his eyesight. Perhaps don't talk. It may be too much for him to…to meet you now, after a separation of so long… I have not told him that you have come. Please…act with caution."

At the doorway Sima turned to face the rabbi, and placed her finger to her lips. "Shhh," she mouthed.

"As you wish," the rabbi murmured, head bowed.

Strong bolts of wattage ripped through her with every step she took closer to the bed. As though they were slides that had gotten stuck in a projector, her movements, it seemed to her, slowed. She took in the bandaged head, the morphine drip, the computer-display of his vitals, and she felt herself weaken. *He is smaller than I remember*, she thought. *But that's his chin, his bold jaw.*

It's Aaron.

Aaron!

At long, long last…!

She stared at him, wanting to grab him, rip off all the wires attached to him, and take him home with her. "Aaron…" she whispered, lifting her fingers and touching the bed railing. Did it just spark on contact? "Aaron, it's me, Sima…" A twitch of movement lit across the lower portion of his face. A rush of sisterly love—she had forgotten what it felt like, it had been dormant for so long—erupted within her. Tears sprang up unconsciously and fell down the sides of her face, meeting at the foot of her chin before she thought to wipe them away. "Aaron," she whispered, petrified to wake him, petrified not to. "Aaron, can you hear me? It's Sima…"

This was when he should have opened his eyes. Instead, his head shook slightly. "Wha—? Sima?" he mumbled. "Can't be…"

She took his hand. "But it is, Aaron. It is. I've found you…at last."

He became very still. A startled stillness. The very air around them suddenly became charged, and threatened them both with dissolution. Sima felt her resolve faltering. She questioned herself, and her hand loosened its hold. *Please*, she begged telepathically, *let me know I was right to come. Nothing else matters anymore, just your approval…* She looked at the rabbi standing two feet away from the foot of the bed, his arms clasped behind him, his head drooped. A clamping of her throat, like a large, gloved hand, threatened to close up her air passage. Time stood, like a tombstone, unmoving. She felt the admonishments of Aryeh and Henya brandishing her soul with scorching tar.

Suddenly there was movement in Aaron's hand. His fist tightened around hers, and she saw a smile cross his face. Relief swept through her. She had been pardoned, her presence accepted! She tightened her grasp of his hand, almost laughing, dangerously close to hysteria. Nothing existed outside of them. The world could end now, and she wouldn't even notice. She did not want this moment to stop, the next moment to begin! Not just yet. She simply wanted to grip Aaron's hand and never let go of it again...

A nurse entered the room. She was the same height as Sima. They beheld one another with something akin to curiosity. Around her striking face she wore a loose, lightweight-chiffon, gray headscarf. "Oh, *bonjour. Désolé de déranger, je dois faire ses signes...*" She directed her words at Sima.

Sima blushed and turned to the rabbi. "What was that? I speak no French whatsoever..."

"She doesn't want to disturb; she just has to take his vitals," said Rabbi Wechter.

"Oh, I can speak English, too," the nurse said to Sima, her words heavily accented. "I apologize—I did not realize you do not know French. There is no need for you to leave the room for this—you can stay."

Rabbi Wechter looked at his watch. "*I* need to leave now, though. I have a meeting soon, and I promised my wife to be home tonight for dinner. I will bring you food, Mrs. Hertzberg. No, say nothing. You must be starving!"

Sima smiled in gratitude and did not persist in her resistance.

When the nurse left, it was just the two of them. She pulled a chair closer to the bed and leaned her head toward her brother. "Aaron..." A hesitancy, so paralyzing, overcame her as she tried to cancel the last twenty years.

"Yes..."

"I don't...I don't really know what to say."

"Why say anything?"

Sima stopped herself from answering. A dialogue without words? Was that the best way to proceed? "Okay," she offered. "Then I'll just stay here next to you. Without talking. As you like..."

He smiled again, and she felt his arm relax. Time lapsed softly, with both of them—magically, it seemed to Sima—having lost the need to explain themselves. Oh, the decades were there, dangling between them. But, in his chivalrous philanthropy, her brother seemed to have dropped any charges; he was not calling for words. After all, people evolve. Nothing and no one remains the same. There would be time to talk later. For now, though, there would just be the basking...

And then: "Sima?"

"Yes?" she felt herself gush. *Ask me anything, Aaron, anything at all!*

"How did you know where to find me?"

"I was watching footage of the Paris riots on a news site," she whispered. "These sites have their uses, I guess!"

"Oh, that," he muttered, and she watched the sides of his mouth turn down.

"I want to say," she countered, "that I think you were very brave."

"Not brave, Sima," Aaron corrected her. "Just angry."

Sima found herself nodding, not only at her own unproductive anger over a political situation that had gone on all her life and that looked endlessly hopeless, but also in acknowledgment of her brother's anger—an anger that had, in the past, provoked him to act in ways beyond the pale of acceptance, bringing grief to both him and all who loved him. Was his anger still a haunting presence? Or had he, perhaps, found something into which it could be channeled? After all, was he not trying to save lives...?

Silence took over again. Sima watched Aaron's chest rise and fall, slowly, restfully. He appeared to have fallen asleep.

She placed both of her hands around the back of her neck and pressed deeply, stretching her head from side to side, feeling the muscles pull free of their tight cramping. It always happened to her when she was stressed; her neck muscles and shoulders would stiffen. There was so much she wanted—needed—to say. Most important of all, Aaron *had* to come home. Now that he was "found," the game was up, essentially, wasn't it?

But this is Aaron we are dealing with, she told herself, as her own eyes began to droop. *He will have his own take. I'll have to be careful.*

Oh, so very careful.

When she awoke, it was getting dark outside. She washed her hands and sat back down. The nurse had returned and was positioning herself to begin the evening meal process with Aaron. Each mouthful was carefully arranged on the spoon and handed to the temporarily blinded patient for him to control. It might have been humiliating, had the nurse's manner not been so soft and pleasant. Sima silently congratulated her for a difficult enterprise executed with such grace, while at the same time her stomach turned to watch the ease with which her brother chewed the non-kosher meat. *Has he abandoned everything?!*

"Mrs. Hertzberg?" She startled at the call of her name. She looked up. Rabbi Wechter had returned. "I have some food for you." He handed her a small package.

She smiled gratefully. "Thank you! I really appreciate this." She proceeded to open the bag and examine its contents: a corned-beef sandwich with mustard and pickles, wrapped in paper towels and covered in aluminum foil; a plastic container of coleslaw; a bottle of mineral water; a peach; and two cookies. The heady scent emanating from the meal made her realize how desperately hungry she was. Salivating, she got up to wash her hands.

"And you'll come back home with me, okay?" said the rabbi. "My wife insists that you stay with us tonight. There will be *shalom bayis* problems if I return without you!"

Sima made the *brachah*, took her first bite of the sandwich, swallowed, and then said, "Yes. I will come. Thank you again."

"And for you, Aaron, I also have news..."

Aaron turned his head to face the general direction of where the rabbi stood. He did not say anything but waited for Rabbi Wechter to continue.

"When I was home, I received a call from France 2—you know, the French national television channel," the rabbi said and then paused, as though waiting for the significance of that information to register. Nothing. "They want to interview you."

"No!" snapped Aaron.

Both of Rabbi Wechter's white eyebrows jumped up. "I might have known that would be your answer, but perhaps think about it first. You—"

"Nothing to think about, Rabbi," Aaron interrupted, his hand up. "The answer is no."

Rabbi Wechter swung a glance at Sima, who had stopped eating. He tipped his head toward her, and then turned back. "First hear me out, Aaron. I think that much I can ask from you." He waited.

"Go ahead, then," said Aaron, his reluctance palpable.

"No one needs to know who you are. You can stay right here, in this bed; they can come to a hospital room. You're all bandaged up anyway. Incidentally, the nurses told me that the bandages are coming off tomorrow afternoon, but France 2 wants to come in the morning. You can give a fake name, or just be known as the 'Jewish defender' who got hurt. Look, I think it's great that they are even willing to air something from our side of this mess. I think you could do a lot of good for Israel. All you'd need to do is answer their questions—that's it. You did *nothing* wrong, Aaron. *Nothing!* You don't need to justify anything. Just answer the questions and tell the truth."

The words hung in the air.

"Will you be there?" Aaron said, after a while.

"If you want me there, sure."

Aaron turned to Sima. "And you?"

"I can sit in the background, if you'd like."

The stillness that governed the room returned. For a long moment, only the sounds of the food tray being taken away, the clink of dishes and cutlery against each other, and the squeaking of the food cart's wheels as it left the room, could be heard.

"Aaron..." Sima hesitated. "Remember you had a teacher you liked, years ago...? He told Tatte something about you being destined for greatness. Remember?"

Aaron smiled. "Rabbi Gold. Rabbi Yona Gold. Nice guy. Whatever happened to him?"

"I believe he is still there in the school. Anyway, maybe *this* was what he meant. Maybe this act that you did—that you might think of as irrational—maybe this was the greatness he was predicting."

Aaron laughed.

"I mean it, Aaron. Defender of the Jewish people...it's a very special thing."

He lifted his hand and tried to scratch his temple, beneath the bandage. "When do I have to answer?"

"As soon as possible," said Rabbi Wechter. "They want to send their team down tomorrow morning, around nine." The rabbi's teeth gleamed white in the soft lighting.

"Okay. I'll do it. But you," Aaron turned his head toward both of them, "both of you had better be there. Remember, I don't know as much about the Israeli-Palestinian conflict as you do."

"Aaron, what you know is precious. Our relationship would never have come about if not for what happened with the Stern family, may they rest in peace."

Sima looked up, surprised. "You don't know each other? You're not Aaron's rabbi? How long have you known him?"

"Not long. And no, I am not your brother's rabbi. Though perhaps," he grinned, "I am the closest thing to that. But come, it's late. You both need to sleep now. There will be plenty of action tomorrow. *Au revoir,* my friend. Mrs. Hertzberg, I'll be waiting for you downstairs in the lobby, whenever you're ready."

The rabbi left the room, but Sima stayed behind. She crouched close to Aaron's ear and whispered, "I've brought something for you, Aaron."

"What?"

"I have a letter..."

"From?"

"From Tatte."

Silence.

She waited.

Finally he spoke. "Tell me about it tomorrow, when I get my eyes back."

Now it was her turn to grin. "Yes," she said. "Perfect. Tomorrow." And with that she skittered out of the room.

28

They did not talk again until they were both sitting in the same black car that Sima had been driven in earlier, the one from which she'd first seen the rabbi coming out of on Campagne de Blocage. The driver nodded to Sima, as though he had expected her to be with his employer, and that none of this was unusual.

"They took away my driver's license," the rabbi said to her in explanation, from the front passenger seat. "I have had a few heart issues." He turned to the driver. "Home, please," he said in French.

Paris in the night can be beautiful, Sima thought as she stared out the window. She was a long way from Long Island, both in body and spirit...especially in spirit. Was she really the wife of Aryeh Hertzberg, mother of five daughters, social worker at an elementary school? Right now, it seemed to her that she was Aaron's sister, and nothing else. All the little, and not-so-little, details that made her who she was, seemed to shrink to obscurity here in Paris, with its lit-up, curvy streets, antiquated buildings, cobblestoned pedestrian walkways, and hanging plants...*everywhere*. It was as though everything was conspiring together to make her forget all else. *No wonder people come here to distract themselves*, she mused. *Life can be a burdensome thing, but one stint here, and you can actually make yourself believe all is well!*

"Tell me about Aaron," Rabbi Wechter said, interrupting her thoughts. He turned to face her.

"What do you want to know?"

"Tell me whatever springs to mind."

Whatever springs to mind... In her mind's eye, she saw her brother, now a teenager, growing more and more sullen. Turning his anger inward. Why hadn't she tried harder to reach him? To be more of a close sister to him? Her heart felt heavy when she saw him through her social worker's eyes. She had so perfected her avoidance of thinking about Aaron, having had ample time to turn it into a craft, laboriously fashioning it into the only justified option. Now she cried out from inside the vacuum of her own mind: *He was just a lost little boy! Impulsive. Yeah. Given to an explosion now and then. Was that so very, very bad?! He was just a young, misunderstood kid, trying to navigate his way through the labyrinth into which he was placed. I see these kinds of kids every day. I could have cured him...maybe. At least helped him out...*

But what was I then? Just a child myself...

Sima wanted to blame her father; she'd done that for much of her life, though it brought her little satisfaction. *Tatte knew nothing of childhood, its rites of passage, its stumbling blocks, its innocent mistakes... He never understood how to use failings as a mechanism for growth. To him, every failure meant descent; every mistake meant eternal rejection; every stumble attested to his only son's intrinsic flaws. Perhaps he saw in his son the worst of his fears, incarnate—walking, talking, breathing in oxygen. For Elchanan, Aaron should have been born a man, fully formed. Never just a boy.*

Oh, Tatte! Aaron could have been so much more, if only you would have let him! If only you had spared him your condemnations. If only you would have held your tongue, Aaron could have risen above all your dire predictions.

"Okay," she finally said, breaking free of her thoughts. "But first, tell me, why is it important to you?"

The rabbi looked quizzically at her. "It is important because... because Aaron is important."

"Are you also a therapist?"

"Oh, no!" The rabbi laughed and slapped his thigh. "Just a simple rabbi, who tries to help people find their way. Aaron is lost. Has been for some time."

"Too much time?"

"Pah!" A few drops of spittle flew from his mouth; one rested on the top of his seat. "Never. Surely you know that. But—it will take time. Now, tell me what you remember about your brother from twenty years ago."

"He was...he didn't...he...couldn't adjust. He just couldn't figure out how to be in the society into which we were born."

"And you? Did you figure it out?"

"I was a girl."

"I'm sorry. I don't understand."

"The girls had it easier, I think. To be considered a 'good' girl was easier than a 'good' boy. When we were growing up, where we lived, it was like a culture of put-downs, where the kids emotionally killed one another. My father and the teachers were not trained to teach sensitivity. They themselves did not have it in them. I have a theory..." She let her voice taper off.

"Go on. Why did you stop?"

"Sorry. I haven't shared this with anyone yet. It has been on my mind recently, but I don't know if I have the words to explain it."

"Try."

"Okay. My theory is that the teachers—or adults in general—of our coming-of-age generation, had needed to steel themselves against their own harsh emotions in order to survive their awful childhoods. You know, the Holocaust, the rise of Communism, deprivation, displacement and perpetual fear... So because they never processed their own emotional experiences, but rather shoved them away, when it came time to raise the next generation, they simply didn't have the tools to do it properly. Aaron, and others like him, got swallowed up..."

"So they cut something out of themselves, something integral, and then, when they needed it, they could not find it. Is that what you are saying?"

"Yes, I think so. That's about it."

"Hmmm…"

"Please. I-I don't know that I am right. It's just a theory."

Rabbi Wechter nodded and turned back around.

A few minutes passed before Sima spoke again. "I apologize. I don't mean to sound so irritable. It's been a long day."

Rabbi Wechter smiled. "No need to apologize."

The driver stopped the car in front of Rabbi Wechter's home. They got out, and Rabbi Wechter opened the gate. "You know, this 'culture of put-downs' you speak of…this is not the Torah's way," he remarked, as she walked through the arch.

"Oh, I *know*. I *know* this very well. It is *not* the Torah's way at *all*. But…for some odd reason that I cannot explain…it *was* the way in our little corner of London."

A aron eyes the bag of candy. He scrutinizes the height of the uppermost shelf from where he sees the brightly colored corner of its packaging. He calculates the measurement of different pieces of furniture that might be useful: the blue table, the yellow chair, the orange crayon box. Now, while everyone is playing and his teachers are distracted, he needs to maneuver the base: the blue table. Bit by bit, inch by inch, Aaron pushes the table so that it is parallel to the red painted shelves in the corner of the large nursery classroom.

As a little preschooler, he is already making his own way.

Table in place, he needs to bring the yellow chair, quietly, toward it. He wants only the yellow chair. He likes it. It is a heavy chair, made of wood, and it feels like his *zeida*: old, warm, and dependable. Not like the new chairs made of resin and metal. He schleps the chair along the classroom floor and heaves it over the top of the table. He stands on the table and looks around. Everyone is busy with something, and no one has noticed him. The teachers are chatting excitedly amongst themselves. Good. Things are going according to plan.

Now he manipulates the chair into the center of the table, a little to the right, so it is close to the shelves...and its stash of goodies. He climbs onto the chair, reaches, and flails his hand. No. Not tall enough yet. He needs the orange crayon box. That will give him the necessary altitude.

He climbs down from the chair and then from the table. He looks around and spies the orange wooden box that is speckled all over with colored wax. It is on the floor, surrounded by nursery children in the midst of discovering their artistic flair. He runs over to them and empties the crayons onto the floor. The children squeal with delight at the pleasure of having all the colors now easily available to them. He hugs the empty box and brings it to his construction site.

He puts the orange box onto the blue table, and once again he climbs. He places the waxy, flecked orange box onto the yellow chair and begins to mount it. This time, in his excitement, he does not notice that in the teacher's corner, the chatter has died down. Three pairs of adult eyes are now watching as Aaron stands on the orange box, reaches out his hand, and clasps the bag of candy. Triumphant, Aaron turns, leaping from the box on the chair to the table, and then, in a flourish, his face red, he bounces and tumbles onto the floor. At first the grown-ups in the room hold their breaths for him, but when he stands up, holding his cache and running to the furthest corner of the room with it, one of them swoops down and picks him up, his legs still running in mid-air. Large, muscular arms carry him to the teacher's corner: the worst of all possible places.

"Aaron Bulman! What. In the world. Are you DOING?!" Her face is twisted, her breath on him, her scowl so large he thinks she will eat him.

He does not respond, but his hand tightens its grip on the bag of candies, and that tightening makes a crinkling sound.

"Aha! So that is what it is all about!" She snatches the bag out of his hold.

The room has become quiet. The children stop what they are doing and look up. Teacher is holding Aaron Bulman. Teacher is angry. Teacher is holding a bag of candy. What will happen to Aaron Bulman? Will he get spanked? Will he have to sit in the corner 'til the end of the day?

"Thief!" she cries, in a pitch too high to bear. "That is what you are! Aaron Bulman! A little thief! And, if you don't watch out, that is what you will grow up to be!"

AARON:

S o this is what it has all come to.
　　Sima.
　　Here.

Standing before me, in the flesh.

Why had I never even entertained the possibility? Was I thinking that my hiding from my past could go on endlessly?

Did I get any warning from Yisrael about news sites' footage? Surely he would have sent a text to alert me. When these bandages come off, I must check my phone. First thing. Maybe one of nurses could check for me. Or perhaps he simply didn't see this footage.

"Zere vill come ze day of reckoning, Aaron, and zen vat you vill say to the Ribono Shel Olam? Tell me. Vat? I vant to hear! Ehh…?"

I don't know, Tatte.

I have never known.

One day passes, then another, and another. All meaningless. There is only nothingness, drifting toward more nothingness. This darkness that I have to weather right now…it does not even bother me. This darkness is…soothing. Yes. That is what it is. Soothing. It absolves me. But tomorrow I will see again.

Tomorrow I will see how the years have treated my sister.

I wonder what I will feel...

And the letter!

Tomorrow I will have my first contact with my father in twenty years. I will read the letter he wrote to me. What a round number: twenty. It's almost as though this was planned. As though it's a plot point in a novel. I wonder what Tatte wrote. I am curious. When was it written? How long has it been since he passed on, to the Next World—to Olam Haba, *as I called it in my youth—to rejoin his father, and his father's father, and all those magical people who trod the planet before me? I hope Tatte is happy, for what would be the point if he isn't?*

I wonder...is any of the old anger left inside me? It's been there so long, it may have stopped hurting. For so long it just sat there, like an overly large pet, sleeping in front of the fireplace. Just there, shedding its hairs. Every so often getting up, letting me know it needed to be fed.

And I have allowed for this.

But if I ever turned the anger on myself, I never would have survived; it would be like a drowning man who has, by his own foolishness, caused his own drowning.

And now they need my help.

To do something heroic.

For those people...who have hurt me.

And whom I have hurt.

Can the past be remade? Can forgiveness ever be more than mere hope? When they called me a thief, I batted my eyes; but when they called me a murderer, something broke inside me. I remember the sound of my inner self shattering, the ping-ping of crystalline particles falling in my core, the prickly shards of my soul as my footsteps trudged on and waited for the restitution of my person in the form of Arkady's hospital discharge.

And how, pray tell, was I to know that Arkady had been sleeping in the room above Rabbi Isaacs's office?! Please, can someone tell me, how was I to know? And how was I to know the flammability of the carpet in that room? And how was I to know how quickly one can die of smoke inhalation? How in the world was I supposed to know?

SUMMER, 1995
LONDON, ENGLAND

ELCHANAN:

O*y voy voy!*
     Noon? Already? Day iz going fast. Very fast. Must get up and daven. Tell to G-tt mine sorrows. Pour them out. Oy, Aaron, Arele, mine zun! If only I could turn the time backvards! If I could, I vould. Mebbe do it over, better. I vould. Anytink to take avay zis feeling. I tought dat tings vere bad back in Soviet Union. But compares to zis, dat vas notink. Unt vhy? Becoz I do zis to mineself. Zat iz vhy. No NKVD did zis to me. I done zis to me. Unt now I cannot live no more. Oy voy voy!

     I can still see mine tatte. He still alive inside me. No one, not even mine Greta, can share dis picture viz me. Vhen he vas taken. Vhat he says to me: "Elchanan, you de man now. Learn Torah. Keep de mitzvos. Take care of your mama." Unt I try to listen. I try all my life to listen. It vas difficult. Yes. But at least I try. I took care of Mama ven she had de baby. She vas sick, and de baby, a little girl, she not breazing ven she born, so I bury her, by de brook, near to de birch trees. I put stone dere, a big von, to mark it. Mama and I, ve go dere every year on de yahrtzeit of vhen she born and die. Ve pray dere.

     I should go back. See if it still dere. Before I die, I should go visit von more time. Mebbe I daven dere for mine Arele.

Mebbe it vill help.

Oy, I remember de vay Mama very sick. All de rest of her life, she very sick. I vork, I run errands, I make little of money—and all goes on de doctors. All de monies I make, I give to de doctors. I vant to live, and I vant Mama to live, but Mama don't vant to live. She don't care. She eat little, but I make good foods for her. But still she eat little. Ven I'm grown, I says to mineself, I vill leave Soviet Union. Vhen I'm grown.

Oy, zis feeling. It is not good. Mine chest. It is not good. I know zis feeling already. I had it before, many, many years before. It vas after Mama die. Mebbe I could have saved her. Mebbe I could have brought better doctor. But he charge. Oy voy voy, vhat he charge! Too much. So Mama die. Dat is first time I have zis feeling. Like mine chest is rock-hard. Like de pavement. It is not good.

Mebbe I gonna die.

Vhen I coming to England, vhen I meeting my Greta, vhen ve getting married, all zis feeling is going away. I can breaze again. I can svallow big. Arele, you don't know notink. Vhat I tell you, you don't know notink. Vhen you born, you make us happy. Mine Greta, she happy. Now ve have one of each. Sima'leh unt Arele, a girl unt a boy. Ve so happy. For first time in my life, since I'm six years old, I feel complete.

But Arele, you is making trouble. From vhen you small, you is making trouble. Always in de trouble. Always the principal is calling Mummy, he telling Mummy vat you did. He saying you breaking vindow, he saying you stab Lerner boy lung, he saying you not sitting properly. Mummy complaining to me. I don't know vhat to do. I don't understand. Vhy you break vindow? Vhy you stick needle into Lerner boy lung? I don' understand. Arele, tell me, you can't sit? Here, I show you how to sit. I show you. Here. You sit. Like zis. Sit. Good. Now come here. Come here, Arele. Come right here, 'cuz I need to give you a frask across your face...

Oy voy voy!

Oy, zis feeling. It is very bad. I need to get up, outta bed, unt I need to go downstairs, unt I need to daven. I need to pour out zis feeling from inside, so I can breaze again. Vhy I am vanting to breaze again, I do not know, but I don't vant to be like Mama. I vant to still live.

Vhy?

I cannot answer zis qvestion.

Mebbe because I still have Sima and little Henitchka. She my sveetie. Vhat a vonderful child. Sima is also, but not like Henitchka. No. Sima is serious. Always vatching. Always she is tinking. I vonder vhat she is tinking.

The day. It is moving fast. I must go down.

Here, let me take out my tefillin. I bring the black box to my lips. My G-tt, His vords are inside de black box. "Hear O Israel, de L-rd is our G-tt, de L-rd is Von." Yes, He is von, but not all Israel vants to hear dat. Not all. Not mine Arele. He don't vanna hear.

Oy, Arele, vhere are you?

Ze day. It goin' avay. I need to pray. For you, Arele, unt for me. I vant to breaze again. Not de kind of air dat has smoke in it. Clean air. Not smoky air. Five months I been breazing smoky air. I valk into your room, I smell your bed. Smoke. I touch your clothes. Smoke. I open de curtains. Smoke. De air. It is tick vit it. Vhy you do it, Aaron? Vhy? Do you know Rabbi Isaacs don't look at me no more? He pass me in shul—notink. I am shamed. Unt Arkady? He back, but he looking terrible, Arele. Terrible. Unt he cough, a lot. Unt peoples saying iz your fault.

Everyvon suddenly interested in Arkady.

Making me sick!

I tying de black straps round my arm. I looking at my arm. It did bad tinks, sometimes. It hit. It shouldn't have done zis. It is a strong arm. Stronger dan I vanted. Mebbe, if I vas veaker, mebbe my arm vould not have hurt you so much. Vhy did you do so much troubles vhen you younger, and den you so qviet vhen you is older? I don't understand. You not like me. Not like me at all. Vhen you is born, I say, zis is my son. I have son, who vill be like me. I love Hashem, my son vill love Hashem. I can be righteous. My son vill grow straight and be righteous. And he vill be even better dan me. He vill learn Torah. He vill not be unlearned like me. Shhhhhh.

Shhhhhhhhh.

Oy voy voy!

A t first it was just soft knocking, with long pauses. Then it stopped altogether. Then it came again, a tentative forcefulness.

Must I wake up? Sima thought. *Already?* Sleep dragged her back to its safety and warmth.

The knocking came again. A female voice, with a sweet, French accent, whispered, "Sima, Sima... It iz alrrready seven sirty... You must wake up now, my dear, if you want to be on time for ze interview..."

Sima bolted upright, eyes wide open, her whole body tingling. "Coming!" she called. "Thank you for waking me."

She looked about her. The bedclothes matched the wallpaper—both were white satin, dotted with small bunches of lilacs. The quilt gave off a powerful, floral fabric-softener scent. She had been too tired to notice these pleasant details when the rabbi's wife had shown her to her room last night.

Mechanically, she mumbled the *Modeh Ani* prayer, before throwing on her robe and stumbling into the nearby bathroom to wash her hands.

It came to her while she was brushing her teeth: Today they would read the letter! Today, after the interview. *I must find the right moment for it. Oh, please help me, Hashem!*

It was almost eight when Sima emerged, as ready as she would ever be to take on the day. Madame Wechter pressed a package of food into her hand before escorting her to the staircase. "Zere be time later, I hope, to know you betterrr," she said. "For now, zis help you. My blessings to you, sweet one."

Rabbi Wechter was waiting outside for her. "I trust you slept well, Mrs. Hertzberg?"

She nodded and rewarded him with a small smile before getting into the car.

When she entered her brother's room, she inhaled his tension; his body was stiff as a corpse. *How rotten of us to do this to him*, she thought. *But it seems there is no choice.* Poor Aaron. His large jaw was so white, his vulnerability displayed in a way that would shame him if he knew.

The same nurse from the day before was opening the curtains and chatting with him amiably in French. Sima walked over to the window to help her. She was grateful to this nurse who seemed to sense Aaron's discomfort, teasing and coaxing until she got a smile out of him, even a chuckle.

Sima peered down onto the street below. How different the streets of Paris were, compared to, say, London, or New York, or anywhere else she knew. Narrower. Darker. More angular. In contrast, the room looked brighter than it had the day before. A fresh bouquet of light-pink roses had been strategically placed on the night table, together with a clear water pitcher and a few plastic cups.

"Good morning, Aaron," she called to him, quietly celebrating that she could wish her brother a simple morning salutation. She walked to his bed and bent near his ear. "Ready?"

"No."

"I want you to know how utterly brave I think you are," she added in a whisper. "You don't have to do this, you know."

Rabbi Wechter glared at her, white eyebrows meeting in the center of his forehead.

Aaron gave her a tepid smile. "I think it's too late to back down now. Is Rabbi Wechter here?"

"Ahem, indeed. How can I help?" The rabbi pulled a chair close to the bed.

"I was thinking, through the night, to simply say it as I see it. No embellishments. But if I don't come across articulate enough, Rabbi, you might have to jump in and speak for me. You owe me that much. I never wanted to do this."

Rabbi Wechter blinked. "Aaron! Of course! I will be sitting right here, by your bed, and will speak for you if and when the need arises. That has always been the plan." The doorway became dark. "I think they are here," he said in a low voice.

Three casually dressed men ambled in, pulling filming gear on wheels. Behind them strutted a dapper couple, he in a dark gray, skinny-fitted suit; she in a scarlet sheath dress, with lipstick of a matching shade, and white-blonde hair, waved to perfection.

Sima backed into the space between the night table and window and observed first the female interviewer. She could not read her. The look on her face was calm, even happy. She laughed easily. But when her face was at rest, she looked hardened. Her eyes were golden brown, with flecks of sun darting from them, yet they did not give off any warmth.

The male interviewer was not as dashing up close as when he had first entered. In fact, his face was a tad odd, Sima thought, with a forehead that jutted out ahead of the rest of him, giving him a more solemn intensity.

She glanced at her own reflection in the window. She was wearing a simple, light-blue, A-line dress with a blue and yellow flowery-print scarf for sparkle. Not exactly spar-worthy. Her wig needed freshening up, too. When she had put it on earlier that morning, she could smell the sea on it from the day before. It was not an unpleasant scent, but the salt had left the hairs less than soft. She ran her fingers through the strands, trying to put more life into them, but eventually gave up and went back to watching the scene around her.

Everyone spoke in rapid French. Sima could not understand much. Occasionally the rabbi intervened, but Aaron did not contribute a word.

By 9:45 a.m. the chairs were arranged, the cameras set up, and everyone knew their place. It was decided, much to Sima's relief, that the entire interview be conducted in English. For Aaron's sake. The editors would decide later whether or not to add simultaneous translation. Finally satisfied, the lead cameraman hit "start."

"Good morning, viewers. Here we are, in the American Hospital of Paris, where a man is recovering from being struck on his head during the riots outside the synagogue at Campagne de Blocage this past Sunday." The woman smiled brightly as she spoke to the first camera. Sima was surprised at how negligible her accent was.

"There has been considerable unrest in the Arab community here in France over the conflict that rages in Gaza. Many Palestinian sympathizers feel that Israel is responding with excessive aggression that, they say, is not consistent with its need to protect its citizens. With us today is Rabbi Wechter, spiritual leader of the congregation of the Kedushat Tzion synagogue. Good morning to you both. We thank you for speaking with us today."

"Good morning," answered Rabbi Wechter. Aaron merely nodded.

"So, I will be directing my questions to the patient first. Is that okay?"

Another nod was all Aaron gave.

"Can you tell us what you remember of the incident during which you were attacked?"

"Well, I..." Aaron cleared his throat. "At first...I...didn't really believe what I was witnessing. That what I was seeing was actually happening. It didn't seem real at all."

"Can you describe, for our viewers, what you witnessed?"

Aaron turned his face in the direction of the rabbi. "It was a...a mob. Mostly young people. Riled up to the point of violence. And hateful. I...I think it was the hatred of the mob that was the most shocking thing, really. That level of hatred, from one human toward another. It's so shocking, you know, when it hits you like that—square in the face." Sima was relieved to see that Aaron had stopped stumbling over his words. "They don't know me, say, or the rabbi over here, yet their hatred toward us was absolute." Less hesitation, she noted. *Good for him.*

"It's not the same as when you read about it, or watch little clips. When you're in it, it's completely different. It's...it's shocking."

The man took his turn to speak. He and his partner seemed comfortable with one another, well-oiled, slipping in and out of the conversation in perfect tandem. "Did you feel a palpable danger? Was there any time that you feared for your life?" Again, Sima noted the lack of an accent. *These reporters must have studied in the States,* she speculated.

"No. Maybe I should have, but I never gave it a thought. It was all just...it was just so shocking. I was making...I guess...split-second decisions. There was no time for assessing my situation."

The woman stifled a grin. "Was it the 'shock' that provoked you to do what you did?"

"What do you mean?"

"We were told you charged at the militants with a metal chair. What were you trying to achieve?"

"Achieve?" For the first time, Aaron looked confused, and within his confusion, Sima perceived misbegotten culpability. Something crumpled inside her. "Nothing," he answered. "I didn't consider that I was going to achieve anything. I just became...angry. Really, really angry."

"Angry? Could you elaborate?" The male interviewer shifted in his seat.

"Well...that here, in Paris, a place far removed from the conflict, people should behave this way. And for what? What would have been gained? It all seems senseless to me. Senseless violence."

"Yes. I understand. Was there a particular point that caused you to behave in the way that you did? That made you feel so angry?"

"It was...chaos. Frightening. There were so many of these rioters. And they had crude weapons. An axe. Homemade firebombs. They were throwing whatever they could. Garbage bins. Chairs..." Aaron smiled. "I had never seen such behavior. Not up close like that. Never. Also..." Aaron stopped talking.

"Go on," said the woman.

"Well, it was also shocking...to see...how...how everyone inside the synagogue was...cowering. There was fear, real fear there. It was... appalling to me. It got to me, I guess." Aaron shrugged. "When I got out of the building, there was a group of young defenders, Jews, standing around. It all happened very quickly. It is hard to put into words... the hatred, I guess. Something snapped, especially when I heard the chanting. You know, what they always chant: 'Death to the Jews!'"

"So you rushed at them?"

"Yes."

"And what happened next?"

"I must have gotten hit. I don't remember. I just woke up here."

"He is our hero," the rabbi volunteered.

"Oh, I wouldn't say that," Aaron protested. "What did I accomplish? Nothing really."

"But as I understand, you went after them. Is that not accurate?" asked the woman interviewer.

"Yes. That is correct. Because of what I was witnessing—the old hatred. I never thought I would come so close to it. These people, the ones inside the synagogue, had no intention of hurting anyone. They were gathered for prayer. The pro-Palestinians were attacking them. I was merely defending who I consider to be innocents."

"But look at what is happening in Gaza. Israel is not innocent of the deaths of hundreds of civilians. No?" It was the woman again.

Sima stiffened. Aaron opened his mouth to speak, but closed it again. Sima started to perspire. She silently begged Rabbi Wechter to intervene.

"Look, I am a Jew," the rabbi spoke at last, "and no, we are not about to commit suicide just for the convenience of some people."

The woman turned to him, her features hardening. "What's that? What is it you are saying?"

"Let me say this: Israel does not like what Hamas forces it to do. On the other hand, if we were to allow them to continue—without defending our borders—it would be national suicide. Every war waged in Israel has been foisted upon us. We have *always* been unwilling combatants. And no, we will not go quietly into the dark night..."

The woman regarded Rabbi Wechter dispassionately. Sima nearly stopped breathing, aghast at how quickly a simple interview could turn into a political tirade. She chided herself for putting Aaron through this. *He doesn't need this now!*

"But what about the slain children?" the female interviewer continued. "What about Israel's relentless shelling of hospitals, schools, places of worship? This is what the demonstrators are protesting. This is what makes Israel unpopular."

"Of course. I understand. But that is exactly the way Hamas wants to play it. Every time the media gets hold of a picture of a dead baby, Hamas rejoices—while Israel mourns. Hamas can, once again, count on the people of the world to pressure the Israeli government to stop defending its own citizens."

"Against children?" the woman almost spat.

Rabbi Wechter stopped speaking. He folded his arms, pulling lightly at the lower hairs of his beard.

The male interviewer switched his seating position to better face him. "Rabbi, every nation has its own narrative. The Jews and the Palestinians, too. It is hard for many people to come to terms with what Israel chooses to do. My colleague here cannot sit quietly while children are being slaughtered."

The rabbi slowly nodded his head. "Neither can I. It is a painful story. But often times, I am sorry to say, facts distort truth."

"Huh?"

"What we read as facts, in the air, has nothing to do with the truth, on the ground."

Sima watched as two cameramen eyed one another. Helplessness, like a poisonous gas, crept into the room, slowly, silently, taking over the air. Aaron was as quiet and as white as the sheets he lay on.

"Facts like the number of Palestinian children dead by Israeli fire? Is that what you mean by facts? Let me read to you some of the facts, Rabbi." The woman lifted a notebook Sima hadn't noticed she was carrying, and began to read: "In Gaza, 1,320 sites struck; 167 dead, and 1,000 injured. In northern Gaza, 35,000 people left without a home; that's twenty-five percent of one town in that region. Those were the figures up until this past Sunday. Then, on Sunday itself, Israeli missiles killed nine youths and injured another fifteen while they were at a beach café in Khan Younis. These are just some of the facts. On the ground."

The rabbi did not speak. He just shook his head slowly, eyes lowered.

"But you said it, yourself!" Everyone turned back to face Aaron. "You just said it yourself: 'These are *some* of the facts.' Didn't you just say that? 'Some of the facts'? Aren't you missing out a whole lot of *other* facts?"

"Don't bother, Aaron!" called out Rabbi Wechter. "Don't bother. I'm so sorry I got you into this. We should never have agreed to do this interview. These people do not want the truth. They want *their* truth. There is no room for the real truth here."

"No!" yelled Aaron. "I'm gonna speak the real truth anyway! We never wanted this war. We exercised every restraint possible. When the Stern family showed up dead, what exactly did you want Israel to do? Be sitting ducks, that's what!"

The rabbi stood up. "Let me say this, for the record: In the media, the terrible gap between the number of Gazan deaths, as opposed to Israeli ones, is presented as disproportionate use of aggression, entirely ignoring the fact that Hamas puts *their* citizens intentionally in the line of fire, while Israel has poured its resources into defending its people. Now, if you don't mind, this interview is over."

Just then, the hijab-wearing nurse rushed into the room, followed by a doctor. "This interview has to stop immediately. It is not good for the patient!" the nurse called out in French. Her hands and the sides of her mouth were shaking, Sima noticed. She wondered why.

Sima watched as the cameramen exchanged words she did not need to understand. If she could slow down time, she thought, it might be possible to process how it felt to be hated. All she could feel at that moment was an incredibly blinding fear. And regret, that she had had a hand in making Aaron take part in this. Afterward, she would describe what it was like to be in that room, with all that animosity and rancor, so beautifully packaged in scarlet and gray: like a banquet of manure.

"Are you ever coming down?" Aryeh called up from the bottom of the stairs. "It's past ten, and your appointment is in less than an hour. Don't you *believe* in breakfast?" He tried to disguise his concern by inserting irritation in his voice—a mask upon another mask. Then he remembered the thrust of her complaints from the night before, and decided on a different approach. "Tamar." His tone softened. "Please come down so we can talk..."

Tamar appeared on the landing, her hair wet and straggly. She was wearing an old denim skirt and a loose pink top that was growing patches of wetness along the shoulders. On her feet were her fluffy, pink winter Crocs.

"So?" she said, as she came down the stairs, never taking her eyes off him. "Are you going to tell me what I need to do with my life?"

"Huh? No, of course not." He smiled at her, attempting to sound casual. "I just want to make sure you eat something today. And..."

"Yes?"

"Maybe we can talk more...about the things that are bothering you. About the things you brought up last night. I've been thinking... Maybe you are old enough to hear the truth." They walked into the kitchen together, both of them averting their eyes but sensing the other to the point of awkward. He turned, and her eyes flickered; she washed her hands, and he threw a towel over her shoulder; he opened the refrigerator, and she moseyed toward it.

Aryeh poured himself some coffee. "You want some?"

"Okay. Thanks."

He poured her a mug. "Did you sleep well?"

"I'm all stuffed up," she answered, between sips. "It's hard to sleep when you can't breathe through your nose."

"Yeah. I know the feeling." He sat down in his usual place at the head of the table. In front of him was toast, cream cheese, and half a chocolate Danish from two days ago that he couldn't bring himself to chuck. He pushed the Danish toward her. "Here. Eat something. How long have you been on antibiotics?"

"Since yesterday. I'm feeling a little better, but..."

He waited. "But what?"

She looked at him, throwing him a relaxed smile. "It's just...nice. I mean...to be home. Right now. 'Cuz it's so quiet. Just us. So open and empty and relaxing." She looked around her mother's kitchen that no longer gleamed. "See?" She pointed to a patch of cereal morsels left on the table. "Look! Crumbs! So unclean, it's practically *whole*some!" She chuckled to herself. "It's just nice to be here without..." She looked at him, catching his eyes staring back. "It's like, there's no pressure to be, or do, or become... Know what I mean?"

Aryeh nodded. "I think I do. Believe it or not, I think I know what you mean."

Tamar pulled at the chocolate Danish; it crumbled in her fingers. "So...when is she coming home?"

"I wish I knew." He was so matter-of-fact, it stunned her.

"What do you mean? You don't *know*?" Her surprise reassured him; at least she knew theirs was a good marriage. Then her eyes narrowed. "Are you keeping something from me, Abba?"

"Nope. I wish that were the case. But it's true; I don't know when Mommy is coming home." He smiled at how she was squinting her eyes to process what he was saying, enjoying that this nugget of information was being received badly. Then he added, "She has an open ticket. And I haven't heard from her since Monday."

"*O.M.G.* Abba! That is so *unlike* you. So unlike the *two* of you!"

"Hmmm, and that's a good thing, right?"

"Yes." She smiled uncertainly. "I guess so. It's just that...you and Mommy never acted like this before. Is...is everything okay with the two of you...?"

He grinned inwardly. "Yes, Tamar. Things are terrific between us, *baruch Hashem*. It's just that some stuff needs to be taken care of by a person alone. Mommy needs a bit of time for herself now; she has some things going on that she'd like to work out on her own. And I respect that. I want to give her the space she needs. I don't want to be in the way."

"So...you're not angry with her?" She kept her eyes on the Danish.

"No, not at all. Though of course I miss her, and I would love to hear from her already."

Tamar turned her attention to buttering her toast. No words were spoken for a few minutes.

She began to nibble. "So..." she tried again, not looking up, "are we going to discuss it?"

"Discuss what?"

She rolled her eyes. "Mommy's brother?"

Aryeh felt his heart swell with anxiety; so small a thing, yet did he have clearance to share? "Okay. What are your questions?"

She faced him. "I want to know why Mommy cut him off from her. What did he do that was so, so terrible? Why was it kept a secret from me? From us? And also...how did you and Mommy think you could possibly get away with it?"

Aryeh inhaled long and hard. He held his breath, watching his daughter, who now met his stare with unwavering boldness. He began to speak on the exhale. "I think you may be right. We need to discuss this. So..." He sat a little straighter. "I am going to take a chance and come clean with you. Your mother's brother, Aaron, hasn't been cut off, as you misstated last night and again this morning. He went *missing*."

Tamar's mouth dropped involuntarily. "*Missing?*" This was not at all what she had been expecting. "As in, you don't even *know* where he is?"

"Correct."

"Oh." She looked down. "That's different."

"How is it different?"

"I thought Mommy cut him out of her life. But if he just walked off one day and never came back, maybe he's just *dead*?"

"No."

"How do you know?"

"Because he's recently been spotted. In Paris."

"In *Paris*!" she exclaimed, her mouth forming incredulity matched only by the wideness of her eyes. "My goodness! Paris?! That's so... so..." She stopped.

"So what?"

"So...crazy! I don't know what!"

"I guess so." He took a long sip of coffee.

"So, you're saying that you *do* know where he is?" Tamar pressed.

"No. I mean, we didn't know, all these years. But this war in Eretz Yisrael...it uncovered where he had been hiding all this time. At least, that's what Mommy believes."

Tamar's forehead furrowed with incomprehension. "Okay, I'm really confused now. What does what's going on in Eretz Yisrael have anything to do with anything?"

"I was getting to it. Here's the thing: you know that there have been riots in many main cities around the world because of the situation in Eretz Yisrael now, right?"

"I heard," she said, rolling her eyes. "These people make me want to scream and—"

"Yeah, yeah," he interrupted. "It's inevitable. Point is: While Mommy was in England, visiting Bubby, she saw a clip on one of the news sites, and on it she thought she glimpsed her brother getting hurt during one of the riots in Paris. So, Mommy being Mommy, she's gone out there—she is there right now—to investigate!" He ended with a shrug and took another sip of his coffee.

"No way! You're kidding me!"

"You wanted the goods. Here they are."

"So this is the 'stuff she needs to work out on her own' that you were talking about?" Tamar asked.

Aryeh nodded. "That's right."

"Wow. So Mommy and her long-lost brother finally met up in Paris." Tamar's eyes sparkled with dreamy notions.

"Actually, I have no idea whether or not that occurred. All I know is that Mommy went to Paris—nothing more than that. Like I said, I haven't heard from her since Monday. She's gone AWOL on me."

"Are you worried?"

"Yes and no. You know your mother by now. She's one determined person. I think she will be okay. And you know what they say about no news being good news, right?"

Tamar grew quiet. "So, we don't really know when they will be coming home..."

"They?"

"Well, Mommy and her brother, of course."

"Don't assume anything, Tamar. From what I gather, your uncle Aaron is an iffy character. I wouldn't be sure that he's gonna want to follow Mommy here."

"Okay, Abba. Here is the million-dollar question: Why did she *behave* as though she had cut herself off from him? Why did she never mention him all my life?"

"He was a wild kid, Tamar, from what I gather. She's told me some stories, but I'm sure there are many more. He stabbed someone once."

Tamar's jaw dropped again. "Really?"

"Apparently. And that's not all..."

"What else?"

"You really want to hear?"

"Yes."

"Okay. He set fire to his principal's office, almost killing the janitor of the building. There was a warrant out for his arrest, I believe."

Tamar closed her eyes and placed both hands over her ears. She'd heard something along these lines last year, of course, during that terrible incident when she'd been accosted by Raizy and her gang. But hearing the details straight from her father was another story altogether... "Is there anything else?" she asked faintly, recovering slowly.

"Not that I know of, but...there could be." They eyed one another pensively.

Aryeh sighed. "This may have been *lashon hara*. Perhaps I should have been vaguer, and not told you these specific incidents with Aaron. I...I just want you to understand why Mommy never mentioned anything about him to you or your sisters. She didn't want your lives to be tainted."

"And what about *you*? Why didn't *you* say anything to us?"

"What do you mean? This was *Mommy's* domain. I had to follow her instructions."

"But you're talking to me now about it. How come?"

He stopped all movement. "Tamar, when my child comes to me for help, and I have something that could be of help to her, I am obligated to make my own decision, regardless of others."

"So you don't feel bad speaking to me about all this?"

Aryeh smiled. "No, sillyhead, I don't. Besides, we have yet to hear how things went in Paris. Maybe there has been a turnaround."

They slipped into an easy silence, both of them eating quietly. After a while, the landline rang. Aryeh stood up to take the call in his office.

He was fiddling around on his computer when Tamar popped her head in the doorway. "Abba, can I ask you another question?"

"No, you may not. Your ration has just expired. Please wait until the light turns green."

Tamar smiled. "Seriously."

Aryeh rocked his chair on its hind legs, like a little schoolboy. "Sure. Fire away."

"Did you read my letter?"

"Tamar," he said, letting the chair fall back into place with a loud thump, "in the spirit of the honesty that we have just established between us, I feel compelled to say yes. Yes, I did read it. But believe me, I only did so out of love and concern for you."

Sima was the first one to move as the room emptied of TV crew and hospital personnel. She ran straight out into the corridor and rushed toward the nurse, tapping her on the shoulder and causing her to twirl around so fast, it was accompanied by a perceptible whoosh. She took both of the nurse's hands into her own, looked meaningfully at her, and said, "Thank you."

The fluorescent light caught the nurse's eyes, startlingly large and coffee-bean brown, surrounded by thick, dark lashes. "It was the least I could do," she mumbled, readjusting her hijab that had loosened. Then she straightened. "So...today is *the* day!" The nurse's hands were still in Sima's. "Excited?"

Sima's eyes narrowed in confusion. "Oh, you mean for his eyes. Yes! Yes, I am very excited about that!"

The nurse thought for a moment, then withdrew her hands, turned sharply, and walked back into the room. Sima followed her. Seeing Rabbi Wechter standing at the foot of Aaron's bed, the nurse stopped and addressed him. "I'm so sorry about tha—"

"No, no, no!" The rabbi waved his hand up to stop her. "Do not assume the guilt of something you were not part of. No need to apologize. This had nothing to do with you. If anything, you helped out by putting an end to the whole sorry scene."

She gave him an unsure smile, nodded slightly, and left the room again. Sima pulled up one of the chairs left haphazardly in the room— remnants of the morning's debacle. She stared into the bandages covering Aaron's forehead and eyes, wishing she could see what lay beneath, if only to gauge how badly his soul was hit. She took his hand. "Aaron..." she whispered.

"Why?" He turned toward her. "Why are we so despised?"

Rabbi Wechter coughed. "We said no..."

Aaron turned toward him. "Sorry?" he asked.

"We said no, and that started the whole hate-fest rolling." The rabbi leaned on one of the heavier chairs, one hand on his waist. His face looked ashen. "Eons ago, we said no to their prophet, Mohammed. *We have our own*, we said. *Thank you for thinking of us*, we said. *But no*, we said. *We're okay*. And so the conflict began."

"Rabbi..." Aaron's voice seemed to rise slowly out of a quagmire; a last-ditch attempt at expiation; his words levitating, or so Sima sensed, as though one could reach out and touch them. "Please... don't be offended..." His strain was evident. She closed her fist tighter around his hand, but he fought her to release it. She dropped it and continued to stare into the white gauze that refused her entry.

"It's just that...and I've thought about this for a long time... Well... it seems to me...that of all human inventions, religion has to be the dumbest." He let out a long breath. His whole body relaxed in the triumph of his having finally put into words that which had been plaguing him for too long. And before anyone could say anything, he added, "And the deadliest."

Sima felt her spirit plunge. Aaron was now further away from her than he had been yesterday. The dream, now that she'd finally found him, of rescuing him and bringing him back to the Torah life she loved, suffered a massive eclipse, brought about by her own encouragement and foolish zeal, her infantile desire to have everything neatly in place, her overstepping. She wanted, needed, to give herself a good, hard kick in the shins. *I have not spoken to my brother in twenty years. What was I thinking, making a forced hero out of him?!*

I don't even know him anymore!

"I agree!" the rabbi chimed in, so suddenly it made Sima startle. She whipped her head around and gawked at him. Rabbi Wechter's smirk was impish; he was clearly enjoying the moment. "In fact, I couldn't agree more!" he exclaimed. "Religion is really for the...I think you say...*birds*?"

Aaron lay very still. Some seconds ticked by. Sima could keep quiet for only so long. "Rabbi Wechter, what are you—"

He lifted his hand at her, to indicate that she should not try to contradict him, but rather listen. She clamped her mouth shut.

"It is true," he said. "Religion can so quickly become exclusive, arrogant and self-serving. Even when the fundamentalists are not going around blowing the brains off of the disbelievers. Aaron," he faced the white-gauzed patient, "what you don't understand is that *Torah is not a religion.*"

"Er, what?" Aaron was half-smiling now, seemingly happy to play along. Sima relaxed. *Let's just see where this takes us*, she thought.

"Yes," said Rabbi Wechter. "Try to follow, Aaron. *Yiddishkeit* never was a *religion*. Different religions came out of it—that is true. But, if we think of religion as merely a system of behaviors formed to guarantee a Heavenly reward in the Afterlife—which is what most world religions are about—then Judaism falls very, very short. Of course Gan Eden and Gehinnom exist, but, you know, we are encouraged by our Sages to serve G-d *not* just for the reward. That's because serving Him is *in itself* a reward! It's an honor, a joy, a privilege! My point is, Judaism isn't just about getting to Heaven. It's about bringing Heaven down here."

Aaron wrinkled his forehead. "Can't say I'm following..."

"It's about transforming Earth into Heaven. You don't *have* to wait for any Afterlife to experience that kind of pleasure."

"Okay... Now how exactly does that work?"

"Look here, Aaron. Did you ask to be born?"

Aaron did not respond.

"Did anyone consult you?"

Aaron rewarded the rabbi with a blank would-be stare.

"You don't have to answer," Rabbi Wechter continued, unfazed. "Point is, you are here. And if, indeed, you are here, then that means that G-d desires you to be here."

"I'm not sure I believe all that."

"Let's say you do, for now, for this moment, for this argument."

Aaron nodded, very slightly.

"Then that G-dly desire experiences fulfillment in the very being that is—wait for it—you!"

"And that is *not* self-serving? Huh!" Aaron looked toward Sima, bearing a grin of pure jubilance. She riled within, watching the back-and-forth with alternating delight and despair.

"Wait, Aaron. Listen. When you do a mitzvah, your entire being— that fulfillment of G-d's desire—unifies with Him. You are at the apex of perfection, and the marriage of the physical with the spirit has solidified—through you. At that moment, neither Gan Eden nor Gehinnom matter, for at that moment, it is just you...and G-d."

Silence followed—the kind of silence that asks a question to the ether, but does not expect a reply.

Then suddenly Aaron spoke. "You wanna know what really bothers me? When they told us that we are the center of the universe; that the whole of Creation came into being just for us. I could never account for how we could possibly be so arrogant as to think that we are the point to which everything is turned. Mind-blowingly cocky, if you ask me."

"Aaron, you're being ridiculous!" Sima almost choked out the words, her throat having caught some wayward saliva. "They didn't mean it as—" cough, cough "—an ego-trip! They meant that each person is the center of *their own* universe. And that everything a person does, or thinks, matters..." Cough, cough. She pulled at the collar of her dress to get some air, while struggling to continue. "...every thought, word, and deed. That's what it means. Surely you couldn't have understood that any other way!" Cough.

"You okay?" Rabbi Wechter walked toward her.

"Yes." Another cough. "Just winded!"

They all grinned.

"Well, it still hurt..." Aaron murmured.

"Why? Why did it hurt? Why should *that*, of all things, hurt?" questioned Rabbi Wechter, curiosity and concern framing his face.

It took Aaron a minute to gather his thoughts. "Because... because I had to sit through many an assembly where they would espouse exactly *how* our importance was infinite, in *public*. And yet... in *private*...it was a different matter. Publicly they would be all, 'You are the crème de la crème.' But I always questioned that, because in private they treated us, or at least me, like the 'crème de la garbage.'"

Rabbi Wechter shook his head. "Many people make this mistake: they have a bad experience, or many bad experiences, and therefore they abandon their faith. And what are they left with?" The rabbi stopped talking. He waited. Sima did not know whether to answer. Was Rabbi Wechter being rhetorical? She took her cue and stayed quiet. "*Nu*, Aaron. Tell me. What is a person left with when he abandons his people?"

Aaron's jaw was very still. Sima watched him, his torment vicariously entering her. She was filled with love for him, yet she could not accept his words. The silence grew longer. She opened her mouth, but the rabbi shook his finger to silence her.

Aaron finally stirred. "Is that why people stay?" he questioned, looking up. "Because they don't want to face the world alone? Is that what binds us?"

"Some. Maybe. Probably."

"You?"

Rabbi Wechter smiled. "No, Aaron. Not me. I decided long ago to develop my own connection with G-d. What I have learned, if anything, during the past seventy-three years of life on this planet, is this: Do not rely on *people*. People are just that: people. And as such, they can be relied upon for one thing: disappointment. To be happy, to believe, to have faith, you must go it alone. You may get lucky and meet someone along the way who can help, maybe, a little. Ultimately, though, you're on your own. Faith, you ask? Sorry, Aaron, but it's got to come from you."

He glanced at his watch. "It's past noon. I need to be headed back. Just wanted to be here when you get your eyes back. Ah, well, I shall have to miss it." He stood and put his hand on Aaron's shoulder. "Enough arguing for today. You did well, Aaron. I'm sorry I pushed you to agree to the interview, but you did a good job, despite what people will say when it comes out." His head tilted, and one white eyebrow lifted. "Anyway, I will be back later on in the afternoon. Mrs. Hertzberg, I will bring food for you. Aaron, what about you?"

Aaron did not respond.

"I see. Very well. See you both later." Rabbi Wechter eyed Sima whimsically. "We'll talk. Later."

"Okay, keep your eyes closed, Mr. Bulman. You have to get used to the light," the nurse said in French. She had magical hands, which flew lightly over the bandages that had covered Aaron's forehead and eyes since Sunday night. A small tug here and there and, voila, the wound and unopened eyes were on display.

Sima gasped. The nurse gave her a sharp look, a warning that brooked no fuss. Sima forced herself to paste on a façade of calm, like the nurse, but there was no mistaking the revulsion that swam in her gut when she saw how close her brother had come to losing his left eye. A line of stitches ran from an inch above the brow to just stopping at the lash line, and another crossed both eyes, but at a safer distance. He wouldn't be able to open his left eye right now, even if he wanted to. The stitches would obstruct it. "Your brother is a lucky man, Madame," the nurse intoned, while swabbing the laceration. "The weapon did not penetrate too deeply." She turned to the patient and switched to French. "You can open your eyes now."

Aaron's right lid flickered open to a slit. Immediately, he brought up his hand. "Too much light. I can't see a thing. Sima? Stand here. Cover the light for me, will you? I want to try to see you." Sima stood over his right side, shielding him from as much light as her body would allow. She lowered her face toward him. He tried to focus. "It's just a sooty image, blurry. Too much light." He closed his eye again, and then reopened it. Every time he tried, the image gained clearer proportions, until finally he smiled.

"My goodness, Sima..." he murmured. "You...you look like Mummy."

The backs of Sima's eyes stung. "Yes." She swallowed. "I do. It's true. Well, I look like she *used* to look, twenty years ago. Only, Aaron, she doesn't...she doesn't look like this anymore. She's aged, you know..."

Aaron's right eye stared hollowly at his sister, before shutting and staying closed for a long time. Then he opened it again, looked at her, and, unable to restrain himself, exclaimed, "Wow, Sima, it's just so good to see you!"

He held out his right hand, and she grabbed it with both of hers, tears filling her eyes. If not for her innate sense of modesty, she would have hugged him. In truth, though, hugs had never been a part of their relationship—not when they were younger, and certainly not during the terrible, turbulent teen years. Besides, Aaron was still too medically fragile for an embrace now.

For several long moments Sima stayed like that, holding tightly to Aaron's hand, not letting go until he needed it back.

Afterward, things eased between them, Sima was relieved to discover. There was conversation, reminiscences, and sharing, all accompanied by occasional, spontaneous, and forgiving laughter. She was thrilled to be able to tell him of her marriage to Aryeh, and all that he had come to mean for her. Her daughters, one by one, were fleshed out before him, twirling and curtsying in absence, each gaining his approval as she provided for him the essence of their personalities and who they were.

For his part, Aaron could not get enough of listening to her, and he urged her to fill him in. So sudden had his thirst for her life's details presented itself to him, even he was shocked. The fact that he was not able to reciprocate in the apportioning of the sacred trivialities that make up most people's lives did not bother either of them. He was single. He had married. It hadn't worked. Over.

Yet, for all of the transparency they had just shared, she did not, could not, not yet, perhaps not ever, disclose to him her anxiety about Tamar. How could she tell him that, on their father's orders, she hadn't allowed his name to pass through her lips for twenty years; that even as shame silenced her, still it gnawed and nibbled at her insides?

The lunch trolleys clanked outside in the corridor, their smells wafting in. Sima did not think she could watch Aaron take another mouthful of the non-kosher fare. She stood up.

"Where are you going?"

"Bathroom," she said. "And I need to call Aryeh, my husband. I can't wait for you two to meet." She watched for his reaction. He gave her a weak but sincere smile. "I'll see you soon," she added, and left the room.

That stillness, she reflected as she strolled down the long corridor. *He still has it.* That economy of sound and space.

She could yet feel his hand in hers. When was the last time someone had held Aaron's hand? When was the last time he had been hugged? Had the non-demonstrative love of their parents been a contributing factor to the loss of him? Physical affection in her childhood home had been weaned out to near-absence by the time they were around five.

Her mind leaped to her Long Island home. When was the last time she had given Tamar a hug? Had it been when they had parted at the bus depot, when Tamar had left to camp? She couldn't remember for sure. Or maybe—had she hugged Tamar the Friday night before that, when they'd had their conversation? After candle-lighting? Yes, she had. That she knew.

She tried to recall when Aaron's stillness had set in. It was around the time of his bar mitzvah. That was when everything had become quiet around him. She suddenly remembered the oddest conversation she'd had with him, on the landing at the top of the stairs, in between their bedrooms. He had been twelve, and she fourteen. He had been sitting on the carpet, playing with a Rubik's cube, and she'd been lying down on a blanket, reading by the light coming from the bathroom. It was Friday night; they had just finished eating their Shabbos meal. Greta was downstairs, cleaning up, and Elchanan was sleeping on the couch, his snores drifting up like a deficient metronome, keeping an unsteady rhythm against the ticking of the dining room clock.

"Sima, what was it like for you when you became bas mitzvah?" Aaron *suddenly asked. "Did you feel different?"*

Sima stopped reading and looked at him. "What do you mean?"

"I mean, something is supposed to happen then, no?"

"Like what?"

"I don't know. Something. My rebbi *told us that we are all born with a* yetzer hara *that is constantly telling us to do bad stuff, and that the* yetzer tov *only comes to us when we're bar or bas mitzvah. So...did you actually feel different when you turned twelve?"*

Sima thought about it, turned onto her stomach, and said, "Maybe. I know that for a while now, I actually want to help out more around the house, and it doesn't feel like a chore. But that could just be because I like things to look nice. I don't like mess. So, no, I don't really feel any different."

He placed the cube on the floor and looked at her. "D'you wanna know something? I'm scared of becoming bar mitzvah."

"Why on earth?" she asked, propping herself on her elbows and staring at him.

"'Cuz the way I see it, if my yetzer hara *caused me to get into all the trouble I got into up until now, it's only gonna get worse!"*

"Oh, my goodness, Aaron! Why would you say that? When your yetzer tov *comes in, fully, that will even it out! Things are supposed to get better, not worse!"*

"Not the way I see it." He went back to playing with his cube.

But Sima could not go back to her book. *"Why, Aaron? Why do you think things will get worse after your bar mitzvah?"*

"'Cuz, if my yetzer hara *is so strong, without an enemy, then doesn't it mean that* with *an enemy, it will only get stronger? I mean, the way I'm imagining it, it works like a pendulum: the more you push one way, the stronger the swing-back is."*

Sima rolled her eyes and laughed. "Aaron, you think too much. Go to bed."

Perhaps his silence served him as a moat serves its castle, Sima now thought to herself. Occasionally the drawbridge would come down—but only very occasionally. She recognized within herself a long-forgotten unease when she was with him, as though his brittleness of spirit was her fault, or at least her responsibility. But she had so much to discuss with him, and so little time in which to do it! She had to return to London the next day, and Long Island would be calling soon after that...

The letter.

She still had to present the letter to him. What was she waiting for?

She looked at her phone—it had been too long since she'd last spoken with Aryeh—but the battery was dead. Of course. She rooted in her pocketbook for her charger, and eventually gave up. France would surely be on a different wattage anyway. She would need an adapter.

Noticing the nurses' station that she was passing right now, she approached the desk and saw that the same hijab-wearing nurse was seated behind it. "Hi again," Sima said to her. "Would you be able to help me out with something?"

"I can try." The nurse smiled sweetly at her.

Once again Sima was struck by her goodness and sincerity. "Do you know where I can make an overseas call?"

The woman's face became serious. She looked about her as she spoke, tapping various piles of folders and equipment. "Well, none of the phones here will let you call overseas. I can..." She stopped speaking.

"Yes, what were you going to say?"

"Maybe I can bring an adapter from home. I live nearby, and I'm going on my break soon."

Sima's eyebrows rose with both surprise and gratitude. "Thank you. Thank you so much," she said, and then, as an afterthought, she added, "I wonder, would you be able to do another favor for me?" The woman nodded. "Is there a kosher meal plan in this hospital? I don't think my brother would realize if we switched..."

The woman smiled openly, her teeth gleaming under the bluey whiteness of the overhead lights. "I have been doing that all along."

"You're kidding!" Sima blinked away the sudden gush of fresh tears that poked behind her eyes. "You're kidding..." she repeated, shaking her head. "What kind of angel are you?" She heard her voice thicken as she tried to regain her composure.

The woman chuckled, her dark skin looking more beautiful as she blushed. "I know how much it would hurt *us* if we were not given Halal meat..."

"Please, what is your name? I want to remember you."

She lifted her hand and tapped the side of her head. "Fedora, like the hat."

"Fedora?"

"Yes."

"Thank you, Fedora. You should be blessed. You are a good woman." Sima held out her hand. Fedora took it. They shook. "One last thing..." Sima bit her lip. *Don't cry. Please, Hashem, help me not to cry.* "Would you please not say anything to Aaron about this? He doesn't care about these things...." Fedora nodded, scrunching her eyes to show she understood.

Sima walked back to Aaron's room, her steps feeling tingly. She decided to store Fedora away, to create a reservoir of peace inside her, to have handy for whenever world chaos became too unbearable. *As long as there are people in this world like Fedora*, she avowed, *mankind may still have a chance.*

276 | THE THIRTEENTH GATE

35

enya put down the groceries on the kitchen table. She looked at her watch: 7:18 p.m. She noted the dust that had collected around the sinks and along the countertops. She opened the fridge. Something was rotting in there. She closed it quickly. She would have to give up her cleaning help again, send her to her mother's house. There was no way she could let Mummy spend Shabbos like this. *Well, well, Sima*, she thought, *thanks for all your help!*

"Who's there?" a startled-sounding Greta called, from what seemed like the top of the stairs.

Henya ran to the bottom step and looked up. It *was* Greta, alone, standing and holding on to the banister. "Mummy, don't move. I'm coming." Henya clambered upstairs, reaching the top, out of breath. "Oh, my goodness, Mummy! You're dressed!"

Greta was wearing a pale-blue chiffon blouse that tied at the neck, and a simple gray skirt, its looseness attesting to the severity of her most recent affliction.

"Yes. I am." She sounded almost triumphant. "And I *feel* great, like a million dollars!"

Henya took a closer look. Her mother *did* look better; some color had returned to her cheeks, and she was smiling. "Still, Mummy, you could have waited for me to get here before walking on your own. What if you would have fallen again?"

"Oh, don't worry. I woke up feeling good this morning, *baruch Hashem*. I got myself dressed. I've been dressed all day."

"Well..." Henya could not think of the right response. "That's... wonderful," she decided to say; it was the safest thing she could come up with.

"Henya, do you think you could help me go down into the garden? I have not been there since Sima arrived. I would love to sit there with you. Help me down, would you?"

"Is Deepa still here? Can she come and help?"

"No, no, she left for the day. But I think we can make it on our own. Let's at least try." Greta scooped her right arm through the crook of her daughter's left elbow, and together they struggled to lower her, one step at a time. She was determined. Though they had to stop a few times, Greta's face stayed calm. Finally, they reached the bottom of the staircase.

"What a nuisance, getting me down those stairs! But the night nurse will be here soon, so you'll have the help you need to get me back up. Come, Henya, let's go out. It's my favorite time of day." Greta walked, unsteadily at first, but then stronger as she approached the back patio door. "Ahhh, there it is," she said, sliding the door open to a welcoming breeze.

"What?"

"The 'before-twilight.' When the sun begins its descent. Best time of day. Come sit out with me. I'm feeling young today," she announced as she burrowed her way through the door. "Henya...?" she called from outside. "It's weird, but it feels like a heavy weight's just been taken off of me."

Henya felt the hairs rise along her forearm. *Was I wrong not to support Sima? Oh, I wish I knew what to do! What should I say?*

It's probably best to keep quiet...

Greta settled into one of the easy chairs and spread her hands wide on the weathered resin armrests. "Come, Henya, sit near me." She patted the chair next to her. "Let's watch the pre-dusk together. I used to love doing that with your father, in the later years." She looked so tranquil at that moment: her eyes closed to the dying-but-still-strong sun; her mouth open just a bit, so the air she breathed into it was fresh; her shoulders at rest. The pale blue of her blouse mirrored the sky, the delicate fabric flapping lazily around her thin body. "*Nu*, Henya? Have you heard anything from Sima? Do you know when she will be coming back?"

Henya stiffened. "No. I have not heard a word from Sima."

"Oh. That's odd. I always thought you two were as thick as thieves. Why didn't you go along with her to the spa? You could have done with a break yourself."

"Yeah, well..." She shrugged. "She hasn't called or anything." Silence. Then, "Anyway, Mummy, what did you want to talk about? Have you eaten?"

"'Course I've eaten. A long time ago." Greta stretched out her arm and let it fall on Henya's forearm. Henya flinched and looked up. "I wanted to tell you about this garden, Henya. For years it was a swamp. Tatte and I never had the mind to do anything with it. You remember what a mess it was, no? Then, one day, about two years before Tatte died, he comes to me in the kitchen, carrying a bunch of catalogues with plants and stuff. I thought he'd lost his marbles..." Greta chuckled at the memory, and Henya smiled to herself as she remembered how she and Sima would count the clichés their mother would use to try spicing up her stories.

"But no. He says to me, 'Greta, it's time we fix the backyard. I want to make a special place for us. I want to make a healing garden. Yes?' Well, I was taken aback. It wasn't his way, ever. But you know..." She lowered her eyes. "I didn't tell anyone, only because I thought he wouldn't want people to know, but he was seeing someone—a professional—for a few years before he died."

"What someone? Like a therapist?"

"Not *like* a therapist, an *actual* therapist. A psychotherapist, if you really want specifics." Greta watched her daughter's facial expression, using it to gauge her next words. "Don't look so horrified. I had gone to my doctor about him. I was so concerned. You may not remember this, but there were times when Tatte couldn't get out of bed. I got my doctor to give me the number to this man out in Uxbridge. You can imagine how much he didn't want to go. He missed the first few appointments. But then, one day, I don't know what pushed him..." Greta stopped talking. The hand that was still resting on Henya's forearm lifted. She held it mid-air as though she were calling for a waiter.

"He never missed an appointment after that first time." Their eyes met. "Now, I can't say that I know what they spoke about, but what I *can* say is that...he changed. Over time. He became just a little bit happier about himself."

"So, that's what happened..."

"You noticed?"

"Yes. The last few years, Tatte *was* different. More mellow. More...I don't know...likeable? What was the therapist's name?"

"Oh, I can't remember. But Tatte never called him by name. He always referred to him as, 'the man.' 'The man said this,' or, 'I told the man that.'"

Henya was looking intently at her mother, not knowing if she should exult in this new position, or just pretend that they had always spoken with this level of intimacy. After all these years, her mother was finally opening up to her, confiding. It both thrilled and unnerved her. *What if I say something stupid?* she thought. *Better not to say anything at all.*

"Anyway," Greta continued, "we chose the first few plants for that flowerbed over there." She pointed to the left corner, where the lavender and salmon-pink phlox and red-leaf hibiscus grew. "After we planted them and saw how easy it was, we just went further with it, your father and I. And now, as you can see, we really do have a lovely garden. A healing place. I love to sit here in the early evening, like now, and just breathe and think."

"It *is* lovely, Mummy." Henya looked around, surveying the space with new eyes. "And it's a lovely story. I remember when the two of you would be down on your knees, digging and weeding together. I always thought it was so beautiful, the two of you enjoying this activity as a couple. Did you find it healing?"

"Of sorts. One can never truly be healed, you know. Life has a way of bashing you about. But growing beautiful plants and flowers…it can put you more in touch…"

"With?"

"With Hashem." She looked at Henya quizzically. "You know… nature and stuff. The beauty of it and all." She turned away with a shy smile. "I'm getting all my words mixed up. Not explaining properly. I mean, Hashem always intended to make a beautiful world, you know. Only it takes us people too long to realize it."

"Yes," said Henya, closing her eyes. She sat back in her garden chair, finally letting herself relax.

"Henya?" Greta spoke to her with half-closed eyes. "You know it destroyed your father when Aaron left, don't you?"

"Of course."

"It destroyed me too. Only, the difference is, I still believe he will return. You father didn't always believe that. For a long time, your father felt that he'd lost him forever."

"I know. He pretty much told us to consider Aaron dead."

Greta lifted her head. "Really?" The whites of her eyes grew prominent, and the corners of her lips began trembling slightly. "Oh…I didn't know that. Did he really *say* as much?"

There it is. The stupid thing I was not supposed to have said. "I'm sorry, Mummy." Henya reached out and touched her mother's arm. "Maybe I shouldn't have said that."

"Oh, dear…" Greta's eyes looked past her daughter. "I did not know…I was not aware…" She seemed to be whispering to herself.

Henya bemoaned her lack of guile. *Oh, no, no, no. I've hurt her. Me and my runaway mouth!* "Mummy, I think he was only thinking for our benefit. Mine and Sima's. He worried about our futures. About how we would escape the scrutiny of the community when it came time to find husbands. This, I think, was what was foremost on his mind when he cautioned us. Please, Mummy, let's not dredge up the past. Let's enjoy the pre-twilight..."

Greta sat back again, seeming to shrink a bit into the cushions. "Oh, well." She breathed out. "I have long forgiven him for his flaws." They both fell silent, quietly repressing any explosive thoughts. Suddenly, Greta exclaimed, "Oh, Henya, he had his own battles. We can never really plumb the depths of what he had to go through." And then, with precise, well-practiced skill, her face settled back to itself. "Anyway," she said, "do tell me again, when is Sima supposed to get back?"

"*Oy*, Mummy, I already *told* you." Henya inhaled, a soft turbulence quivering inside her. "I really don't know..."

Most of that afternoon Aaron spent in a deeply healing slumber. Sima sat by his bed, guarding his sleep, until she was no longer able to fight off her own exhaustion. Just before dinnertime, Fedora came back with the adapter. When she tapped Sima's shoulder, Sima jumped, so startled that her extremities prickled from shock. Fedora lay a finger to her lips, warning her not to make too much noise. "He needs to wake up soon enough, but we can do it gently." Sima nodded, collecting herself. "He needs to get up and walk before the day is out and my shift ends."

"Oh?"

"Yes. Too long in bed does more harm than good."

"Agreed. But how...?"

"You will help. Come on, stand on this side. I will stand with you, and he will use both of us for support. Together we will manage."

Sima put her phone on charge and then walked around to join Fedora on the other side of Aaron's bed. Fedora tapped his shoulder. Sima bent toward him, shaking his knee. "Aaron, wake up. You need to do some exercise." His eyes flitted, but only one, the right eye, opened fully. A shiver ran through Sima. He smiled at her.

"You ready to get up?" she asked.

"I was just in the middle of a really good dream..." he said groggily.

"Sorry. But Fedora needs to leave soon, and you need to try your legs out again."

Aaron turned and awarded Fedora with a drunken smile, still clearly held by whatever image he had last dreamed. The nurse placed one arm under Aaron's left armpit, directing him to lean on her. Sima waited until he was sitting up, dangling both legs over the side of the bed. Then she placed her left arm under his right armpit, in much the same way as Fedora, and slowly he dragged himself off the bed. His face was pinched, and he breathed heavily.

"Steady," said Fedora, in her soft voice. "Don't take a step until you feel comfortable."

"I haven't broken anything, right?" Aaron asked. "I should be able to do this. Why is it hurting so much?"

"Bone bruising. It can hurt like it's broken, even though it's not. When you came in, the x-rays they did showed no cracks."

"Wow, this is hard." Aaron's face was red, his forehead beginning to show tiny beads of perspiration. He took one step, then another, with Fedora lending him encouraging sounds all the while, leaning in just so to keep him steady, knowing when to straighten, when to bow. Sima felt his weight shift away from her, and she realized that Fedora was taking more than half the heft. She looked over at the nurse, hoping to catch her eye and send her sincere apologies, but Fedora was too focused to notice.

At last, after they had walked the breadth of the room, Fedora announced, "That's enough for now. We will try again tomorrow." They both worked hard getting Aaron back into his bed. "It will be better tomorrow. Sleep, especially the sleep of night, is a powerful healer. Now that we have begun, you should be walking independently very soon."

Fedora slipped out of the room. Aaron sank deeply into his pillow and placed his arm over his eyes. Sima hesitated before telling him that she was leaving the room to go call her husband. Aaron nodded at her, without moving his arm.

Aryeh picked up on the second ring. "Sima! Where on earth are you?! I've been worried sick. And Henya is furious. Are you in Paris? Did you ever find him?"

"Shhhhhh, stop shouting! Yes. Yes. Yes. I found him! Aryeh, I found him!"

"You're kidding! You found him! And...?"

"He is well. He is in the hospital over here, with a huge line of stitches above his left eye, and another across both eyes. He's got a lot of bone bruising and all. But *baruch Hashem* he hasn't broken anything. I *told* you it was him. *You* didn't believe me."

"I'm...I'm...speechless. I can't believe it. After all these years. You must be feeling very validated. Sima, I'm sorry. But it's true. I thought you were crazy. Turns out, you were. But that's okay."

"Well, I was *right*. And anyway, it takes a certain kind of crazy. But I'm glad—*so* glad!—I did it. I found him, Aryeh. And I am never letting him go again."

"Does Henya know you've found him? Have you spoken to her?"

"I couldn't care less what Henya feels about this. He's my brother, and I love him. Henya doesn't understand the bond we have. She was too young." Sima was laughing, as the backs of her eyes threatened to spring new tears. *Oh, Aryeh, maybe now we can be a regular family again. Maybe now, when you meet him, you two can be friends.*

By the time Sima returned, Aaron was calm, sitting up in bed, testing his eyes by reading a large-print book. She sat down, but he did not look up. Her hands nervously pulled at the longer strands of her wig, separating one from the other—a childhood habit that had transitioned from hair to wig without the least bit of resistance. She did not even notice herself doing it. Aaron finally glanced at her sideways. "What's wrong?" he asked, putting the book down on the bed.

Sima didn't reply right away; her fingers were pulling on some longer strands of bangs, and her eyes were wonky with concentration.

"You remember what we need to do today," she said at last, not looking at him. "Don't you?"

"Yes. Does it have to be now?"

"Oh, come on, Aaron." She let go of her bangs and stared straight at him with large eyes. "I have to leave tomorrow. This is killing me. Do you not want to read it? It's addressed to *you*!"

His gaze turned to the large window and the gray buildings that congregated on the other side of the street. "Let's say I don't want to read it right now. Would that be so terrible? Can't I deal with one thing at a time? First off, there is you, reappearing out of nowhere after all these years. Then today, the interview, which I still have not finished processing. Now you want me to open up even more from my past. I'm stressed! Can't it wait until tomorrow? I think I will feel better prepared to confront whatever is in there, tomorrow."

No sound passed between them for a full minute. Sima had so much to say, but wasn't sure that Aaron would want to hear any of it. Frustrated, she took a deep breath and settled back into her chair. He went back to his book. She grew angrier as the seconds ticked by, compounded by the knowledge that anger had to be the worst of reactions. And yet, that was what he provoked in her: anger and incredulity. This was the way it had always been with Aaron. With this one remark, he had closed the loop. And she felt her impotence as a wound reopened.

She resumed her wig-pulling, again absently. At last, after many minutes had passed, she opened her mouth. "You know, Aaron, I used to think that the main goal of life was to dodge the fireballs."

Aaron scratched the skin around his scar. "Huh?" he said.

"I used to think that life was about collecting pain-avoidance strategies. The more strategies you had, the better off you were."

"Like a Space Invaders game?" He smiled.

"Right. Or, by expansion: the less fireballs you needed to avoid, the more Hashem was smiling down at you, the more agreeable He found you, the closer you were to this state of worthiness. You get what I'm saying?"

Aaron nodded slowly. "And now...?"

"I just don't think like that anymore." She looked away from him. Dusk was settling outside. Lights in the apartment building across from the hospital were turning on. She could see them twinkling between the leaves. "I decided it's not worth the effort. I'm resigned to..."—she brushed an imaginary crumb from her lap— "...to the idea that life is simply and endlessly painful." She turned her gaze to him and met his eyes. "One thing must be established, Aaron: *Everyone* suffers. One way or another...everyone."

Aaron lifted his brow. "Some more than others," he said, before turning back to his book.

She crunched down on her lips, stewing silently. "Aaron?"

"Yes?"

"I have a daughter...who...I'm concerned about."

"Oh?" He turned to face her.

"Maybe you can help me."

"Oh?"

"She's...she's my eldest, and she's...lately...expressed doubts. She's not a rebellious kid, but she... What am I saying? She is rebelling. Which...I suppose...makes her a rebellious kid. Right? But I hate labeling. It constricts. No. She's *not* a rebellious kid. She's just...going through something, having serious doubts. Aaron..." By now Sima had pulled on both sides of her wig, setting it off-kilter, making her look somewhat theatrical. Her brother's eyes did not leave hers for a moment. She looked up. "Aaron, I'm scared."

"Of?"

"I'm scared of what could happen to her if she were to..."

What passed between them, in the mystical absence of articulation, was twenty years: the throes, the triumphs, the stagnancies, the momentums of all those years that they'd lived apart. Both of them were now unsure of how to proceed, of what was supposed to come next. What was it that Sima was after? What was she asking from him?

Aaron opened his mouth to say something, but closed it again.

"Aaron, speak," Sima beseeched him. "Tell me what you think I should do."

"...Love her."

All at once she felt a jab in her chest. Was it not a given that she loved her own daughter? "Of course I love her. Is that all?"

"Yes," he said, so simply that it crushed her, for how was she to tell him that she had kept his existence a secret? How was she to break it to him that she had not mentioned him to her daughters at all, for fear of hurting them as she had been hurt? And there he lay, all beaten up and pure. All he'd ever wanted was just to be loved, to be accepted. She felt ashamed and knew that it was right—that the shame she felt was correct, and that there were probably a great many other discomforts that she should rightfully endure.

"Did you not feel loved, Aaron? Was that it?"

"Well, Mummy loved me, but—"

"*Loves*, Aaron, *still loves*," she interrupted him. Their eyes locked. Instantaneously, she worried: *Did I have the right to correct him just now? Oh, why do I always need to push in and set records straight?! Why can't I just keep still and allow someone else's narrative to have its moment?*

"Aaron, I'm sorry. I do this all the time. I cut in and correct, finish people's sentences for them. It's wrong. I know. I'm working on it."

Aaron shrugged. "That's okay. Sometimes what you are saying is worth hearing, you know. And this was one of those times."

She breathed out, forgiven, relieved. Breaking free from his gaze, she rummaged in her pocketbook a bit, and finally took out the letter. "We need to do this, Aaron. Soon we won't have time. I leave tomorrow, mid-day, and I refuse to leave until this is done. Your rabbi will be coming back soon. Come on, let's do this, while it's just the two of us here, while there is still time."

He averted his eyes from the envelope she gripped too tightly in her hand, and then he nodded.

She needed nothing more. She was at it, ripping the envelope open as though it was a chocolate bar and she was hypoglycemic—that was how forcefully her hands shook.

The lethargy Aaron felt in his shoulders and arms forced him to lean back into the pillows for support. For the last ten years he'd been reprieved of the sin of disappointing his father, freed from that terminal ball and chain. Would this letter re-convict him?

Sima settled herself in her chair, elbows leaning on the bed. "Ready?" she queried, hope doing its best to shine from behind her eyes. The sky, through the window, was turning dusky; smoky clouds were gathering, like clouds of dust or ash. Outside, a car hooted loudly; someone shouted.

Sima turned on the overhead light just above the bed. Aaron held out his hand and took the letter from her. He read the inscription on the envelope, immediately recognizing his father's uneducated scratching: *To Mine Son, Aaron Rephael Bulman.* He held his breath and pulled out three folded pages. He handed them to Sima. "You read," he said. "Out loud."

Permission granted at last, Sima took the papers and began:

To mine son, mine von and mine only son, Aaron,

If you are reading zis, it means I have probably passed on to de Next Vorld. I am not unhappy about zis. It is a good thing. I never really like Zis Vorld anyvay. Vhen a person gets to mine age, he think about a lot of things. He think about dying, and he think about all the things dat happen to him vhen he live. I am not much different, I guess. Even if I alvays think I am, it looks like I'm not so different, becoz I too thinking about zese things a lot.

Aaron, I needs to tell you something. But is very, very hard for me to say. But I think I must to say it, doesn't matter if it hard.

I vants to say I am sorry. I think I did not give you good childshood. I vants to say that I understand now a lot more dan I used to vhen you vas little. I have been speaking to a man about you and about me and about vhat happened vhen you vas small and about a lots of things. Many things. And I thinking, I have to rite zis down. Even if you don't never to read it. Still I have to rite it down, even if it just be for mineself. I have to explain. But. De man say, don't to excuse. So, I not excusing. Just explaining.

You see, Aaron, mine tatte (vhat I give to you his name, Aaron Rephael), he got taken avay from me vhen I vas six. So I vas just learnin how to read and just learnin de prayers, and den he is gone.

I never see him again. And mine mamme very sick most of de time after, till she pass avay. So I never go to cheder. I never get chance to learn. But. I always remember vhat mine tatte says to me vhen he go. He says, "Elchanan, remember dat you are Jew. Learn Torah. Keep de mitzvos." Dat is last vords he say to me. But after, vhen they taking him avay, no one taking me to cheder. No one making sure dat I learn Torah. Vhen de police coming to our door, dey shouting to mine mamme, "Your boy must to go to school." So she just send me to Soviet school.

And I losing all those years.

Aaron, zis is de truth dat I am hiding from everyone all mine life: I don't know how to learn. I can't learn Torah. I don't understanding how.

I am shamed. I always am shamed becoz I don't know how to learn. I can read from de siddur, but I don't understand vhat it mean. So vhen you coming to me vis homevork, vhen you coming to me vis Gemara, even vis Chumash, I don't know how to help you. So I getting angry at you. Vhy you don't try harder! Vhy you don't know zis! Vhy you not paying more attention!

De man explaining, and now I understanding more better. Peoples getting angry, most of de times is becoz dey are shamed or something like dat.

And now, I am thinking mebbe that you running avay becoz you are feeling de same thing. Becoz you thinking, you are not vhat I vanted you to be. But. Now I am thinking, is not important no more. Becoz vhat is de most important thing is that you are mine son. And I don't even know if mebbe von day you vill read zis and mebbe you vill understand.

I vas wrong vhat I did. Hurting you a lots of times. I vish you to know I am sorry.

And another thing: your old teacher, Rabbi Gold, he is coming up to me in shul about tree and a haff years ago. He saying to me dat he vanna learn Torah vis me. So I says to him no, becoz I am shamed dat old man like me vould not be able to learn. I didn't vant for him to see. But he touching mine shoulder and he says, "Is okay, Reb Elchanan, ve can start from beginning, and ve can learn vhatever you want." I am shamed to say zis, but I start to cry. Right dere in de shul. And he vaiting. And vhen I finished, I know dat he know all about it. He musta guessed.

And ve starting to learn dat night, and ve been learning every night for tree and a haff years, and so much opening now for me. So. Now I see dat de Soviets stole mine childshood. But I trying to get it back now. And mebbe the Soviets stealing your childshood too. But I not making excusing, I just explaining.

And von last thing vhat I am learning about vis Rabbi Gold: Did you know dat vhen Mashiach vill come, and he building tird Beis Hamikdash in Yerusholayim, it says dat to get to de Beis Hamikdash, dere must to be tvelve gates? Von for each of de Shevatim, de sons of Yaakov and also deir families. And every tatte teach to his children vhich Shevet dey coming from, so dey knowing vhich gate dey must to walk troo. But it can happen dat a tatte doesn't know vhich Shevet he belong. So vhen dey building de gates, dey building also anoder gate, de Tirteense Gate.

Zis gate is for us. I don't know vhich gate to go troo, so probably you don't know too. So I am thinking that vhen time comes, and it vill be Techiyas Hameisim, I vill meet you at de Tirteense Gate. If you can forgive me for all de things I didn't do for you, vhen you vas small.

Vis all mine love, vis mine broken heart,
Your Tatte,
Elchanan Bulman
March 4, 2004

A tender silence settled over the brother and sister. Sima closed the letter along its folds and slipped it back into its envelope. An intrusive lump had lodged itself just above her vocal cords, obstructing her voice, causing it to crack at least three times during the reading. So much was riding on this letter, she realized. She knew how it made *her* feel, but could never be sure how her *brother* felt about it. In the arena of Aaron's emotions, nothing was ever without complications or surprises.

She handed the letter over to Aaron. He took it, nodding softly. She lay her head down in her arms, on the bed in front of her. Aaron strummed his fingers on her shoulder, a gesture that gave her the go-ahead to cry. And cry she did. Silently. Inside the protective walls of her arms.

When her crying eased up, she lifted her head and whispered, "So he was hiding from himself all along. Now things become so much clearer..." She rubbed her watery eyes and blew her nose loudly into a tissue. "He always loved books...always opened them and smelled them. I took it for granted that he read them." She rubbed her eyes vigorously again. "But now, come to think of it, I do not remember ever seeing him immersed in them."

Aaron nodded weakly.

"How could we ever have known?" She looked at him. "How? He hid it too well."

"I think..." Aaron began, but trailed off. Sima waited.

Aaron swallowed and tried again. "Do you think...perhaps...that I was like a symbol to him?" Sima's eyes narrowed as she regarded her brother. "...of all his failings. After all, I too had a hard time learning, you know..."

"Aaron, *you* had a hard time learning, because *he* had a hard time learning but could never own it."

"He must have equated me with everything that was wrong in his life," Aaron whispered to himself.

But Sima caught it. "*Oy*, Aaron!" Fresh tears sprang forth. "You were trapped from the start. You never could have climbed out of a pit you didn't know you were in. How will you ever forgive him?"

"Maybe...I could start by trying to imagine how stuck he was himself."

Sima smiled now, through her tears. "Amazing," she mumbled, shaking her head slowly. "You are amazing. My little brother..." She wiped her face on her sleeve, and then, without warning, she started to laugh.

"What's so funny?" Aaron stared at her, a half-puzzled grin lighting up his features.

"They call us 'the People of the Book,'" she chuckled, "even when that is clearly not the case—at least not in the typical sense!" She stood up, eyes alive, arms spread out, as though readying herself to address a wide audience. "Don't you see? Our father lived his entire life pretending to be 'of the Book,' so in a sense, he really *was*. No matter that he could not actually *learn* from those books—he loved them just the same, and surely that qualifies!"

Aaron watched his sister, and the feelings he had fought so long *not* to feel suddenly demanded to occupy their rightful space. It was ferocious. His heart gushed with regret, the choices made so long ago, with his smug, self-righteous resentment, now punctured and bleeding by his misgivings.

Look at all the pain you have caused your family. How different things could have been... As the reproachful thoughts whirled through his head, he paled, and then flushed with shame.

Sima eyed her brother, curious at his sudden change of pallor. "Think about coming back, Aaron," she whispered. "Mummy has been waiting for you for twenty years. Your room has not been touched. She buys your favorite yogurt, all the time, and throws it out when it goes bad. Aaron...there's got to be a limit for how long this can go on."

38

Two things happened simultaneously, as though choreographed, that shook up and out any lingering fervor borne of the letter: Rabbi Wechter's return, and the clinking of the supper trolley, as a dietary staff member brought in supper for Aaron. Fedora slipped into the room as well, to help Aaron sit up, in the least painful way possible, so he could eat. At least now that his eyes were available, he would be able to feed himself.

The smells emanating from the grilled salmon triggered Sima's salivary glands, reminding her of her own hunger. She had not eaten since the hurried breakfast she'd had that morning, before being driven to the hospital. It suddenly felt like a year had passed since then.

Rabbi Wechter took one look at Sima's face, and suddenly slapped his hand against his forehead. "*Oy vey*! I completely forgot to take the meal my wife packed for you. It is sitting on my kitchen table, in its foil container. You must be starving." He looked stricken. "You can always eat it when I take you back to my house later tonight, but I think you need something now…"

Sima's uneasy smile corroborated his claim. Fedora stood up straight. Her scrubs rustled as she walked to the door. "I'll see what I can do," she said, and left the room.

"What could she possibly do?" Rabbi Wechter asked Sima, who closed her eyes and imperceptibly shook her head, indicating that he should not pursue this line of questioning. Rabbi Wechter shrugged and sat down on a chair. "*Nu*, Aaron. When can we expect you to return?"

Aaron screwed up his forehead. "To what, Rabbi?"

"To us, of course."

"You said I had never left; that what I think is disconnect is really a connection that is bruised. Remember?"

Rabbi Wechter threw his head back and laughed. "*Nitzchuni, banai, nitzchuni*—'You have won over me, my sons, you have won over me!'" he exclaimed, nodding to himself. "I see you are the son of the 'Red Rebel.' Whether it sits well with you or not."

Fedora re-entered the room, carrying a tray of foil-covered food. She handed it to Sima with a wink. Rabbi Wechter's eyes darted from the food to Sima and back again.

Sima smiled inwardly. "Don't judge me," she said, opening the outer covering.

Aaron looked up.

The rabbi said nothing, but his eyes held both surprise and confusion, tinged with, of all things, compassion. He crossed his legs, unbuttoned his jacket, and pulled uncomfortably at his beard, but still said nothing. Aaron too watched as his sister burned her fingers unwrapping the double-sealed foil. When she pulled the aluminum up, they both saw the large sticker, with its unmistakable kosher label written boldly in black Hebrew letters. Rabbi Wechter laughed.

Sima looked at him and playfully wagged her finger. "Judgments, judgments!" she proclaimed. "Will we ever be free of them?!" She picked up the packet of plastic cutlery and removed a fork. Then she made a *brachah* and took her first bite. "Fedora, is your community considered judgmental?" she asked, her mouth full of pasta and sauce.

Fedora laughed. It was like hearing soft rain splattering on the window.

"No, seriously, I really want to know. Does it go on a lot?"

"Oh, yes." She dismissed the seriousness of Sima's tone with a wave of her hand. "But it does not bother me."

"Well, it bothers me…" Sima sounded a tad petulant. It caught Aaron by surprise, and he watched his sister closely as she continued, "Don't look at me like that. It's always bothered me. Even though I myself am guilty of it. Still, it bothers me."

"Where I grew up," Fedora said, "judgments were commonplace. It was a way of life: everyone judged everyone. Which is why I do not care about it today. A few years back, I made a conscious decision about this: I am Muslim. This is my choice. I want to be Muslim. I believe in G-d and in the Koran. But I also respect other religions. Because I want to. Not because…well…you know." She lowered her eyes, and Sima watched her dark skin become even darker. "Some people take human judgments too far…"

Sima nodded in understanding, feeling, perhaps for the first time, the awkwardness that someone with Fedora's mindset must be subject to on a more-or-less constant basis.

Eventually Fedora left to her other duties. Having finished eating, Sima began to feel her head bang faintly and her eyelids droop. These last two days had been very taxing, and her body was begging her to respect its needs, she knew. She thought of her mother—how she needed to go back to London and be with her—and of Aryeh and the girls. Of Tamar. She tried not to feel torn. She needed to plan, to reach some kind of resolve with Aaron.

Rabbi Wechter stood up. "It's getting late," he said, with an apologetic smile. "Mrs. Hertzberg, will you want to stay much longer?"

She stole a quick glance at Aaron, and then turned back to Rabbi Wechter with a shrug.

He understood. "Aaron…" he said softly. "Your sister needs something from you…"

Aaron crinkled his nose. "What?"

No one answered his question. It lingered in the air, drifting about like the proverbial dove in search of where to land.

When Sima arrived back at Rabbi Wechter's quaint apartment, she ate some of the meal that Madame Wechter had packaged for her. She was surprised by her own hunger; she thought it had been placated by the pasta Fedora had kindly provided her with. As she ate the beef bourguignon and the moistest and most delicious mashed potatoes she had ever come across, she withdrew her phone. She was grateful to have the dining room to herself, as both Rabbi and Madame Wechter had already excused themselves and gone to bed.

-Hey Aryeh, u available?

-Yup.

-What's happening at home?

-Tamar's home, did I tell you? She's sick.

-What?! What does she have?

- Strep and some skin rash thing. Nothing to panic about, I just felt it would be best to pick her up from camp and take care of it properly instead of going the "camp nurse" route... Took her to the dermatologist earlier, he prescribed some cream. Going to pick it up soon. What's happening with you? How's Aaron? When do I get to meet him???

-The million-dollar question. Tell me, what is Tamar's mood? Is she still angry with me?

-Can't say for sure. We had a discussion earlier, but nothing conclusive. You will have to face it all when you get back. Sorry. But that's the truth. Think about what you would want to say to her, maybe write it down.

-Maybe I will. Thanks. Goodnight, my dear! Need to zzzzzzz!

-Goodnight, sweet dreams!

G reta Bulman hadn't slept well. The London air was oppressively torpid; not a breeze for miles. Even the leaves appeared fake in their droopy stillness.

At around 4:30 a.m., she got out of bed and hobbled to open her windows wider, in search of a pitiful puff of wind. At five, the garbage truck came rumbling down her street, a racket of jungle music and a sibilating diesel engine; it was like a giant mosquito had landed right near her front garden. At odd intervals its back hopper would lift off, hydraulic cylinders all abuzz, accompanied by whistles and shouts. She simply lay in her bed, listening to the noise while stewing. *Those garbagemen really have some nerve. It's five in morning, and they are carrying on as though it were high noon. I should report them, but I know I won't. What's the use? They have more rights than I do.*

She turned and faced the wall, her elbow tucked under her head. *I wonder how Sima is enjoying that spa. Fancy that! I raised a woman of the world—one who actually uses a spa! I've never been to one myself.*

She paused in her ruminations. *Henya seemed unnerved when I asked her when her sister is coming back. I don't want to think about that. They have always been good to each other, never too close in development to compete. Aaron and Sima? Now they were really close.* Oy, *Hashem!* Greta shut her eyes tight. *Why must my thoughts always bring me back to him? Is he cold? Is he hungry? Did he ever get married? Under which sun does he spend his days? Does he know his father died? How long has it been since he left? About twenty years, and still the ache never abates...*

How can it? I am his mother...

When the burn at the back of her eyes began to soften, she slowly sat up in bed and looked around the room. She caught her reflection in the dresser mirror and recoiled at the sight of the white hairs sticking out of her kerchief. When did *that* transpire? She tugged the kerchief over the top of her head and adjusted it. She stared again in the mirror. *That's better*, she thought. *Who wants to see the aging process as it's happening?*

She looked down at her legs, wiggled her feet until she'd shaken the blanket off. *Well*, she reflected, *I'm up already. May as well start the day.* As she leaned over the side of her bed to wash *negel vasser*, a sudden thought struck her: *How wonderful would today be if Aaron would just walk up the front path, enter our house, and come back into our lives once again...*

Oh, stop! For Heaven's sake, just stop these thoughts already!

Greta glanced at the clock on her night table. The red lights glowed at her: 5:27 a.m. Too early to call Henya. Then she remembered what Henya had told her the evening before, how Elchanan had instructed the girls to shunt him out of their hearts. *Oh, Elchanan, was that really necessary? Would that have solved things for you? Did you really think it would have been possible, anyway? Maybe with Henya, but I know Sima. She is just like you. You never stopped thinking of him. Don't deny it. Well, neither has she. Extra pressure is all it must have added for her. Extra, unnecessary pressure. Ah, well...we all make mistakes.*

But this one, Elchanan, dear, this one is a bit of a biggy.

She needed to get up. Slowly, slowly, she pulled herself to a standing position. The pain in her hip had mellowed, like smoldering embers that lit up only when poked. She gritted her teeth, telling herself to soldier on. Deepa would not arrive until seven. What was she to do until then? She was already up; sleep had bypassed her. So...how to use the time? She walked slowly toward the bathroom, measuring her resolve against the space between her room and the bathroom door.

The sounds her empty house made had never bothered her before: the creak of a floor board, the flaring of the water heater, the moaning of a wall. Only recently, since her fall, did any extra noise give her pause. Her left hand gripped the molding on the wall as she tottered along the hallway...and found herself closer to Aaron's bedroom door than she had intended. Or perhaps she *had* intended to come this close? She held on to the door handle of his room, telling herself to use it as anchorage, but the faster she maneuvered herself, the surer she was to sneak into that place that she always, purposely kept closed off.

Standing now at the doorway, she peered meekly inside. *Maybe*, she pondered, as she took in the strips of sunbeams filtering through the brown, heavy curtains, *I had wanted to do this all along. How long has it been since I stepped in here?* She could not remember exactly. It had always depressed her to see her son's old Airfix models, his favorite books, his set of Chumashim and Mishnayos, all sitting on their shelves, never moving, the musty smell of his adolescence still lingering on his clothes. She picked up a torn piece of paper sticking out of a notebook on the dresser. She had read it a thousand times. She read it again. It was just a phone number, nothing special, but it was written by *his hand.*

His bed was made. She had made it about a week after he left. She hadn't had the strength to straighten it out any earlier. Then, around a year later, she had purchased new linens for him and remade the bed. But other than a cleaning lady who came in and cleaned the room once a year, no one ever entered here. She had to admit—though she had waged a silent war for this eventuality not to occur—that Aaron's room had morphed itself into a shrine, complete with its own, time-locked energy. She felt like an intruder, like her presence was unwanted in this place. She shuddered as an icy chill came upon her from that horrible notion.

Still, she sat down on the bed. It gasped as it dipped from her weight. This was a new sound, something she had not heard before. *I guess the springs have rusted*, she told herself. *Time does not pass without erosion. Look at me. Will Aaron even recognize me, whenever he comes back?*

There I go again...

...presuming...

She wished, at that moment, for something so simple: Yes, she wanted him back, but oh...to, at the very least, control her thoughts! The images the room brought back were relentless in their cruelty. And, once unleashed, she knew how pointless her struggle to re-contain them would be. Better to submit, she thought. Better to let them wash over her than to try to hold them back...

In her mind's eye, she saw it all: Elchanan's back, his shoulders trembling from the blows he had ministered, his glasses falling to the floor from the impact...the color of his rage, the depths of his shame. Aaron's blood. At first it trickled from his nose, before dripping over the sheets and carpet. Worst of all was his acceptance. Not a finger did he lift to protect himself. Not even a simple lowering of his head. He just sat there, consenting to his father's murderous intensity, slowly wiping the blood with the back of his hand. How pathetic he had looked. Both of them. And something fearful had opened up inside her, as she watched then and remembered now. It had never gone away: that seismic tremor, when her subconscious was made aware of how cold he was inside. Like he was a walking, breathing, undead.

"Aaron," she whimpered, "please, try to find it in your heart to return to us. Please... Your mother's heart aches endlessly..."

When the lament ended, so did her thoughts. Grateful for the nothingness that replaced them, Greta simply continued to sit. Time passed slowly inside that room.

"It's no good," she muttered, finally, and lifted herself off the bed. "It will do no good to brood." She shuffled out of the room, glancing once over her shoulder, before firmly shutting the door.

By the time she got back from the bathroom to her bed, the garbagemen were no longer spicing the stratosphere with their street language and raucous laughter. A semi-perfect peace hovered over Ashley Grove for a while, and Greta could not decide what to do. The dithering itself upset her. Why was she such a burden to herself? Why couldn't she just read something? Or organize a drawer or two, as she had promised herself she would get to, one of these fine days? Why did everything set her into a quandary?

Absently, she maneuvered herself to the foot of her bed. Sima popped into her head again. Well, what else should occupy a mother's mind in her old age, if not her children? It seemed to Greta that Sima gave too much credence to the letter Elchanan had written to Aaron. Greta laughed quietly to herself, a small, indulgent laugh. Elchanan, she knew, had not been a man of words, never striking the right tone in a language not his own. No. If anything would bring back her son, it would not be this letter, she thought, opening the bottom drawer.

Sima's staunch naiveté still marks her a child. Greta shook her head. *Now Henya—she's different. She couldn't care less about Aaron, or maybe that's just how she needs to play it, in order to live her life. One thing I have learned: each must face the world on their own terms.* Greta shuffled around the nightgowns in the drawer, until her fingers hit the smooth coolness of the cigar case. She wrapped her fingers around its sides and brought it out from under the delicate fabrics of its encasement. She closed her eyes and said a short prayer.

THURSDAY MORNING, JULY 16, 2015
PARIS, FRANCE

A aron kicked off his blanket and scrunched it at the foot of his bed. A sudden airlessness came upon his room, making everything feel tight around him. It was almost 7:00 a.m. He eyed the large half-open window. Today, he decided, would be the day of his "Great Return." The piercing shrieks of Parisian birds did not encourage him to eke out another day in a city that had lost its enchantment for him. Today, he resolved.

Today would be the day.

He let one leg fall to the floor and steadied it before lowering the other. Leaning against the night table, he stabilized his weight before lifting himself completely off the bed. Once upright, a slight dizziness rolled through him, bathing his peripheral vision in twinkling lights. He waited for the feeling to go away. With his arms out like a balance beam, he made his way to the window, and held on to the ledge, breathing in the city air. On the other side of the street, a cluster of large horse-chestnut trees seemed to house a flock of shrieking sparrows earnestly complaining about the early daybreak, and how they hadn't been given enough hours of sleep before the rudeness of sunrise's ill-begotten splendor had driven the night away. Aaron leaned his head into the sill, smiling languidly to himself. *Shhhh*, he told them. *It's not all that bad.*

All at once, a thought sang through his mind, fluffy and light with the joy of memory, and he began to recite: *Modeh ani l' fanecha… I give thanks before You, O Living King, that You have returned to me, with mercy, my soul. How great is Your faithfulness!*

He laughed inside himself, and then he cried, and then he *decried.* Decried and bemoaned, that he—the bum, the no-goodnik, from no-goodnik land—should remember (and with such precision!) a prayer that he hadn't said in over twenty years!

Do you hear, Rabbi Zeligbaum, Rabbi Pomensky, and Rabbi Isaacs? I, Aaron Rephael Bulman, the lowest of the low, king of the Ne'er-Do-Wells, an "ois-varf" if there ever was one, have not forgotten how to say Modeh Ani*! How Mummy would* kvell*! Not you, misters. My mother! Yes, she should take credit. But wait…hold your horses. Don't let us get carried away. Was I allowed to say a prayer without first washing my hands?! Oh, no. Should a prayer become enmeshed in the loathsome squalor of my filth and impurity…?*

Vaguely he remembered, had the courage to once more remember, a teaching from his youth: sleep is partial death. *Do not touch any part of your body before washing your hands in the morning,* boomed the collective voices of his youth. Aaron lifted his hands and inspected them closely. He turned them over, staring into the creases of his palms and fingers, the tips of his nails, the dirt beneath them. He twiddled his fingers, rubbed his hands together. What was impurity? How did it feel? Why did his fingers suddenly feel clammy? Like grunge and grime were germinating on their padded crowns. He brought them to his nose and sniffed. Nothing. No smell. Yet, he was certain that they felt—for lack of a better word—*impure.*

It had to be nonsense. A trick of the mind. *Maybe I am not, after all, remembering right. It's been a long time…how could I be sure of anything?*

He held his head in his hands. So many, many things had slipped through the variegated cracks of his memory. How would he ever learn it all again? Why should he bother?

An hour later, Rabbi Wechter was adjusting the black leather *tefillin* box on Aaron's left bicep, wrapping the straps along his arm. He motioned for Aaron to repeat the blessing after him. Then he took out the second box, kissed it, and unraveled the black straps attached to it. He tightened the leather loop around Aaron's head, aligning the black box with the upper middle of his forehead.

"How do you feel?" Rabbi Wechter asked.

Aaron grinned. "As snug as a bug in a rug."

"No, really..."

"It feels foreign...but not in a bad way."

"Okay," said Rabbi Wechter, in a low voice. "I want you to concentrate now. The mind, the heart, the hand. Those are three very different worlds. Your head, Aaron, is the seat of all thought. Your heart," he tapped the black box secured on Aaron's arm, facing the heart, "is the realm of emotion. And your arm and hand," he tugged lightly on Aaron's left hand, "is action. All your thoughts, your feelings, all the way down to your actions, should work in harmony with Hashem. The passages inscribed on the parchments within these boxes contain the Shema prayer, invoking Hashem's Oneness, our love for Him, and the freedom He gave us from Egyptian bondage—to become His nation and to serve Him, without compromise. Close your eyes, Aaron. Cover them with your right hand. Say Shema. It is time."

Aaron lifted his right hand and covered his eyes. He cleared his throat and recited Shema. Then he paused to swallow and opened his eyes, blinking away some tears. "Can I continue?" he asked.

"Please do..."

He closed his eyes again, and continued in an undertone, "*Baruch Shem Kevod Malchuso...*" *Blessed be the name of the glory of His kingdom forever and ever.* Beneath his eyelids sprang his childhood, snapshots of the past: his mother's arms around him, his father poring over an open *sefer* he could not understand, his sisters walking in front of him, on their way to school...

When at last his eyes opened, the rabbi gestured that he should go on. Aaron recited the first paragraph of Shema, needing help in only two places. Only when it was over did he realize that he had been sweating. Was it possible for him to dissect and label all of the many emotions that overwhelmed him just then? There was joy, to be sure, but also fear. Of what? He could not be certain. Was it fear of risk? Fear of the loss of a carefully sculpted self-containment? Electricity trickled through him, reaching every cell of his body. *So this is what "full circle" means*, he thought to himself. Maybe Tatte would be happy now, looking down from Above.

"So? How does it feel to be back?"

Aaron could not answer. He bowed his head slightly. It was enough. The rabbi helped him unwrap the *tefillin*. They worked in silence. When they were done, Aaron posed his question. "Rabbi, I'm having trouble remembering: am I allowed to say *Modeh Ani* before washing my hands in the morning?"

Rabbi Wechter beamed at his disciple. "Yes. You can," he said.

"So I *do* remember correctly." Aaron rubbed his forehead, smiling with relief. "I was worried I'd lost everything in the passage of time. Okay, how come?"

"Come on, Aaron, you can answer this one yourself."

"Because we are to acknowledge G-d in the first moments of consciousness? Is that it?"

"Exactly. No impurity on earth can defile the *Modeh Ani* of a Jew." As he spoke, Rabbi Wechter wrapped the straps of his *tefillin* around the boxes, before placing them back into their navy-blue velvet pouch and zippering it. "Like I said, Judaism is not a religion. We don't worry about getting to Heaven. We simply try to bring Heaven down here, to Earth..."

"Okay, okay. I get it." Aaron pursed his lips. "Now, I think I want to go back to sleep for a bit. Do you know when Sima is supposed to arrive?"

"Oh, she was sleeping when I left the house. There was no reason to wake her up so early. I will tell my driver to bring her here whenever she is ready. Goodbye for now, Aaron." The rabbi opened the door.

"Goodbye, Rabbi Wechter. And...thank you." Aaron yawned and lifted himself, slowly, back into the bed.

Muffled voices floated through the cracks of the door, along with the smell of fried onions and eggs, but she, Sima, was running with Aaron. He looked as he had when he was a young boy, his wispy hair unevenly cut, his black yarmulke piped with silver, a gap where his two front teeth would grow back. He was calling her name. They were in their favorite park. She held out her hand and tried to grab his, but their hands just never seemed to connect.

She looked up for a moment, and then froze. He couldn't glimpse it—his back was to it—but she could see an enormous dog, almost like a wolf, leaping toward them, hackles raised, front teeth showing, growling, barking, frenzied. She wanted to scream, warn her brother, but her voice made no sound. She ran toward him and tried to cover him with her body, but instead she felt herself being lifted above him—floating. Terrified of her lost balance and of the carnage that would soon occur below her, she maneuvered her arms, as though she were swimming in water, trying to reach Aaron, who still had not noticed the danger he was in.

At last she grabbed his shoulders and tried to pick him up, so he could join her in flight. But he kept slipping away from her. And then, as he fell, the enormous dog pounced and blocked her view. She flew off, her mind exploding, an inner sob demanding release.

She awoke in a sweat, pulse pummeling at her throat. She sat up, motionless, focusing first on the small purple flowers embroidered on the comforter and reproduced on the wallpaper, and then on the sun's warm presence outside, pushing its way through the window. Slowly she purged herself of her dream, forcing the images out of her mind. She looked at her watch: it was 8:58 a.m. She threw off the blanket and whispered *Modeh Ani*, thanking G-d for His faith in her to do her best today. She stumbled out of the bed and into the bathroom to wash her hands.

If I catch the two o'clock ferry this afternoon, she thought, *I could be back in London by seven p.m.*

Half an hour later, Sima emerged from her room, her luggage trailing behind her.

"*Bonjour, s'il vous plaît, ne partez pas sans quelque chose d'abord à manger.*" Madame Wechter's voice made her jump; Sima hadn't imagined that anyone was still in the house with her. She walked toward the voice and found her hostess sitting on one of the brown floral couches in the living room. She had been reading a French newspaper, but was now folding it away and getting up, ready to serve her guest.

"I'm so sorry." Sima bit her lip. "I don't speak French." How was she going to get to the hospital?

"Oh, yes. I forget. My English iz not good like my husband's, but I speak little bit. You need to eat. Yes? I have food in ze kitchen for you. Please. Take." And then, as though reading her thoughts, she added, "My husband has car waiting outside. To bring you to hospital, when… er… you…er…ready. Yes?" She smiled. Sima smiled back.

Madame Wechter was a petite, well-groomed woman, exactly the sort Sima would imagine for the respectable stature of wife of the rabbi of Synagogue Kedushat Tzion. She wore a simple, light-gray dress, with two ruffles at the bottom and on the cuffs. A pink apron was tied to her waist, and a three-tiered pink necklace fell gracefully from her neck. On her head, Madame Wechter wore a short, blonde, fluffy wig. A touch of soft pink rouge on her cheeks completed the look. She walked by Sima and took her hand, leading her toward the kitchen.

"You to sit," she said, as she pulled out a chair squeezed between a cabinet and the table and gestured for Sima to take it. She turned to the gas stove and began heating up the onion omelette that Sima had smelled earlier in her dream.

"Thank you," Sima said. She rested her elbows on the table, watching Madame Wechter work. Clearly, this was a woman in possession of herself, she thought, noting the casual elegance with which she operated in her compact kitchen. The room was typical of Paris: sparklingly clean, but minuscule compared to American standards. A tiny stove and fridge, two small sinks, some counter space, wall-to-wall cabinetry, and a table and four chairs plunked right in the center.

Madame Wechter placed a plate of food down before her. "You will need strength," she said. "Please, take *nourriture*."

Sima looked at her, gratitude in her eyes.

"You leave us today? *Oui*? It haz been hard, no? To see your brother, after so long years. How will you part today? He will go wiz you? He will stay? Your *mere*, she still lives?"

"*Oui*," said Sima.

They both laughed.

It was after 10:00 a.m. by the time Rabbi Wechter's car pulled up at the American Hospital in Paris. Sima thanked the driver and walked at an even, rhythmic clip along the sidewalk to the hospital's main entrance. She smiled inwardly as strands from her *sheitel* lifted in the wind. She felt light, less conflicted than she remembered feeling for quite some time, certainly since reading Tamar's epistle. Hope germinated inside her like a weed. She kept telling herself to put a halt to it, that it was too early to suppose anything, but utopia auto-flowered within her heart's vision, and she was helpless to administer it any mindful influence or caution.

She hurried through the revolving door, wheeling her suitcase behind her, and climbed the stairs to the second floor. How well-rested she felt! She was grateful for the finesse of her hosts, and grateful that she had come, that she had done what she had done. She pushed through the double-doored entrance of Aaron's ward and walked past the nurses' station. Spotting Fedora in her usual place there, she gave a wave, the contentedness she felt made stronger for having encountered so incorruptible a spirit as her brother's nurse.

And so it was that, happier than she had allowed herself to feel in a long time, she approached Room 154, a song in her heart, a smile on her lips.

Aaron?

She stopped short at the room's threshold. His bed was empty, his room sterile.

She turned and ran out to the hallway, her free arm around her stomach. She cried out, a thin, moribund wail, as her organs constricted while she fought down spasms of terror and madness. People began to crowd around her, alarmed by her stunted cries. Fedora caught her just as her feet lost their grip on the floor.

"What? What is it?" Fedora whispered into her ear.

"Aaron..." Sima felt her tongue swelling, her speech slurring. "Aaron. My brother. Where...is...he?"

With Sima's shoulders slumped over her bent knees, Fedora peered toward the room. "He should still be..." She stopped talking and turned to call to another nurse. "*Où est le patient dans la Chambre 154? Aaron Bulman? Pourquoi il a disparu? Quand est-il parti?*"

"*Nous ne savons pas. On nous a juste dit de préparer la chambre.*"

Fedora wrinkled her forehead in confusion. "I don't know what to tell you," she said to Sima. "He must have left, by himself. Discharged himself early. They don't know where he went; they just had instructions to clean the room..."

Sima stared up at her, not wanting to process, resisting Fedora's words. At first she went hot, and then terribly, terribly cold. Her upper arms felt heavy, and the walls of the corridor appeared to her as though they were swaying. She battled with herself for poise, pulling herself off Fedora's lap and into an upright position. Flashes of memory from that morning in May, 1995, bombarded her: her mother's wailing... her father's gruff anger...her own unstoppable trembling when they discovered the note on his bed...

Why? Why would he run away again?

Was it me...? Am I to blame...?

Oh, Aaron!

Aaron...!

Someone gave Fedora a glass of water, which she pressed into Sima's face, forcing the cold cup to her lips. The water splashed down the sides of her mouth. She gasped. "Stop! Please stop! I don't have time. Thank you." She extricated herself from Fedora's arms, and ran out of the ward and into a waiting elevator. She punched the "ground floor" button and waited, biting at her knuckles for the doors to close and for the elevator to begin its descent. Every moment counted now!

Once in the lobby, she ran through the revolving doors and out into the street. Looking both ways, she hailed a taxi, entered, and barked, "Campagne de Blocage. The synagogue. Please. Quick." The driver, an older man whose blue veins could be followed from his temple down his neck, followed her frenzied gesticulations through his rear-view mirror, nodded in comprehension—*Okay, madame, I understand you're in a rush*—and sped off.

When he'd pulled up at the curb near Rabbi Wechter's shul, Sima opened her purse and shoved some bills into the driver's hand.

A confused expression spread over the man's kindly, weathered features. "Excuse me...is too much," he said in broken English, awarding her with a half-smile.

Sima hardly heard what he was saying. Did he want more money? She looked again into her purse and took out another bill. "Is this enough?" she asked impatiently, her right foot already out of the car, one hand pulling at her suitcase.

The driver laughed. "Oh, you English people... Here, this your change," he said, stuffing some bills back into her hand.

She grabbed the money and alighted from the car. Turning toward the shul, she noticed that the police presence had whittled down to one lonely-looking lad holding his gun gingerly across his forearm, like a cherished newborn. Most of the yellow police lines had also been removed. She marched through the white gate and down the paved path along with her suitcase, swinging her free arm menacingly, as though fighting with the air.

She pulled at the glass doors, but they did not budge. She looked for a bell, and found a small, hidden one behind a pillar. She pressed it. Waited. Pressed it again. Nothing. A third time. She peered through the glass, using her hand as a visor, and was relieved to see a man approach the door. It was not Rabbi Wechter, but maybe he could direct her to him.

"Do you speak English?" she demanded, as soon as he opened the door.

"A little," he replied.

"Where is Rabbi Wechter?"

The man pointed inside the building, to the left of the sanctuary. Breathing fast, Sima followed his directions and came into a large office with four cubicles and two closed rooms at the back. The man indicated that Rabbi Wechter occupied the left office at the back.

Sima walked right up to the door and knocked urgently. Not waiting for a response, she opened it. The rabbi was sitting by his desk, speaking casually on the phone. *He is either completely oblivious, or completely callous*, she thought.

He looked up, saw her, and paled, his smile instantly fading from his face. "*Je dois partir. Je te rappellerai. Je suis désolée. Oui, oui, je vais appeler bien tôt...* I have to go. I'll call you back. I'm sorry. Yeah, yeah, I'll call early," he said into the receiver. Then he put down the phone and faced her.

She knew immediately that he had no clue why she was there. Her heart beat furiously. "He's gone!" she said.

"What do you mean, 'gone'?" Rabbi Wechter asked.

"He left. I got to the hospital, and his bed, his room…they're empty! They don't know where he is!" She staggered to one of the armchairs that lined the back of the room and collapsed into it. "He left without a trace!"

"But I was just there this morning! He put on *tefillin* with me. He gave me no indication…"

"Did I pressure him too much?" she interrupted. "Were the two of *us* too much for *him*?" She covered her face with shaking hands, unable to stop her whole body from trembling. Rabbi Wechter remained still, looking through the window, out into the parking lot behind the building.

"Mrs. Hertzberg," he finally said, after she began rooting in her bag for tissues. "Some people don't want to be found."

"Noooooooo!" She leaned forward, clenching her fists and teeth. "I can't live with this anymore!" she cried, striking her chest violently. "I stole my father's letter from my mother. She doesn't even know I'm *here*. What am I supposed to tell her now?!"

Rabbi Wechter did not reply. Retreating into gloomy silence, they both considered their next step. Suddenly, Sima looked up. "Hold on! You have his number. Right? You must have something!"

Rabbi Wechter did not move. Only his eyes turned to meet hers. Then he shook his head slowly. "Mrs. Hertzberg, I cannot, at this point, take the chance of giving you his contact information. I am so sorry. I did not realize he is still at risk to run. Please, understand…"

"*No!*" She stood up. "*Don't* ask *me* to understand! *You* need to understand! This is my *brother* we're talking about! My mother's son. You cannot withhold this information from me. With all due respect, Rabbi, who are you, anyway? A stranger, as far as I'm concerned! You have no right to…to—"

"Correct. I have no right. But I feel I must anyway. Do you have any idea how easy it would be for him to fall away again? Change numbers, place of employment, address? Clearly," he paused, "he isn't ready yet."

Sima searched inside herself for a counterstrike, but found that she had nothing to say for herself.

She has nothing to say for herself... There she is, eleven years old, standing in the hallowed chamber of the dean's office, looking forlorn in the thick, suffocating smoke that crams and pollutes the air from the many packs a day that the dean goes through. She watches the small gray puffs fall from his mouth with every word he speaks on his phone, as he ignores her. The large, sunny windows overlooking the recess yard in the back of the building do nothing to dispel the stale vapor that hangs in the room. Not an inch is free; there is no place to run. It comes at her like a filthy cloth brought over her face every time she takes a breath.

She was sent there this morning because her teacher had said, "Well, girls, if you act like babies, I shall have to treat you like babies," and she had had the gall to retort, "You cannot treat us like babies, because our parents pay tuition for you to treat us properly!" And her teacher had her brought to the dean's office, for "intolerable chutzpah." And he hasn't even acknowledged her presence yet.

When he finally does notice her, it is simply to tell her to continue waiting. "I have a number of pressing issues to attend to, Sima Rivka Bulman. I do not appreciate that you are here."

She waits. Finally, he puts down the phone and turns to face her, his fingers already clutching another cigarette.

"So, Sima Rivka Bulman," he says at last. One hand snags at his lighter. "I hear that you have been rude. That you have spoken out of line. That you have told your teacher how she is to treat you and your classmates. Is this true?"

"Yes," she answers, trying not to breathe.

"Then, what do you have to say for yourself?" That was the refrain they always used. It was the very opposite of refuge; a mocking refrain. She didn't want to answer. "Well, Sima Rivka Bulman, I'm waiting. What do you have to say for yourself?" Whiffs of new smoke gently add to the already crowded air.

"My parents pay tuition for the teachers to teach me," she finally says. "I am here to learn. Not to be treated like a baby."

"Ahh." The dean sits up in his chair, a small smile creaking out from the sides of his mouth. "Well, I have something to tell you, Sima Rivka Bulman: Your parents do not pay tuition. At least not this year. Your father asked for an extension; he said things are very tight for your family right now." He stops for a moment to let it sink in, and then continues, "So, Sima Rivka Bulman, what else do you have to say for yourself?"

Only Sima finds that she has nothing else to say for herself. Nothing else at all...

"Give me my brother's number." The words slipped out of her mouth.

"Mrs. Hertzberg, I want to tell you about my son, my second oldest. Avraham Yehuda, his name is."

Sima had no interest in listening to him. If biting animosity could be harnessed into weaponry, she could not—at that moment—trust herself with this man. But having nowhere else to go or be, she begrudgingly sat back down and stared at the floor. "Go on," she said with a sigh.

"It seemed that wherever he was, trouble was. Like it stalked him." Rabbi Wechter closed his eyes, a small smile playing at his lips. "One day the principal of the school—his name was Rabbi Pinter—calls up and tells us to please stop taking Avraham Yehuda to an early morning *minyan*, as he is obligated to daven in school, like everyone else. My wife said to him, 'Rabbi Pinter, my husband *never* takes Avraham Yehuda to an early *minyan*. Why would you think he does?' Well, there was this awkward silence on the other end of the line, and then he said, 'Mrs. Wechter, I don't know how to tell you this, but your Avraham Yehuda has not been davening with us all year, since he says he attends the early *minyan* with his father. Which means he's been lying. Which means that he has been lying to you too, telling you that he's davening in school when he isn't. Which means he hasn't been davening. Period. Which may mean that you have a greater problem on your hands.' And my wife, she made a very wise decision right then and there. She said to the principal, 'Leave this to me. Don't do or say anything.' And later, when we thought together about what to do, we decided that perhaps the best thing would be to do *nothing*."

"Nothing?"

"Yes. Nothing. You see, Mrs. Hertzberg, *tefillah* is called 'service of the heart.' When it comes to davening, there is nothing anyone can do for anyone else. It's a very personal, individual thing. Avraham Yehuda wasn't yet ready to daven. He didn't see the need for it. We had to wait for the need to awaken within him. Had we used force, he may never have had the opportunity to find it within *himself*—which is the only place that really counts."

"So where is he now?"

"Oh," chuckled Rabbi Wechter, "Avraham Yehuda is married and has a bunch of kids. He lives in Eretz Yisrael. He runs a small publishing house there, and you can be sure that he davens every day, three times a day."

Sima remained unmoved. "I see, I see...but it's just so...so...*hard!*" She dabbed her eyes with her sleeve. "What if I give you my word that I won't call Aaron until you say he is ready?"

"What if I give you his number as soon as I know, for sure, that he's ready?"

"I don't like giving you control," she said, without looking at him. Then she added, "Not specifically you. Anyone."

"I understand. What if you don't hear from me for three months? If three months pass, and I haven't given you his number, then I will admit I failed, and I will give you his number anyway. Three months. That's all I ask."

"So what am I supposed to do now? Just go back home and sit tight?" Rabbi Wechter's face suddenly looked tired. She felt a pang of regret. "Sorry," she mumbled, and closed her eyes. "It's just that... twenty years of waiting—it's interminable."

"It will end. Be assured, it will."

Silence. Then Sima spoke up again. "You know, Rabbi Wechter, I have, over the years, been very hard on myself. I've often reproached myself about why I didn't try harder when Aaron and I were younger. What stopped me from reaching out to him more? I always think, or fantasize, that I could have made him happy. That I could have brought him to see the light. Why didn't I?" Sima was looking directly into the rabbi's eyes now as she spoke.

"Well, now I have my answer. There are only so many times you can fail at something, before you give up altogether." She placed the palm of her hand over her heart. "I can't bear this pain!" she whispered. "I want so badly to forget about him, forget about wanting to save him. I practically did. But I'm here now, again, and nothing seems to have changed."

Rabbi Wechter shook his head. "How wrong you are, Mrs. Hertzberg," he murmured. "*Plenty* has changed..."

T here was no one waiting for her at the dock. Not that she expected anyone to be there, waving a colorful handkerchief, drying an eye, calling her name. Those things only happened in plays or in books, with other people. Not with her. Alone, she yanked at her suitcase and followed the crowd down the gangplank and into the line at Customs and Immigration, passport in hand.

An hour or so later, when she got off the train at Victoria station, she again looked around, foolishly, for someone, anyone, to meet her. Who had she expected? Henya? *I've let everyone down*, she thought. *I have nothing to show for my travels.* But even as she had those thoughts, a little voice inside her whispered, *But you saw him! Spoke with him! Cried and laughed and ate with him! You could tell them all: He is* alive! *That's not nothing!*

She arrived back at her childhood home in Ashley Grove in the early evening, and let herself in. It was very quiet. She inhaled deeply. Ahhhh, the smells of her youth! The Persil detergent that her mother used; the musty wood smell of the bookcases, standing in pristine order; the particular scent that the old gas stove gave off...they were all working in harmony, letting her know she was home.

She went into the kitchen, took out a carton of orange juice, poured a tall glass for herself, and made a *brachah*. As she drank, she stared out at the backyard, at the tops of the tall conker trees behind the furthest wall, noticing how violently they rippled when the harmless summer winds flitted through them. She had gotten to halfway down the glass, when suddenly the house seemed to breathe too heavily, too closely; the clock ticking through the living room wall a little too loudly, a fly bashing itself, kamikaze-like, against the window. An odd and unexpected fear crawled from her neck down her back. *Maybe*, she thought, *maybe the juice is too cold*. She gulped the last few drops and ran out of the kitchen and up the stairs.

Knocking lightly on her mother's bedroom door, she strained her ears to try to hear the sounds of her mother's even breathing. When she heard nothing, she turned the doorknob and burst into the room in a panic. Her mother's bed was unmade and empty. The curtains billowed in from the open windows. Then her eyes caught the mess on the floor at the foot of the bed: nightgowns, all thrown about in a muddle, and the empty cigar box, open, lying on its side.

Sima gasped, and a cold pang of wretchedness mushroomed like a great toxic cloud within her. She flew across her mother's bed and grabbed the phone on the night table. She dialed and drummed her fingers while counting the rings.

At last someone picked up. "Hello?"

"Henya? Henya, is that you?"

"Yes. It is." Henya's voice sounded flat.

"Where is Mummy?"

"Where should she be?"

"Don't play games with me, Henya. Just tell me where she is. Is she all right?"

"She's right here. In my house. Sleeping, actually. She's in the guest room."

"Oh..."

"Well, what did you expect? She couldn't stay by herself after discovering your little pilferage."

"Did you tell her where I was?"

"No, of course not. Doesn't matter, though, does it? She's furious with you."

"I'll get it back."

"*What?* You don't *have* it? Sima, what in the...!"

"What should I do? He took it!"

"Who? Aaron?"

"Yes. Stop barking!"

"I'm not barking. You are!" There was a pause. "You saw him?" Henya's voice softened a tiny bit.

"Yes, Henya. I did."

"And?"

"And what?"

"And...? Is he coming home? Where is he?"

Sima swallowed. "I don't know... I actually don't know the answer to either of those questions."

"Sima?"

Sima could not speak; a rock-like substance seemed to be blocking her windpipe. Her grip tightened around the receiver, and her eyes, once again, filled.

Henya spoke again. "Maybe you should go home. To Long Island, I mean. Things were calmer here without you."

"I'm going back as soon as I can, Henya. Just as soon as I can." A small tear trickled down Sima's cheek as she replaced the receiver. Two minutes later she lifted it again and redialed. "Henya?"

"What now?"

"Don't you want to know how he is? Don't you have any questions? Don't you want to know what we spoke about?"

"No." She paused. "I am perfectly fine. Tatte told us what to do about him, and that's what I've been doing ever since."

Sima absorbed this new blow. A foreign and unwanted distaste for her little sister brewed softly in her stomach. "Okay. Fair enough. Where will Mummy be for Shabbos?"

"Here." There was another pause. Then: "Sima, you shouldn't have gone. You shouldn't have taken Tatte's letter. True, Mummy lived to give that stupid thing to Aaron. A waste of her energy and emotions, as far as I'm concerned. But still, you should have left it alone."

Just as well, Sima thought. *I have nothing to tell her anyway.* "Okay. Thanks."

"For what?"

"For taking care of Mummy."

Silence followed. Then: "Sima?"

"Yes?"

"Please don't call again. Okay?"

"I can't believe you don't want to know what happened…"

Click.

That night, the tossing Sima did beneath her old quilt should have counted as exercise in a fair world. The house's desertedness preyed on her sleep; the ingredients of restfulness—comfort, security, and a sense of well-being—all shunned her. In their place, inescapable in the dark quietude of that night, were the feelings of shame, guilt, and anger. Paramount to her misery was the notion that she had only made things worse; that her meddling had been counterproductive; that all she had learned in both her training and practicing of social work had failed her at the time of her most critical need. *All the good intentions in the world*, she thought, *haven't helped reduce the damage I have wrought, to have pushed him further away…*

Eventually she got out of bed, turned on the old computer, and attempted to compose a letter to Tamar.

Dear Tamar, she typed, and then deleted it.

She began again:

Dearest Tamar, my sweet little girl, my firstborn,

How can I tell you how sorry I am? I had no idea this would happen to you. None. I never intended for you to hear about my brother "from the street." I just couldn't think of a time when I could tell you about him. I realize now how feeble that must sound to you. I think, deep down, that I wanted to tell you, to talk to you, about him, my brother Aaron, to tell you everything. But if I am to be honest (and I really, really want to be), I was scared. I did not want you to carry this burden.

I now see how wrong that was. But one thing you need to know, Tamar, is that I never wrote Aaron off. Not ever. He has lived inside my heart all these years. Ask Abba. He knows this for a fact. He and I have discussed it many times. I always pined to reconnect with him, always davened that wherever he was, he should be happy and healthy. Bubby and I speak of him always. Only, I would make sure none of you girls were in earshot when we spoke about him. It became so second-nature for me, I didn't even think about it. It was always our little secret, Bubby's and mine. And now I understand that that little secret ended up hurting you. Ironic, no? How I wanted to protect you, and ended up hurting you. I would like to think that by the end of camp, when you come back home, we can hash all this out together, and then, with baby steps, we could try to rebuild. Maybe...

She paused to reread what she'd written...and deleted the whole thing again. All of it. Then she got back into her childhood bed, brought the covers up to her chin, and tried, once again, to fall asleep.

It was ten minutes to eight when Sima opened her puffy eyelids and took in her surroundings. She had awoken in too many different beds over the last week to make waking up pleasant. Besides, her head pounded from lack of the refreshing sleep so long denied her. She rubbed her temples, trying to conjure small reasons to slide out from under the warm bedclothes and into the next moment. Had it not been Friday, she would have called the airline, packed her bags, and flown back home immediately, relishing the fact that she would be at her own kitchen table in time for supper with her family. The dip into her "gene pool" had left her half-drowned and shaken. She needed Aryeh's solid, understated strength, the consistent texture of his spirit, the mostly unsullied quality of the life they had built together. She had been away for less than two weeks, yet it felt like perpetuity. But flying on Friday was way too risky, so her return trip would have to wait until after Shabbos.

Which meant that Shabbos would be spent right here, in her mother's home...albeit alone.

After showering, davening, and eating, Sima felt better. She needed to shop for Shabbos—and shopping was always a good distraction. Letting herself out of the house, she calculated her best route to get all the things on her list, and realized that Henya's house, on Morley Crescent, was pretty close to all the stores she needed to get to.

She smiled inwardly. It seemed as though the decisions were being made for her. Buoyed now by what she deemed beyond her control, she strolled up the slight incline of Ashley Grove and turned onto High Road.

Henya, just you wait. I'm a-coming!

Sima's hand hovered over the black iron gate that opened to the path leading to Henya's front door. She checked her watch again: 10:05 a.m. A rush of trepidation unfurled within her, making rubble of her insides. She was unwelcome here, by both her sister and mother; seething, as they were, at her perfidy. *Best not to think*, she told herself. *Just keep moving.*

The clanging of the gate, as it closed quickly behind her, caused her resolve to buckle. *When did that gate get upgraded?* she thought. *It's funny how things get noticed when you least expect to notice them.* She looked around her. *Henya's been busy. I don't remember those white flowers, nor these stunning beds of bluebells. Good for her!*

At the frosted-glass front door, she pulled her shoulders back and lifted her head, drawing her breath in. An attempt at confidence? A bid? A plea? ...Or perhaps just a whimper. She rang the bell.

From behind the door she could hear running, a young girl's squeal, the doorknob twisting and the bolt pulling, until, at last, the door swung open. Her eight-year-old niece stood there, wearing a salmon-pink linen dress and an enormous matching bow. Upon seeing Sima, her freckled face lit up with a grin, revealing the gap where her two front teeth would one day be.

"Hey, Aunty Sima! You're back!" the child shouted with exuberance, flying into Sima's open arms as only a child, whose freedom to feel is sacrosanct, could. Sima held her close, smelling her blonde hair and missing her own daughters.

By the time they parted, Sima noticed that Henya was standing a few feet away, wearing a green paisley snood, a full face of makeup... and a frown on her lips.

"I need to talk with Mummy," Sima said, her eyes darting with discomfort.

Henya did not say anything. As Sima walked past her, no words passed between them. The little girl watched the non-exchange in confusion, her smile fading fast.

Sima knew that Henya's guest room was at the back of her house, with its own patio door leading to the garden. She made her way down the carpeted hallway, passing the kitchen, her brother-in-law Michoel's empty office, and the back staircase, until she came to another closed door. She turned to see if anyone had followed her, and was grateful that her sister had been kind enough to let her brave this showdown alone. She knocked. Was that Henya's form in her peripheral vision? If it was, she was choosing to ignore it.

From inside the room, a faint, "Come in..." could be heard. Sima opened the door and looked around. The drapes were closed, the nightlight still on. There was that faint whiff of overripe cantaloupe again. On the day bed, in the corner, lay Greta, looking so much weaker than Sima had left her.

Twenty thousand guilt pangs fluttered through her. She waited a moment, and then took a few steps in.

Greta lifted her head. "Oh..." she said. "You..." She did not smile. Her lips had no color to them; they just blended into her skin. Her cheeks were more sunken-in than Sima had ever seen them, certainly since the last time Sima had kissed her goodnight.

A rancid flow of chemistry fulminated within her. "Mummy, I can explain..."

Greta inhaled deeply, the fingers of her left hand spread over the top of her comforter. Sadness poured from her eyes. "I never thought you would hurt me, Sima. Never thought you were capable of it... But to lie...to steal...I don't know what to think anymore."

"Mummy..." She closed her eyes and felt a prayer fly from her lips: *Please, Hashem, make this the right thing to do. I don't know what else I could* do. *Make this work.* "Mummy...he is alive. Mummy...I saw him...*I saw Aaron.*"

The words...they flittered in the air between them. She could almost see them, phosphorescent in elegance, and just as dangerous to ingest. For those few fearsome moments, while her words hovered, she wished she could suck them back in, wished her mother had suddenly gone temporarily deaf, so she could protect her from their poison. What had she done?! How could she shock her elderly mother in this way? Cardiogenic shock was a real thing!

How foolish of me!

She watched her mother's face. She saw a flash—fleeting and fragile—of understanding, and then of electric joy. "You...*saw*...him?"

Sima nodded, slowly.

Greta held out her hand. Sima stepped forward. When she took it, she tried not to be disturbed at how dry and thin, *papery*, it was. Sima turned it over and traced the blue popping, pulsating veins with her eyes. She lifted her mother's hand to her face and placed it on her cheek, only then realizing that she was crying. Greta stretched out her other hand and stroked Sima's other cheek, with a love and a sweetness known only to mothers. "You *saw* him..." she repeated. "You *saw* my Arele..." For a few minutes, that was all that was necessary. Within the silence, much tenderness crossed between them. Sima's heart slowed and swelled under her mother's affectionate strokes.

"So..." Greta stopped stroking and held her daughter's chin up, a fountain of hope spilling from her wet, blue eyes, all over the tiny room. "When is he coming home?"

So there it was: The moment that could kill.

Sima's body tensed. Her breathing stopped. White with fear, she considered her options. "Soon..." she managed to whisper, blinking into her mother's stare. "He said he's coming soon."

"Tatte's letter, eh?" The smile stretched in Greta's face; her eyes became pools reflecting the illumination from the nightlight.

"You're not angry that I took it to him, are you?"

"I *was. Furious*, actually. But not anymore. Not now. You saw him, Sima. Isn't that what counts? So it wasn't *me* who gave the letter to him. It was you. Still. You *saw* him. Tell me, how does he look? Is he healthy? Does he look well? *Oish*, I have a thousand questions! I want to hear how it happened! How did you track him down? You see, Simale, I *knew* he was still alive. I just knew it…!"

Sima told her. She recounted all the details of Aaron's heroism, which made Greta laugh and laugh.

"So much like his father! Who knew?"

Sima laughed along with her. "Yup! He certainly is." She was grateful for the distraction; it meant that her mother was not pelting her with uncomfortable questions to which she had no answers, like, *And where is he now?*

When their laughter died down, Greta looked at her daughter breathlessly. "And he *is* coming home, back to us, right?" she finally asked.

I certainly hope so, Sima thought, silently denouncing Rabbi Wechter. Aloud she said, "Yes. He…just needs some time and space right now, to digest all that just happened. You can understand that, right? So anyway, Rabbi Wechter cautioned me—he's the rabbi who became close to Aaron in France…I told you about him…?"

Greta's momentary confusion cleared. "Yes. Yes, you did. Sorry, I can't keep up. *Nu*, so what did this rabbi say?"

"He told me he imagines Aaron will be ready soon, but we shouldn't pressure him at all. Let him reach out to us and come on his own. He…suggested not contacting him for about three months or so. Although hopefully by then he'll have already made contact with us himself…"

"Three months…" Greta intoned. "Ah, well, I've been waiting for him this long, I suppose I can wait another three months…" She swallowed. "Maybe."

On Shabbos morning Sima walked to shul. *Has it only been one week since I was living in a state of familiar unknowing?* she wondered. *And now, one week later, now that I know what I know, am I any better off?*

To distract herself from herself, she decided, while walking, to look around and absorb the many changes that had taken place to the buildings of her youth, both their exteriors and their general purposes. She noted that the large, gothic building that stood in the center of High Road, which had been home to a private all-girls Catholic school back when she was a kid, now had the strains of *"Nakdishach"* streaming out of its open windows, with gaggles of beautiful chassidic children playing in its front courtyard. It made her smile. She enjoyed watching the little boys in their black velvet caps, freshly brushed *peyos* flattened by the breeze, their fathers in black, silk caftans and tall *shtreimlach*, and their mothers in their tailored suits and matching pillbox hats, holding the hands of their daughters in their swishy dresses, all crisp and oh-so-clean.

How dare they call us "dirty Jews," she thought, as she walked toward the entranceway of her childhood shul.

She opened the thick, double doors and strode into the lobby, without noticing the compact desk tucked into the corner, manned by the Mr. Nosson Kopshtimer of her youth.

"Ahem!" Nosson Kopshtimer called out.

"Wha—?" Sima's hands flew to her chest. Then, as her eyes adjusted to the darkened lobby, she finally noticed—and recognized—the man by the desk. "Oh...Mr. Kopshtimer!"

"*Sima Bulman?* Is that really you?!" His brows furrowed in concentration. "I haven't seen you in ages! When did you beam into town?" He was smiling now, clearly apologetic at having frightened her.

"It's Sima Hertzberg now. *Oy*, you really scared me!"

"I know, sorry about that. I just didn't recognize you, and it's my job to stand here now, as part of security. You can't be too careful about letting in any unfamiliar people, these days..."

"Yes, I know all about that... I'm here visiting my mother. How have you been, Mr. Kopshtimer? How is the ol' shul holding up?"

"Well, you can see for yourself. If they have me sitting here, instead of attending shul upstairs with the regular *minyan*, it's not going as good as it could. Old story. Something to do with money..."

Sima smiled. "You know, it's true. Old stuff, old issues. Still and all, I always love coming back. You're never quite free from your childhood, right? Much of my earliest memories took place right here in this building. That's why I enjoy coming to visit here..."

"Good memories, I hope?"

"Hmmm. Mostly."

"Go on. Tell me the difficult ones."

"Maybe some other time. Right now I want to daven."

As soon as she entered the hushed hall, she felt a surge of nostalgia. It happened every time she came back here, like clockwork. *Nothing ever changes in this place*, she thought. *It's like it exists in a time capsule.* She took in the walls, the chairs, the *mechitzah*, the siddurim—piled or scattered, closed or open. She could even locate the three seats that she, her mother, and her sister had occupied decades ago. Now, of course, they were being used by other people.

Even the women in shul had not changed all that much. They stood or sat, softly swaying, whispering their words into their siddurim. In the corners, groups of girls giggled in low voices. She could hear the rich voice of the *chazzan*, coming from the men's section, and she remembered what it was like to hear the soul-stirring strains of her father's voice, back when he had led the congregation—before Aaron had broken his heart for good.

The memories filled her with greater melancholia than she was prepared to handle. She suddenly felt the need to leave, and would have done so, had Mrs. Perlstein not found her and—without any regard to the sanctity of where they were standing—hugged her in a tight embrace and welcomed her back to her old digs. There was so much noisy enthusiasm in Mrs. Perlstein's affection that others looked up from their siddurim and joined in welcoming Sima, causing her misgivings to lift, ever-so-slightly.

"Oh, Sima!" gushed Mrs. Perlstein, finally releasing her from her enfoldment. "It does me good to see you, it really does! Tell me—" here her face fell in respectful concern— "How's Mummy doing? I did hear she fell. I called your sister and left her a message, but she did not call me back. So tell me, is she okay?" She tugged at Sima's shoulder.

Sima nodded. "Yes. *Baruch Hashem*, the doctors say that she will hopefully make a complete recovery."

"Oh, *baruch Hashem*!" She grabbed Sima again for a small squeeze. "Oh, that is so, so good to hear! Is she up for visitors? Maybe I can come by this afternoon..."

"Ahhh...I'm not sure she can handle visitors just yet. Maybe by next week..." Sima said. She quickly chose a spot—close to where she had sat as a girl—and opened her siddur.

After davening ended, the congregation descended the stairs to partake of a catered kiddush to mark someone's father's *yahrtzeit*. Sima followed the crowd, and as she did, the powerful smells from the kiddush room—chopped herring on egg *kichel*, cucumber salad, smoked salmon pate on crackers, *babka*, and schnapps—unleashed a horde of images and scenes long lost within her subconscious.

She didn't—*couldn't*—stay long, and soon made her way back up the stairs. She was almost out of the building when she spotted Nosson Kopshtimer staring at her from behind his desk in the front lobby. He looked shy, like he wanted to say something to her, but didn't know how to do so appropriately.

"Good Shabbos," he finally said to her, bowing his head. "So...care to share a not-good memory? I'm just curious..." His toothy grin; wispy, fragmented beard; and sallow skin reminded her of something he had done many years ago, long before that wispy beard had turned gray.

She stopped walking. Should she share the memory? Would it serve a purpose? Would it avenge what they all did to Aaron? Uch! No. There was no point. "I don't know...I guess it's a mix. Mostly good memories, but some bad. I guess I am pretty ordinary. Ask anyone, and they will tell you the same thing. Mostly good memories, a bit of bad."

"But there *were* bad memories, eh?"

She breathed out. He was asking for it. Why? Did he really want to go there? "Yes, Mr. Kopshtimer. Like I said, good and bad." She turned again and almost made it out of the doorway, when she turned back.

Nosson Kopshtimer had not moved. He wanted something. He wanted the little memory that his presence, and the kiddush downstairs, had provoked out of hiding. How odd! *He* wouldn't remember it. *He* wouldn't have cared about it. Yet it had happened, and she remembered it well. It was such a small incident, but, Sima realized, an accumulation of such incidences can be devastating in the life of a child. Should she tell him? There was no one else around; he wouldn't be shamed in front of any listeners. She opened her mouth. "In fact, Mr. Kopshtimer, I have a memory..." She closed her mouth again.

"Go on. Why did you stop? What's the memory?"

"It involves *you*."

"Then I want to know it even more." His smile grew, but his eyes told her he was worried.

"Okay. Here goes. We were in the kitchen, downstairs, myself and two of my friends. Devorah Hirschfeld and Esti Koegel. Do you remember them? How could you forget? You left us in charge of setting out the food." She watched his eyes as she spoke. One tiny sign of mockery, and she would walk out. "It was a thrill to be working in the kitchen—I mean, for us young girls. We felt important and responsible, cutting up those cakes and laying out that herring. I know that now it seems childish, but in the mind of a child—and we were only around twelve, thirteen at most—these things are important.

"Anyway, you came in," Sima continued, noticing how Mr. Kopshtimer's eyebrows lifted, "and you surveyed the scene. Something got your goat. Perhaps we were being too giddy and loud. Perhaps you had just come away from being told off about something yourself. Anyway, point is, you turned to me, and *only me*, and said two words: 'Bulman...out!'"

Nosson lost his smile and lowered his head. Sima went on. "Why you chose me to leave the excitement of that kitchen, I will never know. You probably don't remember it. Trust me, Mr. Kopshtimer, it isn't something I dwell on. But when I come back to this shul, and I happen to see you, I cannot help but remember the incident..." Sima stopped talking and let the silence take over. Against her will, she felt a tiny bit gleeful as she watched how guiltily he was digesting her words.

"You know...there are many things I have done in the past that I regret," he said, in a voice so contrite that she actually believed him. "But who was I? I was no one important. I didn't think anything I did or said would make a difference to anyone..."

A wind blew in from the street, warm and blustery. Sima's *sheitel* hairs swirled around her face. She pulled them from her eyes. "In the mind of a child, you were the adult. And you created a bad memory for a child. By now, you *must* know that every person in the whole world has the capacity to create memories for children, whether good or bad." The wind stopped. They both stood in the shul's double-doored entryway without talking, without moving. She was determined to see this through, now that she had begun. *For Aaron*, she told herself.

"How—how can I make it up to you?" he murmured.

You can't, she thought. *Oh, dear G-d, what am I trying to do? Nosson Kopshtimer did not orchestrate the catastrophe that is Aaron. It's not his fault. Or anyone's. But it is all of our faults. It is the fault of every person who demeans a child, who visits humiliation upon a child, ping ping ping, in tiny increments. Making minuscule holes in his or her soul.*

"There *is* one way to make it up to me."

"Oh...?"

"Be kind," she said, her hand already holding the edge of the open door. "Especially to children."

Nosson Kopshtimer nodded.

Sima blinked and smiled. "Good Shabbos, Mr. Kopshtimer."

"Good Shabbos."

The wind picked up on her way home. Her *sheitel* flapped about. The women she had passed on the way to shul, who were now on their way home, held their little hats tightly to their heads. A *shtreimel* blew off one of the men, and landed in the middle of High Road. A double-decker bus screeched its brakes, allowing the *shtreimel's* owner to jump over the iron railings, pick up the fallen fur hat, and return it to his head. The man gave the driver a thumbs-up, and the driver tooted three short, friendly sounds on his horn and waved, before driving off. Bits of paper flew up from the pavement and scurried around in mid-air before gently being returned to rest.

Sima felt lighter than she had allowed herself to feel since Aaron had gone missing again. And then she remembered how she had once heard the feeling of happiness described: like being visited by Great-Aunt Agatha; it's sporadic, elusive, and enchanting. She simply appears, without prediction or announcement, bearing gifts of warmth and inner light. Her philosophies are no great shakes: simple, simple, simple is the crux of it. And it works every time. Without rhyme or rhythm, Great-Aunt Agatha shows up, unclutters the pipes, and unclogs the drains, letting you peer, however fleetingly, into clarity.

Sima took a long, deep breath. Her steps led her to Ashley Grove, as her mind began the long process of emptying itself of thought, of stopping the need to make everything better, for her mother...for Aaron...and finally...yes...for Tamar.

They stepped out of the car, she with apprehension gnawing at her stomach, and he with a restlessness he hoped would be resolved by the time they drove back. He threw her a hapless smile. She took off her sunglasses, wiped the sweat off the bridge of her nose with her pincers, and returned the glasses to their spot. They did not talk. Aryeh walked around the vehicle to her, and together they made their way across the grass to the low-roofed building with the makeshift sign that read "Main Office."

Sima's lower abdomen went into tiny spasms as they opened the door. The usual array of women and girls were standing around, some sitting, some on their phones. At first no one noticed the Hertzbergs, but eventually the silence that Sima and Aryeh had brought along with them caused the others in the room to stop what they were doing and look up, if only for a moment.

"Hey," said Rivka Grossbard, one of the head counselors who had been helpful the last time Aryeh had come. "I recognize you. Tamar Hertzberg's father. Right?"

"Right." Aryeh nodded.

"So you must be Tamar's mother," she said, looking directly at Sima.

Sima smiled and nodded.

"You told her you were coming? 'Cuz I think she's at the pool now. She never mentioned anything about her parents coming for a visit. Want me to go get her?"

"Please," they both said, together, which made everyone look at each other a little wide-eyed before getting back to whatever business had been at hand the minute before. Rivka left the building via the small door in the back, the one hardly discernible to the uninitiated. Sima and Aryeh exchanged a glance.

Five minutes later, a shocked and disoriented Tamar followed Rivka Grossbard into the room from the door in the back.

"Mommy...!"

"Hi, Tamar, darling!" Her arms automatically grabbed her oldest daughter by the shoulders, and she pulled her close. Usually, she would close her eyes and enjoy the purity of the moment, its fullness untainted. But this time it was different. The rigidity of Tamar's back; the way her body refused to yield to the embrace her mother was offering... Her daughter's hesitation felt like a bucketful of cold water had just been poured over Sima. It took no more than a nano-second for successive and disquieting denunciations to flit through Sima's mind: *She is ashamed because this is too public... She is dazed because of our sudden, unannounced arrival... She doesn't like me...*

Immediately, Sima dropped her arms, stepped back, and looked at her daughter with new eyes, searching her face for a clue as to why she did not return her affection. But Tamar's face was blank—or maybe it was a small measure of alarm Sima was sensing in her features? Her heart dipped. *She's afraid of me. My goodness, she's afraid of my reaction. How awful, to be afraid of your own mother!*

Sima held out her hand. "Is there somewhere we can go to talk privately?"

Tamar took her mother's hand and looked over at Rivka, who nodded her approval. "Go ahead, Tamar. You can have some 'off' time now."

"Come," Tamar said, pulling her mother toward the main doors. "There is a place I wanted to bring you, for a year now." She stopped and turned to them. "I just can't believe you both came! This is... well...weird. Unexpected, but I guess...in a way...nice." She smiled cautiously at both of her parents. They smiled back, the awkwardness of the moment sitting heavily on all of them.

They followed her out into the sunshine. Traversing the grassy parking lot, they came to a thick wall of trees that had a small opening where a path of dried mud had been established over many years. She took a few steps into the trail, and then turned back to look at her parents' feet. "It's a little bumpy to get there...do you think your shoes are up to the challenge?"

Sima looked down at her beige, high-heeled sandals. She breathed in. "I'll be fine, *mammela*; you just lead the way." Aryeh silently condemned his forgetfulness, from the last time he had worn hopelessly unforgiving footwear. *Oh, well*, he shrugged, *all for a good cause...*

They trekked through overgrown foliage, on a path of rough stone. Pieces of undergrowth jutted out haphazardly, everything doing their very best to banish any hopes for an easy, dexterous reconciliation. *Perhaps*, thought Sima, *it was unwise to have driven over here. Maybe we should have stuck to the original plan and waited for camp to be over before having this talk.* She looked over at Aryeh, whose eyebrows were creased in concentration as he navigated the uncivilized terrain. *Stop overthinking*, she told herself. *We're here now. What's done is done. Let's just hope this works... Please, Hashem, give me the right words to help my daughter.*

At last they came to a clearing, down in a ravine, where a dilapidated stable stood off to the side, in contrast to an otherwise charming oasis, complete with a small brook which Sima would have loved—in a past life—to explore. The heat, from which they had been protected up until now by the canopy of green, now hit them with full ferocity. Sima covered her forehead with her arm, her eyes stinging from the sweat that was dripping into them. Tamar, dressed in a neat blue skirt and billowing button-down shirt—that Sima had no recollection of buying for her—seemed the most at ease, save for the slightly breathless way in which she pointed to the stable and said, "There. In there. Come…"

They walked: Tamar in the lead, Sima behind her, and Aryeh bringing up the rear. The door was open. The odor hit them first: the musty "horse smell." Tamar smiled again as she led them in. "You get used to the smell after a while. It doesn't bother me at all anymore."

"But why…?" The question fell away from Sima's lips. Tamar was watching her mother, wearing a new, slightly bolder expression on her face. Sima wisely stopped talking; she'd let her daughter fill in the gaps.

"Why have I brought you here, Mommy? Is that what you want to know?"

Sima nodded.

"Because this is the place where everything changed for me."

Sima's hand flew to her mouth. "Did someone hurt you here?" She was barely able to whisper the words.

"No, Mommy. No, no, no. No one hurt me here. Well, not really. Except…maybe…*you*."

Lines appeared on Sima's forehead. She scratched her right temple. "I'm sorry. I don't understand…"

Aryeh cleared his throat. His wife and daughter turned to him. "Tamar, is this the place where you first heard of your uncle? Is that what you are saying?"

"Yes. Three of my 'frenemies' stood right there." She pointed to the triple-stacked piles of hay cubes, and then looked back at her mother. "Apparently, I was the only person not to know about your brother. The only girl in the whole camp who had thought of her family one way, and then went on to discover that it was one big lie…"

"Oh, come on, Tamar!" Sima swiped at a fly that was dangerously close to her moist forehead. "Your family is *not* one big lie. *I* am not one big lie. This is going *too* far! How about you ask me why I did it? How about you extend to me the courtesy of explaining my decisions, instead of harboring this secret for a…whole…year…" She stopped talking, her eyes growing wider as she understood the folly of her own words.

She looked quickly away from both her husband and daughter, her eyes darting to the crack in the slats behind where Tamar stood. No one spoke. The dead air hung from them, around them, the smell cozying up their nostrils. Finally, in a low voice, Sima asked, "Was it to punish me? Is that why you chose not to tell me this whole year?"

Tamar's eyes filled. She opened her mouth to speak, but closed it again. She shrugged and looked down, letting the tears spill.

"Sima?" It was Aryeh. "I think Tamar needed the year to process. I don't think she thought of it as a punishment. I think she just needed time."

Sima turned back to her daughter. "Is that true?"

Tamar took a deep breath, trembling slightly. "Yes. Or maybe, not fully. I wanted to know how keeping such a big secret felt. I wanted to experience being you…"

"And…?"

"It wasn't fun. It ate me up."

"Then why are you so angry with me? Don't you understand how hard this has been for me?"

"Exactly because of that. Because it *didn't* seem to bother you at all. You were living this lie and doing it *so* well. I kept wondering, how could she do that? How could she pretend to such a degree of perfection?" Tamar's eyes did not waver from her mother's. "That was when I started to hate you."

"Tamar!" Aryeh stepped forward.

"No." Sima waved him back. "No, Aryeh. Tamar is right. I also hate me. Or at least, this part of me." Aryeh stopped moving. Sima looked back at Tamar, who suddenly looked very small and vulnerable. "Tamar, I can explain it all to you; spill it all out; tell you exactly what happened, in sequence. I could apologize for my stupid decisions. Or, I can just walk away and let this fester between us. What would you like me to do, Tamar? You call the shots."

Tamar's shoulders drooped while she considered her options. For a long minute, all three stood without changing position. "I don't know," she finally said, in a petulant whisper.

"Tamar..." Sima changed her tone. She sounded now as though she was pleading. "Tamar, I want to tell you something, something I have discovered that really shook me." Tamar looked at her curiously. "It is this: some grievances don't have an expiration date. That is to say, some conflicts go down to the grave.

"In my youth, I had never considered the possibility, but when my father died without setting eyes on my brother since he was seventeen, well, that's when I grew up. Maybe not enough for you, but it was a wake-up call for me. The very idea that bad blood can coagulate right there in the grave, if it doesn't get cleaned up beforehand..." She stopped talking, letting the silence work its magic. Finally, all those years of training paid off. In the silence, that was where the best work happened.

"Okay," Tamar mumbled. "I'm listening."

"Maybe...maybe we should all sit down and get comfortable," said Sima. "It's a rather long story..."

She began with the story of the original Aaron Rephael Bulman, his arrest and the consequences of her father's difficult childhood; moving on to Aaron and the summer of Matthew; the humiliations that people casually threw at her brother; the stabbing; Aaron's struggles at school; his quietness; his lack of self-determination. She described Rabbi Isaacs's office going up in flames, and the near-death of Arkady. She concluded with her wild flight into riot-torn Paris, ending with Rabbi Wechter's promise of three months.

At some point she revealed her father's instructions to the two young sisters. She cried as she retold how she had been simply *enduring* for so long, so that by the time she became a mother, she hadn't had the capacity to break free, and now she acknowledged that this had been one very long mistake.

But then something irked her, and she asked Tamar, "In any case, how do you think you would have fared had you known about Aaron?

Would it have made your life any better? Was there nothing I achieved by keeping his existence quiet? Nothing at all?"

Tamar stayed silent.

"Anyway," Sima continued, "I am different now. I am more whole today, in my brokenness, than I have ever been. I really think so. I saw my brother, and nothing can make me go back to that other person, the person I was trying to be, before. You know—the woman with the perfect life, who has everything in place, who has never had to encounter any mess... Look, Tamar, if you cannot accept me, well... that's okay. I am not perfect. Neither was my father. And neither are you. I hope you can understand that."

Tamar nodded.

"I think we'd better get going," Aryeh said, looking at his watch. "Tamar has responsibilities, and we have to pick up the girls soon."

They stood up, brushed off the hay from their clothing, and made their way toward the stable's door.

"One thing I want to add," Sima said. She stopped walking. "It's something I've learned, an enormous lesson from all of this. I want to articulate it."

"Go on..." said Aryeh, watching Tamar peripherally.

"It's that...that the most important role of any parent is to support their child, in whatever the child decides to do, whatever choices he or she makes, and whoever he or she becomes. Unless, of course, it is harmful, whether to the child or to anyone else. But if it's not, then I think that this kind of parental support is *essential*—however hard, perhaps even agonizing, it may be for the parents."

Tamar walked over to her mother, arms outstretched. When she folded herself into her mother's embrace, Sima could physically feel the weight lifting off her daughter. It was a hug to last forever.

Aryeh stood by and watched, not even noticing the tears that fell freely into his beard.

They were quiet as they made their way back through the foliage, Sima and Aryeh concentrating deeply on not spraining their ankles on the patchy terrain. When they reached the grassy field and began walking over to their car, Tamar broke the silence.

"Mommy?"

Sima turned to face her.

Tamar looked down. "I-I'm sorry," she said in a low voice.

"For what?" What could Tamar possibly be referring to, when she, Sima, felt the guilt fall so heavily on herself?

"The letter..."

"Oh. That." She waved her hand and looked over at Aryeh, and then back again at her daughter. "Actually, I am rather grateful for that letter. It was honest. It was raw. I won't say that it didn't hurt me, but...I needed to hear those things."

"I want to apologize for hurting you. For the letter's tone."

Sima took Tamar's shoulders, her eyes brimming. "You know, Tamar, I don't really feel that I deserve your apology, but...it means a lot to me. I...I'm... Thank you."

AARON:

B us Number One.

   That's gotta make you laugh...or at least smile.

   Bus Number One. One! Could any other number be as apt? As germane?

 The crowd, like the heat, is beyond belief—but I will sit in the corner of this bus shelter and do what I do best: people-watch. Was it a good idea to come here? Let me find out.

 There is a lot of noise around me, particularly from the women. They do not stop mothering their offspring: "Come here, Natalia! I said here*!" "Did you put on your sunscreen this morning?" "Why are you wearing your red flip-flops?" "How many times do I have to tell you...?" And on it goes. The heat is quite something, and I find I am reaching for my water bottle every minute, but it gives me no satisfaction. I don't know why.*

 Internal check-in: There is too much tension inside me. I thought, in coming here, that I would be surrounded by disruption, chaos, and the smell of fear, but I am not finding much of it. Interesting to note. After all, is this not a country at war? Yet, as I look around, I see no signs of conflict. I understand that the fighting is taking place in the southern areas of this tiny country, but surely I should encounter worried women and anxious children, no? I do not. Everyone seems to be carrying on as though nothing unusual is happening, and it makes me wonder about media coverage.

The wounds in my chest and forehead are smarting in the heat. I need to refill my prescription for pain medication. My stitches are itching. Sweat is pouring into them from my hairline. I wipe away the sweat beads, but they return anyway. What's the point?

Hmmm, a little girl with dark, brooding eyes is looking at me. What is she staring at? Then I remember: my scars. They must look scary to her. Maybe she thinks I am among the wounded soldiers. The thought makes me smile. I look back. She is still staring. Her mother calls her name. "Yael," she says, "stop staring!" The girl finally turns away from me. It feels like relief.

I suddenly think of Eitan and Uri. I should contact them, now that I have taken so drastic a step, to enter their country in the middle of war.

The men around me are mostly quiet. Some are traveling with wives and kids. Most are bearded. All seem focused. One carries a toddler; another jostles a little girl on his knee. Three young men arrive and talk loudly to my right. They laugh a lot. One slaps another on the back. They are speaking Hebrew, and I do not understand what they are saying, both because of accent and speed. But they interest me all the same. They are religious—sporting long, dangling peyos, *the traditional black pants and white shirts, and white* tzitzis *strands falling down the sides of their pants. Like I used to dress. They seem happy. It's odd. For as long as I can remember, the combination of "religious" and "happy" was an oxymoron.*

I find myself drawn to these religious men. I watch them in fascination, and they don't seem to notice or care.

One thing is sure: this is a land of contradictions.

Bus Number One is finally here. My goodness, look at all these people! So many of them, all Jews. I am being crushed by Jews. Hot, sweaty, temperamental Jews. They are piling in, all of them, into Bus Number One, as though it is the last bus on Earth. Never have I been so physically close to my people. Why do I feel like laughing? I am on a bus—that is all. It is Bus Number One, and it goes, I am told, to the center of the Jewish world, the Kosel. Or Kotel. Depending on political and historical leanings, you might say. And I feel like laughing.

I don't.

I just continue to stare.

And thank G-d that no one notices me.

Naturally, there is no place for me to sit. I content myself with holding a pole, thinking about the fact that I am not used to such boisterous crowds. Where I come from, it is considered rude to be so noisy. But then again, where I come from, I would rather not be.

So there.

The bus takes off. We pass old streets that teem with Jews. I stare and stare and stare. My eyes cannot take in enough. Music is blasting from the many open stores we pass. I think I smell nuts roasting. There are many children about.

I suddenly wonder if this bus is armored. If it needs to be. After all, we will be passing Arab territory, won't we? I look around. Slight panic rises within me. But no one else is looking around with eyes of doom, and so I tell the panic to rest easy. It listens.

I turn my stare outward. The window closest to the pole I am relying on provides me with soul-stirring views. Across the road sit three young boys on a bench. One of the boys has a thick book on his lap, and he is explaining something to the other two. They watch him intently. The image makes my soul ache. I strain my eyes to catch a glimpse of this book that has captured the attention of these mere children. Is that... could that be a Gemara *they are reading?*

I am in shock. Voltage runs through me. My hands tighten their grip on the pole. It slowly dawns on me that I need not go anywhere at all, but watch the world from right here, on this corner. If I get off this bus and sit on that bench, I could be satisfied for hours. Simple streets. Simple people, going about their business. Yet nothing is simple in this land.

Nothing.

Statements are made with every step, with every cream-colored brick, beige with age. Quiet statements, spiced with easy defiance and casual devotion. I am moved to the point that I feel the telltale stinging in the back of my eyes, and I blink rapidly. What is it that these people—my people—say, as they place foot in front of foot and keep their inner eyes focused straight ahead?

Tough on you, Planet Earth!

So there...!

Yep, that's it. That is what they say.

Tough on you!

I smile inwardly.

My head is beginning to pound. I take out my water bottle, and my fingers inform me that it has warmed up in my knapsack and will taste like dishwater that has been allowed to sit. Still, I open it and empty its foul contents into my mouth, allowing some to escape by way of a dribble down the right side of my chin. It is so hot that I welcome the streak of coolness, and let it fall over my collar bone and under my shirt. I do not wipe it off.

We are on an incline now, but the bus has stopped mid-road. I read a sign, written in triplicate—Hebrew, Arabic, and English; it informs me that up this mountain is the Old City. A wave of muscle spasms flutter through me, involuntarily. Internal check-in: frenzied activity.

I inhale deeply and close my eyes, both hands holding tightly to my pole. Perhaps this was a mistake, after all. Perhaps I should have just let Sima take me home. My mother's face, her delight...why have I waited so long?

But I am the curse of my family. The problem child. How could I return?

Oh, what am I doing here? What do I hope to achieve? Connection? I focus on my breath, and the bus begins to move again. The bricks are changing. The closer we get to the Old City, the more majestic and domineering they appear, like they are shrieking, "Listen, you, and you, and you! We have things to say. We have earned our resplendence. We bear witness, thousands of years of it! Open us up at your peril, for our contents are neither pretty nor tranquil. We are royal, and you, O mortal being, are sullied."

The bus has stopped moving again.

The rumbling of the engine has not stopped, but we are not going anywhere.

Someone in the front of the bus—the driver?—calls out that there is traffic, and that we will be stuck for a while. "How long is a while?" I hear someone call out. No one answers, but everyone shrugs.

We Jews are funny creatures.

A mother hands out hot fruit to hot little ones in strollers. Bamba bags are opened by children sitting on the dirty floor in between seats or on the laps of their parents or older siblings. Again a sound comes from the front of the bus. This time it is the sound of singing.

Singing!

I look up. A white-bearded man in a long, black, open jacket and white shirt is, indeed, singing. I can only see the top of him; the crowd blocks my view. It does not take long for others to join in his song. And, unbelievably, I know the song they are singing! The women smile at one another as more and more men take up the song, and soon it seems as though the whole bus—the whole world—is united in singing it.

The song is a parable: The whole world is a very narrow bridge. And the main thing to recall is to have no fear, no fear at all... The old man is standing now, smiling and encouraging us. Some people, who were not singing before, look at each other, and I can almost hear them thinking, Well, why not? What do we have to lose? We are stuck here anyway. *More and more people join in the song. Someone taps my shoulder, and with his smile invites me to join, but I am reluctant to join. I would rather just watch.*

He taps my shoulder again, and before I can stop myself, I am singing too. With strangers. I am singing! I close my eyes, open my heart, and belt out the familiar words, over and over again...

I do not want to re-open my eyes. Please, can we sing this song again? Please, people of Bus Number One, let's sing it again. *I open my eyes and look around. Everyone is in a better mood. The bus moves further up the incline and turns.*

I stop breathing altogether. I am drinking in with my eyes the sight that opens before me, as the bus makes its turn. The sun is pitched at the perfect angle, striking the thousands of white stone slabs that mark the graves of those lucky enough to be buried on this vast, majestic mountain. This must be Har Hazeisim, Mount of Olives. It is a mountain of graves, from its foot until its top. I want to be buried here when my turn comes. I wonder if it is possible anymore. I think of the wet, gloomy cemeteries of England and France. No, I think. Here, *I almost say out loud,* here is where I want to be buried. *This cemetery has stood unchanged for centuries. Maybe I should get off this bus and bow to it, thank it for being here, for not turning into rubble, for not denying our legacy and attachment to this land. I want to embrace these slabs and kiss them. From where is all of this sentiment coming?!*

Oh, Mount of Olives, no wonder we hold our land so dear. Oh my goodness, who knew graves could be this beautiful?

The window lets in a hot breeze, and the sweat on my face congeals. I wipe it off and continue to stare, because that is all I can do. The old man has started another song—and unbelievably, I know this one too. I close my eyes again, and I sing. As the notes leave my throat, I feel more alive and freer than I have ever felt before.

I was dead...but now I am alive.

The incline is getting steeper. The sign we slowly pass says, "To the Western Wall." I feel a swelling in my heart. I look around to see if anyone else is as charged. Sure enough, a surreal noiselessness has settled over the whole bus. The bus is turning now, a sharp corner that is navigated by a wide, outward sweep as it turns right.

Up we continue to drive, a short bit of road, until we arrive at the last bus stop of the journey, the one right by the Kosel Plaza. There are about a million Jews waiting to take this same bus back home; these people have completed their prayers, already emptied themselves of their angst. They are waiting in the quiet heat for us, the latecomers, to disembark.

And we do. In one solid mass. Belongings are collected, children are organized, and we passengers get off the bus and walk, in one motion, toward the metal detectors, and then out to the slope leading up to the glorious plaza. I cannot see anything anymore, for the sun and the whiteness of the stone combine to make my watery eyes squint too much, and the stitches throb so...

I am dizzy. My mouth is parched. I hold my head, and suddenly I feel exposed, undressed, because I am without a head-covering, a yarmulke. I cannot turn to see the Wall while bloisen kop... Is that my father's voice I hear, calling, asking me, "Why are you bloisen kop?" Whether it is or not, this is something I need to address.

To the side I spy golden sinks. I turn toward them, and the water is blessedly cold. Near the sinks I find a wooden fixture where yarmulkes of every size and color are made available for people like me, people who didn't remember to bring a yarmulke, who couldn't imagine feeling so strongly the need to have a small piece of fabric placed upon the seat of their thoughts.

There, now I am ready. I walk past the women's entrance toward the entrance for men, and suddenly I freeze. I cannot take another step. This is all too much. I need to go back to who I was before this war. To simplicity. To the nothingness that filled my days. I turn around and search the crowd. But for whom?

And all at once, I know:

For Tatte.

He said he would meet me here.

He said all I had to do was wait for him by the gate.

I cannot go in without you now, Tatte. Please, come now, Tatte, let's go together. Until you come, I will wait for you. I will wait, because I do not know what else I can do. I want to come back, I want to love you, I want to forgive you, but I cannot do this without you, so please, come, and we will go together. Please, Tatte...come...

The tears flow freely now. Finally. And it is relief that accompanies them. My body lets go. I still cannot go to the Wall. But I can stand here and watch what's going on around me, for eternity. Or at least until my father comes to deliver me from my own impasse.

I do not know how long I have been standing here, watching, as men and boys stream past me toward the enormous stones. They lean on them, speak to Hashem, and then take their leave. I find myself envious of the ease with which they access the Divine spark within themselves and attach it to the Omnipotent. I wish I was able to do that. But for now, I content myself with just watching them do it.

It is growing dark, and I still have not moved from this spot. A bride passes by on her way back from the Kosel. Her family crowds around her, accompanying her up the plaza, toward the stairs behind it, where I think the Old City is housed. Then she is whisked away by her father and mother, in a flurry of good wishes, and once again I look around for a sign from my own father. "Tatte," I say aloud, "find me. I am lost..."

From behind me I hear someone approach. My skin tingles. I whip around. A man of medium height, with a graying beard and a black hat, is saying something to me, but I cannot hear him. "Sorry, what?"

"I said, you've been standing here for a long time. Is there anything you need? Can I help you out?"

I cannot find the words to tell him that I am looking for my deceased father. I shake my head. My throat contracts. I try to swallow, but it hurts too much. I give up. He is speaking to me again, and again I cannot hear him. "I'm so sorry, I cannot understand what you are saying."

"I said, are you hungry? Do you have a place to eat, to sleep?"

I take a chance. "Tell me, sir, have you ever heard of the Thirteenth Gate?"

He smiles broadly. He picks up his arm and lays his hand on my shoulder. "Yes. Of course I have."

I stare directly into his eyes. "I think I just walked through it."

EPILOGUE

To: simah@gmail.com
From: henyaleipzig@sympatico.com
Date: September 20, 2015
Time: 03:18 a.m.

Simaaaaaaaaaa! Come! Get on a plane, bring your whole family! Aaron is back! He's back! He just walked in a few minutes ago, and Mummy can't stop shaking. She is so happy. I have never seen her so happy!

You need to be here! He's asking where you are...!

Maybe come in for Sukkos? Bring everyone! This is a time to celebrate! He looks so good!

He even has a yarmulke on his head. Can you believe that?!?!

Call me as soon as you see this email. I know it's the middle of the night for you, but this can't wait!

Or, you know what, I'm just gonna call you myself, as soon as I finish typing this! I don't care if I wake you. This is worth it!

Just come!

OJPM